Cathleen

Thunk you f
Support.

Enjoy

CAMERON'S
QUEST

Also from David Carraturo, the continuation of the Columbus Avenue Boys Trilogy-*Cameron Nation: Going All-In to Save His Country* and *Columbus Avenue Boys: Avenging the Scalamarri Massacre*.

Hollywood Book Festival-2012 Honorable Mention *Columbus Avenue Boys*.

Kirkus Reviews-*Columbus Avenue Boys*: The author aptly manages frequent leaps, sometimes with dark humor. As the two timelines converge, the novel picks up pace with stellar results: a Fed goes undercover and a seemingly insignificant character returns to chuck a wrench into the FBI's scheme. Blending plot with real-world events and people—**Watergate, George Raft and Frank Sinatra—adds a dash of authenticity to the epic. A mob story with the prerequisite hits, casinos and Italian food, but augmented by a strong sense of camaraderie.**

Midwest Book Reviews-When you're in the mob, you're in for life...so getting out is quite the difficult task. *Columbus Avenue Boys* is a story of the mob set in the 1980s. Three boys grew up closely tied to the underground of the Gambino crime family. As a family patriarch reveals that the Gambinos have strong links to the many deaths of their ancestors fifty years ago. Wishing for them to break free from the mob, the three must work closely together to bring down the Gambinos while retaining their own lives. ***Columbus Avenue Boys* is a riveting tale of criminal intrigue, HIGHLY RECOMMENDED READING.**

CAMERON'S
QUEST

DAVID CARRATURO

CAMERON'S QUEST

iUniverse books may be ordered through booksellers or by contacting:

iUniverse
1663 Liberty Drive
Bloomington, IN 47403
www.iuniverse.com
1-800-Authors (1-800-288-4677)

ISBN: 978-1-5320-1218-1 (sc)
ISBN: 978-1-5320-1217-4 (e)

Library of Congress Control Number: 2016919988

Print information available on the last page.

iUniverse rev. date: 12/21/2016

Along with my Samajumia3, I want to dedicate this story to the memory of my Aunt Joan. I hope you are enjoying catching up with my parents and having a hot cup of coffee in Heaven.

Prelude

The Bloodlines

DECEMBER 24, 1966

A high pressure system had amassed over western Canada signaling the harbinger of a massive Arctic flow into the Northeast. From Washington D.C. to Boston, temperatures had plummeted to sub-freezing levels. The Nor'easter methodically crawled along the coast and by early afternoon, the New York City area was officially in a White Christmas.

Most of the mom and pop stores had heeded the storm warnings and closed earlier in the day. Only the essential establishments had continued to brave the elements until the last possible moment. The tiny village of Tuckahoe, nestled north of the Bronx, had many Italian-American's whose Christmas Eve meal was steeped in religious tradition. The few shops which carried fish, macaroni and even lambs head; the main ingredient to *Capozzelli Di Angnelli* had a steady flow of customers who braved the winter wonderland.

By 6 p.m., the hard working proprietors had decided to call the night complete. Collectively, six men of various ages exited a butcher shop, a macaroni store and a restaurant. They locked the doors and turned off the lights. The contingent of salt of the earth, family providers bunched together and meandered as one. These hardened men were related in some sort of way-by blood, through marriage, once-removed, had gone through this Christmas Eve ritual for over a decade. After the quarter of a mile boisterous trek in the worsening elements, the ensemble entered a small, inviting home to rejoice in the birth of their Lord, Jesus Christ. Awaiting their arrival were parents, grandparents, wives and children who had been busy preparing the meal.

"Michael darling, where are your gloves?" A beautiful wife with a bun of brunette hair and wearing a festive red apron greeted her husband with a hug and kiss as he painstakingly discarded his flannel jacket caked in melting flakes.

"Maria me love, you think I'd never experienced a cold night before. Ireland's plenty chilly," Mike said in a jovial and sardonic Gaelic brogue to his wife of three years. Even though he was new to this country, he was not new to harsh weather.

The men removed their jackets and accepted the warmth of Christmas cheer placed in their hands. Mike had grown comfortable to his new habitat and would not trade where he was for the world.

Joe Cavazzi, the patriarch of the bunch raised his glass, "A toast to this great economy; God Bless the Holiday season, Salute!" Over cheers and shouts, all in attendance concurred. This critical time from Thanksgiving to Christmas had been profitable. Thankfully this year had been good for all, not every year was festive.

Vince's stern voice bellowed, "Hey, I thought your other son-in-law was supposed to help you out today?" Michael had been relieved the retired gunnery sergeant had taken a quick liking to him. He raised his glass and accepted the accolade.

Joe smiled and said "Mikey's still auditioning to be my favorite son-in-law; a real hard worker...was with me bright and early. The good-for-nothing came by before lunch with an outrageous excuse before he disappeared on a secret mission."

Two rambunctious tots wearing red, feety-pajamas darted out from a makeshift fort. They shot at each other with cap guns and dove to safety behind a chair and the love seat in the crowded room. With his first cocktail in need of a refresh, Mike absorbed tough love, parenting lessons.

"You two, knock it off! Show some respect in your uncle's house," Greg, the owner of the best pizza place in town, snapped at the terrors fueled by too many chocolate bars. They heeded the warning and carefully retreated from the back of the Christmas tree to the protection of their mother, who sat on the love seat.

"Hon, you better speak to your boys in a better tone. Let them play. What do you expect with waiting for Santa Claus to arrive? You've scared them to death," Dina reprimanded her husband while enjoying a cigarette. She kissed the boys on their foreheads, stubbed out her butt and returned to the kitchen to assist the other mothers and grandmothers in serving the first course of the *Feast of the Seven Fishes.*

"Okay, time to eat," blended female voices bellowed from the direction of the hearty aroma in the kitchen. In a controlled, chaotic manner, the throng ambled to the dinner table. Nobody took any old seat; they all knew their place and when they reached their designated spot, they sat.

Rocco Albanese stood. The big man was imposing, but his baritone voice was filled with love as he surveyed the room with his eyes moistening. "Let's take a moment to say Grace along with a special prayer for my boy, Ralph." Quiet enveloped the table as Rocco quoted a passage from the Bible. Tears rolled down his cheeks as he raised his wine glass in the direction of his middle son. Ralph sported a buzz cut and wore a red cardigan sweater with black corduroys. He turned twenty in basic training and was home on a short leave before being deployed to Vietnam.

After the prayer and well wishes had been extended, Rocco's youngest son, Jimmy Boy, stood to make an announcement. "Dad, Mom, I'm enlisting after graduation. Al has a family, but I can't let Ralphie be the only one to come home with war medals." The strapping teen made the proclamation with his chin held high.

"Think through your decision...war is not glamorous," Vincent stated. "You'll have to cut your hair, too. You can't go looking like one of those bugs."

"Dad, do you mean the Beatles?" Rita giggled. Mike enjoyed when Vincent's daughter educated her father on the latest fad sweeping the country.

"Beetles, bugs, wasps, whatever; I don't like the way the young folk have been acting. They come into the bar and play those crazy songs on the jukebox. What a racket...beatniks. Where's the country going?" Vincent held the bowl of *zeppole* for his wife and aging mother before he took a few of his own. "Regardless Ralph, remember to listen to your platoon leaders and the veteran NCO's. Be safe, and keep your head low; God Bless You!"

"I will sir, thank you."

While Rocco's youngest sons would be serving their country, his oldest had a family to support. Alfonse and his best girl, Rita, had married after graduation, and their son was born in the spring. This was not the only bundle of joy to bless the close-knit, extended families. Dina and Greg's third son was born earlier in the year. Mike and Maria had two of their own. Their precocious toddler was on her grandfather's lap, sucking a bottle and losing the fight to stay awake. On Independence Day, they had been blessed with a son. He was napping on a large blanket in front of the Christmas tree with the other infants.

In between courses, Mike stretched his legs by the counter and refilled his wine glass. Mounds of food were on the table and the four-gallon jug of homemade red was blocked on the counter near the sink by a bowl of salad. With a clear line of sight to the spectacularly lit Christmas tree, he moved his gaze and admired the luminosity. This life was new to him and he considered himself blessed to have been readily accepted. Italian and Irish blood blended well. He prayed his angels would appreciate the closeness, love and support of a family, which should not be taken lightly. The innumerable amount of friends these children would make would come and go, but because of the bloodlines, those within these four walls would forever be bonded. They would stand by each other to face challenges head on, whatever they may be.

He chuckled to himself, *so far so good*. The boys were getting along fine...just fine. The prized trio was lying bundled amongst the Nativity Manger, presents and ornaments. The superstitious Irishman believed the little ones must have read his mind. Comfortably asleep, Michael proudly viewed Christopher and Baby Salvatore bookending Little Anthony. In a coordinated movement, they extended their arms and grasped for each other.

Michael took a long sip. The alcohol warmed his throat. He took another healthy drink. Turning his gaze to the hubbub of the dinner table, he envisioned how life would transpire for them all before thinking better of his utopian vision. He recalled an old Yiddish proverb spoken to him by a Jewish customer before Hanukkah-*Mann traoch, Gott Lauch*.

Man plans, God laughs.

1

A Gem Amongst The Pile Of Coal

OCTOBER 1, 1983

The hours Rusty Greer billed the University of Texas paled in comparison to the absolute time he logged each month. He was a proud alumnus of an elite college football program, with fond memories of the Longhorns 21-17 defeat of Notre Dame in the 1970 Cotton Bowl Classic forever etched in his brain. An undersized defensive end, he saw scant playing time. The sole reason he was on the amazing squad was because his mother's second cousin was the defensive coordinator. He had vowed allegiance.

Thirteen years had transpired, and he scoured the country for the next crop of athletes to help his program remain amongst the best in the nation. He had focused his attention in Louisiana, Florida and Texas, but because of the success of high-caliber programs in the North, he had been mandated to evaluate talent in Pennsylvania, Ohio and New Jersey. For this weekend, the burly redhead visited Ramsey to gauge the talent of a stud lineman at one of the best programs in the country, Don Bosco Prep. In addition, a wealthy supporter of the UT program had a nephew who was a highly regarded running back at a high school located on the New York side of the George Washington Bridge. After the Don Bosco game, the Bronxville Broncos were playing an away game against their crosstown rival. At 6'2" 230 pounds, Jack Randall played fullback. He was the returning sectional player of the year with a legitimate shot at college football. Greer had taken the challenge of signing players located north of

1

the Mason-Dixon to heart and had vowed to turn over each stone. After losing four bowl games in the last six seasons, his alma mater could not have a fifth.

Rusty's routine was to arrive early to observe pregame drills. Hobbling past the concession stand with a paunch belly supported by two reconstructed knees, he breathed in the intoxicating aroma of hamburgers, hotdogs and sausage sizzling on the outdoor grill. Sporting a beaming smile under his red beard, he made a note to circle back for one or three of those sausage and pepper sandwiches.

Not wanting to be distracted by the Bronxville fan base praising their star, he sat amongst the hometown section. Randall smoothly ran through simulated drills. Greer removed a black, fine tip marker from his shirt pocket and perused the homecoming program. The seasoned athletic evaluator would rely on his years of experience to determine if the small school phenom was Longhorn caliber material. Great athletes made sounds, collisions and movements that ordinary players did not. Jack Randall was bigger than most of players he was set to face. Rusty was prepared to be dazzled with gaudy statistics. He would search for the intangibles.

The home team won the coin toss and received the opening kickoff. As expected, they did not go far; three plays totaling five yards ended with a short punt. Rusty sat in the rickety, wooden bleachers for a better view. Jack "Hammer" Randall proved his dominance quickly. Three running plays for 57 yards, and he was celebrating in the end zone. A short drive and punt by the demoralized home team followed; *this poor squad was outmanned.* Six well-executed plays later, with Jack powering, the Broncos had a first and goal at the eight yard line. After a timeout, three substitutions ran onto the field for the defensive unit. The locals cheered, rallying their scrappy bunch. A tall, husky kid wearing jersey number 80 rattled the side of his black helmet with his hands, as he galloped toward the huddle. Jogging onto the field was a beefy interior lineman sporting number 75. Alongside him was a slimmer player, a linebacker or cornerback in jersey number 10.

"About time Coach Dee!...punishing the boys," a man with an Irish brogue cupped both hands around his mouth and shouted to the direction of the field. "Show'em what your made of!"

Randall took the handoff on a counter play. Number 10, from his outside linebacker spot darted parallel to the line of scrimmage and met the larger Randall below his ribcage. The impact was a thunder clap. The assassin straddled over the prone body and pumped his fist.

"What the hell!" Rusty blared as Randall was decleated.

"You ain't seen nothin' yet," an Italian man, straight out of the *Godfather*, informed the visiting scout.

On the next play, the Bronxville quarterback faked a handoff to Randall and attempted a bootleg option pass around the end of the aggressive, outside linebacker. The trickery did not work. After pumping his arm, the QB ran for his life toward the visiting team sidelines but was effortlessly tossed and he rolled into a gaggle of his teammates.

"Hey Big Al, by the end of this game the quarterback's gonna' be hanging from a hook in your butcher shop." Greer realized the witty bunch had to be the family members of the three players who had recently entered the game.

Third and long, Randall grabbed a short toss on the opposite side of number 10 but made the miscalculation of pausing. Greer opened his mouth in amazement. In pursuit, number 10 leaped over a blocker and once again, violently collided with the former jackhammer. After three minutes of being examined by the trainer, the Bronxville falling star made his way for a rest on the bench. Greer had officially closed the book on Jack Randall. Perusing the homecoming program of the Tuckahoe Tigers, he opened a new book on number 10 and anticipated the remainder of this small town rivalry.

ON THE FIELD

After annihilating the running back for second time, Chris Cameron was amped and felt amazing. He needed the stress relief but was not upset with Coach D'Arco. Making the three best players sit out the first twenty plays was warranted. They had missed curfew before the biggest game of the season as Sal's dad had a moneymaking opportunity to offload merchandise. *Robert Young of Father Knows Best he was not.*

Sal Esposito and Tony Albanese had a steady clientele who took their chances on college and pro football betting sheets. Chris did his part by assisting with the peddling of bootlegged, movies. Utilizing Zio Gregorio's ten video cassette recorders, Chris would reproduce VCR cartridges, as he bided time studying for honors classes.

The night before each game, they ignored the curfew mandate and scrambled around town collecting weekly wagers and peddled items which had fallen off a truck or had been pirated. The end of the night would be ritually concluded with a bountiful feast at a local restaurant or diner. They had the misfortune to run into Coach D'Arco and the rest of the coaching staff at midnight the previous evening. After successfully peddling fifty copies of *The Big Chill*, they were flush with cash and set to feast on twin burger platters at the Odyssey Diner.

"Heh-Heh, Coach D how're you tonight?" Tony had said after he viewed his perfectly coiffed mane of dark brown hair in the window reflection.

As the Tiger head coach paid the dinner check, he glared at his three best players and quipped, "Cee, did these crazy mental patients kidnap you again?" The former Colgate University linebacker folded his arms, waiting for an answer; his forearms protruding power.

"No excuses, we should have been home," Chris docilely answered.

"You could call this our lucky, pre-game ritual," Sal quipped.

"Yeah, our record is one and two, how lucky for us? You guys fucked-up. I hate to do this but rules are rules." The coaching staff circled them. "You guys are suspended for at least the first few plays."

They had taken the risk, and the reward of coveted weekly spending money was in their pockets. The suspension paled in comparison to what Chris was in store for ten minutes later. Entering his living room, he kissed the foreheads of his mother and father. His dad was sitting on the sofa, his head bobbing to the side, while his mother's head lay nestled on his lap. Chris flipped the television switch off.

"Christopher...Colleen called six times to speak with you," Sabina relayed from her bedroom. His sister walked toward him holding the portable telephone. "Your sweetheart was upset." On her tippy toes, she kissed his cheek. At six-foot-one, he dwarfed her by five inches. Two years earlier, they had been the same height. "Good night baby brother, get some rest for the game tomorrow."

Stringing the cord from the kitchen and through the hallway, Chris took the portable phone into his bedroom and shut the door. While dialing Colleen DePasquale's number, he sat on the edge of his bed cradling the receiver in his neck as he untied his sneakers.

"Hey Coll, I thought you'd be asleep."

"Where the hell have you been? I've been trying you for three hours. Aren't you supposed to be on a curfew or something?" Colleen's sultry voice was one of the reasons he was crazy about her, that and she was a total Betty. Venom was seeping through the lines as Chris defended his tardiness.

"Chill out babe, I had to run and do some errands with the guys. I have to make a living. I'm not from the manor. My parents don't throw twenty dollar bills at me when I go out."

"You think I'm a spoiled, rich girl, huh? I didn't agree to date you because of your finances...or lack of. I thought you were a genuine guy and you made me feel special after I moved from Saddle River." Chris had fallen for Colleen the second she had arrived, midway through their junior year. She took the seat beside him in calculus. Luck was on his side as she was also half-Irish and half-Italian. He did the math and surmised they would eventually go out, but took two months to pop the question.

"No, all I want to do is take you out to legit places. Heck, I don't have a car, and you drive me around...it's embarrassing." Chris was lying on his back, staring at the ceiling.

Then the hammer came down.

"I think you are a tremendous guy; cute and fun to be with, but I don't want to date a boy with a chip on his shoulder. You believe you're beneath me on a stupid social ladder. You have to prioritize. School and sports, which you seem to do amazingly well at? Or your friendship with Sal and Tony?"

"Coll, it's more than a friendship. We're the Columbus Avenue Boys for a reason. Shoot, I think you're the bomb...but I can't make promises about changing ingrained behavior since my first day in diapers for Christ's sake."

After an awkward silence, she concluded a well-rehearsed soliloquy. "It's been fun, but I met a great guy from Bronxville, and he doesn't have the emotional baggage you have."

IN THE HOMETOWN BLEACHERS

Rusty scanned the stands and grinned. He loved the feel of Saturday afternoon football. The smell of the fall leaves and the aroma from the grill made his heart aflutter. The band blared *DAT-DAT-DAA-DAA, DAT-DAT-DAA-DAA.* The crowd applauded as the hometown, defensive unit charged off the field. A cheerleader from the top of a pyramid hollered her affection for number 80. He had blocked a field goal attempt to keep the score a 7-0 deficit, as the first quarter came to an end. The undersized squad donned in their worn and dated, black and orange uniforms encouraged each other.

"Sal Esposito, Sal Esposito he's our man, if he can't do it, Eddie can. Eddie Adams, he's our man..." The cheerleaders sustained their excitement for the spectators as the players jogged to the far end of the field for the second quarter.

The Tuckahoe offense clapped in unison and charged out of the huddle. Rusty took note of number 10. Chris Cameron lined at tailback. The quarterback faked him the ball and dropped three steps to throw. The wobbly pass sailed over the head of number 22 and out of bounds. The crowd oohed and aahed. Cameron had laid out a charging defender with a crippling, cut block. The next play was a run. Cameron followed his fullback and shredded a tackler before cutting outside for a twenty-four yard gain.

"So the kid can play offense, too," Rusty whispered to himself. The three gentlemen in front of him turned toward his direction.

"Hey Red, you're in for a treat. Me boy is a wee-bit mad and I have a strong feeling he's going to take his frustration out on these rich lads today," the Irishman said as he extended his hand. "My name's Michael Cameron. My Chris is number 10. To my left be Sal Esposito's, dad and to my right is Tony Albanese's pop." The men waved.

The offense came to the line of scrimmage. Cameron went in motion toward the Bronxville sideline. As the ball was snapped, he cut back sharply and threw a devastating block on the outside linebacker. Eddie Adams scooted around end on an eleven yard keeper. At midfield, Cameron took a toss and followed blocks from his fullback and pulling guard. He paused, planted his right foot and surged. Pushed out of bounds after an eighteen yard run, Cameron slowed his gait and handed the football to a cheerleader who was clapping her hands on the hometown sideline.

"Chris loves to bust balls? My boy and Colleen had an argument last night. You see her face when he tossed the ball?" Rusty listened intently.

The Tuckahoe drive ended two plays later after the fullback fumbled at the 10 yard line. While the Tigers had talent, Rusty could see why they had won only one game-*too many blunders*. He was not disappointed and wanted to see Cameron play defensive. He made his way to the concession stand for a late lunch and to view the action from field level.

This drive ended quickly. Cameron and Albanese stripped the Bronxville running back of the ball, mauling him like a pack of lions pouncing on a wounded gazelle. *What was the Bronxville kid's name again?* The Tigers had the ball on the Bronco sixteen yard line. A burst by the Tuckahoe fullback tied the score at 7-7.

Rusty stayed along the pavilion and studied the action. He eagerly partook in two sausage and pepper sandwiches; *they call them wedges in this part of the country.* The horn on the scoreboard blared, ending the first half of play, and the Tigers trotted off the field past the concession stand and toward the locker room. One of the last to make his way off the field was Chris Cameron. The Tiger stud had removed his helmet and was talking animatedly with an assistant coach. Rusty could see the kid was put together well. He had a rugged jawline flowing through to a bull neck, which was at least seventeen inches thick. Cameron's height and weight stated in the program understated his true size. He was over six foot tall and weighed more than two hundred pounds, not the smaller measurements officially listed.

The University of Texas scout scoffed a third sausage and pepper wedge into his mouth and walked back to the bleachers. During the second half, he was going to see if Cameron was the real deal.

"So your kid's a hardnosed player," Rusty asked as he shuffled past the elder Cameron in the stands. *His father had good size, too.*

"Yeah, he and his cousins have played like a bunch of jackals since they were babies." Mike Cameron tapped Greg's arm.

Greg Esposito snuck a drag on his cigarette and blew the smoke to the sky. "Hey Red, I don't know who you're here for, but seems his boy has your attention. Listen, I shit you not, all of our kids can play but Mike's kid is worth watching. He'll knock the crap out of these pansy asses without trying."

Al Albanese weighed in on the conversation, "Chris was always fast, but he grew last year and has size, too. The kid's a straight A student, reads defenses and analyzes game film with the coach to devise the scheme they should use. With his athleticism and a big brain..."

"Fuhgeddaboudit!" the three men roared and returned their attention to the game.

The second half sealed the deal. Rusty cherished these moments when he had found a gem amongst the pile of coal. The clock ticked to zero to complete the upset special; Tuckahoe 28, Bronxville 7. Scanning his notes on Cameron he nodded approvingly; 178 yards rushing including a 46-yard TD burst toward the end the game, an interception returned for a 55 yard score, a jarring hit to cause a fumble and eleven tackles. He starred the crucial, intangible items. The kid was fast with good footwork and was tenacious in blocking and tackling. He was smart and not afraid to stick his head in the action. This kid had to be made a part of the Longhorn secondary. Some New York toughness could be what was needed to retain national championship stature. Greer scanned the throng of fans exiting the stands until he found who he was looking for.

"Mr. Cameron, may I have a word with your boy," Rusty made his interest official, handing over his business card.

"The University of Texas you say? So, you be wanting to court Christopher, huh?" The proud father radiated. "Let's get you an introduction."

OUTSIDE THE LOCKER ROOM ENTRANCE

Though his weathered face gave the impression of being ten years older than his forty-four years, Mike Cameron conveyed a sense of happiness with life. A naturalized citizen for three years, he had achieved the American dream. Born in County Wexford along Ireland's southeastern coast, his formative years had been a nightmare, to say the least. His mum had died when he was a baby. His dad was a rough and tumble man who worked on the Irish motorway by day and drank heavily. A member of the right-wing Fine Gael party, the elder Cameron confronted many in the pub about his political beliefs. Raised by his loving, maternal grandmother, Michael had attempted to avoid his father's wrath. Grandma Dorothy would mend his wounds and read passages from the Bible. She instilled a strong work ethic in the face of harsh conditions endured throughout his childhood.

After his grandmother's death, Michael fled to Dublin and his father's violent condition. By the late 1950s, the Irish social welfare system had improved the quality of people's lives. Sordid tenements were demolished and replaced with bustling housing developments. With the demand for workers, the eager teen was employed as an apprentice for the burgeoning use of electricity in the country.

Michael received a message his father had died of a heart attack. With practical experience under his belt in the electrical trade, he felt the need for change. The true catalyst was when John F. Kennedy had visited his ancestral home at Dunganstown, near New Ross. JFK's relatives had done well after leaving the Emerald Isle for America; why not give it a go? Michael Cameron had no regrets. As he walked side by side the gregarious, college football scout, he too imagined future Cameron generations had an opportunity to succeed as the Kennedy clan when they left County Wexford in the 1800s.

"Hey dad," the sweat-soaked son greeted his father. Chris had been speaking with teammates and friends.

"Wonderful game my boy. You licked them good, fine effort," Michael extoled as he prolonged an affectionate, father-son embrace. "Christopher, this is Mister Rusty Greer. He be a football scout for the University of Texas."

"Hello Chris, congratulations on an incredible game. I've been in football for more than a few years and something tells me you have more Saturday afternoons in you. The way you hit people...a dang' freight train!" Greer patted Chris's shoulder pads in admiration. He glared at Mike and back to the shocked teen. "May I call and send you information on the Longhorn football program? I'm not making any promises, but we need hard-nosed men in Austin on the defensive side of the ball."

Father and son lingered on the field and took in the moment. The elder Cameron had tried to be a good role model for his family. With limited financial resources, he had spent a great deal of time working double shifts as a foreman at the General Motors plant in Tarrytown and assisted at the family pasta shop. With free time, the good father was engaged in all aspects of his son and daughter's lives. Michael treated Sal and Tony as his own, and he took the boys to baseball and football games, played catch and cards or board games with them. While Greg Esposito was not the best fatherly role model, Michael was similar to Al Albanese. They were kindhearted, church-going men. Neither educated nor rich, they wore their love and emotion on their sleeves and did everything possible to keep their families afloat.

2

Judge And Jury For Any Punishment

NOVEMBER 6, 1983

Situated across the small and crowded bedroom, the Dream Machine set on the dresser flipped from 5:59 to 6 a.m. The black, Sony radio instantly came to life, *"Islands in the stream...That is what we are..."* While the catchy tune was climbing the Billboard charts, the familiar voices of Dolly Parton and Kenny Rogers were the last Chris wanted to hear.

The muscular teen opened his eyes. His head throbbed. Bed covering and sheets were crumpled on the floor, and the chill of the fall morning was felt on his body. Staggering over to snooze the alarm, he stumbled on Sal's lower back and tripped between Tony's outstretched legs before collapsing on his mattress.

Chris sat upright in his twin bed. He moved his hands to his temples to appease the spinning and quell the pain slicing through his brain. His palms were covered with a hardened, black substance. The discovery of more of the same on his forearms and collarbone confused him.

"It's alive," Sal's voice crackled as he called from his makeshift sleeping bag.

"We were worried about you, Cee, glad you survived," Tony groggily added. "I think you ralphed twenty times. Heh-Heh, I had a bucket under you for hours as you puked your guts out."

The tremor of footsteps was felt approaching the closed bedroom door. "Uh-oh, the fun's about to begin..." Sal and Tony chimed in before they covered their heads under their respective pillows and tugged the blankets as far as they would go.

Michael Cameron entered with a crisp knock. The family pet, a white cockapoo with chocolate-colored spots bolted in, leaped onto Chris's lap and sniffed inquisitively. Wexie was named after the family's ancestral town in Ireland. The mixed-breed was a present to Chris for his birthday. He had wanted a car but fell in love with his four-legged shadow and her warm, hazel eyes.

Michael Cameron ambled to the decade-old, Panasonic Quatrecolor television set which shared space on the dresser next to the alarm clock. He clicked the knob and turned the volume as far as possible. The seventeen-inch screen blared to life. After a few seconds of attention grabbing, Chris' father lowered the ear-piercing noise, walked over to his son and sat on the edge of the bed. A Mason jar filled with a yellowish liquid along with ragged towels was placed on the night stand next to a lamp.

"This'll take the tar off you. Scrub hard, don't miss a spot; even those blotches on your back."

They sat staring at the muted morning CBS Sunday news. Violence had erupted in the Middle East. A tragic video montage was broadcast of the destruction caused by a suicide truck bomb at the Israeli headquarters in southern Lebanon. The caption at the bottom of the screen stated ninety casualties. The talking head segued to a clip of President Reagan. The video was a replay from October when the President had given an address to discuss another suicide bombing of the Marine barracks in Beirut that had killed 241 servicemen.

Chris refocused his attention, stammering for a moment as he found words to defend his actions. "First terrorists and a war in Grenada; it's, it's, a crazy time in the world ..."

The senior Cameron cut him off with a fiery brogue, "So smart... straight-A student! My boy, you are better than this. How do you want your friends and family to think of you? If you ever try this stunt again, for the first time, I will tan your hide...make you wish you were never born. I brought you into the world and I can take you out. You're lucky Salvatore and Anthony carried you home." He perused the two mounds lying prone on the floor. "You two are not foolin' me at all."

The disappointed father stood and smacked the back of his son's neck. "You'd be sorry if your mum knew what happened. She's at the shop and thankfully was asleep when you were carried stumbling into the house last night. Get yourself clean and be at Bella's in an hour."

Chris collapsed onto his pillow. Wexie licked his face. He had scant memory of the events from the preceding evening. As was typically the case, their crew did not have a venue to host festivities. Early in the night, as they aimlessly roamed the streets, Chris, Sal and Tony were approached by a car driven by Ernie, an acquaintance from the adjoining town of Eastchester. The derelict wanted help to break into the garage of a mansion he had been casing. The owner was away on vacation and Ernie had been tipped off by a kid who did liquor store deliveries. The detached garage at the end of a long, dark driveway had been stocked with cases of wine and booze. The three bored teens thought partaking in the heist would be fun. With a foggy head, this was all Chris had remembered.

"Cee, first rule when you have never drunk hard liquor before is to NOT guzzle a whole bottle of *Canadian Club*." Tony, the neat freak, was folding his blanket. "And rule number two, never roll around on the roof of a garage which had been freshly tarred when you're shit-faced."

"Holy fuck!"

"Yeah Mr. Football star, and you ruined your varsity jacket. Tar all over the leather. You're lucky we didn't have any feathers. Heh-Heh...if my old man caught me in the condition we brought you home last night he would have lit my ass like a Christmas tree; not the love tap Uncle Mike kissed you with on the back of your neck."

"For my dad to raise his tone, let alone clip me shows how upset he was. I deserve a beating, even if I don't have a clue of what I did." Chris shook his head.

Sal filled more gaps of the lost night. After they had sold three cases of adult libations, Chris had commandeered an entire bottle for himself. He toasted his fruitful final season as captain of the Tuckahoe Tigers on top of drowning his sorrows caused by the sustained spurning by Colleen. She made moving on official; after his repeated attempts to woo her back, she had started dating that rich jerk. On the positive side, the team had won four of their last six games to finish with four wins and four losses. Chris had an outstanding season. His last game was a more dominating performance than the one he had versus Bronxville. In another upset win against a tough opponent, the Dobbs Ferry Eagles, he logged two touchdown runs on offense, a diving interception, a fumble recovery and fourteen tackles. On top of this, the scout from the University of Texas was in the stands to witness his athletic prowess.

"This whole crazy month blew me away-the bad with Colleen dumping me and the good with the whole Longhorn thing. Promise, I will never do anything stupid again. Beer only from now on. I never want to taste eighty proof again," Chris swore to his two lifelong buddies.

"Shit happens, Cee! We knew your drunken messiness was a glitch. Get a move on, your dad ordered you to be at the shop in an hour and you already burned ten minutes," Tony commanded as he handed Chris the Mason jar of kerosene.

NOON, SAME DAY

The Cameron boy had a rough morning as he helped prepare homemade macaroni with his mother and sister. Chris nursed a hangover with the jolt of caffeine from three Pepsi's. Sal and Tony had family work commitments of their own.

Sal's passion was cooking and he loved to assist in the kitchen of his parent's family-owned restaurant. Opened in 1959, Ressini's was one of the longest standing establishments in town. He could spin a thin crust pizza pie to perfection, but his real talent was in creating veal, sausage and chicken specialty dishes.

Ressini's was not open to the public yet. The late day dinner crowd was still hours away. Regardless, the kitchen was bustling with staff preparing take-out orders for Sunday football and family parties. Illegal ways to juice the return were part and parcel with any business conducted by Gregorio Esposito. Amongst the food prep bustling, Gregorio hustled in and out of the restaurant to the parking lot and the trunk of his sedan. Packing up catering trays had consumed this sunny fall afternoon, but collecting envelopes of sports betting cash and selling swag augmented the meal deliveries.

Sal loved to be in Ressini's more than he hated to be around his old man. Gregorio was a rough, tough guy who had migrated to Tuckahoe in the mid-1950s after Bensonhurst became too hot. His first pizzeria had mysteriously burned to the ground, but he had collected a healthy insurance claim for the accident. With the proceeds, he had opened Ressini's. Since his teen years, he had knocked around as a soldier for a few Mafia crews in Brooklyn. Westchester County was no different. Greg had repeatedly found ways to work the system. In and out of jail for a good portion of Sal's formative years, nobody was surprised when his two older brothers had moved across the country as soon as they could.

"All right, let's move, another order," Greg roared as he slammed the receiver to the phone below the bar, crushed out a cigarette and tossed a sheet of paper at his son. "Sally boy, everyone loves your Veal Marsala. While you finish, I gotta' go see someone about a new thing; gonna' get hot VCR's for fifty bucks a pop...we should be able to sell'em for a hundo." Greg lit another cigarette and scurried through the kitchen door.

Sal wiped his hands on an apron and strode over to check the stove before studying the latest order to fill. "Sal sweetie, you finished with the tray of *manicotti*? Smells fabulous, baby." Sal's mom complimented as she came through the swinging doors and eyed the meal-to-go in the perforated tray on the sterile, metal counter.

"All set ma, I'm waiting for the broccoli rabe to drain, and the Grassi's dinner will be set. A new one came through. I may need your help." Sal had resentment for his father, but he adored his mother.

Also a Brooklyn survivor, Dina Scalamarri Esposito was a strong, tough woman who gave as much as she received. She prayed to the sky, did a sign of the cross, and quoted her marriage vow "till death do us part." Dina had stopped numerous beatings and had the battle scars to prove her involvement. Her youngest son was in awe of her ability to keep the restaurant afloat when his father was doing time or siphoning cash.

Dina taught Sal the nuances of the restaurant and gave him culinary tips, but his love for food came from hanging around the Cameron household. With chaos and raucousness the norm in his dysfunctional household, Sal had spent many days and nights as a welcome guest of his mother's cousin. Sal gravitated to the kitchen and since the age of ten would be by the side of his Aunt Maria.

The afternoon progressed. Chris finished at Bella's and assisted Sal with the last of his catering deliveries. Afterwards, they walked diagonally from Ressini's, across the street and over to Albanese's Butcher Shop. The place was jammed with a queue of customers waiting to purchase the fresh cuts of beef, pork and lamb. A glance behind the counter stymied Sal's desire to go to the back room to hang out with Tony. His apron was covered in animal blood as he frantically moved about. Joanne, his thirteen-year-old sister, had a serious smile as she greeted patrons waiting in line with an order book and pen to jot down their requests. Alfonse was wrapping four large packages in brown paper and twine on the linoleum counter.

Chris and Sal mulled about by the front picture window, swatting at flies as they viewed the activity on Columbus Avenue. In reality, they had all lived a few blocks away from the main Tuckahoe thoroughfare. Given all of their family businesses were located on Columbus Avenue, the genesis of their moniker was formed.

They kept a keen ear open to the small talk by an impatient father and son who had been waiting in the back of the line. "My tennis match is in a half hour. Why isn't this line moving faster?" A teen in a blue and white windbreaker wined.

"Teddy, please. Your mother wants pork tenderloin for supper tonight, and Grandmother and Father will arrive by half past four from the city," the middle-aged man who had a bright yellow sweater wrapped around his shoulders pacified his son before returning to peruse the latest issue of *Barrons*. He snapped the fold to punctuate his dissatisfaction.

"This freak show gets slower and slower. Why do we come all the time?" The son rekindled his exasperation in a contemptuous tone.

"Ssshhh, this place has the best meats in the area. Don't stare. We will be done soon enough."

The freak show comment was directed to Alfonse Albanese. Tony's father had been a handsome, jovial man who never missed Sunday mass and treated people with respect. This trait was shared by his wife, Rita, and their two children. Two years earlier, he had been diagnosed with cancer of the parotid gland. To stop the spread of the disease, his jawbone was partially removed. The once vain, gentle giant became self-conscious of his appearance. As difficult a time as Alfonse had, his son took occurrences exponentially harder. Always highly emotional, Tony would come to tears easily and if the situation appeared to put him down or disrespect his family, he would summon an inner strength that combined with his size transformed him into an uncontrollable wrecking ball.

Tony had been feared amongst the school kids for over a decade. As a chubby seven year old, he was teased by a junior high boy and his gang of followers as he walked home from the playground. Crying as he entered his house, his grandfather asked why he was so upset and why was there a pack of kids mulling around the front yard. Through tears streaming down his face, Tony blubbered that the boy had teased and challenged him to a fight. His grandfather grabbed him by the shoulders, looked into his eye and demanded he defend himself. Five minutes later, Vincent yanked Tony from the chest of the bully while his grandson finished pummeling the twelve year old with wild punches to his bloody nose.

The majority of the residents in town knew Alfonse and empathized with his medical condition and cheered his cancer recovery. This was not the case for passersby and customers of the butcher shop who were not from the neighborhood. Particularly hard to Alfonse were the well-heeled residents of the affluent communities and their snooty, spoiled teenage children who tended to treat him as a circus attraction. While Tony had only two ears, he relied on the extra four *orecchio's* of his Italian blood brothers to inform him of insolence.

Sal and Chris gave icy stares as they continued to observe the pompous father and son complain about their trivial inconvenience. For their entire lives, the Columbus Avenue Boys had lamented about these people who may have lived a mile or two away in geographic distance; but light years away in terms of family wealth and perceived, social stature.

Chris and Sal departed the butcher shop and sat on the hood of a silver Mercedes. "How dare they talk about Uncle Al," Sal declared as he rattled the parking meter in anger and speed bagged the fiberglass head with his beefy fists.

"Tony don't need to hear about this, especially when he's holding a meat cleaver," Chris responded as he raised his leg to the top of the hood of the Mercedes and tied the lace of his Converse, high top kicks. "Maybe we need to explain they need to show an ounce of respect, especially in a place of business."

The collective net worth of the Cameron-Albanese-Esposito households was not impressive, but if their family bond were weighed as gold they would be gazillionaires.

"Is he the scumbag who's dating Colleen?" Sal playfully punched Chris on the shoulder.

"Hell no! Going into the Bronxville game, I had a feeling she was dating the quarterback. I clawed his eyes when I tackled him. I saw Colleen with the fag at the movies the next week and the pussy had a scar on his pretty, little cheek." Chris stopped his diatribe. They noticed that the father and son had exited the butcher shop.

"Young man, can you get off my car-it's not a park bench," the father sternly remarked. Sal walked over to the flustered son, took the packages from his hands, and opened the door of the German import. He placed the items on the floor of the back seat and slammed the door shut.

Chris hopped off the hood and marched to the father, who was equal in height and size of the teen, but had rounded shoulders. "Hey Mr. Park Bench, you have a problem. We overheard you talking smack." Chris sneered as he motioned toward Albanese's Butcher Shop. "Who the fuck are you to think you're better than him...and us?" Chris was in the face of the probable advertising or Wall Street executive, and his open mouth was spittling over the man's nose as he barked.

"Da, da, dad...You want me to call the police?" the frightened lad called out.

"Heh-Heh, Teddy bear; you won't need a cop...but, you may need to call an ambulance," Sal indicated as he squeezed the kid's shoulder. "You may need one, too." Sal's face changed from playful to stone cold killer. The boy gulped. "What's the emergency room charge when you're diagnosed with shitting a brick?"

"Young man, I ..." The father wagged his finger at Chris.

"Don't you *young man* anyone you piece of garbage...put away your finger!" Chris poked his appendage on the chest of the deflated man. "You need to go back and apologize. Explain why you and your son were disrespectful."

With a crowd of local townspeople forming, the Bronxville man admitted defeat. He took his son by the arm and humbly walked back to Albanese Butcher Shop.

SUNDAY AFTERNOON DINNER

Salvatore Esposito, Anthony Albanese and Christopher Cameron were more than best friends. The seventeen-year-old, high school seniors were distant cousins who had christened themselves the Columbus Avenue Boys as soon as they could speak. They were inseparable.

Their families had lived within spitting distance to each other since before they were born. While Chris Cameron's father was "off the boat Irish," his mother's maiden name was Scallo. Maria was a traditional, Italian-American woman who loved to cook, cherished her children, and adored her husband. Her cousin, Dina had moved to Tuckahoe after her marriage to Gregorio Esposito. Rita Albanese was a cousin of Maria and Dina. Her family had lived in town the longest of the three.

For the better part of three decades, a late afternoon, Sunday meal was the norm. Rectangular tables were set through the dining and living rooms of the Albanese's quaint home, which they had shared with Rita's parents. With fifteen family members feasting on platters of fried veal cutlets, roasted potatoes, escarole and broccoli a carnivore's delight was upon them. The growing teens attempted to outdo each other. Today they were betting on who could put away the most veal cutlets in one sitting.

"Maybe when you're not hung over Cee; today...no chance. Nine cutlets, and I coulda' had four more if I hadn't had three servings of roasted potatoes." Tony, in a black Billy Joel concert T-shirt, raised his arms in a championship gesture.

"Next week, I'll take my title back. No more hard liquor for me." Before he answered, the hung-over teen had waited for his mother and the rest of the women to leave the room, as they cleaned dishes and prepared dessert. "How the heck do people drink eighty proof crap?" Chris inquired of his father and the rest of the men at the table.

Mike Cameron snickered and debriefed Tony and Chris's grandfathers of the events of the prior evening. "Seems my boy thinks he's a big shot. Bit off, or should I say drank off a wee bit more than he could chew, er' swig."

"Being drunk don't make you a man son, only makes boys who think they're men act stupid," Grandpa Joe interjected from the end of the table.

"Hey Chris, you know what we did to galoops who were shitfaced when I was back in Brooklyn?" Gregorio scooped a healthy portion of salad onto his plate. "We'd follow them like a cheetah hunts a wounded animal...Don't be a mark. Be the hunter, not the prey."

Vincent, who was called Poppy, gave a final bit of worldly advice, "Christopher, consider yourself lucky. I hope this was one of those life lessons." He met Joe and Mike's eyes before turning back to Chris. "Don't let this happen again. Besides, if you pull this crap in when you are away at college, you could get a big ass redneck to whip your hide. Sal and Tony won't be by your side."

These weekly dinners had become the setting for therapy sessions, interrogations, judgment and jury for any punishment. No secrets or off-limit topics was the rule. Chris knew he had to get his act together. School and sports had come easy for him, yet he had always been defensive and uncomfortable out of his inner circle. He was a popular student and respected son of Mike and Maria, yet he rarely socialized, budgeted his schedule to the minute with sports, school, homework and making a buck anyway he could. His temper was as ferocious as Sal and Tony's and usually ignited when he had been slighted due to his lack of money, good clothes and other luxuries the kids who lived farther away from the train tracks seemed to have in abundance.

The Columbus Avenue Boys galvanized wherever they went. They shared the same beliefs. The volcanic trio could be dormant or active and steering clear made perfect sense unless they invited you into their private discussions. Many in school had to proceed with caution whenever they were near. One minute, Sal could be telling a joke to a bunch of kids, but if he sensed mocking or skepticism in his direction, watch out. His demeanor would be commanding confronting the poor soul. Tony was perpetually short of cash. For a frugal person, he could not quell his thirst for collecting record albums and thus emptying his pockets of cash. He was hooked on the *Columbia House* record club. After the enticing deal of ten records for one dollar, he had added to his collection of musical artists at a breathtaking pace. To offset the outflow of cash for music, he rabidly chased down delinquent customers who owed him betting sheet.

3

The Olympic Flag

FEBRUARY 8, 1984

Chris sat upright, his legs folded Indian style on his bed with two pillows supporting his back. Wexie sighed and slowly opened and closed her eyes as she burrowed in the open space on his lap. He gently stroked the top of her head and behind the ears. His canine queen exhaled and gave up trying to keep her eyes open. This was the pooch's favorite spot. Since Wexie became a member of the Cameron household, Chris praised her if Saby or one of his parents had attempted to remove her from this position.

"Wexie, do you want to go with Sabina?" As Saby would attempt to seize the family pet from Chris's lap, Wexie would tense her body and snap as hands moved close. Wexie was his bitch, and the eighteen-pound cockapoo would transform into a ferocious pit bull, growling ferociously and doing anything in her power to retain the position of protecting her man.

As he pampered the pup, Chris sat reading one of his favorite authors, John Jakes. He had enjoyed *North and South*, which was the first of the trilogy of the saga of an American family in the Civil War era. He was halfway through the second installment, *Love and War*. These novels were not on the senior year reading list, and his hectic academic load had waned. On pace to graduate near the top of the class, the last difficult marking period had ended a few weeks back.

"Come out tonight. We're heading to Louie Gee's house for a party, his parents are away."

"I'm still sweating after my work out. Figure I'd finish reading this book. I'm beat anyway."

"Wait, you're reading a book...for fun? Cee, what am I gonna' do with you?"

"Later, if anything good happens, call me."

Exercising and reading historical fiction novels were his distraction, as he had awaited his fate for college life. Pie-in-the-sky dreams of professional football were not a reality, but he wanted to give the next level of competition a try...badly. He had a good head on his shoulders and had mapped out his future. After receiving a business degree and playing ball, he would enter the suit and tie world and be a consultant or accountant or something. He was a perfectionist and meticulous in his preparation. When locked into a subject matter, the facts, data or formulas was not work anymore. Academic scholarships from Fordham, SUNY-Albany, Villanova and Fairfield had come in the mail. He had received football scholarships to play at Rutgers, Maryland and Dayton. Holding off on committing to these offers, he was teased with the allure of the upper echelon program at the University of Texas. Based on his research, UT had the best of both worlds. They had an outstanding curriculum with a world class, sports program. He was on edge and had raced home to check the mail every day, but still the Holy Grail had eluded him.

"Christopher, time to eat," Maria Cameron ordered, lightly tapping on her son's half-opened door. "Let's go, it's gonna' get cold."

"Smells great mom, love your veal chops." He and Wexie bolted for the dinner table.

Halfway through the meal, as the family unit partook in small talk, the telephone rang. "Expecting David to call," Sabina blurted as she jumped to answer the phone. A moment later, she spun around. "Christopher, it's for you. Fred...from Texas," Sabina coquettishly stated, handing her brother the receiver.

"Chris? Hello son, this is Fred Akers. I'm the head coach for the University of Texas Longhorns. A letter is in the mail. You'll receive written confirmation tomorrow morning." The voice on the line spoke confidently, in a scripted fashion.

"Yes sir." Chris was trembling. His parents had stopped eating and focused on their flabbergasted son.

"We would be proud to have you on our football program. The University of Texas has extended you an athletic scholarship to play for the Longhorns. I hope you take into strong consideration this offer to come to Austin. After an eleven win season in 1983, we believe you can help us continue to perform at this level."

Chris repeatedly express thanks his new head coach then once he hung up, shouted, "I'M GOING TO TEXAS, THE LONGHORNS WANT ME!" In the mood to carouse, he grabbed his tar-stained football jacket but did not care, as he bolted toward Ressini's.

He walked directly to the bar. Tony was standing next to an empty stool discussing the betting lines in the sports section of the *New York Post* with his grandfather. Poppy still bartended three nights a week to keep busy. "Thought you weren't coming out?" Tony called out.

"Changed my mind...the University of Texas called...Coach Akers himself...Offered me a scholarship."

Tony grabbed Chris' shoulders, shook him and whaled.

Poppy rang a bell dangling from behind the bar and called out to the ten patrons in the dining area, "Christopher made us proud." Dina and Gregorio came from behind the register to commend him, as Sal made his way out of the kitchen. He was balancing two chafing dishes with a big paper bag on top.

"What's all this about?" Sal said as he placed the items on the counter.

"Sally, the Longhorns want me."

"Wow, I am proud of you." Sal embraced Chris seconds before Tony rejoined the trio. "I'm almost done. Help me deliver this order; a big Wednesday night party. Let's jam tonight."

Tony and Chris helped Sal prep the remainder of the items and placed them in the trunk of Gregorio's Ford Granada.

Chris's good fortune did not yet end. Alfonse Albanese, out of breath, walked into Ressini's with his wife on one arm and a white shopping bag in the other. Michael and Maria Cameron were in their wake discarding their coats and sporting proud smiles.

Alfonse scooped Chris up in a warm embrace, his legs dangling in the air. "Let the boy go, you'll squeeze the life out of him," Rita demanded of her husband.

23

"We were all hoping you'd get the scholarship to Texas. I saw this in a store at the mall for you." With a huge smile, Alfonse presented a black cowboy hat from the bag and placed the gift on the top of teen's head. All those in the restaurant renewed their merriment. Vincent popped a bottle of champagne.

They drove the mile and a half from Tuckahoe to Bronxville. Chris was adjusting his cowboy hat in the reflection of the side window and from the back seat sang *Home on the Range* in a horrible Texas accent. Sal and Tony improved on the acapella rendition to the tune. Sal studied the directions and turned off of White Plains Road and to Tanglewydle Avenue before reaching their destination-27 Oriole Avenue.

"Hot dang!" Chris deadpanned as they exited the car and peered at the colossal mansion. "Is this a hotel?"

"Bartholomew J. Thiessen, friggin' loaded pansies; screw'em, a hundred dollar order," Sal noted as he handed Chris a tray from the trunk.

With arms full, they reached the front porch after what seemed like a five-minute walk. Tony rang the bell. Rhythmic chimes sang an Old World tune. Set to ring again, a quartet of teenagers, hoisting beer bottles, opened the door and chuckled. The Columbus Avenue Boys entered. No adults were present. *Van Morrison's Caravan* blared from a stereo, and the unmistakable smell of marijuana smoke resonated throughout the room. Chris was in awe of the enormous television set in the biggest living room he had ever seen. The picture quality displayed the opening to the Winter Olympics in Sarajevo in colors he had never seen from his nineteen inch black and white screen back home.

The room erupted in jeers. The Olympic flag ceremony was replayed. An embarrassment and slip-up, the Yugoslavian flag had been raised upside down by the host country.

"Ha-ha, must have had those Tuckahoe kids raise that flag. Stupid bastards...Hey Tex, did you guys from the ghetto raise Yugoslavia's flag?"

"Hey girls, let's play MASH," a dweeb in a yellow polo shirt blurted as he handed pieces of paper to all in the vicinity. The acronym stood for Mansion-Apartment-Shack-House and was a popular game where kids were asked to predict their future.

"Hey Colleen, didn't you live in a shack? Mansions are a lot better!"

Chris ignored the disparaging remarks and placed the items nestled in his arm on top of a counter in the kitchen. After completing the task, he walked to the foyer to wait for Sal and Tony. The petty barrage persisted. Not being able to contain himself, he ambled over to the direction from where the catcalls had originated.

"Nice jacket, they shit stains?"

"Where's the rodeo, hoss? You scoop horse shit?"

Seated at a long couch were Jack Randall and his Bronxvillites; comingled amongst the collection were a few girls. One happened to be Colleen DePasquale. She sat next to a kid with his arm wrapped around her shoulder. Chris eyed her and she sheepishly waved hello. *What the fuck,* he thought. He sauntered over to give a proper greeting.

"Hey Coll, how've you been?" Chris ignored the posturing from the boys on the couch. Four of them came to attention and surrounded him.

"I'm okay...funny seeing you at this party." She took a sip from a plastic cup of clear liquid.

"Listen...great news, my scholarship to UT happened. I had wanted to tell you...yes, it's funny." Chris leered, sizing the huddle forming around him. "You Jack Randall?"

"Yes, I guess you're Cameron? See you're bragging about going to Texas? Shit dude, I'm playing for Yale in the fall. Screw your Texas bullshit. Ivy League's where the money's at." Randall was three inches taller than Chris.

"Congratulations, good for you. I do have to thank you; I don't think I'd have been noticed by UT if not for you...amazing. I had wondered since we kicked your ass...why would someone as big as you squeal like a pig?" Chris puffed his chest.

The room full of the children of the elite gasped. The moment of silence was broken, and the preppy hoard chuckled uncontrollably, as Randall had flicked the cowboy hat off of Chris' head then grabbed the front of his tar-stained jacket. Randall pushed Chris backward and took a swing. Chris raised his right arm and deflected the left hook. Ducking, he surged ahead and drove into Randall's midsection. They pretzled clumsily to the hardwood floor with Chris on top. The teens threw punches wildly.

Sal and Tony raced in from the kitchen and tossed bodies aside. Lamps crashed to the ground, beer bottles broke, furniture pieces and tables moved asunder. Girls screamed in panic. Chris gained control and banged Randall's head hard against the stone fireplace. Sal and Tony pushed their assault. The prissy bunch scattered. Chris whaled on his instigator with a flurry of punches. Tony grabbed a folded chair and wildly orbited the projectile around his head.

"Fuuuccckkk!" Chris screamed as he stopped the thrashing. "My hand...God Damn Iiittttt!" He gingerly held his left wrist and staggered to his feet. "Piece of garbage!" Randall flailed in a prone position on the floor with his head and nose bloodied. Chris kicked him in the ribs, grabbed his cowboy hat, and placed the signature item back on his head before turning toward the direction of Colleen. He blew her a kiss.

The Columbus Avenue Boys walked away. Before their retreat, Sal snapped with dissatisfaction, "What...only a five dollar tip? You cheap bastards." They boisterously sauntered away.

Ten minutes later, Chris was in the emergency room at Lawrence Hospital. In the melee, his left wrist had been broken. He returned to the waiting room with his arm supported in a sling. Two Bronxville cops were questioning Sal and Tony. Chris was next on their list.

The boys were charged with aggravated assault. Luckily, since the get-together was unsupervised with alcohol and drugs served to minors, the charges were dropped by the parents of the Thiessen boy who had hosted the get-together. The elder Thiessen was a well-regarded corporate attorney in New York City. After he had spoken to the arresting officer and a few witnesses, including Colleen DePasquale, he had realized any further police investigation would do more harm to his family reputation if the incident went to a trial or was further publicized.

Unfortunately, Chris found out Jack Randall had asked his uncle, the substantial University of Texas booster, to call the school's athletic director. He voiced outrage; a prized recruit was a hoodlum. Less than a week later, a stern letter was sent to the Cameron household. Chris' scholarship offer was pending review.

4

A Chip On Your Shoulder

APRIL 2, 1984

Sal dried his freshly rinsed hands on a stained white apron. He snatched a damp towel. After wiping perspiration off of his forehead, he used the towel to remove a flat metal plate which was sizzling in the brick oven. He admired the signature appetizer dish of mini-bruschetta loafs topped with his specially marinated peppers, red marinara sauce and cuts of bacon.

"Those for paying customers or for your friends?" Gregorio interrupted his son. The oval slices simmered and the budding chef added the finishing touches of parsley flakes and parmesan cheese to his eatable work of art.

"Dad, don't bust my balls. I charged ten bucks, and they pre-paid." Fifteen high school classmates had been invited to Ressini's to watch the NCAA Basketball Championship game between Georgetown and the University of Houston. The game was billed as a marquee event-Patrick Ewing and the Hoyas versus the Phi Slama Jama Cougars, led by Hakeem Olajuwon and Clyde Drexler.

"If the cops come, I'll kick your ass till tomorrow," Gregorio growled as he scrutinized the crowd.

"Don't bug out. All they want to do is watch the game. Besides, I was able to scurry action. We have pools and side bets all over the place. You'll get your cut." Sal knew his father didn't give a shit about serving alcohol to minors. The cops never bothered him and he loved getting the taste of easy action.

Sal decoratively arranged the bruschetta on a serving dish. He knew his friends would not appreciate the extra care he put into the appearance of the appetizer plate, but he still went through the exercise of serving the highest quality and visually appealing dish.

Screw his dad. The old man was aging rapidly and intent on gambling and allowing the restaurant to deteriorate. The original Ressini's Restaurant was torn down during the urban renewal project in the late 1960s and re-opened a half a block away on Columbus Avenue. A small bar area divided two dining room's with underutilized space upstairs for opportunities when multiple events were booked. Unfortunately, in this day and age, large parties were rare occasions. Sal remembered when he would hustle for tips when Gregorio organized casino nights in the spacious upstairs venue.

"About time!" Tony barged into the kitchen to assist with the assortment of trays. The bruschetta was accompanied by a mound of calamari fra diavolo. For those with weaker pallets, mozzarella sticks and chicken fingers were served.

"Chris here yet?" Sal removed his apron and checked his hair.

"Walked in a minute ago, he's saying hello to your mom and Poppy. Guy's making us look bad, brought his school books."

The buzz of the crowd enveloped the hosts. The raucous pack of fans slapped backs, extended high-fives and razzed each other as they viewed the basketball game displayed on the television set anchored to the wall in the far corner of the room. Moments after they realized the trays of food had arrived, the hoard flocked with empty plates and utensils to feast on Sal's creations.

Chris made his way into the room. In one hand, he held a spiral notebook with papers protruding from within. In the other was a red plastic cup with foam overflowing. He placed his book on an empty table then downed half the cup in one gulp.

THE COLLEGE DECISION

After two agonizing months, the disciplinary review by the University of Texas was completed. While Chris would be invited to play for the Longhorns, for his first year he was a walk-on but luckily invited to camp with no scholarship. The scholarship offer he had received was revoked. If he behaved, maintained above a 3.0 Grade Point Average, performed at a satisfactory level in football and did twenty hours of community service during his initial semester his situation would be reviewed. He was a stellar student and highly motivated to play football. These stipulations were not going to be a problem. Thankfully, with the support of Rusty Greer and his position coach, Dean Campbell, he pieced together enough federal aid to fund the first year of his tuition, books, room and board.

Giving him even more incentive, one night Grandpa Joe and Grandma Julia had called him to their basement apartment. While his grandparents owned the small row house, they had agreed to relocate as the Cameron family grew; an amazing gift of generosity Chris had never forgotten. They modestly handed him a tattered shoe box. Chris opened the cardboard top and his jaw dropped. As they had gifted his sister a year earlier, bundled together with worn rubber bands was eight thousand dollars in small bills. Since their grandchildren were born, they had sacrificed regularly; a dollar here, five dollars there, maybe a twenty. All of the squirreling away of nuts for the winter was for Sabina and Chris' college education.

"Congratulations my boy, go kick ass and knock'em dead!" While Grandpa Joe was prone to profanity, Chris had to chuckle. Grandma Julia had grabbed his cheeks with her boney fingers and demanded he be the best football player and student.

With his broken wrist mended, Chris found alternative ways to control his temper. The transformation had been encouraging. He had discussed this dilemma with Sabina during a brother-sister therapy session. This was good practice for her. She was a freshman at Iona College with aspirations of becoming a social worker. With an A in the introductory psychology course under her belt, Chris deemed her the best person to turn toward to address his quandary.

"Little brother, I'm gonna' give you my diagnosis. You have what we call in the psych world, a chip on your shoulder." The beautiful brunette grasped the troubled teen's shoulders and kissed his cheek. "Chris, you don't get reality. You're the town golden boy, and your lack of money means zero to anybody."

"Why do I resent what I don't have? Those rich punks piss me off. I want to spit on the BMW's they received for birthday presents, and I'm sick of wearing third-rate clothes." Chris held his sister's hand and squeezed hard.

"Don't you think proving them wrong will be sweeter when you succeed more than they do? They received good fortune on a silver platter. You would be succeeding with hard work. Our macaroni store's profitable because of your math skills and expense control ideas. You are the best athlete to come out of Tuckahoe in two decades, and you are going to graduate near the top of the class. Oh, and screw you. I had to pay for college. Admit it; you'll get your free ride back."

After extensive soul searching, the siblings determined Chris needed to release his anxiety. Since any blowup would shatter going to college for free, he was determined to persevere. They put a plan in place. Whenever Chris put pen to paper to map out a solution, he carried through with the mantra. Sabina asked him to help at the homeless shelter. This experience enlightened him to people who had worse upbringings. In addition, if he went on a three-or four-mile jog or worked out with weights in the morning, he was relaxed throughout the day. This had changed from his routine of rushing his exercise at nighttime. Chris had a propensity to be on edge if he had not trained his body. This would continue in the coming weeks, even as he rejoins the baseball team and worked his wrist to full strength.

Always a regimented and focused person, Chris could not remember a time when exercise was not included as a part of his day. Being the fastest runner on the football and baseball teams, he was an alpha male and thrived to stay ahead of the pack. When he reached his teen years, he embarked on a weightlifting program. The three boys had been around the same height as pre-teens, but when puberty kicked in, Crazy Salvatore and Baby Anthony grew. They became Big Tony and Sally Nuts. Chris held a celebration when he passed the six foot mark this past summer but his larger cousins busted his balls and shrugged the event off.

"Chris, feeling okay?...you sick, my brother?" Sal playfully chided on a summer day as they lifted weights.

"Get real! You call this sick, asswipe?" Chris raised his shirt to reveal a chiseled six pack. "I gained five pounds but measured myself and grew two inches since May. Six-one and a hundred and ninety five pounds... screw you homos."

"No friggin way; thought something was different about you. Till you're packing over two hundred pounds, you're not officially in the real men club. Besides, the only good six pack in my book is one that is chilling in my refrigerator," Tony kidded as he finished a set of bicep curls. While he puckered up to his reflection and bowling ball bicep in the mirror, he informed Chris clothes shopping would be in desperate need before the first day of school. "You're gonna' have a problem with long pants; you're in the flood zone. Your jeans'll be above your ankles."

"Shit, we better hustle. Sal, does your dad have anything in the hopper for us?" Chris lay on the bench and pressed an easy set of one-hundred and thirty five pounds.

"Friggin' old man always has something to make money, but I get *squadouche*; the other day I caught him stealing fifty bucks from my wallet."

BACK AT RESSINI'S

The Tuckahoe High hoard had scrounged funds to bet via final score pools and bracket scoring. Chris had an inventive way to extract riskless cash.

"Yo, we're gonna' offer ten thousand dollars to the person who completes a perfect bracket; charge ten bucks, it's free money."

"What if we lose?" Tony said slightly panicked.

"It's mathematically impossible. You could hit the lottery three times before coming close." Chris was correct. Twelfth-ranked Richmond upset fifth-ranked Auburn, eleventh-ranked West Virginia topped sixth-ranked Oregon State, and tenth-ranked Dayton bested seventh-ranked Louisiana State.

By half time, the game's eventual outcome was obvious. Georgetown had the dominant squad and multiple players were on their way to double digit scoring. With Patrick Ewing leading the Hoyas to their place in college basketball history, Chris spent the second half of the game outlining a term paper for social studies class.

The Houston Cougars called a time out and the broadcast went to commercial. After parroting Clara Peller "Where's the beef?" line as he watched the *Wendy's* advertisement, Chris wrote diligently in his notebook.

"Didn't you get your scholarship brah'? Take your foot off the pedal and have fun," Phil Maffei, an acquaintance he kept his distance from humorously prodded. He turned a chair around and sat.

"Nothing is ever one hundred percent Philly. Besides, doesn't mean I have to mail my results in. What are you gonna' do, stop learning after high school? Never stop bettering yourself."

Chris scribbled three bullet point topics. The world events paper was focused on the last of the U.S. Marines being pulled out of Lebanon.

"Dude, I have my dad's tile install business to fall back. I go in on Saturdays, sleep in the back room for eight hours, and he pays me a hundred bucks. I'll get smart guys like you to work for me when you get home sick and come crying back to Tuckahoe."

The room went silent. Chris closed his notebook and coolly chewed the last bite of his mozzarella stick. Phil gulped and his protruding Adam's apple expanded. Fear had manifested on his face as he attempted a coquettish smile.

"Enough Christopher!" Poppy had witnessed the last of the exchange and demanded order. Chris and the mass of youths went silent. "School tomorrow; end of the night." No one, young or old questioned the authoritative voice of Tony's grandfather.

"You have a problem running your mouth and...your nose." Chris tapped Maffei's right nostril with his index finger in recognition to the teen's alleged cocaine use. "Watch yourself till I go to Texas...you made my shit list...right on top." Chris raised his notebook and sneered. Maffei quickly gathered his belongings and scooted to the parking lot with his cohorts.

In the aftermath of the altercation, Chris paced the room and glanced out the window. Maffei and his Guido buddies had not yet departed. They were sitting on the hood of his Firebird and smoking cigarettes.

"So much for controlling your temper," Sal stated as he cleared plates and glasses. The rest of their friends had trickled out of the restaurant. The three cousins were alone.

"Lucky Poppy came...shit. I would have re-broken my wrist."

"Damn, I have major problems too," Sal chortled.

Tony placed dirty items on a tray and wiped a food stain from a table. "Don't forget me. Dudes, chips are on all of our shoulders. Fuck'em, we don't need any of them."

"I thought I had my anger under control," Chris said. "Shit, if a pissant can tee me off over one stupid comment, what the heck am I going to do when a redneck crosses me?" During the soul searching with Sabina, he had thought long and hard about his upcoming freshman year.

"Clean slate. Cee, this'll be the best thing for you. You're half a country away, and dudes will be worse off. The colored guys on scholarship came from living in shacks in the friggin' country. You focus on surviving and kicking ass. The last thing on people's minds will be where you came from." Sal slapped his cousin on the back. "Put the book away Eggbert, grab a rag, and wipe those tables in the corner."

5

Not An Original Columbus Avenue Boy

JUNE 1, 1984

Friends in the right places were always advantageous. Rickie Mullino happened to be one of them. Because of a learning disability, he was left back in school twice-kindergarten and the first grade. The day after his thirteenth birthday, he had walked into the local beer and soda distributor and applied for a job. Even though he could barely lift a case of soda, he was hired to stock shelves. Seven years later, the twenty-year-old high school senior, practically ran the place as the night manager. Before closing, he made sure to place three cases of beer by the dumpster. After waiting the customary five minutes, his friends would grab the libations-low quality crap like Meister Brau or Black Label-and bring the cases to a rendezvous point.

"This shit is piss!"

"Who the Hell cares, it's free!"

"Where else you getting beer, dude?"

As soon as winter had turned to spring, the boys of the Tuckahoe High senior class had met religiously to celebrate their imminent graduation. The countdown was less than three weeks away. The festivities were held after dusk in the woods behind the Parkway Oval field and close by where they had played ball their whole lives.

"A toast to Ricky Mullino-give the guy a beer." Tony raised his can and saluted. Sal handed over a twelve ounce Black Label.

"The owner isn't stupid guys. He lets me take the crap before he's ready to toss em'out. Nasty if you don't guzzle ice cold, but a beer's a beer." Ricky took a long swig. "You losers would drink anything!"

The close-knit Tuckahoe community had a history of taking care of its own. The old folk joked to their grandkids and nephews, "Better not marry an Italian girl from town because you could be related." Chris, Sal and Tony were all generationally linked. They were not unique amongst their peers, though the Mullino-Bellacosta-Alberetto *famiglia* had deeper ties, going back to the 1880s. Ricky's father was a mailman and had been active with his kids with Cub Scouts, sports or charity drives. He coached Little League and had never missed a game Ricky or his brother played. While Ricky did not continue with athletics, his kid brother had talent. Joey Mullino had made varsity baseball as a sophomore and played shortstop alongside Chris Cameron on the left side of the infield.

While not an original Columbus Avenue Boy, Ricky was amongst the inner circle. However, he had shied away from the gambling activities. He had devoted most of his time to "working at the Bev!" and hoped to get into law enforcement. Ricky loved to instigate his friends into stupid arguments about mundane matters. "Yo Jim Bug, Robin Yount's one of the best players...on pace with Ty Cobb for lifetime hits."

"Rick, you're kidding me. Friggin' Ty Cobb had four thousand fuckin' hits. No way the Brewer guy is better than him." Jim Clemenza had received his nickname at the age of nine. He had a propensity to bug his eyes when tackling in football. As far as they knew, Jim Bug had the most extensive baseball card collection in the world and he lived and breathed statistics.

"At this stage in their careers, Yount had forty more hits than Cobb... just saying!" Ricky turned his head and almost spit his beer out. He didn't give two shits about Robin Yount, but Chris had fed him these stats to prod their friend. Jim Bug was inclined to overreact. This exchange could end with the Bugger rolling around in a wrestling match before the night ended, but these indiscretions were all good. You never knew when another memorable moment would be created.

"Yo, Frankie Zip...Yanks suck or what?" Ricky called from across the field and Frankie, wearing a Yankee cap stormed over.

"Please with your friggin' Mets. They get one good pitcher, and you think they'll be good again. Winfield, Guidry and Mattingly. Who the Mets have? Gooden, Strawberry and Hernandez."

"Spankees suck, Spankees suck, Spankees suck!" Sal, Chris and Tony chanted around the diehard Yankee fan, Frankie Zingaro. The banter was all in fun, most of these guys had been classmates since Ms. Pellner had taught them their alphabet back in the day.

After a dozen years, their friendships were entering a new stage. Chris would be off to college in Texas. Scotty and Mark were going to serve their country in the Marines. Ricky would bide his time at the Beverage Mart until he took the police test. Eddie was a carpenter apprentice for his father. Sal would try his luck at community college, but in reality he was all about the restaurant. Jim Bug had an uncle who was an electrician. Joe V was set on laying carpet with his dad. Tony would follow in his father's footsteps at the butcher shop and Frankie thought he may buy the deli he worked at.

Alas, no Jim Bug moments occurred, and Frankie Zip had stopped defending the Yankees and ragging on the Mets. Sal and Tony were not ready to go home and would wander around like nomads with the dim prospects of finding some chick to do the nasty with. Ricky and Chris headed home. They had commitments early the next morning. Chris wanted to be hangover free for his run and gym session before his shift at Bella's. He was in prime shape, physically fit and prepared to be a Longhorn.

As the pair climbed the vibrating, metal steps of the walking bridge which spanned the railroad tracks and connected the Parkway Oval with Columbus Avenue, they saw in the distance the flashing lights of an ambulance in front of the Mullino home.

THE NEXT FEW DAYS

Some events will never be forgotten. For Chris, this was the blood curdling scream of Mrs. Mullino as the rear doors of the ambulance were slammed shut by the paramedic. Ricky had comforted her as they watched the flashing lights disappear into the distance.

Luigi Angelo Mullino passed away in transit to Lawrence Hospital. The cause of death was a cerebral hemorrhage to the brain. The forty-four year old had no symptoms beyond complaining on the morning of his death that he had a slight headache.

On three prior occasions, Chris had been to wakes and funerals for older relatives. This was the first time he had to pay his respects for a friend who he had a conversation with a day earlier. Chris, Sal and Tony hugged Ricky and Joey. When they tried to utter words of sorrow to Mrs. Mullino, she consoled them more than they did her. Chris did not sleep for days after the ordeal and spent hours doing yard work for Grandpa Joe, using the solitude to think about the man who he admired and friends he respected.

Four days after the funeral, Chris was walking with Wexie when he bumped into Joey Mullino on the street corner. The Mullino's Boxer, Max, was on a leash. The two dogs sniffed each other hello as only they do.

"Hey Joey, how are you doing? Where's Ricky?"

"He went to his job. They begged him to take time off, but he's going nuts at home. We have relatives coming and going. Mom's a mess. They have her on valium. The school counselor stopped by. Hell, he's graduating in two weeks. The teachers waived his finals. Ricky's taking the police test. If he needs recommendations, a few teachers were sure to oblige. Anyway, he thinks enough people will vouch for him with Chief Johnny living next store and Manny from the Beverage Mart."

Chris's demure voice cracked, "Wha, what about you? You have to stay focused. You're a great athlete. We missed you the other day in the playoff game. Lucky we won but you not flanking me at third base hit home. You okay to play on Friday?"

"Our Uncle Phil's religious. He spoke with us before the wake. It's God's plan...whatever that means?...a lesson is always learned. He assured us our father was proud and he would be upset if we would've stopped living because he died. The guy barely had money but made sure to give his family the best in life. I want him back...I need my dad, Chris!"

"Maybe he was watching from up there when we scored in the last inning to win. He wanted you to have the chance to play."

"Hell yes, I'm playing."

Chris wrapped his arms around his young friend and they sobbed together.

The event changed Chris immensely. Even through catastrophe, the Mullino's were rich beyond their wildest dreams. They had love and admiration for each other and the community embraced them, in life and death. Chris had a tremendous support network, wonderful parents and an existence he would not trade with anyone. He did not need money. His family bond made him the wealthiest person in the world.

6

Wild In The Wood

JUNE 24, 1984

The early morning sun lying low on the eastern horizon was accompanied by a refreshing breeze wafting in from the Atlantic Ocean. The low tide ebbed and flowed in the distance while seagulls squawked as they foraged for food on the low tide beach. Vince Scala and Joe Cavazzi had awoken at their usual 5:45 a.m., drank coffee, and went for their customary four mile walk. This was different from their normal trek around the Village of Tuckahoe. Today, they did their exercise on the boardwalk in Atlantic City.

"Not bad, feeling an ocean breeze," Vincent commented to his friend of nearly fifty years.

"The misses are excited. Vince, to tell you the truth, I am too. I'm worn out. My bones are old, and I swear I have'ta pee all night. Florida will be fun; we earned it!"

The Cavazzis and Scalas had made monumental decisions. They would be departing the friendly confines of Tuckahoe to live the rest of their years in snowbird paradise-Port St. Lucie, Florida. After thirty-five years at the Tuckahoe Department of Sanitation, Vincent had submitted his papers for retirement. He took his beloved to enjoy their first vacation in twenty years. With friends sprinkled along Florida's east coast, they had stayed a month and came back with news-they were proud owners of a two-bedroom condo in a community where three former Tuckahoe residents belonged. In conjunction with the decision, the Albanese's bought Vincent and Teresa's house.

The economy was vibrant and after three decades, Bella's macaroni could not be kneaded fast enough and profits were rising as more yeast was added. Mike and Maria Cameron approached Joe and Teresa with an offer to buy their business and small house. With a newfound nest egg, Joe and Maria did not take long to go on their first vacation since JFK was president. They had been more than curious to find out why Vincent and Teresa were tanned, invigorated and excited. The Cavazzis purchased a unit in the same complex. The turn of events made total sense as both of the families had cohabitated with their in-laws and the time had come to pass the reigns.

Exercise complete, Vince and Joe entered the main entrance of Resort's Casino. Gregorio was hunched over a craps table. At 7:30 a.m., the exciting late night crowds were long gone. He and one other gambler were resolved to change their luck.

"Hard Six, yes baby!" Greg took a long drag on his cigarette before stubbing the butt out in the overflowing ash tray on the shelf below the rail. "Nother' one of these hun." Greg tilted his coffee cup, addressing the middle-aged, morning shift waitress.

"Whataya say, get your bankroll all back yet?" Joe tapped Greg on the shoulder as he doubled his pass line bet.

"Nine, nine, centerfield nine," the boxman called out in a nasally monotone.

Greg turned to Joe and Vince and lit another Viceroy. "If this number hits, I'm doing all right. What time we heading out?"

"Last I saw Irish Mike, think at 2 a.m., he was smoothing out our return to the mother ship." Greg nodded as Vince gave the travel update and refocused his attention back to intently watch the dice land on the green felt; a four and a two. He collected his winnings.

The male elders, consisting of three fathers and two grandfathers, had concocted a plan during the Friday afternoon luncheon on the day the boys had graduated. The women were in jovial moods. With this as a backdrop, Mike Cameron stated the men should chaperone the teens to Wildwood for their post-graduation celebration. Sal, Chris and Tony were headed to the Jersey Shore the next morning with friends. The women rolled their eyes. Wildwood was conveniently located forty-five minutes south of Atlantic City. Shadowing their young adult sons as they went "wild in the wood" was not the true intention of the parental concern.

"Maria darling, we be taking your dear old dad and his *compare* Vince for what could be their last trip to gamble before they leave."

The five men piled into Mike Cameron's 1977 Impala station wagon with Chris, Sal and Tony for the three and a half hour trip. After a fifteen minute inspection of the boy's living arrangements they hauled ass to Atlantic City for their own fun.

"You guys better behave yourself and watch the booze." Alfonse set the ground rules as the boys unloaded their luggage. "Sun and excessive alcohol don't mix. Remember, we're a phone call away."

Greg interjected with a final bit of fatherly advice, "If you need to call us, your ass is grass!"

Greg ended with a good role at the craps table. He collected on four numbers before the shooter hit his point.

"Nine, baby, another win! Hey, take me down my friend. I'm outta' here," Greg instructed the dealer before he addressed a gentleman in a black tuxedo standing behind the velvet rope. "Think you can give me a comp for breakfast? I've been hitting the table hard for the past six hours." The pit boss nodded and came back a few minutes later with a voucher for the breakfast buffet.

After Greg traded in his stack of multi-color chips at the cashier's window, he, Joe and Vince walked toward the elevator bank. Mike and Al were waiting.

"Come on guys, breakfast's on me," Greg boasted.

"Good, let's get the boys. I spoke with Rita. Anthony called yesterday. He was homesick by Saturday morning...missed his bed...what can I say guys, us Albanese's are emotional, momma's boys. I miss Rita, too." Al had dated his future bride when he was fourteen and she was twelve.

As they took full advantage of the free buffet, the men chatted proudly of their children. Greg was in a good mood after his two thousand dollar turnaround at the craps table.

"My Sally boy would have something to say about the shit they serve. I ride the kid, but he's gonna' make hay as a cook, or should I say chef." Greg took a final stab of his omelet before pushing the plate away.

"I give him a lot of credit. He overcame a reading comprehension problem and plowed through his junior and senior year nicely. What he get, a few B's and C pluses?" Mike complimented Greg's son. Noticing the blank expression on Greg's face, Mike continued with his praise before Greg finally interjected.

"He'll do all right. School ain't for him, but cooking is; he'll take a few courses at Westchester Community College."

Mike could tell Gregorio was as surprised as anyone about the news. In reality, he had no idea how Sal did in any of his school years or his ultimate plans.

Big Al returned with another plate of pancakes. "What guys? I'm hungry." After his facial cancer surgery two years earlier, Alfonse had lost over a hundred pounds. Once he was given a clean bill of health, he reverted to his forty-eight inch pants size.

"Anthony's going to have a career as one of them bodybuilders," Irish Mike complimented Big Al.

Yeah, he has my looks, of course, and I swear he grows more muscles by the second. He'll be able to rip the meat apart barehanded. With Sal's car, they're gonna' join the exercise place over in Yonkers and get YUUUGGGEEE!" Al boasted, mimicking his son's pronouncement.

Greg had finally made his son happy with a surprise without an ulterior motive; the graduation gift of a 1974 blue Cadillac. Sal was on cloud nine when he was handed the keys.

"And our golden boy." Greg raised his hands toward Irish Mike. "Chris smacking heads in Texas should be a sight to see on Saturday afternoons."

"Yes, well the lad does have those stupid anger problems. Had everything in the palm of his hand and needs to work to get the scholarship back. An opportunity like this is once in a lifetime and worth fighting for. Bella's will be here when he gets back, but playing for them Longhorn's won't." Irish Mike adjusted the Orange Longhorn cap on his head. Chris had surprised him with the cap after his visit to the campus in May.

"Even if football don't pan out, Chris is supersmart. He's has a good head on his shoulders...he'll do fine. What's he gonna' study?" Big Al had finished his pancakes.

"Ever since I can remember, especially after he helped me study for my citizenship test, the boy's had a fascination with American history and commerce. It'll help when he comes back to run the store." Irish Mike became Irish-American Mike in the spring of 1981, ironically, the same day President Reagan was shot in a failed assassination attempt.

LATE MORNING IN WILDWOOD

Michael Cameron made the left off of New Jersey Avenue and onto Garfield Avenue. The rollercoasters of Morey's Pier stood silent in the distance. Lively Saturday night fun on the Jersey Shore had been replaced with the Sunday morning sleep and hangover. The side streets were littered with bottles, cans and cardboard containers.

The elders took sarcastic, witty pokes at their offspring as they exited the vehicle. Times were different from when they were young. A weekend of debauchery was not in their thought process way back when.

"I was working fourteen hours a day in Dublin as an apprentice for an electrician at their age," Mike commented.

"Yeah, well this wouldn't have gone well with Rita if I went with friends for a weekend without her."

"You don't wanta know where I was at eighteen." Vincent had enlisted at seventeen and on his way to Peking as part of the China Marine Detachment on his birthday.

They didn't think the boys would be waiting outside with their bags packed, but did at least hope they would be awake; *the time was 11:30 a.m. for Christ's sake.*

"How are you Gilly, my good man? Did our boys cause you any trouble?" Mike greeted Gil Aliberto who was born and raised in Tuckahoe. Gil in his youth had spent his summer vacations at his family's shore house working at T-shirt shops on the boardwalk. As a retired fireman, he had fixed the condemned structure across from his family's place and rented to hordes of teenagers all summer long.

"They did good, well behaved boys...all of them. They were lucky. I rented two rooms to a bunch of girls from Philadelphia. From what I saw, they seemed to hit get along quite well...Hey Gregorio, Sal's a good singer."

Greg ignored the compliment and flicked a cigarette butt into the middle of the street and walked over. "So they did all right?"

"They can come back anytime. They're in apartment 2A." Gil pointed to a set of wooden steps on the side of the porch.

Irish Mike climbed to retrieve the boys. The yellow, vinyl-sided structure was comprised of three levels and partitioned into separate apartments. The Tuckahoe contingent was lodged in a unit on the second floor. The anxious father knocked, and with no answer he banged again. Sal bustled to the door dressed in a pair of gym shorts. He opened and let his uncle enter.

"Me God...is this what twelve years of education has done for you. Christopher, Salvatore, Anthony, it's time to head home. Any more of ya' coming with us? We leave in ten minutes, with or without ya." Mike left the room rolling his eyes as he returned to the sidewalk below.

The smell of stale alcohol and other foul stenches lingered in the abyss of the small apartment. A multitude of teens were flopped on the floor and on couches in contorted states of slumber. Empty beer cans comingled with containers of Chinese food and pizza boxes on the counter of a galley kitchen. In record time, the trio crawled and shimmied into the hatchback and fell back to sleep for the entire ride home.

The leisurely life of a high schooler was officially over. The time was upon the Columbus Avenue Boys to become men and enter the real world.

7

Hook'Em Horns

The fresh grass was thick with the early morning dew and predictions of the Indian summer continued to look promising. Tony had been at the butcher shop since dawn frantically working and had not had the chance to check the weather forecast. For the first time in four decades, Albanese's Butcher Shop would be closed to the public. Alfonse had informed customers to place orders in advance and remember to pick up their cuts of meat over at Ressini's.

Gregorio would have one of his workers handle the transactions. Ressini's would also be closed for the better part of the day, as was Bella's Pasta Shop. Additionally, Mario's Barber Shop and Zingaro's Deli would have "Closed For Business" signs on the busiest day of the week. In reality, the closures made perfect sense. Most customers would be out of town. This fact was confirmed by the chartered bus idling in Depot Square and set to depart. Forty-eight men and women were boarding the *Greyhound* charter. Coolers and baskets were filled with an overabundance of food and drink. Another fifteen cars were filled to the brim with town folk sipping coffee and partaking in small talk. They were set to caravan across the George Washington Bridge to the Meadowlands.

The Penn State Nittany Lions and the University of Texas Longhorns were scheduled to kick-off at 11:05 a.m. While most of the 76,000 fans tailgating would be donned in the blue and white of Pennsylvania's favorite

45

university, the contingent from Tuckahoe would be sporting variations of burnt orange and white.

An hour later, the brigade of army ants disembarked and camped in the far back corner of the stadium parking lot. Men arranged tables, chairs, barbecue grills and emptied contents from cardboard boxes and brown paper bags. By 8:30 a.m., most in attendance were sipping homemade red wine, which flowed generously from non-descript four liter jugs. Appetizer plates of *sopressata*, sharp parmesan cheese and marinated peppers, were unwrapped for the feast. Loafs of fresh Italian bread were stacked in a cardboard box on the blacktop pavement.

"All right Sal, get the other half of this banner," Tony and Sal unraveled the design created by Joanne and Sabina. In burnt orange, the sign read *Tame Those Lions-Go #20-Chris Cameron!!* The banner spanned the length of the bus and when secured firmly in place, the entire crowd let out a collective holler and cheer. They saluted Chris with wine and early morning, eye-openers.

Maria Cameron and her mother Julia clenched Rosary beads, and whispered a silent prayer. After the moment, they rejoined Teresa Scala, Dina Esposito and Rita Albanese. Chafing dishes of broiled potatoes, steaming broccoli rabe, sausage and peppers, fried chicken cutlets and eggplant parmesan were organized on long, rectangular tables. These items would complement the beef tenderloin, chicken legs, hamburgers and hotdogs which were moments away from being tossed on the grill.

Sal jabbed Tony in the ribs and admired at the cadre of mothers. "God forbid if they ran out." In actuality, triple the amount of those attending could be fed, and they were happy to share the feast with any passersby.

"You guys came all the way from Texas?" Three bearded men in Penn State jersey's had wandered by to say hello.

"No, we're from Westchester. This guy's son plays for Texas." Big Al, in a formfitting, XXL Longhorn jersey nodded to Irish Mike. The proud father was decked out in Longhorn apparel and animatedly telling a story about his son's accolades in double session drills while giving a two handed UT salute to Greg.

"My lucky charm, Sally tell me Texas is gonna' cover the six point line."

"Chris don't expect to get any meaningful playing time today, Greggie. He did say their defense was spectacular and no way Penn State could contain their speed.

Check us out; we both put our bet in with the bookie...two hundred times each. Cee's tip could win us each a thousand bucks!" Sal and Tony did not gamble excessively as Gregorio's bad luck was fresh in their minds. However, they had confidence this wager would pay off.

"Poppy, if I win Ricky and I are gonna' take a road trip to see Chris after we finish helping you move to Florida." Tony took a bite from his plate of cured meat and cheese.

"My frugal grandson, a thousand bucks would go a long way for you," Vincent laughed.

This was the last weekend when the Scalas and Cavazzis would be residents of Tuckahoe. Sal had to stay and work at the restaurant. He was struggling to stay motivated at community college. Tony would drive the U-Haul to the Sunshine State while Ricky Mullino would follow in his own car. Assuming the wager panned out, after offloading the furniture and boxes they would continue west to Austin for deep-pocketed, college fun.

The large cluster of Cameron well-wishers had gorged for close to two hours; nary a vegetarian was in the bunch. After scrubbing the area clean, the loyal subjects queued in front of Irish Mike to receive their tickets. Chris had called in favors from his new teammates. A game this close to New York was rare and since most of the players had never been out of the south, they were eager to bargain. He gave away complimentary tickets to home games for the next two years in exchange for sixty tickets. The situation was win-win. Penn State was expected to have the dominant number of people in the stadium; hence any cheering for the University of Texas side would be inspiring. The gaggle from Tuckahoe promised to be loud and boisterous as newly indoctrinated Longhorn fans.

"Hook'em Horns!"

ON THE FIELD, 3:48 REMAINING
IN THE FOURTH QUARTER

CAMRUNNNN...CAMRUNNNN...CAMRUNNNN. The chant
emanated from a small pocket of the stadium, behind the visitor's bench
midway through the third quarter and moments after Jerome Johnson had
scored on a two yard run to put the Longhorns up 21-3. After the squads
changed sides for the fourth quarter, the volume grew and had spread
throughout the stadium. Johnson scored again to make the score 28-3.

"Hey number twenty!" Cameron sprinted over to the Longhorn's
secondary coach, Dean Campbell and bucked his chin strap. "Go in and
replace Jerry Gray."

The crowd erupted. Cameron tapped the All-American safety on the
shoulder pads and joined the defensive huddle. The eleven players clapped
in unison, and Chris took his spot as the sixth defensive back in the Dime
Package employed by the Longhorns when they had a big lead. He stood
eight yards deep, situated between the two inside linebackers.

"Nice play, Stevie!" Steve Braggs, a star cornerback tipped a pass
over the middle. As the ball was deflected, Chris simultaneously laid his
shoulder pad into the opposing wide receiver.

With less than two minutes remaining, the Longhorn defenders
trotted off the field. Penn State's final offensive drive of the game had
stalled. Chris's fan club went berserk, as he raised his arms in appreciation
and gave a special wave to his mom and dad.

Chris high-fived Coach Campbell. "Thanks, you made my family
happy."

"Keep sticking players across the middle, and I'll be thanking you.
Good job kid. I had no chance of surviving after the game. Luka Brasi
would have made me sleep with them fishes if I didn't put you in." Coach
Campbell's voice was intense, but Chris saw him chuckle. Alfonse Albanese
had been crazily cheering. His penetrating voice had besieged Coach
Campbell for the past hour.

When the final horn blared, Chris ecstatically ran to the stands.
He leapt over the railing and kissed his parents and Sabina. A swarm of
hands slapped his shoulder pads in congratulations and he soaked in his
mini-reunion before being summoned to the locker room. He anticipated

a fond farewells when they boarded the bus before heading to the airport, and he knew this was the last he would see his parents for the foreseeable future. While he loved the friendly confines of Tuckahoe, surprisingly he was hooked on UT country and had no intentions of leaving anytime soon.

TEN WEEKS EARLIER

Soon after his birthday, Chris Cameron boarded a Greyhound bound for Austin. When he had arrived at the northeastern border of the Lone Star State, he immediately fell in love with the diversity of the landscape. He had pictured cowboys riding around on horses and tumbleweeds rolling on the prairie. As he made his way toward the capital city, he saw sprawling ranches, oil rigs, cow pastures, thick woodlands and many lakes and streams.

He stepped onto Red River Street and was immediately blasted back by the furnace which was Texas in July; 107 degrees for the third straight day. While the heat was nothing he had ever felt before, *Africa hot, playwright Neil Simon would say,* he did not waver from the extreme conditions.

After getting acclimated at the Blanton Residence Hall, he changed into running shorts and sneakers before walking across the Quad in search of a place to jog. He traversed south on Guadalupe Street and took the early evening run slowly, snaking west to the Shoal Creek Trail for a rural jaunt he could never experience in Tuckahoe. He navigated through the wooded terrain, circled east and eventually completed the excursion fifty minutes later by the entrance to Texas Memorial Stadium. He admired the structure which was a far cry from the rocks and dirt he had played on at Tuckahoe High.

Though training camp was not for a month, Chris had wanted to jump right in to the campus life. If homesickness struck, he could be back before the fall semester at Iona College commenced. He attended a morning history class that focused on World War Two. For the remainder of the day he exercised at the world class, sports complex.

Chris completed his first college class with relative ease and received an A. He would take four courses for his first semester. Prior to football camp he declared a major in economics and quickly found being a football player provided him with an easy way to set the ideal schedule.

"Mind if I work in?" Chris had made a few friends with football players who were taking summer classes.

"Sure CeeJay. Hey did I hear you saying to Alton you have no classes scheduled on Monday or Friday?" Ron Grunther, an African American twin to Sal Esposito asked.

"Ron, man I still don't believe you're a freshman. Yeah, I'm taking four courses. I have class non-stop on those three days, but the flip side is I have loads of free time to study and workout."

Chris had received major kudos from his workout partners for his strength in the weight room, especially on the bench where he had surprisingly out did them all by pressing 225 pounds for nineteen reps. However, he took returning player recommendations to heart and focused a great deal on his speed work.

Junior fullback Rhett Williams enlightened him on what to expect. "Ain't no bodybuilding contests CeeJay. Sheat, we're big and strong and better be able to hit like a motherfucker or we wouldn't be here in the first place. This game's all about speed, and Coach Akers is all about IT! A few words of advice, y'all better get lightning quick. They moved me from linebacker to fullback during my freshman year cause' my lateral movement was considered sub-par. Forget about wearing all those thigh and knee pads...even your cup. Travel light, don't need any undo weight on your body."

Chris took the guidance to heart and conducted sprints, stairs, jump rope and agility drills until the cows came home. His hard work had paid off. One hundred and forty players were in camp the first day, with twenty-one in the pack of defensive backs. By the end of the third day, the number of safeties and cornerbacks was nineteen and the players in camp had dwindled to 122.

Chris embraced the high intensity of Coach Campbell. Only 5'5", the former Longhorn safety had played fearlessly in his younger days.

"If you lay into a receiver in the upper chest, I guarantee he'll not want to raise his arms to go for a pass across the middle by the third quarter... Don't cut your nails, scratch the motherfuckers when you strip the ball... You see a pile, go right for the ankle and twist the fucker, make'em come out for a play...hold the ball carrier, as he's heading out of bounds, let your support trailin' you come and strip the ball...Turnovers, turnovers, turnovers!"

UT had an infinite amount of talent on both sides of the ball. The information Chris had received before training camp was spot on. As he handicapped his competition, he was the same size or bigger than most in the secondary. At 6'1", 205 pounds his physique was ripped muscle and he had clocked his best forty yard dash time ever, 4.6 seconds. But, he did notice an edge to a few of his peers, especially the black players, which he fed off. Chris thought his lower middle class upbringing was meager, until he spoke with others he had met. Most came from squalor upbringings and had survived horror stories in the own right. They knew the opportunity at a major college football program was their lottery ticket to the NFL and in life.

A marked difference was apparent between the freshmen and upper classmen who were veterans of multiple off-season work-outs, training camps and high intensity practices. They knew what to expect. Fights broke out between players on a regular basis, and depending on the circumstances the skirmishes were left to simmer on their own. Chris had one of these altercations. In an isolation drill, a tailback had to choose between four openings that were denoted by blocking dummies laid out vertically and spaced five yards apart. Chris showed his athleticism. On the whistle, he mirrored the runner dancing past the first obstacle. Chris leapt over the second dummy and made the tackle three yards behind where the drill had taken place. In the process, he laid out two players who were standing in line.

"OOOO-AAHHHH...YO CeeJay, nice hit

"Lay off New York...I'm supposed to make my move before you come across!" Chris tried to help him from the turf but the runner tossed the ball in his face. Chris pounced on the upperclassman and smacked the sides of his tormenters helmet.

"Run three laps to cool your ass." Coach Campbell dragged Cameron by his collar, forcibly pulling the rookie to the side, yanked his shoulder pads and whispered through his helmet earhole, "Exactly what I want from you...keep the aggressiveness up!"

Some called Chris "Sinatra" in reference to Old Blue Eyes song, "New York New York." Chris loved the accolades. "Fly him to the moon, he's leaving today…Sinatra knocked him sidewaaaaays!"

The inter-squad scrimmages showed he had weaknesses. Among his lowlights was when Jerome Johnson ran him over on a sweep. Later in the series, he was pancake blocked from an immense, offensive lineman. Regardless, after the two-a-days were complete, he thought he had a legitimate shot of receiving playing time on special teams or garbage time at the end of blow-out games.

A hyper-extended elbow derailed his dream of suiting for the home opening 35-27 win versus Auburn University. When the injury fully recovered, he had made the traveling squad for the game against Penn State.

THE REMAINDER OF THE SEASON

Chris was pleased with his initial season and first semester. He had bided his time on special teams. Unfortunately, while the Longhorns had high expectations, ranked number two in pre-season, they lost four of the last five games.

He graded out okay. In limited playing time he had recorded three tackles from the safety position, two tackles on kickoffs, tipped a few passes and made no glaring miscues. He was in the coaching staff plans for the 1985 season and his athletic scholarship would be reinstated. In the classroom, Chris took an easy course load and posted solid grades.

Similar to life in Tuckahoe, Chris did not have time for socializing. His free hours were consumed with football training, class work, and studying plus community service. He made friends; two of whom were his roommates. He had first met Ronald Grunther during summer classes and workouts. Ron-Ron, was a mammoth of a young man. Born and raised in Denton, Texas, his father was a preacher and the mayor of the city while his mother was a nurse. Grunther player linebacker and studied education, with plans to be a teacher. He had accompanied Chris to the food banks and homeless shelters around Austin.

Jason Rodgers was their other roommate. The tall, lanky tight end from Stillwater, Oklahoma, was the gregarious son of an oilman. The energy business had been kind to the family before it was not. He lamented about the boom-bust cycles. Three years earlier his family could have easily afforded tuition. Now in dire economic straits, without a scholarship, attending the university would have been difficult for Jason's parents to pay his way. His mom was sick with cancer and with two older brothers also in college, the Rodgers were struggling mightily.

Besides a few keggers, the roommates rarely went to parties. Chris had similar interactions which he had with Sal and Tony. He even tutored Jason for an algebra class. They would spend time playing poker and telling stories of life back in their hometowns. Sal and Tony brought Chris' stories to life. Tony and Ricky had visited in October and they were ready to play out a scene from the movie, *Animal House,* and go to a toga party, but all they did was hang out at the quad after the disappointing tie to Oklahoma. Sal paid his visit during the week after Thanksgiving to fill Chris in on the latest and greatest escapades of his dear old dad.

Zio Gregorio had used his early season windfall as an opportunity to bet the football schedule even harder. The results were not good. He had success when Chris fed him sporadic tips. Chris had been optimistic, and while the Longhorns had a ferocious defense, he noticed cracks in the offense around midseason. They were not scoring enough, and injuries had taken their toll. Sal and Tony were given the warning; the mighty Longhorns were due to falter. His buddies bet wisely, and they capitalized in four of the last five games. Gregorio gambled recklessly, and he had a long history of spending five dollars for each time he won. When the dust to the college football season settled, he was deep in the red.

Chris was succeeding in a different environment and invigorated by the experience. For Sal and Tony, the few months since high school they had lived an existence similar to the time before graduation.

This was about to change.

8

Eight And Six

JANUARY 20, 1985

On any given Sunday, Tony and his dad would be at the butcher shop before dawn and work till midday. However, with the automatic mincer breaking the day earlier, they had been scrambling to fix the contraption all night long. Not able to get it to function, Tony booked home in the middle of the night. "Old Betsy" was retired to the garage once the new model had been purchased. If they needed to replace the new unit, the profits earned over the holiday season would be grounded up.

"It's a crazy cow eat cow world in the butcher business." Alfonse lamented to Anthony as they sipped coffee and finished the last of the cold pizza which Rita had dropped off during the late night repair session.

"The saying never gets old, Dad."

The elder Albanese had used the bovine line for maybe a million times over the past fifteen years. An old snapshot of Tony slicing his first cut of tenderloin at the age of five was taped on the wall behind the cash register to prove how long they had been working side by side.

"Dad, you remember the nice lady...Mrs. Dellacroce, a friend of Nonna Teresa...I forgot to mention to you...she's going *baats*' but made a point to tell me her grandkids and whatnot, loved the meal. She only gets her meats from Albanese's. I came around from behind the counter and gave her a big kiss."

"When a customer comes in to give you a compliment...son, it's the best. Nothing in the world replaces the feeling of...we did good again. With

54

all the craziness we're under with deliveries and multiple orders, fixing machines and crap, don't get any better than this."

Eviscerating all kinds of meat, slicing chicken and cutting pork tenderloin had been in Albanese blood since the 1920s. Born in the Fordham Road section of Bronx, Rocco Albanese had moved to Tuckahoe after the war. The butcher shop was opened in 1946. Alfonse and his brothers, James and Ralph had all loved to play in the freezers, haul carcasses, and spend time with their dad. The boys grew muscle by hanging large sections of beef on the rail. Hard, sweaty work, but if you wanted to provide a quality product you must love your craft. After high school, Ralph and James joined the army while Alfonse earned his stripes in the trade.

Sadly, in the early months of 1967, Ralph was killed in action in the Vietnam War and in June 1968, James lost his life. The ordeal was a heart-wrenching time for the Albanese household. Saddened with the death of two sons, Tony's grandfather gained a tremendous amount of weight. He succumbed to a heart attack, leaving his dad as the sole survivor of the family business.

Alfonse did his best, but many a time his best fell short, especially after Joanne was born. Thankfully, the Albanese's lived with Rita's grandparents in the small, two-family house on Circle Road. If not for the rent from tenants in the apartments located above the butcher shop, the Albanese's would not have had the cash flow to survive. Over time, they saved and one of their proudest moments was when they were approved for the mortgage to buy the house. Still destined to perpetually be house poor; nevertheless, the mortgage was paid on time.

As was the norm, after this long day, father and son were in need of a thorough cleaning. They relished the transformation to dapper don. When not in white aprons, they would dress to impress, with hair perfectly coiffed and smelling of cologne. The tradition had been passed through the generations.

"You almost ready Anthony...game's in a half hour."

"One minute, Dad, my finishing touches." Wearing a white, sleeveless tee-shirt, he viewed his handsome appearance in the mirror. *Sharp, as usual.* He turned sideways and flexed his tricep. The defined horseshoe shape was the secret to his strength and confirmed by his four hundred and five pound bench press.

After the surgery to remove part of his jaw, Alfonse had become self-conscious of his appearance but soon realized his friends enjoyed his company because of his bubbly personality and kind heart. His son had a hard time and reservations about continuing in the family trade. On the slide, Tony had been asking around for job opportunities. He put his name on the lists for the fire department and inquired about opportunities with Con Ed, the phone company, you name the union shop, he applied. He cried himself to sleep, clueless about what he would do in life; Sal had the passion for cooking, and Chris was super smart and his college experience would be his foundation for a successful career. *What did he have?*

"Yo Erik, your dad's a bigwig at Ma Bell, right?"

"Yeah, he does all right."

"You think you can ask him if his department's hiring. I hear the union benefits are great."

"I'll ask man, but he's been bitching about cut backs. To tell you the truth, I'd be first in line."

What had remained fun and energizing was when he collected betting slips at the high schools, pizza joints and delicatessens around town. At 6'4" and 260 pounds, his ferocious reputation had not waned in the least. He harnessed the power of intimidation. At home he remained sweet Anthony, but around the neighborhood he was growing accustomed to the moniker of Big Tony.

AT RESSINI'S

"*Miami Dolphins, Miami Dolphins, Miami Dolphins number one, they are the Miami Dolphins, Miami Dolphins, Miami Dolphins...*" Greg Esposito gregariously sang the old pep song for all to hear. He was decked out in aqua and orange and wearing an NFL jersey; number 13 with Marino emblazoned on the back.

Sal's dad would bet any side of a wager, regardless of the team or horse involved. *Heck, even a cockroach race would entice him to throw a few bucks for action.* The only exception was when the Dolphins took the field. A fan since the days of the "No Name Defense," the franchise had recorded the only undefeated season in NFL history back in 1972. This season, Miami had been dominant and earned their trip to Super Bowl XIX. They had covered the gambling line in thirteen games and Gregorio was out for blood in the finale against the San Francisco 49ers.

Sal knew the real story. Besides the good fortune he had betting the Dolphins and University of Texas games, for the most part, he had not fared well. Going into the most heavily wagered day in sports, Gregorio had lost close to $20,000. To get even, he hit the bookie hard and had laid out an additional $5000 in pools to augment his action for the day.

"Hey, hey, Maestro, it's Greggie. What's the line and Over-Under?... Dolphins getting three and a half...good, good! Over-Under's fifty. Give me a two thousand time teaser; I want the Dolphins and the Under." Sal watched in disgust as Gregorio locked in a parlay bet. If both sides won, he would take home $40,000, and his bookie would owe him money for a change. If both sides lost, another $22,000 would be added to his debt.

"Dad, all locked in, huh?" Sadly, Sal still wanted some semblance of a father-son moment.

"Yes, Salvatore...GO FISH!"

Thirty people had been invited for the Super Sunday party. The Dolphins were set to kick off. Stanford Stadium was packed and a beautiful, sunny day was upon the two teams in northern California.

Greg and Irish Mike gave each other a high five after the 49ers muffed the opening kickoff. The Niners were pinned inside the ten yard line as the Dolphin delivered and held Joe Montana's high-powered offense.

"Yeah baby!" Greg screamed as Dan Marino led the Dolphins to the first score; a field goal, 3-0. "I'm ahead six and a half to zero already. Three points, too; need scoring to stay low."

The course of the game would not be all in the Dolphins favor. On the next drive, the 49ers took the lead 7-3. The Dolphins countered; before the end of the first quarter, Dan Marino connected on a two-yard touchdown pass. In the second quarter, the 49ers showed why they had lost only once during the regular season. San Francisco went into dime coverage to take away the deadly passing game of Miami's heralded, rookie quarterback. The defense stiffened, and the 49er offense meshed. Joe Montana drove 53 yards and completed an eight yard pass for a 14-10 lead. A quick score increased the 49ers lead to 21-10 and another touchdown followed. The Dolphins rallied with two field goals to end the half at a 28-16 deficit.

The Dolphins had shit the bed with zero chance of a miracle comeback. The long-time, degenerate gambler lit his tenth cigarette of the game and exited past the jovial hum of the room. Worried, Sal peaked out back and saw his dad pacing in front of the garbage container.

After three more cigarettes, Greg came back in for a fresh pack of smokes and mumbled as he passed his son, "not a friggin' party for me!" He stormed back out.

The 49ers had filleted the Fish. They scored another touchdown and added a field goal in the third quarter to extend the lead 38-16. Gregorio re-entered the festivities with three minutes remaining.

The unlucky gambler walked by the television and flipped the middle finger for all to see before removing his Dolphin cap and flinging the headpiece against the far wall. Sal followed him into the hushed bar area. Greg poured a short glass of whisky, lit another cigarette before he gulped the shot. Sal had a lump in his throat as he perused the many sheets of folded papers of all sizes with the numbers for the nine pools his dad had participated in. Five hundred bucks, loser; 49ers five-Dolphins one. One thousand dollars, loser; 49ers nine-Dolphins nine. All horrible number combinations and not a winner in the bunch. He unfolded a yellow eight by eleven with a bold star scrawled on the blank side, the $2000 pool run out of the pizza joint in Mt. Vernon. Smiling, he handed the sheet to his father.

Greg marched into the party, a shit-eating grin plastered to his face as he clenched the paper with the grid of numbers displayed. "What was the score at halftime?"

"Think 28-16."

"Oh my God, I won twenty five grand! Niners eight and the Dolphins six!"

"My good friend, you better sit...seems you won plenty more." Irish Mike had a beaming smile as he put his arm around Greg's shoulder. "The score at the end of the third quarter was 38-16...eight and six again!"

"Holy fuck, another twenty five grand!" Greg was shaking and pulled over a chair to sit. Irish Mike stood in back, playfully massaging his shoulders.

"Two minutes left, still 38-16." Sal was grinning from ear to ear. He did not have many father-son moments and was soaking this one in as he took the seat alongside his dad.

Collectively, the jovial bunch of partygoers rooted for Greg to catch his break.

"Hold the ball"..."DE-FENSE-DE-FENSE-DE-FENSE"..."Incomplete, 49ers get the ball...They're sitting on it...Montana's taking a knee. TEN-NINE-EIGHT-SEVEN-SIX-FIVE-FOUR-THREE-TWO-ONE-ZERO!" The 49ers were the champions of the world.

"The final was...Holy Shit! I won a hundred and fifty thousand bucks!" Greg screamed in a horse and gravelly voice. The veins in his neck bulged. Sweating profusely, he grabbed his left wrist and keeled over.

9

Enzo

JANUARY 23, 1985

The rustic cowbells rattled and clanked denoting a customer entering Albanese's Butcher Shop. Since Wednesday mornings were relatively slow, Alfonse ran to the hospital for a quick visit. Thankfully, Gregorio's heart attack was minor, and he was resting comfortably while tests were conducted on his ticker.

Tony lowered the volume of the radio and the snare drum solo to Bruce Springsteen's newest hit, *Born in the USA*. He greeted his guest, an anticipated visitor but not a paying customer. The meat mincer machine had needed repair, and thankfully still under warranty.

"How are you doing today, sir?" The patch above the technician's left chest pocket read Scott and his blue overalls reeked of stale cigarette smoke.

"I hear your grinder's on the fritz. Let's see what I can do," the chrome-domed, mechanic proposed.

"Take your time. We appreciate you coming; cold as a bitch!" Tony smiled slightly and escorted Scott to the back room. *There was something about this guy which his father had mentioned but he couldn't recall the gist of why.* "You want coffee or something?"

"No thanks; I have a busy day. You have the warranty?"

"My dad left the pink copy in the tray." Tony pointed as he reached for the telephone receiver and dialed. "Yo Cee, what's going on my brother?"

"Nothing buddy, an hour to kill until my accounting class. How's Zio Gregorio and Sal?"

"The heart attack was triggered by his nerves. He smoked a pack and a half of cigarettes during the Super Bowl. The night was awful. My dad and I were in shock."

"You two cried?"

"Well...come on...friggin' emotional moment, you should have seen Sal's face. He may hate the guy, but he's upset." The whirring of an electrical screwdriver came to life in the background. Tony walked closer to the front door. The cord was stretched like a clothesline.

"What's all the noise about?"

"Our friggin' mincer crapped out. The guy's fixing it...Christ it's cold as a bitch," Tony declared as he viewed the frigid morning along Columbus Avenue. The howling wind rattled the large picture window.

"Yeah, we can't get away from winter either. It's twenty five degrees in Austin."

"So hysterical listening to Uncle Joe and Poppy bitch the other week about the weather. They moved south to get away from the cold."

The Columbus Avenue Boys had gone to Florida after the bowl game loss. Chris took a bus east while Sal and Tony drove south. They met in Orlando and traveled to Port St. Lucie together. Their plans to catch major rays and work on tans fell apart. From Texas to New England, bitter temperatures had engulfed the region. The orange crop had been in jeopardy of failing. Besides the lack of tanning, the two week vacation was great and included their first visit to Disney World with the old folk. Unfortunately, they lost needed beer money after being schooled in shuffleboard, pinochle and poker; *life lesson number one: Don't play anything competitive against the elders.*

"When you coming home?" Tony asked Chris as he glanced at the repairman closing his toolbox.

"Gonna' be a while. Have spring drills in April before classes end. My roommate Jason Rodgers...you remember J.R.?...well his dad owns an energy company, and I may help out at an oil rig about fifty miles away. Pay's good, keep me busy till summer school."

"Repair guy's done. I'll give Sal and Zio Greg your best. Call you later with any updates."

"I'm finished, nothing I can do, my boy. Something jammed in the motor and the whole thing's shot," Scott deduced as he placed reading glasses in his front pocket.

"Whatya' mean? Warranty should cover repairs," Tony snatched the pink document and read aloud as he walked back to where Scott was standing.

"Only for six months, boy; read the fine print before you go wasting my time to come out in this weather. You should have studied better in school. You'll need a new one." He pointed a finger toward his head in a mimicking gesture. "Here's the catalogue; you and your dad take a peek... lots of pretty pictures and no big words."

Bingo! Tony remembered his dad say Scott was a complete prick because he was educated on all the latest and greatest. Alfonse bit his lip because of the good deal. The guy had done work at Ressini's and Bella's. He was a heavy gambler and had a reputation for bilking customers when he was on a losing streak.

"So our good deal had limitations, huh?"

"Young fella, every deal has limits. My business card's clipped to the brochure. Call me when you decide." Tony was attempting to explain they did not have $5000 to replace a machine they had purchased in good faith six months and two weeks earlier. Scott ignored him as he buttoned his coat, lit a cigarette, and left in silence.

An hour later, Tony filled his dad in on the unexpected and unwelcome news. Alfonse cursed aloud, something he rarely did. Obviously, they did not have the extra money in the till to absorb this expense. A horn tooted outside the butcher shop window. Tony grabbed his coat and a small bag. His father's bad mood had migrated to him.

"Who pissed in your *Cheerios*? Why are you grumpy?" Sal asked. He was behind the wheel of the Cadillac and they were on their way to the hospital.

"This motherfucker bamboozled us. Our mincer broke, and he's saying the warranty don't cover repairs anymore. New models are running close to five gee's."

"No fret, maybe my dad'll give you the cash. Has a hundred and fifty large comin'. Gonna' walk around town like a big shot...you know the old man had already spent the winfall ten times over in his mind while he lay stewing in the hospital bed."

"You're in a better mood," Tony noticed.

"He was moved from ICU to a regular room."

"You think he'd lend us the money? Would go a long way...still, not the reason I'm pissed. Motherfu..." Tony slammed his fist on the dashboard.

At the hospital, Sal and Tony walked quietly down the corridor to room 618. The room was semi-private, but the bed adjacent was vacant. They reached the partially opened door. A man was visiting with Gregorio, as he ate lunch in a chair by the window. The visitor was not a doctor. He was a tough guy, husky with a bald head and wearing a full length, black leather coat covering a maroon turtleneck. The boys knew him as the dude who showed his face at Ressini's for the past few weeks. Sal and Tony stealthily waited in the hallway until the conversation was completed.

"Greg, glad your heart's all right, but enough with the formalities." The man gripped a plastic cup of vanilla pudding on the lunch tray. He sniffed and placed the dessert back in its original spot.

"Yeah, I hear you Enzo. Good news...your chit will be paid in full. Only problem is, I need to get out of this place first." Greg's heavily stubbled face was gray and his reddish complexion was replaced by a more ashen tone.

"Forty-five grand on the book...sorry boss, but this big a number increases a thou' each day you don't pay. I'll give you a grace period of two days cause of your predicament before the juice starts running."

"I'm in a fuckin' hospital bed, Enzo! Are you kidding me? Coulda' died...you'd have squat. I never failed to pay before. Relax."

"Let me give you free medical advice...you better get your ass outa' this place filled with sick people. You may be a patient again. Clock'll be ticking!"

Enzo reached to the bottom of Gregorio's bed and retrieved a black, skully hat which was lying on top of the sheets. He fitted the hat on his head. Sensing the imminent departure, the boys hid by a supply closet. When the coast was clear, they doubled back.

"Yo dad, how are you doing? Ouch, you need a shave." Sal kissed his father.

"My mom thought you'd enjoy these." Tony kissed Zio Gregorio's cheek and handed over a box of Linden chocolates.

"Perfect timing guys, wanna' earn a few bucks? Sally boy, when you reopening the restaurant?" Greg picked out a small cube, sniffed and cracked a dark chocolate open. "Coconut, my favorite." *For a man with an acute heart condition and who had been physically threatened moments earlier, he was unusually upbeat and care free.*

"January's slow, Dad; won't hurt to stay closed till next week. Mom decided not to open until we knew more about your condition. Besides, you know in the dead of winter we lose money by staying open in these weather conditions."

"What you need us to do for you?" Tony refocused on the important topic.

"Go collect my winnings for the Super Bowl pool; two grand for both of you if you get the dough to me by tomorrow."

"Sure thing, we'll go this afternoon."

"Good, good. Go to Polazzo's Pizza and Pasta; the joint on Lincoln Avenue in Mt. Vernon. Ask for Tommy something or other...oh yeah, Tommy Forgione. He's a bartender. I'll call and tell him you'll be by. Damn, I need a smoke...friggin' hospitals."

Tony had a bounce to his step at the opportunity of extra dough in his pocket and to save the day for Zio Greg. They spoke of how to spend the windfall. "Joan Anderson," Tony blurted out the name of his high school crush. She was a senior at Tuckahoe High, but they were not an item when he was in school. Her father had forbid her to date until she turned eighteen, which was last week.

"What about Joanie?" Sal tuned the radio to the introduction of the Howard Stern Show.

"Saw her yesterday when I stopped by the school to see a few people. One thing led to another...she squeezed my arm and practically begged me to take her out." Tony flexed his eighteen inch mammoth bicep for added emphasis. "An extra couple of thou' will go a long way to wining and dining her."

Sal shook his head. "She's out of your league, bro; no seriously, sweet girl. All you need to do is flex. She'll throw dollars at you like one of those Chippendale guys."

"You mean the characters we saw at Disney?"

"Heh-Heh, no they're Chip and Dale. I'm talking about those homo dudes in the G-strings who dance around for the old broads." The banter continued as they entered Polazzo's Pizza and Pasta.

No customers were in the main dining area. The room was populated by busboys setting tables. The lounge was adjacent to a hostess stand and the entrance was through a fluorescent, scripted sign above the archway which spelled out "LIBATIONS." A guy was standing behind the bar. His arms were folded above an immense potbelly.

"You collecting for Gregorio? They nodded. The man handed over a thick envelope, turned his body and flipped through the Daily News.

Sal counted the bills on the top of a table. After a few minutes, he raised his head.

"What are you doing, Mr. Forgione? My dad's expecting a hundred and fifty thou' not twenty-five. He called you to say we'd be coming...don't BS us," Sal's voice grew louder and angrier.

"Listen you little punk." While the man's belly was immense, he stood well under six feet tall and his slouched shoulders were the exact opposite of the torsos of the strapping teens. "Tell Gregorio he may get his money... soon. But no friggin' way is he getting the whole amount. I didn't expect one guy to break the bank, especially in my biggest pool. Besides, he'd piss it away."

Tony glared to Sal in disbelief. As he did, four older guys appeared by the archway. The intimidating henchmen were built the same as Tommy Forgione and wielding baseball bats. Tony sized murderer's row, took a deep breath and blew out forcefully. Sal did the same. The defeated pair's eyes met before they meekly exited the establishment.

Once they drove safely away, Tony exploded, "JeeeSuuuSS Christ! Do we have PUSSY taped on our back?" He slammed his fist on the dashboard. This time the hard plastic cracked.

"I hear you, my brother. Let's call Cee, get his advice to figure this shit out before I go tell my dad."

Back at the butcher shop, they called Chris to lament. Tony was steamrolled by the douche bag repair guy and they were swindled big-time by the chubby bartender. Chris listened as Tony relayed the details of the story.

After a minute, Chris responded, "Is Jo-Jo's still into acting?"

"Joanne, yeah. She's doing plays and is in chorus. Why?"

Tony and Sal moved close to the receiver. Chris proceeded to give the details to his plan. After they hung up, Tony placed another call to Sabina Cameron.

LATER AT POLAZZO'S PIZZA AND PASTA

Tommy Forgione was more relaxed than ten hours earlier. He had to be shadowed by four bodyguards, as he made multiple stops at bank branches in Bronxville, Yonkers, Woodlawn and Mt. Vernon before finally arriving for his bartending shift. With a duffel bag filled with close to half a million dollars, he had to take precautions to secure his welfare. Besides the added muscle, he carried a snub nosed Smith & Wesson.

Forgione was a long time bookmaker and an aspiring entrepreneur. The forty-two year old, divorced father of two sons had built a vast network of friends, associates, bookies and gamblers that he had cultivated through two decades of hustling. His Super Bowl pools were extremely popular and added forty grand to his pocket. However, he had a pleasant surprise after strong-arming the two punks who came to collect for a degenerate gambler. The guy had won a hundred and fifty thou' but had a heart attack after finding out he had won. Screw him, he had sent kids to collect. Tommy would wait him out. Maybe the degenerate would have another heart attack and croak or the mob would whack him for not paying a gambling debt.

His makeshift bodyguards had earned their pay for protecting him. They scared the shit out of those two punks. When the bruisers had walked into the bar, he was intimidated. Four baseball bats neutralized any potential threat. He would still need the protection to escort him home. The unexpected windfall was stored in his duffel bag tucked below the bar and a few of the winners of other pools had not showed to collect. He was floating close to $300,000 until they were all paid-in-full.

"Well hello ladies, what can I do for you?" Tom greeted three attractive, young women who had entered the empty lounge. For a Wednesday night, this was a pleasant surprise.

"I'll have a glass of white wine. Sandy what do you want? Rosie, you're driving. Be responsible, only a club soda," the redhead demanded of her friend.

"Do you beautiful girls have ID?" He was going to serve them anyway, but he had to go through the motions.

"Sure." The redhead handed over her license. He studied the card and handed back with an air of authority.

"I'll show you mine, if you show me yours?" The cute brunette named Sandy giggled as she handed him her entire wallet. "My boyfriend broke up with me tonight. You better pour one of those slippery nipples or something. In fact, make mine a double!" The three cuties triumphantly laughed.

"You girls are legit." Tom inhaled, sucked in his stomach and gave a coy leer to the stunning trio. *My, my; a blonde, brunette and a redhead.*

"Well, how old are you handsome? Let's see some identification. Bet you're no older than twenty-nine," the recently jilted Sandy speculated.

"I'm older ladies." He removed his wallet and slid out the driver's license. The blonde studied the picture and data intently.

"Oh my God...Sandy, he lives in the building next to you on Bronx River Road?" She blew cigarette smoke to the ceiling.

"No way, let me see ...yep, I'm your new neighbor Tommy boy. I moved into the area a few months ago from New Rochelle." She raised her eyebrows and smiled before angling her face toward him. The professional barkeep had his lighter ready and lit the beauty's cigarette. She blew smoke over his shoulder.

The ladies talked amongst themselves and drank a few more cocktails. Out of the blue, as drunk women tend to do, they had a petty argument about female bullshit. The blonde and redhead stormed out in a huff, leaving the brunette stranded.

"Screw them. Can I use your phone?" Sandy's eyes were moist. Tommy bent behind the counter and handed her the receiver. After a few seconds, she ended the call, "SHIT...do you have the number of a cab company?"

"I get off in ten minutes, I can take you home. We're neighbors, would be my pleasure." Tommy crossed his fingers as his hired hands made their way into the lounge.

"Will you? Tom, you are such a doll."

"Hey guys, I think I'm all right. This young lady's gonna' escort me home." He grabbed a stack of cash in the duffel bag and handed a few bills to his friends.

Tommy quickly rang out the register, grabbed his flannel coat and the duffel bag. He and his damsel in distress exited into the cold night. He opened the passenger side door and hurried around the front before sitting behind the wheel. Hopefully, he'd have a good story to tell when he sauntered into work the next day. With a devilish grin, he beeped the horn at his cohorts who were also leaving Polazzo's.

They drove off, winding west along Lincoln Avenue. He crossed the overpass of the Bronx River Parkway before making a right onto Bronx River Road. As usual, no parking spaces were available. He went about his nightly exercise of circling around the block to find a spot. He made a left, driving the steep hill of Glen Road.

"Jackpot!" Finding a parking space this close to his apartment was a rare treat. An older model Cadillac was pulling out. He parked under a barren tree by a row of overflowing garbage cans. The icy wind howled. Tom and Sandy made small talk in the front seat of his Honda Civic.

"The heat feels good. The warmth finally kicked on as I have to leave," Sandy said, as she placed her hands in front of the vent. "Oh, this is my favorite song." She increased the radio volume and seat danced to *Like A Virgin*.

Tom saw his opening, "Madonna...are you like a virgin?" He glided his hand to Sandy's jeans. She let him explore, and he nervously massaged her knee and thigh. In response, Sandy gently stroked his fingers with her petite hands before moving his index finger to her lips. Smiling demonically, she kissed the appendages and reached to turn the volume of the radio higher. Tommy scrunched back in his seat and she unzipped his fly to rub the growth forming in his pants.

A WHILE LATER

Tommy Forgione was awoken by the sound of piercing screams coming from outside his car. Sandy was standing on the sidewalk by the opened passenger side door.

"THAT'S HIM. OH MY GOD...OFFICER, IS MY COUSIN ALL RIGHT!"

A police officer wrapped his jacket around Sabina Cameron's shoulders as she tensely smoked a cigarette.

"DO NOT MOVE. PLACE YOUR HANDS ON THE DASHBOARD!" a large African-American officer barked. He drew his revolver at the barkeep.

"Waa, waa, what's going on?" Tom's lips were oozing blood and his eyes and cheeks were puffy. Readily complying with the officer's wishes, he flinched and grabbed for his ribcage which was covered by a torn shirt.

"Scumbag, get out of the vehicle, slowly! You have the right to remain silent, anything you say..." Forgione was yanked from the vehicle with the help of three of Yonkers' finest. A large crowd of spectators had formed around the crime scene.

"NO...WHAT IS THIS...SON OF A BITCH...I WAS FRAMED... WHERE'S MY BAG?"

Two officers had opened the back door of the Civic. They removed a hysterically crying Joanne Albanese. Her shirt was torn, and she was flailing her arms over her head. Sabina raced through the pack of police officers and consoled her cousin. The dark-haired angel bawled into the older girl's shoulder.

The officers continued the search of the late model Honda. A gun was located under the passenger seat while a gym bag with a stack of money along with a vial of white powder was in the trunk. Tom Forgione was hauled off to jail. He was arraigned the next morning on kidnapping, attempted rape of a minor, and drug charges.

Sabina Cameron and Joanne Albanese sat in the back seat of a Yonkers police cruiser. The door was open, but the heat was on high. A female officer was taking their report of the altercation. Sabina gave her rendition of the fabricated story in which her brother had concocted and Sal and Tony had flawlessly planned. Joanne sipped hot chocolate in silence.

"I...I...I met him at this restaurant in Mt. Vernon. He was bartending; thought he was a nice guy. My friends and I had a fight. I was stranded and in a bind. He insisted on taking me home and agreed to get my little cousin at the movies in Bronxville. Something weird happened once he saw her. He snapped and changed into a pervert. We asked him to drive us home, but he ignored our request. He made a lewd comment about having a better idea. He groped me, and when I refused to give him a hand job, he pushed me out of the car and sped off. I'm lucky I remembered where he said he lived." Sabina winked at her little cousin and took a sip from her Styrofoam cup.

"Sweetie...Joanne, can you tell us how you were able to fight off the bad man? You are a brave, little hero," the officer implied.

"Well, I kicked and punched with all my might. He wasn't gonna' get me...my parents and older brother taught me to defend myself."

Sabina, aka Sandy...pleasured the unsuspecting, Tom Forgione. His eyes were closed in anticipation. Tony yanked open the door, as Sal pounced in. Tony wrapped a pillow case around their prey's head to muzzle his screams and control his movements. The pair slammed the swindler's face into the steering wheel and kneed and kicked his ribs until he was unconscious. Jo-Jo superstar came from offstage, hopped into the backseat and curled in a ball, ready to shake and cry on cue. Sal and Tony transferred the bundles of twenty, fifty and hundred dollar bills into another duffel bag. They left ten thousand dollars and the cocaine under the seat before sneaking away into the night.

A week later, Sabina and Joanne dropped the charges of kidnapping and attempted rape. They did not want to go through this horrible ordeal in a courtroom. Forgione pleaded to a Class A misdemeanor drug charge, paid a stiff fine, and was ordered to perform thirty hours of community service.

10

Deezz, Dem and Doze

MARCH 1, 1985

The economics department of the University of Texas was the largest within the College of Liberal Arts. The professors encouraged their students to think creatively about a wide range of topics for insight into the real world of private enterprise. The workload afforded scant time for an eager sophomore to socialize, as they plowed through papers, compiled research, and attended lectures to improve their performance.

"You're stalking this girl," Jason Rodgers chided, as they walked briskly to attend a guest speaker presentation.

"What? I'm into poetry." Chris managed to find time to enjoy the arts.

"The chick, Ally, has nothing to do with us going? Hope nobody sees us. The least you can do is to ask the dang girl out. Shoot man, I thought New York guys were supposed to be super cool?"

"Today's the day. I think I'm wearing her down." This proclamation had been made by Chris a year earlier during freshman year.

As with his crush on Colleen DePasquale, Chris became enchanted with Allison Wood the first second he saw her waiting to register for courses. He was too shy, and the best course of action was to try his best to be anywhere she was going to be on campus. Baby steps had led to walking; their friendship had progressed to being paired in an economics class study group.

They were conscientiously reviewing notes on the benefits of supply side economic policy. Chris believed he was winning over the tall brunette with his stories of working at his family's pasta shop and relating the positive benefits they experienced with the implementation of Ronald Reagan's economic policies. She was intelligent, and the Woods family was old Texas oil money. Her grandfather was a major benefactor to UT and they were studying in the Woods Memorial Library. Because she had never worked a day her life, Allison was having a hard time finding a real world example to how Reagonomics benefited small business.

"Ally, this was what happened when Reagan lowered taxes. In the late 1970s, we had people coming in to our shop who bitched about not working, inflation was staggering, and they'd buy maybe one or two items. When inflation and unemployment declined, they bought more and considered homemade pasta a luxury they could afford. Our sales increased over a hundred percent from when Reagan was elected in 1980. No wonder he got re-elected in a landslide."

"My granddaddy and daddy were major contributors to the Reagan campaign. They were invited to the inauguration in Washington." Allison gave Chris a cute smile. "However, my older brother...he is a different story. Unfortunately, he backed Mr. Mondale."

"Yeah, my sister voted for the losing side, too. She is of the liberal mindset, bless her soul." Even as kids, Chris and Sabina discussed politics. She had volunteered to pass out pamphlets for Jimmy Carter's failed campaign in 1980.

"Well, we have to introduce them, don't we?" Allison twirled her hair.

"My first vote. I mailed back to New York for Reagan. One for one in presidential elections, I'm undefeated... Soooooo, you think since I'm a Republican, your daddy and granddaddy would mind if I took you out?" His cup of water next to his notes trembled as his knee shook under the table.

"Take me out? Christopher J. Cameron...do you mean on a date? It's about time." The Texas belle placed her hand on top of his forearm. He melted with her touch.

The mood was broken as a paper football whizzed between the lovebird's faces. Chris snapped his head to direction of the errant kick. Snickers and giggles emanated from a column of library books as Chris and Ally rolled their eyes and pooh-poohed their instigators.

The fake college life was growing on Sal Esposito and Tony Albanese. When all you did was workout in a top-notch weight room, go to parties and not have to go to class, how could their pseudo-life not be a blast? This was especially true when you had a boatload of money at your disposal.

"Pummeling the dude was such a friggin' rush! "I never felt so alive!" Tony said as he hugged Chris upon their Austin arrival.

"Swiping the cash and giving him legal trouble was the icing on the cake," Sal satisfyingly greeted his blood brother.

Ricky Mullino had acted as the getaway driver for Sal and Tony to board a midnight *Greyhound* to Texas. Sal handed Ricky three envelopes. One was for Tony's dad with $5000 to replace the broken machine; the second held $50,000 for Gregorio, more than enough to settle his gambling debt. The third was for Sal's mom.

Sal had made a moral decision to hold back the bulk of the money which his dad had won. He placed the money in a safe deposit box at a well-respected Texas bank.

"Dad, would you listen to me...please? You'll get your cash, but stop gambling. You suck and doesn't the restaurant mean more to you?" Sal crossed his fingers and waited for a response.

"Boy, if you're wrong here I will beat the crap out of you. But okay, I hear what you're saying. This was a close call. Enzo didn't hide he was at the end of the line with me."

"Keep the restaurant closed for remodeling, get yourself healthy and recuperate. Ma, hold the money. My buddy's father is a carpenter, and he agreed to do the work for thirty grand."

"Oh, how exciting, baby; new designs are dancing in my brain," Dina ecstatically responded.

"Dad, when I'm back in town, I'll turn over the remainder of the Super Bowl winnings; seventy-five grand. Spend as you wish." Chris and Tony listened.

Chris patted Sal on the back. "The most direct you have ever been to Zio Greg."

"Kinda' easy to be tough. I'm 1400 miles away and making friggin' demands through a telephone line." Sal wiped sweat off of his forehead.

Status reports that Sal had received from his mom were coming back positive, and he beamed the place would be top notch with her in charge.

With time to kill, they were living the college lifestyle of the rich and famous as the Columbus Avenue Boys were $225,000 richer. They had determined Tommy Forgione was garbage and did not deserve the money from the Super Bowl pools. The average yearly income for a family in the United States was a fraction of this sum. Life was as good as they could have ever imagined.

Even though they were teenagers and had no underworld connections, they never challenged the assumptions and whispers around UT that they had to be in the Mafia. "We're playing this shit to the hilt. Why not? We're Italians visiting Texas with rolls of cash," Sal convincingly schemed. "Big Tony, I'm not rocking our fugazi, underworld boat?

While Chris was shy around the female student body, Sal and Tony were not and made fast company with the bevy of sorority sisters populating the campus. The young ladies were drawn to them like flies to honey and enchanted by their rough, tough *New Yawker* speak.

"Hey, yo, yo my friend Cee...I'll have one a deezz, dem and doze."

"Will you say water for me Salvatore?"

"WAATTEER...Heh-Heh, what you mean...a pretty little thing like youse' don't say it right." They notched many marks on bedposts at Duren and Andrews female dorms.

Sal and Tony were going to hate heading back to New York come Monday morning. Surprisingly, the quasi-college life was productive. While Chris was sitting in classes and vigorously courting Allison Woods, Sal had enrolled at the Austin Culinary School for a three-week course on Texas barbecue. Tony spent time working for J.R.'s dad at an oil rig outside of San Antonio. He had assisted in the maintenance of the heavy machines and was paid five hundred bucks for a five-day stint.

They had equally split the take from Forgione. Chris shared his with Sabina since she was an integral part of the ruse. With the cash he had received from his grandparents almost depleted, his cut would go a long way for the remainder of his sophomore and part of his junior year for spending money at the university.

Sal and Tony had close to five grand remaining. They would drive back East in style. The bulk of their fortunes had gone toward the purchase of new vehicles. Sal was the proud owner of a black Chevy Silverado while Tony chose a red, Chevy C/K.

Chris had been perceptive. The economy under Ronald Reagan had been better than what they had remembered as young kids when the peanut farmer, Jimmy Carter, had tried his best to run the country into the ground. The three compadres were flush with cash, driving bad-ass vehicles, and their muscles were bulging. Life was good.

11

Meaner Than A Junkyard Dog

MARCH 8, 1985

The twenty yard, roll-off dumpster had been filled to the brim with beams, tile, molding, sheetrock and carpeting. Sal and his parents stood outside Ressini's clapping their hands and waving as the garbage was removed from the parking lot. As they entered, tradesmen were diligently completing the finishing touches for the grand reopening scheduled for less than a week away.

After his eight day stint in the hospital, the doctors had ordered Gregorio to rest, take his meds, and lay off the smokes. Remarkably, he had done his best to change the bad habits and had even embarked on an exercise regime. Sal had encouragingly noticed for the past four weeks his dad had walked a couple of miles per day and worked out with weights.

"So what do you think, honey?" Dina unveiled the spectacularly renovated Ressini's Restaurant. The last of the parquet floor tiles, a stainless steel bar sink, and soda dispenser had workmen tinkering about. For the most part, the place was ready for primetime.

Gregorio shed a tear, as his voice cracked, "Dina, darling, I'm speechless."

"Angelo, we cannot thank you enough. On time and under budget, you are our hero...This is my husband, Greg."

"Nice to meet you, my friend," Gregorio said. "My wife couldn't stop speaking about the work you did. To see the finished product for myself is spectacular."

"You're the one who has someone who's spectacular. Mrs. Esposito has a fine eye...her vision, not mine." Angelo firmly shook Gregorio's hand.

Salvatore came bouncing out of the kitchen. He had been completing the graphic design for the new menu and sought his parent's approval before running off to get them printed. The menu would be comprised of a lighter fare, with pizza and wedges, complimented by higher-priced pasta, beef, veal, chicken and daily specialty dishes. Sal had been promoted to head chef by his mother, and he had accepted the challenge.

"I'll take my place behind the register and collect the cash. You and your mom did real good."

"Heh-Heh Dad, you ever think you could charge $22.50 for an entree before? The bar has the ambiance of a downtown hotspot. Specialty martini menu's gonna' be killer."

Sal had consulted with Chris to crunch the numbers. With the premium alcohol and wine pricing, if a quarter of the patrons had a two drink minimum, the profit margin would be more than they ever earned before. All they had to do was keep the old man away from the bookie.

"If we fail, I blame you." *Well, the compliments sure didn't last for long.*

"Yeah, okay Dad. I'm going to the printer and the gym with Tony." Sal was in such a euphoric state, and the pep in his step had continued through the unveiling of the restaurant. His good moods were always short lived. Not many people knew his bulging muscles were the result of releasing the massive amounts of anger caused by the verbal and physical abuse he had endured through the years from his father.

LATER, EAST COAST FITNESS CENTER

The clanking of weights at squat racks and bench presses was complimented by the crescendo of sixty-, seventy-and eighty-pound dumbbells slamming to the padded floor. Heavy metal music blasted. This was a typical day of pumping iron at the premier gym in Westchester County.

Sal and Tony had spent a good chunk of the remaining cash on weight belts and wrist wraps for their workouts, nutrition supplements and protein powder to fuel their bodies and of course plenty of stylish apparel with the

East Coast logo. Today, they wanted to get extra ripped before hitting the night clubs hard. After an early powerlifting workout of heavy squats and deadlifts, the night session consisted of super sets of biceps and triceps.

"Ten more reps, feel those fuckers," Sal was on a bench and blasting out overhead tricep extensions with an eighty pound dumbbell.

"Don't be a pussy Mary Jane, do you wear a skirt? Give me five more reps." Tony's arms were growing into legendary status.

A gym musclehead snuck behind the counter of the juice bar and replaced the Def Leppard cassette blasting *Rock of Ages*. Moments later, the sounds of "*We Are the World...We Are the Children...*" was immediately reciprocated with a resounding "BOO" response which emanated amongst the testosterone filled gym floor. The easily convinced juiceheads must have thought listening to the tune over and over again would atrophy muscle growth.

"Turn that crap off, Carlo!" Felix Bannos, the king of them all screamed as he bolted from the powerlifting room.

Bannos and Carlo Volpe joked and pushed each other as only steroided out friends would do. While Bannos gave the appearance of a gorilla in the wild, Volpe stood 5'5" but had defined musculature. Sal and Tony admired the pair from afar.

"The Volpe dude's all right. He let me and Frankie Zip cut the line at *Hoops* the other night. He was bouncing and didn't ask us for ID."

"Yeah, well the other one, the big scary dude, he's a prissy mother fucker...He was in the locker room when I was changing. I happened to open the locker with his crap in it...by mistake of course. Guy almost took my head off...jerk." Tony shook his head in abhorrence before lying on the bench. A hundred and five pounds for twenty reps should shock his system.

"Still man, give the guy credit; and his girlfriend...*madone*!" Sal situated himself for a set of preacher curls.

"Fifteen more reps till your arms are ready for the club," Tony praised his workout partner.

"Dude, you're ripped, too." Sal punched Tony's chest after he followed with a grueling set of overhead extensions. "You want a protein shake? I'm gonna' get a pineapple and banana smoothie with whey."

Massaging his throbbing cannons, Tony walked over to the juice bar. "Ummmh, get me the same as you but with strawberry...banana makes me fart." He made his way back to clean his weight station which was a mess. He had left five, ten, and twenty-five pound metal plates on the floor after his tricep-bicep shredding session.

Tony chuckled as Felix Bannos stumbled in front of him. Bannos had tripped over a plate scattered on the floor, as he admired his appearance in the mirror.

"Yo, Henry...tell these assholes to clean their mess," The manager of the gym disapprovingly shook his head, as he blended Sal's drink.

"Hey, I'm sorry, Felix...my friend, I was coming to clean. My name's Tony...Tony Albanese," he stated, thinking this was a good time to break the ice with the gym superstar.

"I don't give a fuck kid...watch your ass...don't let this happen again." Bannos bumped past him and returned to the powerlifting room.

Over the loudspeaker, Henry piled on. "Will Tony Albanese please put his lipstick and kneepads on...Felix Bannos wants a blow job." The entire gym erupted with catcalls. Tony stood in place with his head pitched. Regaining his composure, he raised his head and caught Sal's eyes from ten feet away.

"Not thirsty anymore, my friend." His eyes were those of a psychopath.

IN THE PARKING LOT

Rewording the Jim Croce song *Bad, Bad Leroy Brown*, Felix Bannos was God's gift to this earth. He was feared on the south and north sides of Yonkers, in the baddest parts of the city, even Getty "Ghetto" Square. At the clubs he bounced at, all the chuckleheads better beware of his name. He stood 'bout six foot four. All the ladies wanted him to be their lover while all the men called him sir. He had a reputation of being meaner than a junkyard dog and old King Kong would swing on a vine in fear of his presence.

Bannos had competed in bodybuilding and powerlifting competitions on the East Coast. He received a standing ovation as a nineteen year old, posing side by side with Lou Ferrigno at the 1976 Pro Mr. America competition. Depending on if he was training to compete in powerlifting or bodybuilding events, he would balloon to 280 pounds of thickness or shrink to 218 pounds of shredded muscle. Posted on the chalkboard hanging in the powerlifting room were his recent achievements-a bench press of 585 pounds, a deadlift of 860 pounds, and a 635-pound squat. His inhuman power was primed for the New York Power Lifting Championship and had been enhanced with a potpourri of anabolic steroids. For this cycle, he bragged about his cocktail mixture of Anadrol, Malogex and Danabol working their magic through his system.

"Hey, Y-O...Marco, Carlo, Billy," in YO-nkers resident fashion, Felix called out to his three comrades in massive arms. "Gotta' meet Jimmy outside. He has a job for us to do before heading to the club tonight."

Bannos had a fearsome reputation. Since maintaining his massive frame was expensive, he was lucky to have a well-paying profession to reinforce his tough guy persona. He and his underlings were employed as soldiers for a Gambino capo. They shook down restaurant and nightclub owners, strippers, coat check girls, bartenders, waiters and waitresses. You name the tree, they shook fiercely. The other week, Bannos & Co., had brazenly demanded a popular disc jockey, Rico Rokz, provide free on-air plugs for a restaurant which their capo had a piece of. The on-air personality with the scratchy voice had initially thought the comment was amusing. After a beating in the parking lot of his apartment complex in White Plains, DJ Rico's rocked face and ribs had agreed to the request.

The three toughs walked out to the sub-freezing, winter night, roughhousing amongst themselves as only the best and baddest would do. "You kidding me? Assholes, you have nerve!" Sal and Tony slid off the freshly waxed hood of a red corvette. The souped-up sports car was customized with the vanity license plate, *FLEX CAT.*

The pair double-timed in the direction of Bannos & Co. Sal surged past Felix and exploded his arms out in a two hand shiver. Marco propelled backward into the brick wall and crumpled to the sidewalk. Sal continued on. Carlo Volpe transformed into a scared midget running around a circus tent. The third fella, named Billy, turned into Wee Willie after a swat across the right side of his face with a hard left hook.

Bannos exhaled and turned. The three steps Tony took toward him were swift. Depending on the circumstances, a grown man could change from being confident to fearful in a split second. Before this moment, nobody had ever NOT feared Felix Bannos.

A closed left fist tomahawked his right shoulder. Bannos' legs bucked as the second half of the combination came swiftly; an enclosed right fist grasping a sharp object. His left eye exploded. Tony punched him with an exposed key held tightly in his fist. Felix covered his face. A flurry of punches to both sides of the skull followed. He tripped backward after a two-arm shiver. A wall stopped his momentum, and his cranium snapped back as he slammed against the brick structure. Bannos staggered in place and tried to counterattack by swinging wildly but the force of the errant punch caused him to trip and stumble to the pavement. Tony dragged him toward the sports car, and FLEXCAT blubbered, "Oh please, please God make him stop." Raised by the collar of his leather jacket, Bannos' head was banged into the hubcap, and his ribs were kicked repeatedly. Not a word was uttered by Tony during the assault, only heavy maniacal breathing as Bannos received the thrashing of his life. A boot met his jaw, his nose and cheek before striking the nose once again.

"No, no, no," The thrashing continued. BAM, BAM! "Stop please, oh please stop!"

A crowd formed.

"YO ALBANESE, enough!" Set to finish him off for good, Tony abruptly halted. Bannos flopped to the pavement, directly underneath his vanity license plate. Mr. Black and Blue Torn Muscle lay prone, bawling uncontrollably.

12

Doing Surprisingly Well Without Us

APRIL 20, 1985

Rita Albanese and Maria Cameron perused the vast assortment of selections of the Red River Grill's breakfast buffet. The eatery was located in the atrium, one level below the lobby of the Marriott Hotel. The women placed items on plates and in bowls-cottage cheese, an egg white omelet, slices of dry whole wheat toast, and oatmeal with a scoop of assorted fruit. Their husbands were impatiently waiting for their beloveds to return with the meal to fuel the rest of their day. The men had been forbidden from feeding their bellies without proper supervision.

"I don't want to hear another word, Al. Sugar bear, you've eaten enough on this trip already. It's time to eat properly."

"Jeez Rita, do you want me to shrivel to nothin'? I'm still a growing boy."

"Maria, luv; what do you expect me to do with these morsels? Me God, after getting us across country in record time, Alfonse and I are more than a wee bit hungry. What do you say, my good man? Let's be goin' on strike!" Maria's husband coaxed his buddy to revolt against the misses.

Michael and Alfonse had been true road warriors, taking turns driving 2500 miles over the past seven days. The first half was primarily on Route 95 South from Tuckahoe to Port St. Lucie for a long overdue visit to their parents.

"Embracing retirement life I see. I've never seen you tanned and relaxed," Alfonse queried his father-in-law over a game of shuffleboard.

"Is my father-in-law feeling any better Vince?"

"Been tough on them, Mikey. The recovery from the fall has been slow."

The Camerons had been melancholy. A few years older than Vincent and Teresa, Joe and Julia were into their seventh decades on earth. They had aged considerably since leaving Tuckahoe. A few scary moments had transpired. Joe had fallen a few times, and as a result he needed a walker. Julia had refused the doctor's request to get an aide to assist her from time to time. Maria and her mom had petty arguments. Julia shuffled around the retirement community in an attempt to show she was self-sufficient.

The latter part of the journey had taken the couples west along Interstate 10 for a visit to see Christopher. The Camerons and Albaneses had never visited the Southern states before and this was their first visit to the University of Texas. This would be the swan song for the Impala station wagon.

"Alfonse, my good man, when I purchased my work horse in 1977 I had followed its assembly from the first bolt. I plan on supervising once again." Mike enjoyed his job as a foreman at the Chevrolet plant in Tarrytown.

"Christopher loved when he visited you at the plant," Maria reminisced.

"Aye, but the lad was mesmerized by how we operated and not the wonderful cars."

"Seems to be doing okay for himself smarty pants; football going along fine and his grades were A's and one B+ for the semester," Maria defended her son.

They were visiting in Austin to cheer Chris on at the inter-squad scrimmage. The Longhorn offense and defensive units would square off in the pinnacle event of spring practice.

"Chris was moved from free safety to strong safety. They have a young squad and talented guys at the two cornerback spots and free safety."

"Did he take the move all right?" Alfonse asked inquisitively as he devoured his 850 calorie meal.

"The boy's optimistic. Took the opportunity to show he belongs. He knew he wasn't fast enough. The speed of the outside receivers was ridiculous. He's in awe of a few defensive backs. I wrote their names; Tillman, Jeffries and Bragg," Michael recollected as he showed a set of color pictures of the three studs to Alfonse. "Coach Campbell wanted to try Chris at strong safety because the two guys ahead of him on the depth chart were seniors."

For the move to the physically demanding strong safety position, Chris had gained ten pounds of muscle to his frame. He would have to cover tight ends, blitz the quarterback, and be involved in the line of scrimmage running game defensive schemes. At 6'1" and 215 pounds, he was the largest and most aggressive defensive back.

"My Christopher is not shy about bragging. For the strength test prior to spring drills, he completed 225 pounds for twenty-four repetitions. No other defensive back came close, and he was three reps behind the hulking linebacker, Kiki deAyala."

"You two guys, all you talk about is football, football, football. Come on, Rita and I are going to call home," Maria ordered as her husband finished his fruit plate.

"Anthony's doing surprisingly well without us," Rita stated. The wives led the way as they walked the steps toward a row of pay telephones located in the rear of the lobby.

"Dina's thinking about filing for a divorce," Maria declared with a sad face.

"Greg was doing better since his health scare. Outward appearances could be deceiving," Rita reflected with dismay as she squeezed her husband's hand.

"Since Rosa had gone through a divorce, Dina wanted her advice. She was going to call to get her opinion." Ten years earlier, the Cavazzi family had cheered when Maria's sister, Rosa had divorced the *skeevoza* Pat Fortuno. The odd marriage had upset her parents for years. Fortuno was a vile character. Happily remarried and living in Houston, Rosa planned to drive to Austin the next day to have lunch with the family.

"Surprised me, too. Dina's seemed happy, bubbly at times. Restaurant's doing fabulous, and Greg hasn't been gambling. He even stopped smoking."

"Well, I'm sure Rosa will get an earful from Dina. She'll have plenty of real good gossip when we see her tomorrow," Rita said as she inserted a handful of quarters to dial the butcher shop.

Rita spoke with both Anthony and Joanne while Maria had a chat with her daughter. Sabina was pulling triple duty while they were away. Thankfully, a bunch of girlfriends had agreed to assist her at Bella's. Besides tending to the store, she had classes most mornings and she waitressed at Ressini's. For the few hours she had to herself, she volunteered at a food bank.

"My Saby, she's the champion for the underprivileged. Bless her heart," Maria commented by the revolving doors of the lobby entrance before the group headed to Texas Memorial Stadium.

"I must have a talk with her, though. She was flippant about us visiting with Rosa." For some reason which Michael could not put his finger on, Sabina did not care for her mother's sister. This perplexed him, because his daughter was a saint whose sole ambition in life was to help the less fortunate and had compassion for all people.

"So, is the butcher shop in one piece?" Alfonse kissed his wife on the cheek and held her purse as she put her sweater on. The windy and chilly afternoon was unusual for Texas in April.

"Yes darling. He misses his mommy, but he was in a great mood. While the store was traditionally slow for the weeks after Easter, because Ressini's was busy they were doing great with the business Sal had given him."

"Sabina reiterated the same about Bella's; unusually busy."

In theory, the three family businesses had operated as one. For the past twenty-six years, Ressini's had never purchased their quality meats, pasta and side dishes from anywhere but the Albanese and Cavazzi stores.

"Well, one thing appears obvious; those young folk are pushing us out. Me thinks they want to retire us."

Since Sal and Tony had returned from visiting Chris earlier in the year, the boys had matured considerably. Sabina and JoJo had joined in with this surprising growth from adolescence to mature, young adults. They had insisted their parents take a long vacation.

"After all you've earned the time off."

"Our friends will help us. They need the extra money."

"When you return good and rested, the businesses would still be standing."

BACK IN TUCKAHOE

Since the grand re-opening of Ressini's Ristorante, customer traffic had been far above the six hundred plate weekly breakeven threshold. This had been especially evident on Friday and Saturday nights

"Ressini's Ristorante, how may I help you?..."Ooohhh, I am sorry, the only times available for a table of six this Saturday are 5:30 p.m. or 10 p.m....Next Saturday?...well yes, we do have 8 p.m., okay a party of eight. Your name please ..."

In addition to the good fortune in the dining room, Ressini's lounge had transformed into the hot spot for young adults to carouse on Thursday evenings. If you arrived late, you would join a line of lounge lizards wrapped around the outside of the establishment with a hope to mingle with the attractive women who flocked to the premier destination.

"Okay Reggie, rules are as follows; if the chick's hot, she gets in without a wait. If a bunch of tools come, make'em wait. We don't want a pirate ship. Make couples wait a few minutes, but no longer...you control the flow." Tony managed the floor security crew to perfection. He had hired ten massive guys, all donned in tight, red T-shirts. Leon, a guy Tony's knew from the gym had a favorite saying-"I'll rip you a new asshole if you give me any trouble tonight!" Nobody doubted he would not easily perform this extremely invasive medical procedure.

Sabina peaked at her watch and exhaled as she surmised how long the three remaining tables of customers would linger. At 10:45 p.m., she was nearing the end of her Saturday evening shift. Exhaustion was setting in after an exceptionally tiring week. While the Camerons eldest child was glad to assist her parents while they were on vacation, her emotions were close to their maximum.

"Ricky, give me two vodka tonics and a glass of Pinot."

Ricky Mullino was biding his time bartending. He was off to the police academy in ten days. He had taken the Police Office Entrance Examination a month after high school graduation. Joey Mullino had recently been hired at Ressini's as a busboy.

"Hey little lady, let me buy you one. Rick, get Sabina whatever she's drinkin' on me." Enzo was sitting at the edge of the bar nursing a scotch. He eyed her figure through her black slacks and a white tuxedo shirt.

"Thanks anyway...I'm leaving after my shift ends...bedtime." Sabina smiled in Enzo's direction and rolled her eyes at Ricky. She returned to the dining room with a full tray.

"Did she make a joke or something...punk?" The inebriated, semi-regular challenged Ricky, who could not hold back a grin after Sabina had exited.

"Na...na...no, Enzo."

"Let me talk with you...Mr. Big Shot."

Ricky scurried into the kitchen. A few moments later, Sal came out. "Enzo, it's kinda' late. I'm gonna' respectfully ask you to leave for the night. Besides, we're closing the bar...last call came and went already."

"All right, allllright...sorry kid," Enzo slurred a halfhearted apology. He tossed back the last of his *Johnny Walker Black* and exited via the side entrance.

LATER, CLOSING TIME

Sabina, Ricky, and Joey sat at a small table in the corner of the lounge. The last of the dinner patrons had departed and they were tallying tips and having a nightcap before walking the quarter of a mile home together. Back in the day, Joey had been Sabina's best babysitting client while the whole town knew Ricky had a major crush on her since before puberty. As co-workers and young adults, Sabina was patiently waiting, and waiting and waiting for him to make his move.

"You two strong men ready to escort me home?" Sabina asked, as she double-checked the service door in the rear of the restaurant. She was tasked with the end of night responsibility. Sal had left ten minutes earlier to shower before heading to a club in the city.

"Hey tough guy...we're not finished, you and me." Enzo emerged from the shadows.

"Enzo, I am more than sorry. Please, I am not going to fight you; you'd kill me." Ricky had his arms up in surrender fashion. Sabina inched close to his side. Visibly shaking, Joey slid behind his older brother.

"Na, not gonna kill you...you're a wanna'be cop right? Well, you need a challenge." With his thick meat hooks, Enzo yanked Ricky by his chest.

His tuxedo shirt tore as Enzo flung him hard against the garbage dumpster where he thudded hard into the metal.

Enzo was unyielding, stomping on Ricky's chest with his thick-soled boot. He yelped in pain, as his ribs cracked. The psychopath was unrelenting with his vendetta. Sabina screeched as she dropped to the ground to blanket Ricky. Joey shielded his brother's body. Enzo stumbled and wildly kicked Joey in the face. With the trio huddled in a protective cocoon, the tough guy slowed his assault and breathed heavy. He stopped his punishment and staggered into the night.

13

A Case Of Amnesia

APRIL 23, 1985

Sal and Tony bullshitted about the Mets promising 14-8 start to the season as they bided their time on Seminary Road, a main thoroughfare near the Bedford Village Elementary School. The guy they were waiting for, Denny Zuletic, was driving a silver Mercedes and dropping his two daughters off at school. An Albanian immigrant, he was forty-eight years old and slightly built with light brown hair. The guy owned DeRosa's Ristorante, a high scale eatery in Greenwich.

"This guy lives in a sweet neighborhood. I hear of few of the Mets players live up here," Sal commented, as he observed the woods of northern Westchester.

"Most of the guys live in the city, but I bet Gary Carter who's a family guy does. Holy crap, a deer!" Tony pointed at the tree line hugging Seminary Road.

"Shit Ton, huge mansions and wildlife are everywhere. This guy did all right if he's hobnobbing with pro ball players; penniless immigrant to fat cat, restaurant owner."

Denny's fairytale story did have a few bumps along the way. Since the doors had opened, DeRosa's had been the target of an extortion scheme from a high-level Mafia figure. After three years, Denny had brought his problem to the attention of the FBI. An eighteen-month investigation followed. DeRosa's and four other restaurants in the area were put under surveillance. The FBI swept in and arrested associates of the Gambinos.

The indictment had stated Santo Tracino and ten of his soldiers had conspired to commit extortion by obtaining money and property from, and without the consent of the operators of restaurants in Greenwich, White Plains, Stamford and Hawthorne. While Denny Zuletic's name was never revealed, he was scheduled to testify at the trial in less than a month.

Sal and Tony were wearing red and white Fox Lane football jackets and baseball caps. As they viewed the silver Mercedes in the distance, they waved their arms for him to stop. The hood to their car was lifted and they played the part of goofy, high school jocks. The side window to the Mercedes buzzed open as the driver slowed to a stop.

"Thank you sir...it's dead...think you can help us?"

"You two must play on the line for Foxx Lane, had a good season. Sure thing, let's have a look," Denny praised the pair as he stepped out.

From the rear passenger side of the disabled Chevy Citation, a third person emerged. Damien Morris was running this show. Simultaneously, Sal and Tony grabbed Denny by his arms as Damien sauntered over. He was a tough guy in his mid-twenties with thick brown hair and a goat-tee. He wore a loose-fitting, bowling shirt over his muscular frame.

"Thanks, we had hoped you would stop...saw you drop your two beautiful daughters at school." Denny did not say a word and shook uncontrollably as Damien guided him over to the opened hood of the disabled vehicle.

"You've got a lot on your plate...Let's say you happened to own a restaurant...the plate reference would be a funny play on words."

"I, I, I, don't want any trouble," Denny whispered.

"Trouble...why would you be in any trouble? This guy thinks we're hooligans. All we want him to do is assist in fixing the car, right?" Sal and Tony nodded.

Denny's body tensed as Damien reached to the back of his pants. He breathed out and gulped as a folded sheet of paper was handed to him. Written on the page was the indictment against Santo Tracino.

"It's not worth the drama, dude. Why don't you go on vacation for a month; take this. It's the least we can do for helping us with the car." The imposing tough guy placed an envelope in the palm of Denny's shaking hand. He opened the packet to reveal a stack of hundred dollar bills. After a few seconds, the restaurant owner nodded his head in concurrence before removing the bills and tucking the bribe into his front pants pocket.

Sal and Tony shut the hood of the car. The trio took off in the Citation. Damien dead-panned, "Guy must think Albania is safer than Bedford."

"This one was easy," Tony remarked from the back seat.

"Been at this for a while guys, wish they were all as easy as this."

Standing slightly over six feet tall with broad muscular shoulders and a rugged jaw, Damien Morris was barely literate, and a high school drop-out. He had been raised by his mother in a public housing project in the Bronx. Not shy about his humble roots, he bragged to Sal and Tony about how he came to be. One of the only white families in the projects, Damien, along with his brother and two sisters had survived as best they could on welfare, food stamps and charity box clothes. When he was three, his Irish father was found dead in an alley; the consequence of years of heavy drinking. His Italian mother was a beautiful woman who had to work two jobs to make ends meet. Her ample breasts had caught the attention of many in the lounge where she bartended.

Damien committed his first crime when he was eleven. "My brother Billy, he's six years older than me, we found mom crying with her blouse torn in the lobby of our apartment building. A black guy who lived in another building tried to rape her; the scumbag volunteered to take her home from the bar. The next night, as the creep was getting out of his car, Billy and I pounded the fuck out of him with spiked bats and rocks. We kicked the shit out of him and left the body a mess on the pavement. I actually thought we killed him."

Soon after this incident, the Morris family moved to Yonkers. By his teen years, Damien lifted weights and boxed. "All I wanted to do was fight, in and out of the gym. My ass was never kicked."

Training out of the Jerome Boxing Club and the Morris Park Gym he had perfected a devastating left hook. Damien was benching more than 400 pounds and flexing 19-inch biceps. He was a slab of muscle when he caught the attention of an associate of Santo Tracino. The capo, who was a bricklayer, overheard Damien bitching about money problems while helping to pour cement. To see how broke the kid was, Damien was offered two thousand dollars to kill a guy who was pinching on a bookmaker's turf. He made the offer by drawing a pistol in wet cement and 2k before smoothing the mortar out to dry.

Damien made good to earn his bounty, and put his trademark two bullets from a 9mm pistol into the back of the skull of his victim as he was mowing his lawn. He left the masonry business and had cemented his reputation. Over the years he had become a feared enforcer.

LATER, IN YONKERS

Sal Esposito exited the Bronx River Parkway and snaked his truck through the narrow streets of the Crestwood residential section. This was his normal shortcut to avoid mid-morning, Central Avenue traffic. Tony had gone to dispose the Foxx Lane jackets and caps. He would dump the garments in a Goodwill bin at a shopping center in Mt. Kisco. Damien Morris had ventured to deal with his assortment of underworld business activities. His territory encompassed northern Westchester and Connecticut and included a wide array of money making opportunities. Sal and Tony had been assigned to his crew by Santo Tracino's son, Jimmy.

Jimmy "Jimmy Tree" Tracino was an old friend of the Columbus Avenue Boys. They had played Pop Warner football during their pre-teen days. Since he had lived in Yonkers, and not Tuckahoe, they had lost touch. They had become reacquainted after Jimmy Tree witnessed the thrashing of Felix Bannos outside of East Coast Fitness Center. While standing over Bannos' writhing body, Jimmy Tree had unexpectedly been put in a bind and needed muscle for a situation later in the evening. A nightclub owner had been shooting his mouth off, saying Jimmy was a punk and if not for his feared father he would be pumping gas somewhere. Jimmy walked into the club with Sal and Tony by his side. They barged into the owner's office and Jimmy beat him with a stapler. The stapler broke apart after a blow to the head. Perturbed, Jimmy continued the assault with the base of the telephone. Needless to say, after getting out of the hospital, the remorseful club owner had a sit-down with Santo and his son. He apologized profusely and handed over a $5000 tribute for any inconvenience. Sal and Tony made an easy $300 apiece.

Sal parked his truck behind the mini-mall and walked around to the front of the building. An insurance agency, tattoo parlor, delicatessen and video rental store were the tenants of the one-story structure. Sal entered Rewind Video and greeted the attractive blonde behind the cash register with a kiss on the cheek before walking into the secluded back room reserved for perusing the XXX flicks. Jimmy Tree was finishing a conversation as Sal tapped on the doorframe. The visitor took Sal's approach as his opportunity to leave. He shook Jimmy's hand, nodded to Sal and departed.

"All is a-okay upstate," Sal gave the coded update.

"Yeah, we'll see. You'll get your taste, soon." Jimmy would pay Sal and Tony $500 each if Denny Zuletic was diagnosed with a case of amnesia before the trial.

"Besides this...Jim...I have a favor to ask." Sal put his arm on his captain's shoulder as they inspected the hardcore porn on the covers of the plastic video cases.

"What's on your mind, Nuts? We don't provide medical coverage," the gangster joked. "Ever have three women at once? My strip club in the Bronx is where you need to go. As long as you keep the lights off...when the switch goes on, *oohfaaah!*"

"Good from far...but far from good," Sal joked in reply. "No, this is business related...the guy Enzo, he's been hanging out at my restaurant. My father, the *stunod*, owed him money last year when he was gambling like a mad man. Anyway, he still thinks he owns the joint and..."

"Enzo? No Enzo in our crew; describe him."

"Big, bald, ugly dude; badass from Mt. Vernon...what's his last name? Pella, Pellan..."

"Pellanigro, Enzo Pellanigro? He doesn't run with us, Sally. In case you haven't heard, your dad hasn't been with our crew for close to two years. Since his gambling took over, he couldn't cover his tribute. My dad stopped protecting his place. He must have built his gambling sheet with Enzo. Bad move. Enzo runs with the Luccheses and has a vicious reputation; bookmaking, loan sharking. The motherfucker ain't going anywhere, anytime soon. Enzo could do whatever he wanted at locations not under our control."

"The bastard beat the crap out of a good friend of mine last week, for no reason. You remember him, Ricky Mullino; played Blue Devils, too. Well anyway, kids gonna' be a cop in the next few months. Don't you think he could be a guy you want to get on the good side of...I was thinking?"

"Sorry buddy. Your restaurant would be a great place for me, but I can't bark up that tree because what a lunatic did to a kid who we don't give two shits about."

"I'll do whatever...if the economics make sense...for you outside my restaurant. But, sorry, Ressini's is off limits. The place is my blood." Sal stood firm on losing control of his family business.

"I hear you, man. Sorry to tell you, you've lost the place already. Made guys can do whatever the fuck they want. You're on your own." Jimmy stopped examining the pictures of tits and ass. "On the bright side, Damien says you guys are scary as shit and intimidating the fuck out of his saps. Work your ass off, maybe you'll get a promotion."

Sal stormed out of the video rental store. Time again to make a call to Chris from the butcher shop.

14

Broken Up

The largest of the contiguous United States, the Republic of Texas encompassed the better part of 270,000 square miles. Traveling from east to west and north to south, one observed a diverse terrain which ranged from coastal swamps and piney woods to rolling plains and rugged hills, and finally the desert and mountains of Big Bend. As a temporary employee of Rodgers Oil and Gas, Chris Cameron believed he had traversed the entire Lone Star State.

For the contracted assignment, he had been tasked to categorize any type of oil and gas drilling activity within the state. For the past four weeks, he had crisscrossed the vast landscape, scribbling on maps and pinpointing locations of upright oil derrick rigs, pump jacks and vehicles of competing companies. He slept in dingy motels and scoffed meals at rest stops and diners. The money was good and he had plenty of time to contemplate the meaning of life. The downside was he had been isolated from civilization, rarely had time to exercise and ate an excessive amount of fast food.

Finally back in Austin, he would devote the next eight weeks to getting in prime shape for the football season and to take two more classes. His freshman year grades were solid. Scholastic times would be challenging as he was contemplating whether to double major in subject areas he equally enjoyed-economics and American History.

The lack of contact with his family and friends had been difficult to handle. He did not know what Sal and Tony were doing and his mother was worried sick. The beautiful Ally had also been on his mind while he was on the prairie. While the courtship was in its early stages, they had enjoyed each other's company and she was the first person he had called when he returned to civilization. Thankfully, she had not returned home to Fort Worth over the summer break.

After the enjoyable weekend with Ally, he checked in on the home front. Sabina was planning to do a stint with *Habitat for Humanity* and would be spending two weeks during August in rural Mississippi to help construct homes for the less fortunate. Bella's was doing well. A friend of the Albanese's had inquired about opening a location with the Bella's name in Yonkers. The franchise would be close to the Hudson River and would not cannibalize any business from the flagship store in Tuckahoe.

With his parents and Sabina's happy news fresh in his mind, he rang Sal and Tony. The problem they had mentioned about the Enzo character was gnawing at him while on the road. Short of killing the mobster, he had not been able to define any reasonable way to squeeze him out of the picture. Chris had not been back to Tuckahoe in a year. His collegiate life in Texas changed him dramatically, and the makeover was for the good. While guilty of losing touch with Sal and Tony, he had a life of his own to live.

This had never been the case before. During the long hours pondering life over the past month, Chris had grown maddened by Sal and Tony's lack of focus. They were no dummies. In fact, Tony was one of the best chess players and still beat Chris regularly. He had tutored him in math and science and once he applied himself, concepts would be grasped quickly and good grades would follow. Tony could tell you the odds on a sports bet in a nano-second and knew all about the butcher trade and fixing anything mechanical. Chris thought Sal was a savant and did poorly in school because he was bored. He was an artist and his creations came out of an oven. He had thrown himself into the culinary trade at a young age and never tired of creating and learning. The classes he took in school were unfulfilling. While he had a reading comprehension problem that was not diagnosed until his sophomore year, he managed to pull C+/B-grades. He could sing and sketch. Conversely, Chris was tone deaf, his drawings were chicken scratch, and he was lost around mechanical objects.

Equally remarkable about his blood brothers was their ability to extrapolate on an idea he would conceive. Chris was a visionary and loved to lay the groundwork for a plan. Once formalized, Sal and Tony would execute to perfection. Whether devising a scheme as five year olds for their parents to give them candy, distracting a teacher while Sal prepared a practical joke, or to play hooky convincing the school nurse they were deathly ill, they had participated in many, masterfully constructed ruses. This early education had matured into the perfectly executed con on Tommy Forgione. Chris had hoped since the last conversation maybe they had figured out a way to handle the Enzo quagmire on their own.

He dialed the phone.

ALBANESE'S BUTCHER SHOP

The mid-morning rush had waned and Alfonse removed his apron, grabbed car keys and went home to eat lunch with Rita. He greeted Sal, who was walking in to see his son. Sal went directly to the back room while Tony locked the front door and flipped the OPEN sign to BACK IN A FEW. Sal placed paraphernalia on top of the sterile stainless steel counter. They diligently prepared three syringes of Dianabol, Deca-Durabolin and Anavar. This cocktail of anabolic steroids was moments away from being injected into their gluteus medius muscles.

After the thrashing of Felix Bannos, Sal and Tony were on emotional highs which made them feel invincible. This intoxication could only be extended if they were perceived as being unequivocally feared. This led to their experimenting with "the juice" and toward the end of the first three month cycle, they were officially hooked. Strong and muscular before the illegal enhancement, they had noticed a marketed difference in strength and appearance. Sal's bench press in February was 315 pounds for three reps. Today, a power set of 375 pounds for ten reps was *like butter, baby*. He had gained thirty pounds of solid beef. His butcher buddy had seen similar results. Any time they entered the sweaty confines of East Coast Fitness; the other weightlifters knew the forty-five pound plates would be commandeered by the burly pair.

Their gargantuan physical appearance helped in many ways. The chicks at the clubs flocked to them. Other juiceheads followed their every move and bribed the pair with cocktails at the bar or protein shakes at the gym to get on their good side. Damien Morris collected gambling debts and laid down the law of the land with ease when S&T walked into a joint with him.

The downside to the drug flowing through their veins was they suffered from acute cases of back acne. In addition, they had grown apart from their parents and were rarely present at the traditional Sunday meal. They used this time to socialize and conduct underworld business with nefarious acquaintances. Sal desired the breathing space anyway. As an added side effect to the drugs, he had experienced mood swings and was prone to snap when his father provoked him. The less he saw of the old man, the better.

Percolating in the back of Sal's mind had been the silence from Chris about the problem they had discussed regarding Enzo. When they had initially spoken about the dilemma, Chris had promised to get back with a solution in short order. This was two months ago. In the meantime, Enzo had induced Gregorio to hire some of his minions to work in the kitchen. Sal had to fire and smack around more than one of the lowlifes for brazenly stealing and dealing drugs. Gregorio did not care this was transpiring.

Tony had finished his injections and was storing away his paraphernalia when the phone rang. Sal was completing his cycle.

"What's going on my brother?" Chris genially greeted Tony from the other end of the telephone.

"Hey, it's alive. Where the heck have you been?" An edge of cynicism was in Tony's words.

"I've been out of commission. Worked the past month for J.R.'s dad driving around the entire friggin' state of Texas. Good money but had little telephone access. I didn't speak with anybody," Chris snapped in a defensive tone.

Sal came on the line after Tony had relayed the update on Chris' whereabouts. "Hey Cee, I'm pissed at you. We spilled our guts about Enzo and crap. The guy's a cockroach, and his hanger-on's are around all the time; it's like playing Wack-A-Mole. My regular customers don't feel comfortable. The Thursday night crowd petered out. Ricky tells me complaints have been called to the police station to watch out for drugs at Ressini's. This has gone from bad to worse. We need him out."

"Finals were a bitch...and job kept me busy so I haven't had time to think this through," Chris continued to defend his actions.

"Yeah, yeah, okay we hear you college boy. You're too busy for us," Sal shot back.

"It's not what I meant at all dude, relax...why not come to UT for a few weeks, it'll be fun. There's a jamming music festival that..."

"Cee, you don't understand what's going on. I can't leave. When I return, the place could be empty. This guy's a psycho, and my dad is wrapped around his finger. And your answer to me is 'relax?' Screw you and your music festival!"

"Sal, rela...I mean, sorry, I've been busy."

"Enough with you're busy...we're busy, too. Jimmy Tree's making us run around busting heads and shit...not what I wanta' do with my life. But hey, the money's too good to pass on and enough to keep the restaurant open...for the time being."

"Hey, I never told you to get into this life, man."

"Oh, I see...you're better than us. You've given enough of your master plans. The well's dry, and you're too busy. Hell man, Enzo's after Sabina too, you okay with it? She's not, but it's scaring her. She's drinking." Sal had transitioned to a more contemptuous tone.

"No Sal, I don't want Saby or you guys to suffer. I honestly don't have an answer for you. What the hell can I do to a made Mafia guy?"

"Get off your ass and help your friggin' blood brothers!"

"I can't...have classes and working out. It's complicated. Shit Sal, I have a friggin' life too! This discussion is a circle jerk."

"Screw you. The friendship's over, stay with your Texas life and friends down there home on the range...you could care less about us...you're dead to me."

"You're dead to me, too," Tony echoed.

"What the fuck? To hell with you guys!"

Sal and Chris disconnected.

As close as the trio was, they were incredibly stubborn. In any case, this had been the worst quarrel which had transpired and half a country away, settling the dispute was highly unlikely under the present circumstances. The argument would not be resolved anytime soon.

The Columbus Avenue Boys had broken up!

15

The Gambino Payroll

AUGUST 24, 1985

The late days of summer were the perfect time to take in the scenery of the Canadian outdoors. With a warm breeze blowing through the early morning air, Sal Esposito and Tony Albanese were dressed identically in red fleece shirts, faded blue jeans and tan work boots. They were in the driver's seat of their respective trucks and hauling Coachmen Camping Trailer's. No one noticed the fashion *faux pas*.

Sal had reached the city limits of Buffalo in less than seven hours. He crossed the Peace Bridge and after a twenty minute traffic delay, headed north on the QEW Highway and pulled into the Queenstown Heights Park a few minutes before noon. Tony took a similar path and arrived a half hour later. They ate lunch separately on park benches in the picnic pavilion; sandwiches they had brought from home in Coleman coolers. After the midday meal, Sal went to the washroom. When he returned, Tony took this as his sign to take care of nature calling.

Entering the far corner stall, Tony removed his black fanny pack which held thirty thousand dollars in large bills and snapped the strap around a stainless steel pipe protruding upward from behind the toilet. After five minutes, he exited the stall and washed his hands. As he stood observing his perfectly quaffed hair in the mirror, a short, fair-skinned man in a loose fitting orange T-shirt ambled past him and into the stall that Tony had occupied.

After a few seconds, the man called out in a French-Canadian accent, "Hello, you left something behind." The inhabitant raised his arm above the stall door and handed Tony an exact replica for his forgotten fanny pack; less the thirty grand.

Tony attempted a comical, French accent, "All set my friend."

Sal and Tony walked separately to their respective trucks. The vehicles were parked in diagonal ends of the park, in shady comfort a few hundred yards beyond the picnic area. Both Coachmans were backed into the overgrown brush with the black Silverado and the red C/K pickup facing outward. Sal drove off first. He was followed fifteen minutes later by Tony. Instead of heading into the woods for a camping trip, they doubled back toward the Peace Bridge border crossing at Fort Erie.

The border agent to re-enter the United States was on the Gambino payroll and waved them both through without inspection. He had participated in this innocuous scam for Jimmy Tree many times over the past few years. Eight hours later, after unbearable late summer weekend traffic, Sal and Tony had crossed the Tappan Zee Bridge and into Westchester County. At close to midnight, they arrived at the final destination, an abandoned warehouse on Gun Hill Road in the Bronx. The campers were disengaged from the trucks. A burly Russian with salt and pepper hair handed Sal a thick manila envelope filled with cash. Tired and in need of showers, they traipsed off to the friendly confines of Tuckahoe.

Inside the warehouse, the trailers were opened. Two dozen women piled out, stretched their bodies, and lit cigarettes. They ranged in ages from eighteen to twenty five. Of Russian or Eastern European descent, they had been smuggled into the country to work at Gambino-controlled cathouses and strip joints. After a few months of performing a wide range of sexual services, these women would be discarded to the streets of Brighton Beach to assimilate with the predominantly Russian community.

The next morning, Tony woke bright and early for his task of the day. He had been looking forward to completing the assignment. At a small, well-kept, brick-faced colonial on the north side of Eastchester, Tony rang the doorbell and waited patiently to be greeted. A seven-year-old girl with long brown hair tied in pig tails opened the door slowly.

"Hi beautiful, is your granddaddy home?" Tony patted her head and smiled as she showed off her new Cabbage Patch doll.

"Can I help you?" the grandfather of the young princess greeted his visitor. Behind the partially opened screen door was Scott the repairman who had bilked him earlier in the year. The middle-aged repairman clearly did not recognize Tony who was wearing a tight black tee shirt and maroon sweatpants. The muscles in his arms were bulging.

"This is about an outstanding matter you have with my associate. You recall some bad luck around the time of the NBA Finals?"

Scott uneasily escorted his precocious granddaughter inside to watch cartoons.

"Why don't we speak in private?" Scott motioned to the direction of a detached garage at the end of the driveway. They walked in silence to the side of the structure. Scott fumbled with a set of keys before he found the right one and unlocked the door. They entered. The garage was more of a workroom. For a vehicle to fit, a wide array of machines, appliances and tables had to be rearranged or removed.

"Heh-Heh, I guess this is one of the older models." Tony strode over to a mincer in a corner. "You don't remember me yet, do you?"

Scott paused and sized the young visitor before his memory improved. "Wait a second; are you the butcher's kid?"

"One in the same." Tony gave a cocky grin and extended his massive arms wide in a presentation fashion. His triceps gave the appearance of sides of beef to be placed into the mincer. "I'm trying to get smarter. Here's a math equation for you to figure. If someone bets the Celtics to beat the Lakers six times in a row but fails to win the last three times..."

"I'll get your money!" Scott blurted.

"Let me finish, it's a word problem...and had the misfortune to double his $3000 bet on those occasions...but two months later had not paid the debt back, what is the answer?" Tony walked over to a set of hand tools. He flipped a screwdriver a few times in his right hand.

"You will get paid!"

"And how are you going to do it? By overcharging my father again? By screwing my uncles? Tony held out the tool for emphasis to his last word. "By kicking a puppy?" Tony jabbed the point of the screwdriver into the wooden table and moved closer to the repairman.

Scott stammered, "Umm, umm, I know what I can do. We have an education account for my granddaughter, but will take a week to process the transaction."

"Seems reasonable...hey, we don't want trouble, pal." Tony showed a wide toothy grin. "When you provide a service, you want to get paid."

Tony eyeballed the room for anything of value to sweeten the deal. Swag was a perk he relished. "Drop off the tools hanging on the wall to Bella's. Bring the slicer over to the butcher shop, and for good measure, throw in an ice maker for Ressini's. Their former owners will have to understand you lost them...*capice?*"

The muscular collection agent squeezed past the oversized beer-belly and exited the garage. Jimmy Tree would get his due, but Tony would get his taste, too. He was growing to love his new job.

BACK AT THE UNIVERSITY OF TEXAS

Chris lay resting on his single bed in his dorm room at the University of Texas. His gray gym shorts with the UT logo on the left leg and matching T-shirt smelled of his sweat of the day. He was too exhausted to remove the soiled garments. A plastic bag filled with ice cubes was wrapped around his left knee. Another ice pack was affixed to his right shoulder. He passed out attempting to study the defensive playbook.

The Longhorns played a bone-jarring scrimmage the day before against the University of Texas-El Paso. While he was not expected to get meaningful action, Chris found himself on the field for four possessions with the first-and second-string defensive units. Early in the scrimmage, an injury had taken out the player ahead of him on the depth chart. He fared well and recorded a highlight reel hit when he blitzed from the corner and decleated UTEP's halfback five yards deep in the backfield. In obvious retaliation, a wide receiver wiped him out with a cut block a few plays later. In the ensuing series, a pulling guard pancaked him, as he was forcing a runner to cut back toward the defensive pursuit. While a smart play on his part, nonetheless, after three impromptu backward rolls, Chris staggered off the field with his head ringing.

For the fall semester, Chris would take four classes. Micro-Economics, English Literature, Computer Programming and Psychology should not be too taxing, he thought. He was optimistic about the possibility of more playing time this season, especially if the injury to the players ahead of him were prolonged.

Since the blowup with Sal and Tony, he had not spoken to his ex-blood brothers. Of course, his sister had provided updates of their whereabouts and life events. Saby informed him they were blatantly using steroids and socialized with an intimidating crowd. She confirmed Enzo was a creep. Since the altercation with Ricky Mullino, they had tried to avoid the gangster whenever possible. Ricky was away most days at the police academy, and he bartended on Saturday nights. Mike Cameron had filled in behind the bar at times and thankfully, Enzo was not brazen enough to come on to Sabina while her father was working by her side.

Chris' squabble with Sal and Tony had extended to his life in Texas. He had taken on an isolationist attitude and was perfectly fine to sulk in solitude. Without warning, Allison flew off to Paris for the semester and would not be back until Christmas break. Ron and Jason did not to take summer courses and had arrived hours before football camp. With the dearth of his best friends on campus, Chris made the best of his pocket of time by taking two classes over the summer semester. He had received B+ in both. The rest of his time, he kept to himself and trained.

16

Upset Of The Year

OCTOBER 3, 1985

The surprising warmth of the Indian summer had continued into its third straight day. With temperature in the low seventies, Sabina Cameron lowered the passenger side window to allow the smoke to dissipate after she lit her second cigarette of the short trip. Tony was driving her to class at Iona College, as her car was being repaired after a fender bender over the weekend. She had scraped the side of her 1979 VW Rabbit against a fire hydrant.

"Told you not to drive home," Tony had warned her. The miscalculation was due to her consuming too many vodka and cranberries.

"I won't do that again. Good thing you knew the owner of the auto body shop. How good a friend is he to do work on the arm?"

"Let's say he owes me one. I'll come get you in a few hours after your classes are over; meet you at the burrito place."

Saby placed her backpack on her lap before checking for her pocketbook. "Oh, and by the way, I'm upset your spat has persisted. Please work matters out. How bad could the fight have been with Chris half a country away?" Sabina exited the vehicle and shut the door. She continued to speak to Tony through the open window.

"Lots going on, Sabe; besides, your brother...he's too busy with school and shit kicking on the prairie to think about us anymore. Cee wrote us off. He didn't seem concerned about the bastard creeping on you."

"This silly spat has gone on long enough. And don't worry about me. I can handle Enzo if he tries anything."

"Yeah, like Ricky? Lucky his ribs healed or he wouldn't have been able to be a cop. His first day with the badge is sometime next month. He won't be at the restaurant to protect you. Chris was wrong, not us. Sabe, you can't put the world's problems or our issues on your petite shoulders. Stick to helping the less fortunate. You've been our Momma Bear, but as you can see, we're adults and don't need your supervision."

"I try to balance everything, and you guys concern me. I have a high average at Iona and you guys are always on my mind. If you want something done, you have to give the task to the person who is always busy and you know I keep myself as busy as possible."

"That you do, and relax...slow down. You don't have to justify anything to us."

"You know I get excitable. By the way, you and Sal better not forget to show at the food bank tomorrow night. You promised to come at least once a month."

"You can count on us. The toy drive at Christmas last year made me cry. I loved being Santa for all those kids; can't wait to do dress up again."

"And would you two attend Sunday dinner once in a while?" Sabina went off on a tangent.

"To tell you the truth, Sal and I have discussed this. Look, with the older generation in Florida, it's not the same. We cherished those times, but all Zio Greg does is piss Sal off. He begs me to stay with him instead of sitting across the table from his old man."

"Maybe this is what maturing is all about? I miss them, too. It's why I go to Florida a few times a year, to keep connected and get advice and such," Sabina said. "I went for a week after the little ruse you asked me to help you with. The dirtbag had his due, but participating in that fashion was out of character for me. Blood is thicker than...oh heck, I'm gonna' be late for class."

Sabina gave her good-bye, and Tony drove off.

THE MORNING ASSIGNMENT

A mile's drive past Iona College, Tony made a right turn onto Lockwood Avenue and parked in front of a three story, medical building. At the office of Dr. Saul Cohen, Gastroenterologist he greeted the receptionist for his 10 a.m. appointment. He filled out a couple of pages of forms with bogus personal data. After a ten minute wait, a short, plump middle-aged nurse escorted him to a private room where she recorded his vital signs. She left the room and an additional fifteen minute passed before Doctor Cohen lightly tapped on the door and entered.

"Mister Annucci, hello, and first visit with us I see." The doctor jotted down notes on his chart.

"Yeah Doc, I've come across a problem I was hoping you could help me." Tony hopped off of the examining table and whispered in the doctor's ear. "This pain in my ass...it won't go away."

"I'm not following you, young man?"

"You keep avoiding my employer when you owe him sixteen gee's...you became a pain in my ass. Follow me, Dr. Larry Holmes?" Tony unfurled the cover to a magazine.

To pass the time while the doctor had made him wait, Tony had brought an issue of *Sports Illustrated*. On the cover was a glossy picture of the heavyweight bout; the one where Michael Spinks had upset Larry Holmes. Holmes had been heavily favored after winning the first forty-eight bouts of his illustrious career. If he had won number forty-nine, he would have broken the record for consecutive wins held by Rocky Marciano. He did not. For the first time in seventy-five years, a light-heavyweight had beaten the heavyweight champ. The upset of the year was not a wager the good doctor had been on the right side of. Since the eight to one favorite had lost, Tony had been tasked to see why the good doctor was late with his money.

"Oh, such a goofy bet-I was showing off at a cocktail party and called the bookie; no way should he have lost," Dr. Holmes rambled. "Well, umh, I am waiting for a few checks to come in from insurance carriers. I was going to call about the delay; no later than the end of the month...promise."

"I see, I see, cash flow difficulties...me too. But, we ain't Chemical Bank. If you're late...someone has to be paid," Tony whispered this bit of information into the doctor's stethoscope.

Thinking quickly on his feet, Dr. Cohen scanned the room. "I have an idea. I'll be right back."

"Don't make me wait." Tony gave a gratifying smile as the doctor bumped into the door frame of the windowless room.

Less than two minutes later, he returned carrying an oversized cardboard box. He opened the top and handed Tony a perforated package. "This is *Tagamet*, a drug for treating upset stomachs. It's a miracle cure and a blockbuster drug. I have samples by the case full. Take them all. I'm sure you could offload with no problems; costs twenty bucks at a pharmacy. Charge five or ten bucks. Each box has two hundred in total. I can easily get you a thousand more," the doctor nervously presented Tony with the offer for extended credit terms.

"Okay...bring these out to my car. I think your John Hancock will be well received by my employer." Tony moved his beefy fingers to the doctor's front shirt pocket and removed the stack of scripts. "All this does is smooth the payment date. I expect the full amount on Halloween...hope I don't have to come back to scare you." Tony walked out of the examining room with the doctor in step behind him. As he past the reception desk, he handed his parking slip to the woman sitting behind the counter. "Do you validate?"

BACK AT THE UNIVERSITY OF TEXAS

Chris Cameron awoke early and trotted over to the sports complex for a workout before his psychology class. After a month of setbacks, he was pleased the knee was close to one hundred percent healed. As he set the treadmill speed to 8.0, his legs moved fluidly and his gait showed no signs of pain. With a one-mile sprint completed, he toweled off before cranking out twenty pull-ups and fifty dips. He continued to the bench press and did twenty repetitions of one hundred and eighty five pounds. He completed this four exercise rotation three times and after fifty five minutes he was sweating profusely, fully confident he would be fresh for the afternoon football practice six hours hence.

All the hard work would not matter. For the first two games he had been relegated to mimicking the Missouri and Stanford defensive sets. His coaches were not in attendance to notice if he had made a good play or not. Regardless, he had regained his top physical shape, studied the playbook and went through practice drills at the highest level.

"Hey Sinatra, walk with me." Coach Campbell had bumped into Chris in the hallway outside of the locker room.

"Sure coach, what's up?"

"If your knee's doing better, we'll be requiring your services this week. Collins' hip is hurt, and he's officially out. I was thinking of making the move anyway. I've been reviewing game film, and changes need to be made after giving up five scores to Stanford. They always seemed to move the ball through the air so easily, and no way can we give John Elway a short field after our offense scores. Heck, we'll be going against Troy Aikman of Oklahoma in a few weeks. This game against Rice University should be a good time to test our younger players and work out the kinks for more aggressive coverage schemes. I'm giving you the heads up; you're one of those players."

"Thanks for the opportunity; you can count on me," Chris assured him with a smile a mile wide.

After the conversation had ended, Chris walked across campus to his psychology class. He barely listened to the professor blabber about Plato and Socrates vision of a utopian state, as his mind was elsewhere. Happy at first, he soon turned melancholy. His parents would be proud of his good news. Could he say the same about Sal and Tony?

Oh, screw it; he had a game to prepare for.

17

This Is No Way To Treat Your Partner

NOVEMBER 27, 1985

The holiday season was always the best time for the small shop owners of Tuckahoe. The rush would last until Christmas Eve. Family get-togethers, holiday parties and end-of-year celebrations required meat, pasta and alcohol. Bella's Pasta, Albanese's Butcher Shop and Ressini's Ristorante met these needs in their own shape or form.

Tony and Alfonse had been hard at work for close to eighteen hours preparing orders for Thanksgiving feasts around town. They were happy to take an impromptu break when Sal strolled in carrying a cardboard tray of hot coffee and a brown paper bag of assorted sweet rolls he had purchased at Solano's Bakery on Fisher Avenue.

"You read my mind, my friend...hey dad, Sal brought you coffee," Tony grabbed his usual; a large black with four sugars. He removed the plastic top and blew gently to cool his caffeine jolt. Alfonse grabbed the medium cup; his triple shot of espresso.

Thanks Sally. Another ten hours to go...don't get any better than this," Alfonse said with his mouth full as he inhaled a sugary pastry in two bites. The cowbells on top of the door clanked. The elder Albanese raised his hand to greet Joanne and Sabina.

"Oh good, you're the man I want to see," Sabina declared as she reached for the small cup with SAB scribbled on the side. Joanne grabbed a jelly donut.

"Who me?" Sal kissed Saby on the cheek.

"You're not gonna' appreciate what I have to say," Sabina cautioned him. "What the hell is this with you not paying me? A hundred pounds of short pasta, which you bought more than a month ago is still outstanding."

"Sally, you're kinda' late with the order you placed with us, too," Alfonse stated in a docile tone.

"I have no idea what either of you are talking about. My mom does the bills, and she pays on time," Sal said, as Sabina handed him the delinquent invoice. Alfonse walked to his drawer, found the copy of his overdue chit and handed the slip to Sal to examine.

"Son of a Bitch! This wasn't me. The scumbag Enzo stole my dad's order forms; must have been one of his cockroaches. The signatures are bogus; these were given to your workers. Four hundred friggin' dollars, mother..."

Less than a minute later, Sal was screaming in the face of his father. Gregorio had been on the phone behind the empty bar when his son had confronted him. While he had attempted to lead a healthy life, Gregorio had regressed back to his old routine of cigarettes and gallons of coffee. His exercise regime consisted of raising his arms and cursing at ESPN. Sal did not fear him in the least. He was the dominant male of the family.

"Dad, where the hell is Enzo? The piece of garbage," Sal demanded as he slammed the forged invoices on the countertop.

"Easy, Sally my boy. What seems to be going on?" Gregorio asked in a hushed tone.

Two of Enzo's associates arrived via the kitchen doors. Razza was a short and wiry Albanian from Queens who spoke broken English. Sean was the exact opposite; a tall, burly Irish guy with a blotchy red complexion from the Woodlawn section of the Bronx.

Sal grasped Sean by the throat, and at the same time seized Razza by the front of his sweater and yanked him off balance. He swung both men around. Sean was wrapped in a headlock, and Sal clenched the back of his neck. Bar stools crashed to the ground, as Sal flung Sean into the metal cylinder foot rest that snaked the length of lower portion of the bar. He effortlessly slammed Razza's head on top of the wooden bar. The minion slumped to the floor, dazed and close to unconsciousness. Sal turned his attention to the bigger man. While Sean was larger than the sinewy Razza, he was dwarfed by the enormous presence of Sally Nuts. He grabbed Sean by his shoulders and drove a right open palm into his Adam's apple, which caused the punk to gasp for air. Sal finished him off with two left hooks to the face and a right upper cut to the ribs.

TONY'S TURN

The entire fracas was an eternity to the victims, but in actuality had lasted for less than a minute. "You want me to remove the garbage, my friend?"

Tony dragged them out by their ankles. In the parking lot, he shoved the disoriented and hurting bodies into the back seat of Sean's late model Grand Am. The keys were dangling in the ignition. *I have an idea*, Tony thought as he drove the car by the secluded wooded area of the Parkway Oval. He smacked the already bruised men around while fishing in their pants pockets. After no cash was found, the big man popped the glove compartment open. *Jackpot!* Tony counted out $640 and threw the remaining wad on top of Sean and Razza's bodies. He secured the delinquent payments in his front jeans pocket and made his way back to Ressini's. He tossed the Grand Am keys into an exposed sewer drain on Lake Avenue and flagged a police cruiser on its way to patrol the quiet park. He alerted the officer of an argument he had witnessed between two men. The fight had escalated.

Rookie PO, Richard Mullino turned on the flashing lights and sped toward the disturbance. He pulled behind the car which was parked suspiciously on the grass landing by the park. Officer Mullino drew his weapon and slowly approached the vehicle. Support from a fellow officer arrived less than five minutes later.

The suspects had been subdued and were lying on the patch of grass. The two men had their arms folded behind their backs. Officer Mullino informed the veteran officer who had arrived at the scene he had witnessed two men arguing. After the altercation became physical, he cuffed both parties until backup arrived to assist. The veteran officer proceeded to walk around the Grand Am. The doors were open and cash was a strewn on the back seat of the vehicle. Proper protocol for expected organized crime activity was to call the FBI.

BACK AT RESSINI'S

Tony re-entered the restaurant as a police car sped past him with its lights flashing. Sal was sitting in the lounge, hunched over a small, circular table speaking intently to his father with his hands interjecting punctuation to every few words. Sabina was busy wiping the bar clean. Blood had been splattered across the tile floor and on top of the counter. Shards of broken glasses were carefully tossed into a garbage can.

Sal nodded with satisfaction at the way Tony had handled the disposal. Gregorio was nervously averting eye contact and staring at an imaginary object behind the bar. After a few minutes, Enzo tapped on the locked front door. Sal gave his approval for Sabina to let him enter. She walked over and unlocked the door. Sabina ignored Enzo's derogatory greeting and exited to the street.

"Where's my guys? Razza and Sean were supposed to meet me," Enzo asked a-matter-of-factly. He had ignored Sal and Tony and addressed the question to a silent Gregorio who did not respond but lit a cigarette and withdrew through the kitchen doors.

"They finally paid their bill for the orders you placed at Bella's and the butcher shop. Mighty nice of them, but they had to go." Sal was in charge.

"This is no way to treat your partner. I was trying to drive business. The money should come out of the till." Enzo unconcernedly picked his teeth with a toothpick.

"Partner? You're not my friggin' partner. You're a freeloader," Sal sternly shot back.

Gregorio re-emerged from the kitchen. Enzo sauntered over and addressed him, "I thought you informed your boy of our arrangement." He turned to Sal with a sly smirk on his face. "Kid, I own half this joint. Sorry for the confusion, thought you knew."

"WHAT THE FUCK YOU TALKING ABOUT!"

"Sally, calm yourself; I've been meaning to tell you. Somethin' happened, and well...I made a deal with Enzo," Gregorio blabbered as his shaking hands fumbled for his smokes.

"What does he owe you?" Sal had a dourer expression on his face. He turned to Enzo for the answer he didn't want to hear.

"Tell him," Enzo ordered Gregorio to confess as he confidently sneered at Sal.

"Sixty...you don't understand Salvatore, I needed one or two more weeks. My luck was set to change, but he cut me off. I hada' go along with his deal."

"You lost sixty thou' on top of the money I had saved?" Sal realized the gambling disease was past anything the old man could control. "We're not finished with this, Enzo."

"Okay kid...enjoy Thanksgiving tomorrow. We need to be good and fresh for the holiday rush...right partners?" The new owner of Ressini's chuckled, as he made his exit.

AT THE ALBANESE HOME, THANKSGIVING NIGHT

Sal and Tony were appalled by the turn of events. Regardless, their appetites were not diminished, and this was their first family meal in close to a year. Sitting at the table felt less special as the elders were away in Florida and the tiff with Chris had continued to fester. In happier times, the table would be filled with fifteen people but for this Thanksgiving meal only ten sat. The mothers still cooked for thirty and would never change.

When the parade of family members sat in front of the television to watch the football game, Sal and Tony situated themselves three feet from the screen and did not move for three hours. Their keen viewing interest was unmistakable to all that they were proud of their estranged blood brother when he entered the game for good with 3:15 left in the first half. After a solo tackle, Sal and Tony observed bold lettering printed on Chris's taped-up wrists.

KYLE FIELD IN COLLEGE STATION

The game was supposed to be close and exciting. Texas A&M had one loss in the conference, to Baylor University in the Battle of the Brazos. The University of Texas also had one conference loss, but had soundlessly defeated Baylor. Expected to be a low scoring affair, the game ended with A&M crushing the visiting Longhorns 42-10.

With a record of 8-3, the Longhorns had fallen out of contention for a premium, college bowl game, and the Aggies had earned the Cotton Bowl bid. On the positive side, Chris Cameron had been promoted to a starting position. He had been elevated to first string, strong safety in the second quarter. He played well, recording three tackles and defending a pass.

The Fall semester had been productive and rewarding for Chris. With a few weeks left of classes, he was on pace to maintain his 3.6 GPA. Allison had returned from Paris and he was happy to hear she had missed him dearly. While he had not had a Thanksgiving with his family for the second year in a row, he was touched by the offer from Ron-Ron for a belated holiday celebration with the Grunther family.

Did Sal and Tony realize he had written CAB in big black lettering on the white tape wrapped around his wrists when he made a solo tackle on the running back in the third quarter? Chris had capitulated, and while he was preparing for the contest, he had made a mental note to send a silent SOS. The feud with his buddies had to end. The *mea culpa* may be awkward to spit out of his stubborn mouth, but he knew within five minutes they would be laughing and telling stories, for *old times never get old*. First things first, focus on the bowl game and then mend the bond with his blood brothers.

18

The Greatest Present In The World

DECEMBER 24, 1985

After the disheartening loss, the University of Texas would be relegated to play Air Force in the Bluebonnet Bowl on New Year's Eve Day in Houston. The coaching staff held shortened practices and with weekends free until intense preparation commenced, Chris visited with the families of his two roommates. First, he and J.R. were invited to the Grunther family's belated Thanksgiving dinner celebration in Denton.

Chris was raised Roman Catholic and lived across the street from the Assumption Church. The Columbus Avenue Boys had dabbled for a short stint as altar boys. When they realized the money being collected in the wicker baskets was not for them to split, they quit. After smacks to the back of the head from their parents, they confessed the real reason was they were bored and would have had a bolt of lightning strike after they did something embarrassing on the altar. The parents had all agreed with the astute analysis. Chris considered Easter and Christmas as the religious holidays, not Thanksgiving. The day was all about the food.

The Southern Baptist Grunther home was different. The Thanksgiving celebration declared the greatness of God and not the greatness of America or football. Pastor Grunther furnished his blessing before the meal from Psalm 106:1-"Praise the LORD. Give thanks to the LORD, for he is good; his love endures forever." Still, Chris witnessed many similarities of Ronald's family to his. The five Grunther kids shared a three bedroom home and struggled to make ends meet. They had felt truly blessed when

Chris' parents mailed a gift of ten pounds of Bella's homemade pasta and a gallon of their famous, red sauce. Chris proudly assisted Mrs. Grunther prepare the pasta course.

Chris had a magnificent time two weeks later when the three roommates spent the weekend in Stillwater with the Rodger's. The Rodgers had hosted a pre-Christmas party as J.R.'s mom's next round of chemotherapy was planned for the week before Christmas. Her breast cancer, which had been in remission had resurfaced. The festivities were subdued, but Chris could feel the warmth. For the past decade, the Rodgers had experienced financial ruin and success before struggling again. They had persevered in the face of overwhelming turmoil.

On his last night of visiting with J.R., Chris had fallen asleep on the couch in the den with tears in his eyes. He missed his family greatly. Paradoxically, he had realized after witnessing the trials and tribulations of his roommates along with the death of Ricky Mullino's dad, he considered himself blessed to be raised in a relatively stable environment.

The time had come to meet Allison Wood's relatives. He had eagerly accepted the invitation to spend Christmas in Fort Worth. On the 26th, he was required to be in Austin. An enhanced defensive scheme was to be implemented for the running attack of Air Force. With money earned over the summer, Chris had purchased a blue, 1979 Chevrolet Monte Carlo that had served him well in getting around campus and for the two road trips to Denton and Stillwater. He drove alone during the three hour trip and pulled into the driveway of the Woods estate before nightfall. Ally had greeted him at the door and introduced her big, strong beau to her parents and grandparents. Chris thought her younger brother, Kelvin was nice. He was a football player from a prep school in the area. Undersized, nevertheless he had dreams of playing ball for the Longhorns.

"So Chris, Allison tells me you're first string in the bowl game as a sophomore...I played back in '65, and her grandfather played in '41. We smaller players couldn't compete nowadays." For all the money he had, Allison's father appeared to be down to earth.

"Dad, will you tell this to Kel? Have him end his stupid fantasy about being a friggin' Longhorn. Heck, he's short and slow as shit; stupid game anyway!" Allison's older brother, Chad, had made a haughty appearance without introduction.

"Watch the cussing son...and the Scotch," Mr. Woods reprimanded his namesake before turning to mingle with partygoers.

"Kelvin, I was your height in the tenth grade. I sprouted before my junior year. Ally says you're super smart. Use your brains, work your butt off, you may push me out of a job," Chris encouraged the maturing teen. He extended his hand to Chad. "My name's Chris, Chris Cameron. I'm a friend of Ally. Nice to meet you...Merry Christmas."

"Yes, well nice to meet you, too...I suppose. Hey, was your car out front?" Chad took a short sip from his ice-filled drink.

"The Monte Carlo? Yes."

"Thanks for telling me. I was going to yell at the maid to park around back," Chad pretentiously sneered before taking a celebratory gulp of his liquid courage.

"You are such an ass, Chad. I wish you'd go back to San Francisco," Ally chastised her brother and stormed out of the room to find her mother to vent.

Chris was left alone with Allison's two brothers. One was a great kid, the other a pure asshole. *Time to show this poodle who the alpha dog was.*

"Chad, I brought presents. They're in the trunk of my jalopy. Would you mind helping bring them in?" Chris put his arm around Allison's brother's shoulder and escorted him outside. Chad did not have a chance to refuse.

When they were alone, Chris grabbed him by his shoulders, cupped his right hand and smacked the side of Ally's brother's head. "Listen closely; I do not play around. I was trying my best to be cordial. The second I saw you, I knew you were a douche. But, I'm a gentleman, and I'm crazy about your sister," Chris spoke intensely, an inch away from Chad's face.

"Look, I–"

"No look I, pal. I've seen your type before. Super entitled, save the world liberal yahoos. I've had to work my ass off for what I've received. Did you think I was going to let a punk ass, trust fund baby disrespect me?" Chris hauled back his right arm but held going through with a punch. Chad cowered. "Are we clear?"

Chad's conduct had turned obedient as he acquiesced, "Crystal...yes. And I do apologize. This was my fourth Scotch." He extended his hand and the cockiness appeared to be slapped out of his system.

118

"Shoot my brother!" Chris wrapped the trust fund baby in a warm hug. "Let's get those presents."

Over the next few days, Chris observed the interactions of the cold and aloof Wood's family and compared them to the closeness and affection of the kinfolk of his roommates. Ron and Jason's relatives warmly greeted, joked and knew minor detail of each other's lives. The Woods were standoffish. The older women were catty, the men were boozehounds and discussions centered on one upping each other. In this setting, Allison appeared to show her true colors. At times, she was an exact replica of the six other women in attendance. The pasta delivery the Woods had received from the Cameron's remained in an unopened box set in a corner of the kitchen and her parents did not acknowledge its arrival.

Chris made a mental note. Ally was not the best for him. Yes, her family could open many doors in the business world, but if he were to turn into one of them, he would never forgive himself. Working toward his degree, he had become especially passionate about the private sector and was thinking about life after college. Bella's store expansion plans, while exciting, was not what he wanted to devote the remainder of his life to. Did he want to work for a big company? The law or educational fields were not professions he felt strongly about either. Was the next phase of his life in Texas or back in New York? How would he kiss and make up with Sal and Tony and what had they been involved in? These topics consumed his mind during the drive back to Austin in solitude.

CHRISTMAS IN TUCKAHOE

The long-departed Scalamarri relatives would have used the phrase, "Esta dei Sette Pesci!" The centuries old tradition of the Feast of the Seven Fishes for Christmas Eve dinner was when Catholics fasted prior to receiving Holy Communion. While meat could not be eaten during the fast, fish could. The seven courses correlated to the number of sacraments. The Scalamarri lineage took the feast a step farther by serving thirteen varieties to denote the twelve apostles plus Jesus Christ. Besides, thirteen of anything was better than seven.

Twenty-two family members and friends had crammed into the Albanese home. The Scalas and Cavazzis had made their first visit since they had sailed into retirement more than a year earlier. The menu included plenty of clams-Manhattan clam chowder, stuffed clams and linguini topped with clams. After a brief rest, fried calamari, scungilli & shrimp fra diavolo, Alaskan crab legs, a cold shrimp platter, baked cod, fried silver fish, broiled scallops, flounder francese and lobster tails with crab meat would be served. The meal would not end until espresso laced with Sambuca warmed their bellies. With red and white wine flowing, many a fun story and a potpourri of current events were bantered about. As an Irish man who never understood the meaning of a short conversation, Michael Cameron was in rare form. Early in the meal, he had swayed the discussion to politics and world events.

"Mike, why do the two religious types in Ireland hate each other? Enlighten me, I never had a reason to discuss this conflict between the Irish Catholics and Protestants until the events became a news story. Are you happy the Republic of Ireland has a role in Northern Ireland?"

"I am, Alfonse. The United States had progressed from these types of conflicts being in the forefront. The U.S. Constitution allowed religious freedom. In Ireland, it's a Civil War and a Civil Rights movement. Our opposition's the Unionists. They're aligned with the Protestant community and mandate Northern Ireland to remain within the United Kingdom. The Irish nationalists, who are mostly Catholic, want to leave English rule for a united Ireland." Mike was passionate about the plight of his ancestral people. The Cameron's routinely had discussions about geopolitics and the world economy around the dinner table. Chris and his father tended to be of conservative thought, while Sabina and Maria had a liberal affinity.

"I don't get these religious beefs. Most wars are fought due to this, and the first people who came to America came due to religious persecution, but to me...heck, it's all about the economy," Gregorio stated. "If you're making money, you'll get along with anybody."

"A true statement in my book, Greggie. We'll sell pasta to anybody in good or bad economic times. The troubles in Ireland have to do with the politics, jobs and who's being employed. The British deliberately gerrymandered the protestant majority. When the political system collapses, violence follows."

"I can see where you're coming from. If someone tries to take over another crew's turf, the one being taken over strikes back," Gregorio answered in a hoarse voice.

"So what's the deal announced last month mean?" Alfonse inquired.

"Lady Thatcher's making the right moves. She's close with President Reagan. I hope this bodes well but time will tell." An attempt to bring about a resolution had been made by Margaret Thatcher and Irish Prime Minister Garrett Fitzgerald. They had signed the Anglo-Irish Agreement marking first time the Republic of Ireland's had a right to have a consultative role in the affairs of Northern Ireland.

"Speaking of Reagan, the economy's humming along," Alfonse bubbly gave a CNN Business report. "I saw on the news the stock market's at record highs. World affairs ain't for me, but I'm always interested in the almighty pocket book."

"Unemployment's dropping, too; the effects of the tax cut have taken hold," Mike stated, as he accepted his second plate of linguini from his wife.

"We need more customers in the restaurant. Hell, first Thursday nights slowed. People are coming in less, even on the weekends," Gregorio despondently countered Alfonse's analysis. In reality, Ressini's slowdown had nothing to do with the state of the economy.

"It's the degenerates who are mulling around the bar," Dina chimed in as she set platters of fish on both ends of the table. "People don't want to be near those types of people."

"I have to agree with your lovely bride," Irish Mike derogatorily stated. "I feel uncomfortable around Enzo. He's surly and won't even try and have a conversation. And come on, I am at my best around people. If I can't have fun in a bar, I'm more than happy to spread the joy to my love and stay home."

"Guy must leave, he's gonna' kill our business. How the Hell did you friggin' screw us again…How?" Sal barked. To this point, he had been silent.

"I don't want to talk about this Salvatore. We'll get through…let things simmer on the stove, okay." Nervously, Gregorio stood and grabbed one of his smokes from the kitchen counter. "I'm going outside. Anyone want to go have a cigarette, Mikey?"

"No my friend, cutting back and saving my last fag of the day till my walk to church." The elder Cameron had a New Year's resolution to quit smoking for good...again. "Oh heck; one more, won't hurt."

OUTSIDE THE ALBANESE HOME

The night was cold and star's lit up the night. On the front porch, Gregorio lit Mike's Winston and then his Viceroy. "Damn, damn, damn it all to Hell Mikey," Greg cursed as he exhaled and blew a stream to the sky.

Sensing Greg wanting to vent, Mike inhaled and stood silent. Greg continued, "Salvatore's right, I am a degenerate. Heck, all my boys have me pegged. Dina curses me during the friggin' holidays. It's my fault John and Robby never come back to New York for Christmas or Thanksgiving, Easter, friggin' Groundhogs day, get the picture? They hate me."

"I don't want to pry buddy, but did you take the little advice I gave you a few weeks back?" Mike took a final drag. He would only smoke half.

"Shit yes, I finally saw the light. Three weeks of Gamblers Anonymous meetings have done me good and at the most tempting time to bet, the playoffs and Bowl games. Not to brag, but I haven't even missed the action. I'm not agitated anymore when a game's on. Heh-Heh, can you image there are other saps worse than me? Through group talks, I've come to realize my anger toward the family over these years was due to this crazy addiction. Heck, I don't need the aggravation. The restaurant has more than enough risk to quench my thirst," Greg passionately stated, as he dropped his butt to the pavement and ground out the smoldering filter with his boot.

"Aahh, but the lure of the easy score," Mike tried to put himself in Greg's psyche.

"I've sold my soul to Satan by turning over half of Ressini's to Enzo and only have myself to blame. No pool or parlay bet could get me out of sixty grand to the Lucchese's. Enzo's not leaving anytime soon." Greg sniffled. "Guaranteed, Ressini's will be burned to the ground or closed in the next few months."

"A clean slate is good, too, keep moving forward and not back." Mike tried his best to comfort his long-time friend.

"I want to work my marriage out with Dina. I love her, Mikey. It's time for me to make amends with Robby and John and beg them for forgiveness. I've never seen my grandsons."

"And how about Salvatore?"

"I have my resolution, too. It's all scripted in my mind to apologize to my baby boy. Do you know there are times when I sneak into his bedroom when he's asleep and look at him? I'm amazed that I had created an amazing, strong kid...heck, strong man? Nervous, but I'm going to muster the courage to tell him as much as we walk to church in a few hours, then I'm gonna' beg the almighty to save me. How's this sound?...Sal, let's talk for a second. I wanted to say this Christmas I've received the greatest present in the world...You. I've been a lousy father, and the beatings I gave you and your brothers, I'm not proud of any of those horrific nightmares. I've been a sick man. Gambling's a horrible disease, and my brain is altered. What you've done with Ressini's, heck your grandmother would be proud to have her name associated with this wonderful place. From this date on, I am going to do everything in my power to make you proud of me. It'll be hard, but we'll survive because of you. You are my greatest gift, and I am the luckiest SOB to have you as a son. You are the man I wish I would have been and I love you. You give me the inner strength to get better," Greg emotionally finished his soliloquy.

Mike sympathetically patted Greg on the back. "Right from the heart. Hey, the air is a wee bit cold. Wipe your eyes, and let's get back to dinner. I am sure Salvatore will find compassion in his heart to forgive you for all the madness."

"One more smoke, be inside in five minutes. Tell Dina to save me a lobster tail, they're my favorite."

After his longer than expected bathroom break, Mike had noticed Gregorio was not back at the table and a lobster tail remained in the middle of his uneaten plate.

"Is he still smoking, Mike? Can you tell him his dinner is getting cold," Dina asked as she pointed to her husband's empty spot.

His shriek stopped the Christmas Eve festivities in its tracks.

Gregorio had fallen to his knees and toppled into a Christmas display on the front lawn of the Albanese home. His eyes were open but he was scared and confused as the paramedics secured him into the ambulance.

19

I'm Gonna Need Your Help

JANUARY 10, 1986

Chris took the first flight leaving Austin on New Year's Day. As he walked toward the baggage claim area at LaGuardia Airport, his dad was there to greet him; his mood was serene. From the moment Michael's long-time friend had been taken away in the ambulance, the family tragically knew this one was worse than his first scare.

Gregorio's condition never improved. He remained in the Critical Care Unit for fifteen days before taking his last breath at 7:51 a.m. on the morning of January 8th. He was fifty-nine years old. Once a virile, strapping man, he had deteriorated quickly over the past year, transforming from the bruising figure of his youth into a shell of his former self. Dina and her three sons were by his side. Gregorio had been heavily sedated throughout and while he had opened his eyes and was alert for a few fleeting moments, he had never gathered the strength to speak.

The petty argument was immediately forgotten. With tears in his eyes, Chris hugged his blood brothers as he entered the Esposito home. Chris and Tony did what friends do; they consoled Sal throughout the ordeal. The boys spent hours reminiscing about life in the dysfunctional household. Sal's brothers and their wives had arrived from across the country shortly after the New Year. Sal got reacquainted with John and Robert after the many years apart. John was twenty-four and married after serving in the Navy. He lived in the suburbs of San Francisco. He and his wife worked for a computer company. Robert was twenty-six and resided in Chicago, working as an accountant for a food company. He and his wife had two toddler sons who had never met their Uncle Sal before. Touching moments were beheld. The rambunctious duo bonded with their hulking uncle, climbing over him and giggling as they were effortlessly tossed in the air. Awkward at first, the family had come together and John and Robby were proud of the way Sal and their mom had worked to keep Ressini's afloat.

The first day of the wake was emotional. Gregorio may have had his problems behind closed doors, but as a local businessman and resident of the community for three decades, he had countless friends and admirers. The Westchester Funeral Home was a narrow, two-story structure located on top of the hill on Main Street in Eastchester. During the bitterly cold days and nights, a steady stream of mourners had queued outside the entrance to pay their respects. The family was touched as the older generation of townsfolk had braved the elements to say a final good-bye.

"Thank you for coming...I appreciate it...How are you?"

"Ooohhh, he was a good man, one of the best...the stories I could tell."

"Be strong young fella, I remember when you were this tall. Your father must have been proud of you."

"Dina, Dina, sorry for your loss. I remember when you moved here, can't believe thirty years has passed."

The comments varied, but the message was consistent. Gregorio would be missed and the Esposito family was in their prayers.

"Uncle Carmine, this is Salvatore." Joey Mullino guided his great-uncle by the arm. The old man had mouthed a prayer by the coffin and stood with confusion on his face.

"Your brother was a good friend of mine," Carmine stated as he wrapped both of his bony hands around Sal's right hand. Tony and Chris were standing tall, bookending him.

"Thank you. I'm touched," Sal whispered into Joey's ear. "How's he doing? Poor guy."

"Alzheimer's...it's getting worse. My aunt has to put him in a home," Joey responded as he escorted his Uncle Carmine over to Dina Esposito. She was wearing a black shawl and sitting sunken, in a decorative chair with wooden armrests. Her eyes were red and swollen.

"I remember Uncle Carmine well. What a shame. My dad used to work on his car. He had a monster sized Skylark, a friggin' tank. Dad says the big old thing collects dust in the garage and hasn't been driven in years," Chris reminisced as he glanced to his father warmly greeted the deteriorating, elderly man across the crowded room. His dad would order him to help Carmine Alberetto with yard work in his immense, vegetable garden while Michael performed minor maintenance or wax the Buick.

Near the end of the first evening session, emotions had come to a boil. Enzo had the audacity to show his face. From the rear of the crowded parlor, Chris watched the exchange unfold.

"My condolences; good man Gregorio," Enzo greeted John and Robert with firm handshakes. He extended his paw to Sal with no reciprocation.

"You're presence is not welcome. Don't try and say a word or go near my mom. I don't want you at the restaurant again!" Sal raised his voice as he inched toward the mobster.

Enzo's face turned flush as the hum of chatter went still. He turned his head and ignored the stares. Walking directly past Chris, he motioned to his two associates who had been mulling near the exit. "The bastard's gonna' embarrass me. Piece of garbage; come on, let's go send him a message," Enzo seethed as he addressed his partners in crime. He had whispered the statement loud enough for Chris to hear. The troupe squeezed past a gaggle of well-wishers.

Chris waited a few seconds and followed the three men outside. Enzo's car was parked perpendicular to the funeral home, in one of the meter spaces on Dempsey Place. Chris waved Ricky Mullino over with his hand as the police officer was directing the pedestrian traffic along Midland Avenue.

"Hey Rick, do you have a second to talk?"

"Kind of, what's up? Hey, tough loss against Air Force. You played well."

"Thanks, we'll be better next year. Did you see three guys cross the street?"

"Oh, you mean Enzo and his crew?" Officer Mullino waved two cars through. "Can't miss the scumbag...speaking of!" He turned to let another car go by. This time he peered inside the vehicle. Enzo was in the passenger seat of the silver BMW.

"I overheard Enzo say he was going to get back at Sal; because he disrespected him on the procession line. He may try to do something to the restaurant." Chris stared at the rear of the BMW as they drove away.

"Let me call this in. I'll have someone do a patrol around Ressini's."

"We don't have time," Chris howled and bolted off.

Still in football shape, Chris sprinted the downhill mile in less than six minutes. He caught his breath on Columbus Avenue, a hundred yards from Ressini's. The street lamps were dim. A sedan was idling in front of the restaurant with its lights turned off. Chris noticed a darkened figure scurry from the back of Ressini's and into the awaiting car.

Chris bolted to the restaurant. He went to where the darkened figure had emerged; the garbage dumpster adjacent to the rear entrance by the kitchen. As he approached, smoke was seeping out through the orange glow illuminating from beneath the lid and the foul smell of smoldering garbage and plastic was in the air. He grabbed at the cover and attempted to flip open but recoiled as the metal was hot to the touch. Reaching into his pocket, he fumbled for the spare key to Ressini's. Unlocking the back door, he ducked inside and came out a moment later with a fire extinguisher and a broom. He placed the broom handle below the lip of the dumpster top and pushed upward. Flames billowed as the top crashed on to the flipped open side of the container. Chris sprayed foam onto the blaze. As he doused the flames, a police car with lights flashing arrived on the scene. The officer had reported the incident and grabbed his portable fire extinguisher to assist in containing the fire. Before responders arrived, the situation had been contained.

While giving a statement, Chris did not provide details of the incident, even though he knew this was a clear warning from Enzo. The message was crystal clear-the mobster was in charge. This matter could not be handled through legal channels.

Sal and Tony had arrived as firemen were in the midst of analyzing the scene. They walked over as Chris was ending his statements.

"He did this...I saw their car," Chris seethed.

Sal grabbed Chris by his shoulders. "You okay?"

"Yeah, I'm fine. Sorry I didn't grasp how real this was." Chris raked Sal's eyes before he turned and did the same to Tony.

"The whole friggin year keeps escalating, this is very real. Guy's not gonna' stop," Tony exclaimed.

The Columbus Avenue Boys walked away from the crowd, toward the sidewalk. Chris stood in the middle and put his arms around their torsos. "You had asked if I had an idea to solve this problem. My brothers, the answer is yes."

GREGORIO DOMINICK ESPOSITO

Enzo had stayed away. The second day of the wake was as emotional as the first and Gregorio was laid to rest at Holy Sepulchre Cemetery in New Rochelle. After the funeral, all well-wishers were invited back to Ressini's for lunch. Vincent Scala and Joe Cavazzi had the most stories to tell.

In his younger days, Greg was a character. He charmed the women, young and old and made them want to return to have a meal. Many of the locals spent late night's playing cards and talking sports for hours on end. Even the old time police and firemen had a soft spot in their heart for Greggie Espo. He knew how to treat customers right.

"Greggie always treated cops with respect. Get them on your side, give'em a free pizza. They'll never forget you. The old Chief stumbled out many times after free booze but the next day he'd book his kid's birthday party. He would do a silly dance all the time a big order came in. Greg was gruff, but, he made me laugh over the years; heck over the decades," Joe retold fond memories.

"He knocked on my door one night, had to be 3 a.m. Teresa's yelling. Hell, at that hour, Greg was the only one who could be there. He's holding a box of crap and could I store it for a few hours? Well, he begs and I finally agree. I put the damn thing in the cellar. He gets clipped. Christ, Dina was livid and refused to post bail. A few days go by and he gets off by paying a fine. I told him, hey Greg are you gonna' come get the box? He had forgotten all about stopping by my house. I never knew what was in the darn thing and to tell you the truth, I still don't want to know." Vincent had tears in his eyes.

"My dad had a solid friendship with you two. Thanks for all you've done," Sal sniffed and reached for a napkin.

"We butted heads but this marine does not play games," Vincent commented as the room chortled.

"To tell you the truth, because of Vincent's toughness with Greg, he saved him from more trouble with the law," Joe surmised as he accepted a coffee from his grandson.

Some of the stories were comical, others were gut-wrenching. If you wanted the scoop on any old-time tale, the best place to hear them come to life was from Vincent or Joe. They had a history which went back to 1935. Joe Cavazzi and Julia Scallo had met on the lower East Side of New York City. Back in the day, they were married at the Scalamarri's banquet hall in Tuckahoe. The Cavazzis had moved to Tuckahoe and a life in the country. The Scalamarri family had relatives around the New York City area with the names of Scallaro, Scalo, Scalle and Scala. This was a result of lazy, Ellis Island immigration officials who could not bother taking the time to decipher the correct pronunciation from their thick Italian accents. A tragic event almost destroyed the family and ended the ownership of the banquet hall; *a story for another day*. At the wedding, Vincent was introduced by his cousin, Julia to her husband, Joe Cavazzi. Vincent was only sixteen at the time. The date was memorable to Vincent in many ways. At the reception, Julia had coaxed him to dance with Teresa Carpinello. Vincent and Teresa immediately fell in love, but they would not marry until eight years later. They both served their country in World War Two; Vincent as a marine and Teresa in the Woman's Auxiliary Air Corp. When they returned to Tuckahoe in 1947, they raised a family. The Esposito's moved to the neighborhood from Brooklyn in 1956. Gregorio had realized he needed help with the restaurant and turned to Vince and Joe to help keep him straight. Since Gregorio was involved in countless racquets, Vince and Joe had been adamant; no shenanigans inside the restaurant. Gregorio could only push his swag away from Ressini's four walls. This had stayed true to form until Vince and Joe had announced their retirement and subsequent move to Florida.

During the luncheon, Chris pulled Ricky Mullino aside. After small talk about him being a rookie on the beat, the conversation progressed to the events of the night of the vandalism. Ricky was adamant about his hatred for Enzo. Their genteel friend had vowed he would love to get retribution for the harm the gangster had caused. Chris was happy to hear this.

"I think I have a way for this to play out," Chris whispered to Ricky. "I'm gonna' need your help though."

"My gun's always loaded Cee. Whatever you need, I'll do what I can."

"Nothing drastic; no need to blow your law-enforcement career. We need the bastard eliminated or incapacitated. If Sal or Tony's fingerprints are on this, all Hell will break loose. Enzo's a made guy and if he's whacked the Lucchese's will go after whoever did it...hard." Chris glimpsed toward the direction of the bar. Sal and Tony were downing shots with John and Robby.

"So, what do we do?"

Chris and Ricky walked outside. The afternoon was cold and windy. They meandered along Columbus Avenue and chatted for the next half hour.

Operation Erase Enzo was in motion.

20

Good-bye Tuckahoe

FEBRUARY 24, 1986

Provided minimal information, Sal and Tony never asked many probing questions. Ignorance was the best defense if they were busted by the cops for the activities they carried out for Jimmy Tracino. Jimmy Tree was only a year older than Sal and Tony, but he presented himself as a seasoned underworld veteran. He oozed confidence and had a vision which was cultivated from idolizing his father. His older brother had wanted no part in the life of crime. Jimmy was the exact opposite. He had been attached to the hip of the respected and feared Santo Tracino for as long as he could remember. Jimmy had trained as a Golden Gloves boxer to toughen his reputation and had gained respect by being ruthless and uncovering unique ways to generate cash for the upper echelons of the Gambinos. Santo became a made member when he was in his late-twenties. Jimmy had paid his dirty dues since his teen years. His loyalty to the Code of Omerta was rewarded with getting his button on his twenty first birthday. What he did to speed the process was beyond Sal and Tony's pay grade. They had no dreams of being indoctrinated into "the family" and had informed Jimmy they would not kill at will for him or anybody. Of course, rough beatings and strongarm threats were fine. Murder was not their forte. Moneymaking schemes were their specialty and Jimmy Tree craved cash more than he needed another cold-hearted lunatic in the crew.

They had strategized about gravitating away from the rougher side and operating a sports book or pushing swag for Jimmy Tree. They had pleaded for this potential career change after dodging a bullet last fall after refusing his request to murder the owner of a sports club on Long Island. The target had been married to a woman who was having an affair with a Gambino capo. The broad had a life insurance policy on her husband. Jimmy's crew had been contracted to make the hit. While Sal and Tony had refused, Randy Sarno, an up-and-comer had accepted the assignment. The dumb bastard botched the hit from the get go and beat to death the wrong guy. The sports club was owned by two people and the one he had killed was a happily married father of three baby girls. Sarno was locked in a federal penitentiary and soon to be facing a life sentence.

As Sal and Tony drove along Saw Mill River Road in the early morning, they had pieced together the method behind Jimmy Tree's madness for what they were about to do. A Federal judge had ruled city and school officials in Yonkers had intentionally segregated the city's public schools and public housing along racial lines. The mandate to the school system was to bus students from the nonwhite areas to schools in affluent neighborhoods. This process was not expected to be implemented for a couple of years. Never one to procrastinate, Jimmy laid the groundwork to take over the bus companies and lucrative contracts.

"Are you Pete?" Tony called to a man through his open window.

"Yeah, what can I do for you?"

"We were hired by a consultant for the bus driver's union. They're recommending you may want to hire people we send; vandalism to your fleet and what not...we should be in the best position to control this type of security for you," Tony remarked as he stepped out of the truck. His arms were folded as he faced Pete.

"What's this all about? I'm not hiring anyone," Pete confusingly asked.

"Yeah, but you will. You'll be in a good position to get the federally mandated contract to bus the colored kids from Getty Square," Sal enlightened the bus company owner as he strode over.

"Hey Pete, you do want a good life for the Maldanado family in Irvington. This'll work out great. We'll be by to hear updates on your hiring plans; if someone quits or what not, let us make a good recommendation on reliable guys to hire."

The two bruisers hopped in the truck and drove off. The way the Tracinos saw the future, controlling the bus driver's union would put them in a dominant position to fleece the school district during contract negotiations. The maintenance of the vehicles could be funneled to their repair yards and performed at inflated prices, and the newly hired workers would have to kick back 10 percent of their paycheck. They could control the snow removal during the winter, and the other seasons were sure to have ample opportunities. Creative ways to make a buck were abound. They would be crazy not to get their sticky fingers into the scam at an early stage.

In Tuckahoe, Sal and Tony went their separate ways. Tony had to relieve his father at the butcher shop. Sal had to swing by the house to retrieve a tray of chicken, which had been marinating overnight in a lemon and herb sauce and prepare for the few patrons who showed on a Monday afternoon. The winter morning was sunny and unseasonably warm. He was optimistic workers would not want to be cooped inside their places of employment.

He parked in the driveway, behind his mother's Chevy Cavalier. Once inside, Sal called out, "Mom!" No answer. Her keys were in a bowl on the end table.

He walked through the kitchen and snaked his way through the small confines of the one story home he had lived his entire chaotic life; silence. He went into his bedroom. A lavender envelope was propped on his pillow and addressed to "My Sweet Salvatore." In an instant he knew what the contents would entail. The unread pages were held tightly in his hand as he lay on the bed and stared at the ceiling. Minutes passed before he exhaled to calm his nerves and began to read the Dear Son letter.

My Dearest Salvatore:

This is the hardest letter I will ever write but the time has come to start life anew. I cannot believe six weeks had passed since Gregorio's death and I am a widow at fifty-three. The last few years with my husband had not been fun and "death do us part" for this practicing Catholic had been a hard pill to swallow. This had been especially true since I met Angelo Palagano. I have to be honest. I immediately fell hard for the contractor as he was doing the amazing renovations at Ressini's. Our friendship grew at a time when your father was *in a real bad place. We strictly had a friendship, until your father passed. The past years had been stressful. I met with lawyers a few times to draw separation papers, but chickened out on multiple occasions. Greg would do something which gave a spark of hope he was going to change, but he always reverted to his old ways. Angelo was my rock at a time I desperately needed support and affection. I cried uncontrollably when Greg's condition had worsened and the prognosis was dim. However, anguish soon turned to guilt. After the funeral, my emotions were more relief before eventually turning to happiness. Greg's passing had allowed me the freedom to be with the man I loved without the stigma of divorce. The life insurance policy I took out fifteen years ago had been a smart investment. The check for $100,000 arrived a week ago. This set in motion my current course of actions. In this envelope is a check for half of the insurance proceeds along with the legal documents to the house. The restaurant has to stay in my name because you are too young to obtain a liquor license, but rest assured, the place is yours 100 percent. I know Gregorio was the main reason for your anger and resentment. As wife and mother, I was not innocent and am keenly aware of the type of person I married. Heck, living on the edge was one of the main reasons I fell for him in the first place. Many prayers had been whispered and tears shed over the years as I forgave Gregorio for his sins and at the same time begged him to stop the madness. You see, the edge sometimes leads off a cliff. The law caught Gregorio three times, and he had spent a total of twenty-seven months incarcerated. In actuality, those were the best times for our family. I never blamed Robby and John for moving away as soon as they possibly could. On the flipside, I admire you for sticking this out and remaining by my side. You are strong, physically and mentally. However, the time has come for me to leave. I am moving to Florida with Angelo. As you read this, I am getting married by the Justice of the Peace. We are heading south and a new life in Fort Meyers. Oh baby, I hate to abandon you, but I was never going to be able to do this face-to-face. Good-bye my sweet baby, good-bye Tuckahoe.*

Love Mom.

The teen's room had not changed since he rearranged the furniture after John had left for the Navy. Cookbooks, sports magazines and an old football jersey were in their customary places. His bed was positioned in a corner which masked unrepaired holes in the plaster wall. When the boys had been bunched in the bedroom, to repair the destruction was a waste of time. The older brothers had taken out their aggravation on the runt of the litter and thrashed him good on many occasions-until the runt grew bigger and stronger than his siblings. The beatings had stopped before his tenth birthday. This was when Sal gave more than he received. Regardless, old wounds took a long time to heal and Sal had never been close to John and Robert. No love was lost when they fled the craziness of the Esposito house. Sal didn't even respond to either of his brother's wedding invites and never stayed in touch. A silver lining in his dad's death was a thawing of the relationship between them all. They would never be close, but at least cordial dealings could be had.

He took a deep breath and exhaled once again. Standing, the colored sheets of paper were crumbled into a ball and tossed into the waste paper basket in the far corner of the room. Before doing so, he folded the $50,000 check and tucked the financial security into his pocket. Oh well, life goes on. Time to get to work.

LATER AT RESSINI'S

While the restaurant was slow on Monday evenings, a busy and unwelcome cockroach was sitting in the corner of the lounge. Enzo Pellanigro ran his bookmaking and loansharking operation meticulously and bragged about his exploits for all to hear.

"I know who all my customers are and what they owe me, to the nickel," he'd loudly pronounce on the payphone, as Sal lurked by.

The scoop on Enzo was while he had no formal accounting studies and rarely attended class at Mount Vernon High School back in the Fifties, he was great with numbers-debits, credits and especially receivables. One category he had never had to deal with was delinquent accounts. The nefarious brute was always made whole; in one way or another. The cash he had generated for his capo combined with his disregard for human life had been favorably viewed by the upper levels of the Lucchese crime family.

Enzo would razz Sal whenever he was in ear shot as he boasted to anyone who would listen. "My Ressini's score has been one of his best... Greg Esposito was the worst gamblers in creation. I took his action personally, didn't layoff one penny. I extended credit until he hung the noose around his neck and tightened the pressure with loss after loss after loss." This ended with Enzo getting a piece of the restaurant at the perfect time. His soldiers had taken the opportunity to steal inventory and peddle drugs for almost a year.

Sal knew he had to toe a fine line with Enzo. If they continued to make the life of his soldier's miserable by breaking their bones or sending them to jail, he would bring his complaint to his higher ups. This was the wrong time for a turf war. Santo Tracino and his son Jimmy had come to an agreement; Sal and Tony would not harass him. Ressini's was Enzo's possession. If they crossed the line, Santo and Jimmy may have no choice but to give permission to take them out. Sal and Tony would bite their tongues, make him feel uneasy, and bust his balls, as he sat at the end of the bar, but in reality that was all they could do. He had sent a message with the mini-inferno in the garbage dumpster; he would torch the place if they made a move and screwed with his livelihood. Sal would do anything to keep Ressini's open. The prospects of seeing the structure burned to the ground was an accident he wanted to avoid at all costs.

Enzo collected his take and met with associates as he ended his night. "Better to meet me at Ressini's than a pizza parlor or an auto body shop. Besides, we can oogle the sweet, tasty Sabina chick when she waitresses." He never wavered from derogatory comments.

As he did when Enzo was sitting at the bar, at 9:45 p.m. Sal popped his head out of the kitchen and barked, "Last call!"

"Mr. Pellanigro, one more?" The bartenders treated him with courtesy and respect. A potential confrontation was not worth a broken limb.

"Nah kid, I'm leaving." The gangster tossed back the last of his Scotch, grabbed his coat, and walked out.

Sal locked the back door of Ressini's. A police cruiser pulled into the parking lot and shined the strong beam of a spotlight in his direction before serenading him with a short, whoop of the siren. Sal quipped, "Hey Barney Fife, did Andy teach you a new trick today?"

"Kiss my ass, buddy. Hey, follow me to Depot Square," P.O. Mullino lightheartedly called out before he kissed the siren once more and sped off.

As the most junior officer on the Tuckahoe Police Force, Rick Mullino was paying his dues, covering for senior officers and working many double shifts during his initial five months on the job. For the most part, the Village of Tuckahoe was a sleepy community and the streets rolled up early. When a high profile arrest occurred, the Chief took note. Ricky was presented a citation after he apprehended the two drug dealers last November. He was onto a promising career in law enforcement.

"Another double-shift?" Sal inquired, as he scooted across Main Street and toward where Ricky was standing.

"Yeah, first one of the week; I'm beat, 7 a.m. comes early for my next one," Ricky yawned and turned his head toward the ringing coming from the payphone in front of the darkened, Carvel ice cream shop.

"Yeah, what's up?" Ricky answered on the fourth ring.

"How'd things go?" Chris was on the other end, calling from Austin.

"All good, he's getting pissed, you can tell. But he goes through the motions, as I do," Ricky relayed his recent run in with Enzo. "I tag him for minor bullshit, say drive safe and go back to make sure Sally closes without incident."

"Good, keep the facade going. Nothing too onerous, continue to bust his nuts. Hey, speaking of Sal, I've been trying to reach him all day. Have you seen him?"

"He's right next to me. Hold on, he wants to talk." Ricky handed the phone over.

"In a bad mood my brother...my mom split today. She left with the friggin' contractor and moved to Florida to get married."

"I spoke with Tony earlier, and he filled me in," Chris said. "I am devastated by Aunt Dina, wish I could say or do more. Please, sit tight a little bit longer, and don't go off on Enzo. It's real close."

"I'll try. The house will be quiet for the first time. Mom always fell asleep with the TV volume on high. Gonna' be an adjustment," Sal serenely stated.

Ricky grabbed the phone from Sal. "Hey, Sabina was pulled over again last week. A buddy of mine from the police academy is on the job in Eastchester. She was drunk; three times since I've been working. Have a talk with her, I'm concerned."

"I'll speak with her, but my sister does not take criticism from me or anyone younger than her too well. It's one of her weaknesses. This'll have to come from my parents. I'll have my father lay into her. I don't see why she needs to get drunk to that extent."

"I guess the plan is for me to continue as is?"

"Not for long, give me a shout if he does anything out of character," Chris reiterated his request.

21

Happy Birthday

APRIL 6, 1986, BETWEEN NORMAN AND AUSTIN

With ample time to ponder in his thoughts as he drove south along Interstate 35, Chris had contemplated a plethora of topics ranging from world events to micro-details of his life. He was at the midpoint of 400-mile trip back to UT. What was the underlying theme running rampant through his brain? *Life was one big rollercoaster.* God made you stronger by taking life's euphoric and prideful moments and balancing with times of despair and misery.

While he was a great student and exceptional athlete, his family did not have wealth or abundance, except in love. He had a special bond with Sal and Tony, yet he could not get a date for his high school prom. He had received a scholarship that was rescinded before he earned back. Bella's had struggled for a quarter century before the business had flourished with franchise locations. College had been an amazing experience thus far but would get harder. His class load had increased with the decision to double major in Economics and American History. He had held his own, but his solid GPA could slip. He had received limited playing time during the first two football seasons, but if he worked hard, more time on the field could be warranted in the fall.

Life could be a lot worse. He could not imagine being a relative of the victims of the Space Shuttle *Challenger,* which had tragically exploded in January. Loved ones had been proud watching the lift-off. Seventy-three seconds later, their lives were devastated. Besides the tragic world event,

Chris thought of how Sal was coping with his mother splitting and the death of his father. Zio Gregorio and Zia Dina had treated Tony and Chris with respect. However, Sal had agonized about his father's reprehensible behavior and while his mother loved him dearly, she had been complicit in the nightmarish abuse bestowed upon their youngest son. The sliver of hope Sal had prayed for was Gregorio could change and show him affection, but the closure had never materialized. The scars of his past had allowed him to come to terms with his father's death relatively quickly and he had taken his mother's abandonment in stride. He was resilient and a survivor. Sal's birthday was today. He was the first of the Columbus Avenue Boys to burst through their teen years. Tony's birthday was a month away while his was not until July.

Chris had his present delivered to Sal while he was working for Rodgers Oil and Gas. This past week he had crisscrossed Oklahoma searching for drilling activity in a similar capacity to what he had been contracted to do the previous year within Texas. The assignment had been a week in duration, and the data he had compiled indicated the energy business was in for a rough patch. World oil prices had collapsed to $10 a barrel. This was encouraging for the majority of the country and bode well for consumer spending. The stock market was at record highs. Staying true to the rollercoaster philosophy, what was good for 95% of the country happened to be bad for the 5% that relied on the energy sector. With life journey in motion, Mrs. Rodger's breast cancer had gone into remission.

Chris returned to the dorm at 9 p.m. He placed his duffel bag on top of his bed and dug out a handful of quarters in a Longhorns coffee cup on the counter next to the refrigerator. He placed a call at the payphone on the wall in the middle of the hallway.

"Hey my brother...Happy Birthday!" Chris greeted Sal.

"Heh-Heh, Cee I am a happy man. Thank you, thank you!"

"Why, you get a new girlfriend or something?"

"No man, shit...of course you wouldn't have heard the good news yet... Enzo's dead! Tony and I have been euphoric all day."

"Thought he was paralyzed?" Chris inquired.

"Must have been complications; he went out of this world the way he deserved to go. Kiss my ass you dead piece of shit!"

In a remarkable turn of events, the world had turned into a happy place again.

SIX DAYS EARLIER

On April Fool's Day, people played practical jokes and hoaxes on each other. Originally referenced in Chaucer's *Canterbury Tales* as far back as 1392, Enzo Pellanigro had countless instances to confirm fools were in abundance on any day a sporting event was played. This year, the tables had been turned.

Chris had never thought of himself as a killer; maybe an assassin on the football field, but never a killer. With the threat to the well-being of his blood brothers acute, he capitulated and had zero qualms about the hard truth of the fair justice which was needed to be served regarding the Enzo quagmire. Sal and Tony had to be as removed as possible so the assistance of "Officer Mullino on the beat" was the solution. Wearing a badge, Ricky was beyond reproach from the gangster. Chris correctly assumed Enzo would view the sophomoric harassment by the rookie cop he terrorized a few months earlier as a punk amateurish move he would have to deal with.

From the plan's inception, he had been optimistic. The mobster must never terrorize again. Chris had prided himself as a meticulous planner. Thinking through the details had consumed his thoughts. All types of scenarios had been war gamed in his mind. He knew the only way to take Enzo out was to make the incident appear to be an accident. An alibi was cemented. He scouted locations for Rodgers Oil & Gas during his spring break from UT. Since oil prices were at uneconomically low levels, scant data would be reported. He had kept his car at an office park outside of Tulsa, as he went through the motions to search for drilling activity between Norman and Tulsa. For all intent and purposes, his whereabouts would be confirmed by multiple, independent sources.

Over the prior three months, he had many discussions with Ricky Mullino to analyze Enzo's activity. Set in his ways, the cocky mobster had never deviated from a routine, even after he was hassled for minor driving infractions. From a rest stop outside of Broken Arrow, Chris slammed down the payphone. Driving non-stop to New York, by nine the next evening, he had parked his car on a side street on the opposite side of the Bronx River Parkway in the Crestwood section of Yonkers. The one wrinkle to the plan was upon him. This was ironed out when Tony met him within five minutes of his arrival, and he hid in the rear compartment of his truck for the next phase.

Enzo would be busy. The NCAA Basketball season had concluded the day earlier with the Louisville Cardinals upsetting the Duke Blue Devils 72-69. Crazy action was placed on the entire tournament. With sixty-four schools to bet on over the three week span of the event, illegal bookmakers had made a killing.

Chris peered out the back window and observed Enzo. In Ressini's lounge, the bookie sat back and collected from the suckers who had to pay the piper or risk having the wrath of dealing with a late payment. Twenty percent juice on a delinquency was incentive for customers to make the commitment whole in the quickest amount of time. Based on Enzo's reputation, the alternative would be harsh and painful.

"These degenerates are never late?" Chis whispered to Tony from his stealthy viewpoint.

"Casinos and sports betting operations lack one bit of service illegal bookmakers have over them," Tony said. "Bookies allow those with lousy credit to place bets with no cash to lay out."

Enzo was preoccupied till closing with his accounts receivable dealings. Tony backed the truck and drove away. Within a minute, he was in front of Carmine's home. Chris had altered his appearance with a Yankee baseball cap covered by a gray hoodie. His face had a growth of stubble. He shrugged and double timed until he was safely in the foyer of the Alberetto residence.

The senior had a vague recollection of Chris, as the teen lightly tapped on the door and let himself into the kitchen. The debilitating effects of the disease had made Ricky's uncle appear ten years older than his seventy years. Ricky had known that the nurse did not check on his uncle at this hour so Chris would be safe from being noticed. He asked about family and the unseasonably warm weather and requested to see the Skylark. Carmine's eyes lit up, reminiscing about a story of Chris' dad from twenty years earlier. In the garage, Chris grabbed an old cap and black windbreaker hanging from a nail on an uncovered wood beam.

After admiring the sturdy chassis, Chris asked if they could go for a ride. Carmine beamed as Chris guided his frail frame to sit on the passenger side. The keys were in the ignition, and Chris turned the switch. He left the garage open and they drove north on Columbus Avenue. After reaching the tunnel entrance to the Bronx River Parkway, Chris doubled back to the Elm Street-Tuckahoe exit. The parking lot of the abandoned Parkway Casino was empty and he backed into a concealed spot by the corner of the building. The big hand of the clock was on the twelve and the small hand was on the ten.

Chris escorted Carmine out of the car. The long-time family friend became acclimated with his bearings. They admired the structure, oblivious to its dilapidated façade of the entrance to the banquet hall.

"A big fire happened...tragic, killed many good people, friends of my parents," Carmine recounted a story from his youth.

"Rest for a minute Uncle Carmine, I want to get something out of the car." Chris set him on concrete steps and sprinted back to the Skylark. Five minutes had passed.

BACK AT RESSINI'S

For the master plan of all master plans, Sal was instructed to mope around during the past week, outwardly worrying about his mother leaving and the struggles to keep the place afloat.

"I was close to moving on, but I overheard the kid say he was waiting for proceeds from a life insurance check," Sal disgustedly overheard Enzo licking his chops to one of his henchmen.

Sal popped his head out of the kitchen and hollered toward the bar area, "Last call...time to go!" The plan had to be synchronized. He had to be robotic and relay Enzo's comings and goings to Ricky.

"No more for me. I've had a profitable day." Enzo was in a good mood with his pockets full of cash. For the first time, he left a five dollar tip for the bartender and didn't finish his Scotch.

Enzo had apparently learned his lesson about barely drinking and driving as Ricky was always at the ready to pull him over for any infraction. "I was waiting by the traffic light in Depot Square. With venom in his voice, Ricky would debrief Sal, "His apartment's in Yonkers. He made tracking him comically easy. When the green arrow was prompted, he'd make the right turn to Main Street. I'd give him a few seconds of false security and then after the next traffic light, I'd light his ass, as he made a left turn onto Yonkers Avenue."

"Shit...friggin' ballbuster." Enzo would express his displeasure by punching the steering wheel as Officer Mullino approached. "I gotta' pee like a racehorse."

"License and registration, please."

"Sure thing officer...five times this month...Do you miss me?" Enzo would blurt out.

"No sir. Were you aware you drove through a yellow light? You're supposed to slow and stop, not go faster." Officer Mullino would study the license. "Please be careful. I'm going to let you go. Proceed safely through our town...have a good evening."

As Sal cleaned the restaurant, he crossed his fingers. Enzo scanned the darkened and quiet streets before spitting in frustration and throwing his arms in the air. Ricky was idling and ready to make his move. When Enzo drove off, Sal bolted for the front door for a better view. At the Depot Square traffic light, Enzo turned the corner.

The lights to Officer Mullino's police cruiser illuminated. Show time had begun.

THE FRONT SEAT OF THE SKYLARK

The flashing lights were visible in the distance, and Chris felt a surge of excitement flow through his veins. Enzo slowed to a stop at the corner of Elm Street and Yonkers Avenue, perpendicular to the Parkway Casino. The frustrated mobster buzzed the window down and waited. The police cruiser parked behind the BMW.

Officer Rick Mullino marched to the vehicle. "License and registration please."

"Here you go kid; nice night, huh?" Chris overheard Enzo bellow from a hundred yards away.

"For some, I've been busy. We received a call. A silver sedan similar to this one was involved in a hit and run earlier this evening." Officer Mullino took a few steps back and inspected the length of the BMW. "Step out of the car please! Can you explain the markings along your front quarter panel?"

"You kidding me? All right, all right; I've been in Ressini's all night. If my car has a scrape, then the hit and run was to me, too."

As Enzo scrutinized the markings, Ricky went into action. "Sir, come with me." The properly trained law enforcement officer pushed Enzo against the trunk of the police cruiser, and handcuffed his wrists. "I don't want you to be messing with a crime scene. For your own good, I have to put you in safe spot." Officer Mullino guided Enzo to the back seat of the police cruiser and slammed the door. The window was partially opened.

"You'll pay for this, punk. I'm not gonna' forget. You better not let ...." He stopped in mid-sentence, as his eyes went wide with fright.

Chris slammed his foot to the gas pedal and turned on the high beams. The old sedan bolted forward and quickly gained speed. Ricky dove to the ground. The Skylark accelerated, and the heavy front end impacted with the back door of the police cruiser. The collision lifted the vehicle off of the pavement. Chris had braced himself by squeezing the steering wheel, but the collision smashed his chest as he surge forward. Luckily, the tightly secured seatbelt held him firmly in place. He kept his foot pinned to the accelerator until the police cruiser tipped into the river bank. He reversed the Skylark and backed to the spot where Uncle Carmine was resting. Chris opened the driver's side door and removed the jacket and cap. He handed the garments to the old man before escaping through the woods behind the abandoned building. He used the darkness of the park to hide his retreat. Five minutes later, he was driving back to Oklahoma and arrived in Tulsa late the next evening.

OFFICER MULLNO'S INCIDENT REPORT

On 1 April at approximately 22:06, while on patrol, I viewed a 1985 silver BMW run through a red light on the corner of Main Street and Yonkers Avenue in Tuckahoe. I followed the vehicle, as the driver made a left turn onto Yonkers Avenue. The vehicle stopped on the corner of Elm Street and Lake Avenue. The driver, Enzo Pellanigro, became flippant as I asked for his license and registration. I ordered him to step out of the vehicle and he twice refused to comply. On the third request, he complied, but as he did so, he bumped into me. At that point, I subdued the driver until I could call for assistance. As I placed the suspect into the back seat of the patrol car, another sedan in the parking lot of the abandoned Parkway Casino had come to life. The tires screeched, and the vehicle surged ahead. I yelled for the driver to stop but to no avail. Originating at over a hundred yards away, the out of control, late model sedan had its lights on bright. I dove to the embankment to safety. The approaching Buick slammed into the police cruiser. The back quarter panel was crushed, as the stationary vehicle with the victim sitting inside took the hit dead on. Parked close to the concrete embankment along the edge of the Bronx River, the collision propelled the police cruiser onto its side. The vehicle tipped over the concrete lip separating the road from the river, which rested six feet below ground level. Initially landing in the shallow water on its left side, the vehicle rolled onto its roof before settling with the undercarriage facing skyward. The flow of the river in this section was four feet in depth. On its side and with the window open, water quickly filled the cavity. With his arms bound, the victim had no leverage to brace himself during the collision. His body was rocketed sideways, and his head and shoulders slammed into the opposite side door before crashing into the window. The victim lost consciousness, and his head was submerged. I dove into the shallow waters and bounced around the vehicle in an attempt to save him. I worked around and grasped the handle to jar open the door. My fingers slipped, and I lost balance, falling onto my back along the muddy bottom. At this point, I grabbed a large rock and slammed the back window until the glass shattered. Crawling inside, I grasped for the victim's legs. Shards of glass cut into my arms and face. The victim was a large man, and with the added volume of the river, he did not budge. Officer Blanco arrived at the scene and assisted me. We pulled on the victim's legs and grabbed at his shirt until the torso was lifted above water level. The victim was still breathing. At this juncture, I performed emergency medical care via CPR, and the victim threw up water and began to breathe. Officer Blanco remained with the victim until the paramedics arrived on the scene. The victim appeared to have his neck broken and was immobilized. A 1972 Buick Skylark was driven away from the crime scene.

With the paramedics working on Enzo, Ricky was helped up the side of the muddied embankment and to the road by the strong arms of Sal.

"What happened? This is a friggin' disaster," Sal worriedly stated as he handed Ricky his jacket to keep warm.

Out of breath, Ricky pointed in the direction of the abandoned Parkway Casino. They slowly walked to the area. The front end of the Skylark was crushed, and the engine was turned off. His Uncle Carmine was sitting on the concrete steps staring aimlessly into space. Mr. Alberetto was in a confused state and suffered from Alzheimer's. He was taken to Westchester Medical Center before being transferred to a state-run health care facility.

22

I Manage The Book

MAY 15, 1986

As die-hard Mets fans, the Columbus Avenue Boys had endured pain and lots of heartache for their entire lives. They had suffered the agony of defeat for the better part of their existence. Too young to remember the 1969 Miracle Mets, they had scant memories of the loss to the Oakland A's in the 1973 World Series.

"Being a Mets fan builds character," Tony Albanese would say to all who came into the butcher shop and view his autographed picture of Tom Seaver proudly displayed with yellowed tape on the wall behind the register. After the 1977 trade of the franchise pitcher, one had to truly bleed orange and blue to admit they loved the Mets.

The Yankees had averaged 93 wins and had won two World Series along with five division titles between 1976 and 1983. Yankee fans blew the horns of Don Mattingly, Dave Winfield, Ron Guidry and Willie Randolph. Over the same time, the Mets had languished in the cellar of the National League, and the best trial lawyer could not win the argument Craig Swann, John Stearns, Joel Youngblood and Lee Mazzilli had been top tier ballplayers. Times changed, and the Queens bunch had become competitive with consecutive, 90-plus win seasons. With phenoms like Dwight Gooden and Darryl Strawberry gelling, and the seasoned, veteran leadership of Keith Hernandez and Gary Carter, the Mets were the toast of the town.

Chris Cameron was isolated in Texas for the Mets' resurgence and dominance of the National League. He had infrequent opportunities to watch the team play and missed games at Shea Stadium. Since they were toddlers, his father or Uncle Al would take them to a few home games each year. The first vivid memory of attending a Mets game Chris had was in 1973 when they sat in the nose bleed seats during a doubleheader against the Montreal Expos. His father had been a fan of the Say Hey Kid, and Shea Stadium was jam packed for Willie Mays Night. One of the greatest players in the history of the game had announced his retirement.

Sal and Tony had gone to a handful of games this season, including the first three of what turned into an eleven-game winning streak. Neither of the trio had ever witnessed a game beyond Shea Stadium. They had plans to visit the new spring training home of the Mets. Their favorite sports franchise was building a massive facility in Port St. Lucie. Tony had been like a wide-eyed, little kid when he visited the construction site earlier in the year with his grandparents. Exploring with Poppa Vince, he was amazed by the size of the earth moving vehicles and the scope of the project. Comically, Tony was also an autograph whore and would do anything to walk away with a scribbled signature on a piece of paper or ball.

Chris was determined to outdo his blood brothers. The Mets had a series against the Astros in Houston, a two-hour drive from Austin. While they had lost the night before, with strong pitching from Ron Darling and a two run bomb by Danny Heep, the Mets were on their way to a convincing win. If the lead held, they would be 22-7 for the season, a blistering clip of fun times for any die-hard fan.

"Let's Go Mets! Let's Go Mets!" Chris screamed into the payphone hung on a wall a few feet from an Astrodome restroom. Sal was on the other end of the line.

"Were you behind the Mets dugout jumping like a mental patient in an orange shirt?" Sal and Tony had been watching the game from the bar in Ressini's.

"Hell yes, I snuck my ass down from the upper deck after the fourth inning. I missed a friggin' foul ball by inches...I should of knocked over the baby," Chris kidded.

"What a season, huh? Our Mets have had been great and…our life has been friggin' fantastic," Sal beamed. "A masterpiece and I am not talking about the Metsies."

Ressini's Ristorante had a resurgence of business. Without the eye sore at the end of the bar, Sal had righted the ship and customers were flocking back. With the windfall of cash when he sold the house added to the funds from the insurance proceeds, all was right in the world.

"Saby says the new Bella's location in Yonkers was doing great. With the few dollars I have coming, I may want to partner with you guys and open another one, in New Rochelle?" Sal unveiled a business offer to Chris.

"Sounds good, Sabe's almost done with college. She'll have the free time to focus on an expansion strategy. She may want to be a social worker, but the capitalist world seems to be pulling her in. Go right ahead!" Chris' parents had more free cash than at any time in their lives. Bella's Pasta had turned into a mini-success story.

"On a more serious note, any chatter about retribution for Enzo accidentally dying?" Chris asked.

"Jimmy Tree had a sit-down about the whole thing. Enzo's capo didn't seem too concerned and was surprised to hear Enzo held out from kicking up from what he earned when my dad lost all the money. The dumb bastard thought the whole thing was a fluke accident and said if he knew what Enzo held out on, he may have taken him out on his own. We presented an opportunity to Jimmy to whet his appetite. He went to bat and claimed Ressini's for his protection. He gave ten gees for the Lucchese's to walk away. Heh-Heh, to clarify, I gave Jimmy the money, and he made the offer," Sal debriefed some more of what had been transpiring. "I reiterated that the business side of Ressini's was off limits, and he reluctantly understood because of what Tony and I have up our sleeves."

THE NEXT MORNING, DEPOT SQUARE

Rick Mullino was walking the beat and coming to an end of his midnight to eight shift. To add to his misery, a steady rain had been falling since dawn. Assigned to the Patrol Division of the Tuckahoe Police Department, badge number 618 had sworn an oath to maintain the highest standards of the law enforcement profession...well, sort of. Tuckahoe was a small town, and thus he had taken an unwritten oath to protect his own.

On the job for eight months, he had recovered from the cracked ribs but had struggled to complete the police academy training. Revenge against Enzo Pellanigro had been in the forefront of his mind and was a motivating factor for his determination. When Chris had sought his assistance to take Enzo out, he immediately agreed. In a small police force where three officers were on duty at once, he'd have flexibility while enforcing the law. As the lowest ranking officer, he received the least favorite assignments. Besides midnights, he worked holidays and Sunday mornings. This made reconstructing the crime scene incredibly easy with a ten minute cushion when he set-up Enzo's toadies. Two hoodlums were off of Tuckahoe's quiet streets, and his version of the event was never questioned.

He was amazed at how Chris had pulled off the Houdini act with his uncle. The move was brilliant. Ricky's aunt was set to shell out thousands of dollars for Uncle Carmine to be cared for at a private medical facility. On the last call, Chris gave him specific instructions on what to do, how to dictate matters and where to physically place Enzo after he handcuffed him. His instincts took over when he saw the mobster clinging to life.

With rain pelting the pavement harder, Officer Mullino was glad to see Tony walking toward him. Under an enormous golf umbrella and carrying two cups of coffee, Tony placed one in his hand and provided cover from the rain.

"Wet as a bitch; sorry I didn't bring you a donut," Tony deadpanned before taking a sip from his Styrofoam cup.

"You're telling me. I get off in twenty minutes. I'm going to go to the gym if you want to work out." Ricky had not lifted weights in high school, but as a police officer he had committed to building his physique.

"I'll come by and pick you up...hey listen, I want to run a proposition by you...off the record."

"Go on...I'm listening," Officer Mullino suggested as he waved to a long-time resident in a passing car.

"Okay, we won't do this if you don't sanction the idea. With Enzo out of the picture, we have breathing room. The upstairs of Ressini's has not been used in years. Sal and I want to operate card games. We'll keep a tight ship, no trouble or nothing."

"What kind of cards?"

"No casino games, they're trouble; only poker. Run cash tables and a tournament...lock the door once the last dinner patron's leave. We want to earn for Jimmy Tree, and while Sal drew the line on any other part of the restaurant for his monkey business, he thought this would be fine. We love card games, running numbers and betting sheets, not breaking bones."

"Seems innocent enough," Ricky responded.

"Based on what we lived through with Zio Greg, the place to be was on the house side of the ledger. Sal's taking $30,000 from his insurance money and using the cash flow to extend credit."

"What's your role?"

"I manage the book. With money involved, nothing will slip. We expect the payback to be quick. Hire experienced dealers and take a 10 percent rake. After we give you and Jimmy Tree a taste, we could earn up to five thousand a night."

"I appreciate the generosity, but you don't need to give me any taste. I'll snoop around and see how you should handle the set-up. Too much of anything's not a good thing, especially in a sleepy village. The chief was not happy when Ressini's became the hot spot on Thursday nights. He was close to squeezing Sal cause he don't have a cabaret license."

"I hear you. Check this out; we'll host a game one night of the week. The other nights the game will rotate. Different operations get a piece in a whole bunch of locations. Nothing gets too hot. This is my best shot to make a name for myself. We could coin money."

23

A Friend Of Mine

OCTOBER 25, 1986

There was no reason to gloat, even after a convincing win against SMU. The Longhorns had mired through a dreadful year. They had been dominated on both sides of the ball, and the coaching staff's low expectations had been spot on-three wins and three losses. Inconsistencies had led to two lopsided losses, the most gut-wrenching one being at the hands of Arkansas. All of their wins were against inferior opponents.

At strong safety and on special teams, Chris did not have many memorable moments. He believed he had retained first team status due to more glaring weaknesses on the defensive side of the ball. To make matters worse, he trudged through a tough course load and was struggling to maintain B averages in his four classes. At the same time, he and Ally had decided to see other people. To clarify, she wanted to date someone else while he thought staying alone was the correct move. To add insult to injury, he was in Dirty Martin's Place, sucking on his tenth beer of the night while sulking through a monster headache, as he stewed over the last few outs of the World Series on the muted television set situated at eye-level, behind the bar. The New York Mets were set to blow the series. Tied after nine innings, the Red Sox had scored two runs in the top of the tenth and held a commanding 5-3 lead. The Mets had been heavy favorites to win and they were down to their last out.

"Mets suck!" Chris regretted wearing his team cap. "They shouldn't have beaten the Astros dude," a drunken Houston fan taunted the New Yorker from an adjacent barstool.

"If the Astros didn't have Mike Scott throwing spitballs, the Mets would have steamrolled them; against the Red Sox, no friggin' excuse. Let me buy you a beer, I'm not in a mood to argue." Chris extended his hand to his fellow barfly who snorted and turned to gloat with his buddies.

Gary Carter lofted a soft single to left field. This was followed by Kevin Mitchell who dunked a flair into short centerfield for another hit. "Yo Ron-Ron, two out rally; I can dream!" Chris clapped his hands and gave a half-hearted smile. "Yes, go baby!" He cheered in feigned excitement as Ray Knight's single to right-center scored Carter to cut the lead to one. Life was in the miracle bunch.

"You still yapping, loser? You Longhorn punks are pathetic," the drunk re-engaged. He was a burly white guy in his early twenties wearing a Texas A&M sweatshirt with a matching cap. His hairy beer belly flopped over his belt buckle and oozed from under his unkempt, T-shirt. Sitting at the bar since before Chris and his friends had arrived, the rambunctious Aggie alum had been fueled by multiple rounds of tequila shots.

The Red Sox changed relief pitchers from Calvin Shiraldi to Bob Stanley. Believing momentum was on his side, Chris laid a Ben Franklin on the bar and coaxed his instigator to accept the bet. "Listen asswipe, hundred bucks. Mets'll win, watch the screen!"

Mr. Texas A&M rubbed his beard. He turned and scrounged a handful of bills from friends along with two crumpled twenty dollar bills buried in his own pocket. He dropped the pile on top of the bar. The bet was in place...Chris raised his hands in celebration. A wild pitch had tied the score. Kevin Mitchell trotted in from third. The game was tied at 5-5, and Ray Knight was on second base. "You fuckin' loser! Old mo' is with the Mets!" Chris gave a two-handed high five to Jason.

Chris watched intently as Mookie Wilson worked the pitcher. He fouled off three straight pitches to draw the count full. On the ninth pitch, the Mets centerfielder dribbled a weak bouncer along the first base line. The slow roller was trouble from the get-go...Red Sox first baseman Bill Buckner stayed back and let the ball play him.

"He missed. Mets win!" The ball skirted through Buckner's legs for the biggest blunder in World Series history. "Suck ass!" Chris saluted a fuck you gesture to his mark with the handful of bills protruding from his two hands. He turned to his pals. Their celebratory huddle bumped into the A&M losers who were a hundred dollars poorer.

The perturbed drunks pushed back. Ron threw the first punch. An Aggie fan crumbled to the floor. Chris was grabbed from the back of his shirt and flung to the ground. His face and chest were stomped by various sizes of thick soled boots. He covered and rolled from the thrashing, as J.R. grappled with the pair. Two Aggies collided against the bar and threw defensive roundhouse punches that landed weakly on J.R.'s back and ribcage. An old-fashion bar brawl was in motion.

Chris staggered to his feet. He seized his bearded instigator by the throat and jerked him by the neck into a headlock. They fell over a barstool with Chris landing on top, pummeling his forehead with a flurry of punches. His Aggie foe attempted to cover his face, as Chris connected. Aggie's nose exploded in a pool of blood. As Chris was set to finish him off, he was hauled from the back of his belt and yanked away from the melee by Ron Grunther.

"We can't get busted!" The three roommates staggered and tripped, as they exited the bar. Chris felt like he was home again. And all too familiar was the feeling he had done something stupid.

When he awoke the next morning, his left hand was swollen and he could barely rotate his shoulder. His condition did not improve over the next day, and he fought through the pain during non-contact drills at practice.

"Okay, huddle with your position coaches for skull sessions and to review game film –Texas Tech's not going to be easy," Coach Akers announced after the final wind sprint.

"Not you Sinatra," Coach Campbell commanded. "All Mets fans are going to have to stay...run for me! Grunther and Rodgers, I heard you two are Mets fans, too; keep CeeJay company."

Their trivial punishment was jogging twenty laps around the football field. The owner of Dirty Martin's Place was a long-time booster of the UT football program. He brought the incident to the attention of a few coaches who happened to have lunch at the restaurant the next afternoon. While not mentioning names, three players, one of whom had been wearing a Mets cap, were involved in the altercation. What saved them was a bartender who had witnessed the incident confirmed the five gentlemen wearing the Texas A&M Aggie attire had been the instigators.

AT RESSINI'S RESTAURANT

Dubbed the Yonkers Poker Tour or the YPT, the schedule was Pat's Bar & Grill in Eastchester hosted a cash game on Tuesday nights. Conrad's in Bronxville had the lock on Wednesday with a crazy, Omaha High/Low game. Peter O'Malley's in Fleetwood invited high-stakes players on Thursday. The Riverview, overlooking the Hudson River in Yonkers held a $50 tournament on Friday's. Tammany Hall in New Rochelle ran high and low limit games on the weekend while Ressini's controlled Monday nights.

Ressini's $75 Texas Hold 'Em tournament had attracted a growing number of players for the past four months. By adding a sweetener of $5 to the prize pool for each participant, the number of players had grown steadily from eighteen the first night to sixty players. Crucial to the success, the high volume of traffic provided an ample supply of prospective players for two to three cash games to operate. Besides Ressini's, under the protection of Jimmy Tracino, Tony oversaw all of the YPT nights. They took in close to $30,000 a week, and Jimmy Tree's tribute was a healthy ten grand; not chump change for a drug-and prostitution-free business.

The success of their poker room had taken plenty of guile and strategy to get established. Tony had been tipped to competing games in the area. For the vast majority, he and Damien had managed to persuade the passive owners to close shop. Tony had a two-prong approach. Besides frank discussions with the owners, if the game remained active, he went the incentive route. He boldly approached a few of the high stakes players and offered favorable terms for chits they would build on his credit book. This approach had been the most effective. What made their venue attractive was the high action element. The influx of wiseguys had money to burn and talked a good game, but in reality these toughs were fish in wolves clothing.

An assortment of characters assembled; accountants, small business owners, construction workers, a TV producer, gangsters, Wall Street types, all walks of life. The nicknames matched-Big Joe, Danny the Whale, and Fat Freddie absorbed plenty of oxygen and requested reinforced chairs. Wild Thing never shaved and perpetually reeked of marijuana smoke. Stevie Garbage worked for the sanitation department but never played a junk hand. KGB was a silent Russian who would consistently win. Brendan the Fisherman was a lanky off the boat Irishman, and he always seemed to catch good cards on the river. Doctor Jay was a chiropractor who snapped opponents in two. Jerry the Barber cut hair for thirty years; at sixty three, his mane was impeccably coiffed while his wallet was trimmed. Smiling Vito received his nickname because when he lost, he would return to his strip club in Mt. Vernon for sex. Dangerous Damien was Sal and Tony's lieutenant. He had a reputation for playing any two cards and either won or lost in rapid fashion. Darius was another Irishman who cut trees for a living. He kept the table entertained with Scotch-induced bravado. Kevin the Preacher was an imposing black man with a deep baritone voice. He would pray to the Lord for a card to improve his soon-to-be dominated hand. Lucky Louie was an over-the-top Mets fan decked in blue and orange apparel. His name did not correlate, but the owner of a highly successful insurance brokerage had ample cash flow to burn.

Lucky Louie was in a good mood even though he had lost a $900 pot; his straight to the Jack had been bested by a flush draw that hit a four of spades on the river. The Mets had been losing 3-0 going into the bottom of the sixth inning of the seventh game of the World Series. Led by a Ray Knight homerun, they had battled back to tie in the sixth inning before taking the lead for good in the seventh inning.

Sal locked the restaurant and had made his way upstairs to Ressini's card room. Tony was operating the game, and this was their biggest turnout thus far. The allure of the Mets seemed to have brought every rounder in the area to watch the game and play cards. Eighty people had registered for the hold 'em tournament and three cash games had been running full since 9 p.m.

Nick Conte, a regular, raised his hand and barked out, "I need a reload Big Tony." He was taken for his final $280. Trip Jacks were bested by a straight to the King.

"Makes twelve hundred for the night Nicky," Tony calculated. He wrote the debit in the ledger of his big black book before counting out sixteen green $25 chips and twenty red $5 chips. "Good luck."

"Yeah, I'll need a friggin' rabbit's foot," Nicky fumed as he retook his seat and peaked at the two cards dealt to him before tossing the mess into the muck.

The room shook after Darryl Strawberry homered in the bottom of the eighth. A surprise single by the pitcher, Jesse Orosco brought in another run to extend the Mets lead. Tony had found his calling. His poker enterprise was growing steadily and Sal's restaurant had been resurrected. To top things off, the Mets were three outs away from winning their first World Series in seventeen years.

The games were high octane gambling at its finest. Experienced dealers moved along at a brisk pace. Adjacent to the cash games, the tournament was at twenty eight players. The last to be eliminated was a newcomer who had been recommended by Nicky Conte. He walked over to Tony.

"Hey big man, what's the wait for a seat?"

"You're third on the list; another half hour."

"Add me, name is Rico...can I speak with you about something?"

"All depends," Tony coyly answered.

"A dead friend of mine used to run this joint. Since his services were in the place, I was thinking about–"

Tony cut him off.

"Rico or whatever the fuck your name is, this place has been family run since before you were born. No dead people you knew or know or want to speak about–"

"Any problem?" Jimmy Tree was standing with his back to Tony and had overheard the altercation. "Tony's with me, Rico. Maybe you need to get a map or something; seems like you're lost. Your dead friend had no deed to this place...understand?" Jimmy picked something out of his tooth with his pinky finger and took a swig from his Budweiser longneck.

The room cheered again. Jesse Orosco had struck out the last Red Sox batter to end the game and the New York Mets were champions of the baseball world. Tony had wanted this to be a special moment. Sal pranced over and gave a congratulatory hug.

"We should be happy, Mets won!" Sal examined the sour expression on Tony's face before grasping the nature of the moment. He placed his immense frame between Jimmy and Rico. "Tree, who's this guy?" The discussion gravitated to the back corner, away from the table action.

"Rico Ianucci, guy's a friend of mine," Jimmy answered before whispering authoritatively into Ianucci's ear, "Your dear departed friend bragged about laying claim to this place. I tend to disagree. Sal and Tony go way back with me."

Rico was a made guy and a mirror image of Jimmy Tree. His father, Rocco Ianucci was a big shot for the Lucchese's and was locked up serving eight to fifteen in an Ohio federal prison for racketeering. Rico had a ruthless reputation for drugs, gambling and loan sharking. A bakery on Allerton Avenue was his front. He had earned his button by taking out three Russian ecstasy dealers who pinched his turf. Rumor was, he chopped off their hands and feet before dumping the bodies in the woods upstate. No fingerprints made identifying the decomposed, third world corpses impossible when they were discovered three months later.

"None of this was going on when Enzo's ass was taking space here. He had no claim to squat for what I do," Jimmy Tree continued to disprove Ianucci's facts.

"Time for you to go, BITCH!" Sal enunciated the last word, which caused the room to go silent. After a moment, the rumble of table talk resumed.

"Okay, no trouble. I'd still like to play another time, you run a good game. Hope we can be friends?" Rico turned to Sal and Tony with an extended hand but addressed the apology toward Jimmy.

Sal and Jimmy Tree escorted Rico downstairs. Sal unlocked the door, and the Lucchese tough walked across the parking lot to his Porsche. "Don't worry Sally. With the cash you guys are bringing in, my dad ain't giving up shit," Jimmy reassured Sal and patted his back before returning to the poker room.

Sal stood alone, staring at the idling sports car. As he took in the cockiness of Rico driving off, he couldn't help get a pit in his stomach.

24

Till Death Do Us Part

DECEMBER 17, 1986

Chris Cameron was heading home. On the tail end of a twenty-eight-hour, 1,800-mile journey from Austin to New York, his Monte Carlo had snaked along in a northeastern direction traversing through Texas, Arkansas, Tennessee and Virginia. After resting in the outskirts of Roanoke, he continued northward on I-40 before merging onto I-78 by Harrisburg. He was determined to arrive in Tuckahoe before nightfall but could not resist the urge to stop at Hershey Park for their world famous chocolate.

With the help of late night study sessions, he had salvaged the semester and was optimistic he would receive B's or B+ and possibly an A in his classes. The football season had been a complete disaster. The Longhorns would not be competing in a post-season bowl game. The bar brawl had hampered him over the final five games. While he remained a staple on kickoffs and punts, he had lost his starting spot in the secondary. His shoulder injury had not been healthy enough for the grueling pounding. The highlight of his dismal year was a blocked punt against Texas Christian and a fumble recovery on a kickoff against Baylor.

This would be the longest extended time he would spend in Tuckahoe since the summer of 1984 and his only documented time back during his two and a half years away. For Zio Gregorio's funeral, he had stayed less than two weeks.

Upon his arrival, his mother smothered him with food and affection. Maria had many sleepless nights worrying about the health and welfare of her baby boy and she wanted to make sure he was okay. She must have sensed him coming, as Chris had opened the front door to the aroma of his favorite meal. A plate of pork chops with hot cherry peppers and roasted potatoes was simmering on top of the stove. Within minutes, he was properly fed and his dirty laundry was dirty no more.

Later that evening, Chris partook in father-son bonding time at the Riverview Grill. Michael had bought his underaged son a few beers, as they chatted. Michael had asked Chris to watch his sister closely during the time he was home. Sabina and her parents had many arguments about her late nights and the young men she had been carousing with. She appeared to have two distinct personalities. Her passion to help the underprivileged was noble, as was her vision and management of Bella's. This determined young woman would transform into an emotional wreck if she consumed alcohol to the point where Michael had stopped purchasing adult beverages for the home. At twenty-one, Sabina was defiant and had all of the answers to life. She viewed her overindulgence as a fun way to relieve the anxiety of her day. Sal and Tony had mentioned specific incidents in which they intervened while out at nightclubs to save her from dirt bags and lounge lizards. Ricky had a list of incidents for her being pulled over for driving under the influence. She never received a ticket, but he had encouraged her to be responsible.

Chris and his father spoke about college life and plans after his senior year. He still had no clue but was absorbing a well-rounded course load. He was captivated with the nuisances of different sectors of the economy and how they intersected and fed off each other. He enjoyed the oil field scouting assignments. When Michael had taken him to visit the car factory as a boy, Chris could not get enough of how the assembly line operated. During his stop at Hershey Park, he took the factory tour and absorbed the history of Milton Hershey. The chocolate man's amazing philanthropic work was sure to appeal to Sabina. For a Christmas present, he purchased a book on his life for her to read.

After the catch-up time, father and son went upstairs to the private room. Mike Cameron had regularly participated in the weekly poker tournaments. While never venturing to sit at the crazy cash games, he competed well in the fixed dollar amount, elimination tournaments. He had earned his way to four final tables and had $1200 in winnings to prove his success. His best showing was a second place finish at Conrad's Pub back in October.

"Dad, you want another beer?" Michael nodded yes, and Chris signaled the attractive, auburn-haired waitress by raising two fingers. "Heineken, Holly." Chris and his father were both alive in the tournament but seated at separate tables. Eighteen players remained.

Tony worked the room. The clock beeped. "Okay, blinds are one thousand, two thousand; seventeen players are left." Number eighteenth cursed after pushing all in and busting with 9-10 of diamonds against a pocket pair of queens.

Chris mucked an inferior hand, stood and took a sip, as he stretched his back. "My dad kills them, huh Tony?"

"He holds his own...won another hand, he's on fire." Tony clapped his hands in the direction of Irish Mike raking in a pile of chips. "Hey look who finally arrived."

Sally Nuts' intimidating presence was noted by all. He nodded to Tony and Chris, as he walked around the room, shook a few hands, and joked along the way. The waitress handed him a beer. He was in good spirits.

"Oh Christ...Heh-Heh...this table's seating all professionals. Hey Uncle Mike, I'll give you a twenty buck bounty if you take Marcus out." The scrawny plumber shook his head and whined about his miniscule chip stack. Sal whispered in his ear, "Not for nothing, you better win tonight. You still owe me two grand." Marcus went back to concentrating on his two cards.

A few hands later, a disappointed Chris stood. The tournament dreams had ended when his two pair was counterfeited with a higher two pair on the river. He evaluated his dad's chip stack. Still alive and with a healthy amount, Irish Mike would be in good shape for the final table. Chris stood in back of his father's chair and massaged his shoulders. Michael allowed his son to peek at his two cards, a pair of fours. Chris concealed his excitement as another four fell in the window of the flop. Chris walked over to Sal after the three players in the hand folded to his father's 5000 chip bet.

"I'm proud of you guys. This place is hopping," Chris surmised, as he perused the jam-packed room with satisfaction.

"It's all cause of Big Tony. He's a wiz, runs this like a big time accountant. Heh-Heh, who'd a thunk?" Sal admiringly bragged, as Tony wrote diligently in his black book and simultaneously took a stack of bills in exchange for a handful of chips to a player who was set to enter the cash game.

"I may sit at the cash game," Chris contemplated as he counted out $200.

"Don't bother Cee, save your chump change. We call that the grown-up table. Those guys have been playing for hours, and they've bought in for thousands; game's sick. Even the kiddie table will run you four or five hundred to stay competitive. The stakes are for real. We took home eleven thou' the other night," Sal proudly mouthed into his blood brother's ear.

"Crap, why the hell am I going to college? When I get a job after graduation my entire salary will be twenty-five grand...if I'm lucky."

"You stay where you are. You'll see our gratitude under the Christmas tree. What you did can never be repaid, but your world ain't in the underworld." Sal put his hand on Chris' shoulder.

"We protect each other in different ways," Chris asserted, as he raised his beer bottle in a salute.

"Till death do us part," Sal concurred as he chinked bottles with Chris and took a deep swig before slamming his beer on a window sill and marching toward a guy who had entered the room. "Can I help you friend?"

"Yeah, maybe; I wanna' talk to two guys named Tony and Sal," the muscular, middle-aged man in a black leather coat inquired.

"Lot'a Tony and Sal's; sort of like yelling Maria in Spanish Harlem. Odds are, someone's gonna answer," Sal responded as he eyed his visitor.

"I hear you, pal. If you happen to see these guys, we need to talk. Name's Angelo, Angelo Mats. Jimmy Tree can tell you about me. Enzo's business is not finished." The named stranger was of average height and ensconced in a thick wool sweater which added to his bulk. He did not seem intimidated by Sal's commanding presence.

"We're kinda jammed, no room for spectators. Enjoy your Christmas, my friend." Sal shook Angelo's hand and escorted the wiseguy to the stairs. With a stone face, the messenger departed without a glance back.

"What was he all about?" Chris asked.

"Goes with the territory, I guess. We've grown guarded about the influx of...shall I say...undesirable characters at the poker games during the past few weeks. Forget about the cops, we're worried about the robbers."

"Thought Jimmy Tree squared matters?"

"He'll call them over for a private discussion or to talk outside. They never cause any trouble. These pricks are pawns sent to observe. With the tables filled like they are, it's easy to see why they're snooping."

The ghost of Enzo had spooked the Columbus Avenue Boys. An exorcism was needed to rid them of this demon.

25

It Was An Accident

In an overcrowded courtroom of the Federal District Court in Manhattan, harsh prison sentences were imposed on leaders of the Italian Mafia. Sentences ranged from forty to a hundred years. With evidence obtained under the Racketeer Influenced and Corrupt Organizations Act, U.S. Attorney Rudolph Giuliani had indicted eleven organized crime figures. Charges included extortion, labor racketeering, and murder for hire. Eight of the defendants were found guilty on all counts. The Lucchese's were crippled, as its entire hierarchy was sent away for life. Of the remaining three defendants, one was granted a separate trial, while the other two died before the trial began. Gambino Underboss Aniello Dellacroce passed away after a long struggle with cancer. His boss, Paul Castellano, died from unnatural causes. The Gambino ringleader was shot to death before Christmas outside of a steak house in Manhattan. The news outlets had widely surmised Big Paul's murder was at the hands of John Gotti. A protégé of Ainello Dellacroce, Gotti had risen to prominence but had raised alarms by selling drugs, which was taboo among the old-time Mafia hierarchy.

Gotti had taken advantage of the Mafia Commission in disarray and had received tacit approval for the hit. The definitive murder request was sanctioned after Big Paul had breached long-standing, mob protocol by not paying his respects at Dellacroce's wake. After the hit, Gotti cemented his place at the top of the most powerful crime family in America.

The Gambinos stole millions from construction scams, hijacking, loan sharking, gambling, extortion, prostitution, drugs and countless other disreputable activities. Santo Tracino had an unquenchable thirst to make the illegal dollar and went way back with John Gotti. They had met in the early Seventies, running in the same Brooklyn crew, and had cemented their trust while serving time together at the Lewisburg Federal Penitentiary. Gotti ran out of the Bergin Hunt and Fish Club in Queens while Tracino operated out of the basement of the Acropolis Diner in Yonkers. The sons of these powerful gangsters gained experience and stature under the tutelage of their powerful sires.

With the Dapper Don in charge, Santo had been elevated to a powerful position. He ran his operation like the CEO of a Fortune 500 business and had no tolerance for those who were not streetwise. His underlings had been put on high alert. Turf wars had flared with rival crews. With their backs to the wall, Lucchese, Colombo, Bonanno and Genovese soldiers had been mandated to earn more by encroaching on protected turf.

Before their gambling venture, Sal and Tony had participated on extortion and debt collections with Damien Morris. Of late, they had rarely seen their crew leader. Damien had recruited a fresh pack of wildings to squash threats to undermining Tracino's power. Tony recalled an infamous Damien recollection. A shyster had millions of dollars of drywall work coming out of the World Trade Center. Even though he knew he was being robbed, Santo did not want to risk not getting his taste from this lucrative scam. The bullshit artist skipped out on a meeting with Santo. Damien happily put two bullets to the victims head as he opened his car door in front of a synagogue in Staten Island.

In another incident, the decomposing corpse of a Genovese soldier was found in the trunk of an abandoned sedan in the lot of a warehouse in the Bronx. Damien had put three bullets in his head. The Genovese crackhead had brazenly robbed a tanning bed salon that was a front for Tracino's top ecstasy dealer.

SATURDAY

Promoted heavily in the weeks prior to the event, Tony was ecstatic by the turnout for his marquee poker tournament. Held at the expansive top floor of the Calabrese Social Club in New Rochelle, the event was a huge success. He had a knack for this and prided himself on operating the best game in the area. The bye week between the NFL playoffs and Super Bowl XXI was the perfect time to quench the thirst of hardcore rounders. The Trojan horse for the captive audience was the upcoming game between the New York Giants and Denver Broncos. The first New York team to make the Super Bowl in seventeen years was reason enough to lay some green on Big Blue. Tony drew the bodies in the door while Sal catered the food and hired the gorgeous waitresses. The final table would split $45,000 in prize money. With three cash games running full tilt, they were set for a twenty grand night. Jimmy Tree had stopped in earlier for his taste, twelve thousand dollars from two of his best earners.

Cards were in the air for the tournament promptly at 6 p.m. Seven and a half hours later, the final table was set. Chris, Irish Mike and Big Al had been knocked out early. Chris was heading back to college in the morning and bummed a ride home with the old men. With a rare night off from walking the beat, Ricky Mullino was in solid position with 82,000 chips.

"Okay guys, take your seats. Let's get this show on the road," Tony announced.

"This is the best I've ever done. My ass is gonna' play tight as hell. Pocket Aces or Kings is all I'm going in with," Ricky said.

"Sixth place gets you three grand and first place is twenty-five grand. Play smart. Hope I'm handing you a fat envelope, my friend."

"Christ, it's almost my entire salary. Maybe if I win, I'll play with the big boys." Ricky had dreams of sitting at the $5/$10 no-limit game which had been running hot since three hours before the tournament began. Over a hundred grand in real money chips were in play on the green felt.

"Heh-Heh, yeah right; a ten person wait to sit there. Check out Jose in the Cincinnati Reds cap. Guy bought in for eight hundred and has won over eleven grand. Friggin' guy works for Con Ed," Tony tried his best to dampen Ricky's zest for action or how he saw it; guaranteed destruction. "All right, take your seat tournament players. Bobby, shuffle-up and deal."

The nine men and one woman who had been on bathroom and smoke breaks settled in for the final push. Five minutes later, the tenth place envelope was handed to Joanne, a black woman from Mt. Vernon. This doe was superior to the majority of bucks in the room. Two thousand dollars would provide a formidable bankroll for her cash game seat.

Ricky peaked at a Four of Hearts and a Nine of Spades. He tossed his cards into the muck, drained the last of his Coors Light and shuffled off.

"You see the look on his face?" Sal chided Tony as they watched Ricky bustle along the narrow hallway and disappear behind the restroom door.

Moments later, three brutes in ski masks and black sweatsuits barged into the poker room. They moved swiftly, speaking vehemently as they approached. Two progressed along the outer aisles brandishing handguns for all to see.

"Place your heads on the tables, nothing cute! Fold your arms behind your neck," the leader of the pack confidently demanded as he trailed in the center of the melee. He was grasping a Remington Shotgun. His cohorts tipped the table of a high limit game to its side. Poker chips, glasses and bottles crashed to the floor. A deathly silence fell amongst the room.

The badass marched to Tony and tapped the scary front end of the shotgun three times on top of the rolling bar. This cart was being used as the makeshift bank. A case of chips and a metal box of cash were stored on the unseen shelf located below the counter.

"No troubles, my friend." Tony slowly lowered his arms. *Am I the only one who crapped in his pants?* Trembling, the big man handed two handfuls of hundred's and twenties to the assailant.

"The lower shelf, too!" Tony bent down again and re-emerged with a thicker stack bills. The gunman nodded to the associate on his right. His accomplice, who was half the size of Tony, darted over and pistol whipped the big man above his right ear. Tony staggered backward toward the wall as the attacker snatched the mound of bills from the counter.

"We're not playing games, asshole!"

"All of you... don't be stupid and no one will get hurt. Empty your pockets...you first." The lead gunman aimed the muzzle at Fat Joe. "After you're done, go to the back and face the wall." Joe's obese body shook uncontrollably as he emptied $3000 into one of the brown paper bags opened in front of the cart.

During the next five minutes, each player followed the commands without opposition. Besides the hundred and fifty grand Tony relinquished, the two bags were filled with an additional $50,000. The two gunmen grasped the bounty and backed toward the exit door and disappeared down the steps. Their leader surveyed the room. Seeing all were compliant, he made his retreat.

IN THE RESTROOM

Ricky Mullino thought to himself he had jabbered on for far too long during the break. His excitement was bubbling over, but he had to take a crap. By the time he had finished the pep talk with Tony, the line for the restroom had grown to four deep. The call for the final table came, and he reluctantly sat. After the tenth place finisher was eliminated, Mother Nature could wait no more. He hurried off; hopefully when he returned another player or two would be eliminated. With seventy-four thousand chips, the perfect opportunity to play safe was upon him.

Ricky had weaved his way through the empty tables and walked hurriedly past the stairwell entrance of the upstairs room to the Italian club. The restroom was across from a narrow coatroom. He locked the door from behind, unsnapped his black, nylon fanny pack and hung the strap over the door hook. Even in civilian clothes, Ricky carried his Heckler & Koch P9 wherever he went. He had purchased the West German, semi-automatic pistol at a gun show at the Jacob Javits Center a few months back. He loved the feel of the double-action trigger and kept his weapon stored inconspicuously in the fanny pack.

As Ricky sat on the bowl, he discerned the bustle of the poker room had waned. The thump of a table crashing to the floor startled him. Sensing alarm, he removed the revolver from the fanny pack. He slowly turned the knob and opened the door slightly. Surveying the room, the shrill of voices ordering the submissive throng of players to empty their pockets roared. The perpetrators were unaware of his presence. Fifty feet away, they were pre-occupied and facing in the opposite direction.

The trained law enforcement professional checked the cartridge and decocked the hammer of the H&K P9. Settling himself, Ricky warily exited the restroom and darted across the hallway to the darkened coat room. Stuffed with jackets and coats of all makes and sizes, he was easily concealed. He skirted along the doorframe, remaining hidden behind the garments. There was an unobstructed line of sight to the action. Ricky bided his time to determine when to make the safest move. Glancing out at the room; the first gunman had backed out and retreated down the stairwell. Ricky heard his heavy footsteps trample the stairs. The second gunman followed but paused for a moment to straddle the open door. His back was to the exit, as he bustled down the flight for his retreat. The third gunman mimicked the movements of his two companions. Less than ten feet from the exit, he lowered the shotgun.

"Police! Drop your weapon!" Ricky ordered. The criminal stopped in his tracks. Officer Mullino circumspectly inched out from the shadows. He kicked the exit door shut, barring the other assailants from re-entering. His H&K was leveled at the perp.

The gunman cautiously raised his free hand high in a defensive position while the other hand grasped the barrel of the shotgun. He slowly placed the shotgun to the floor but began to tremble and his fingers lost their grip. As the weapon tipped, Officer Mullino dove for safety. He was not fast enough.

The blast was deafening. The buckshot penetrated Ricky's upper torso and blew his body backward into the wall of the hallway. Dead before he collapsed to the laminated floor, his chest cavity had been torn apart. Blood, bone and cartilage painted the corridor.

An off-duty fireman tackled the gunman. Another player scampered over and secured the fatal weapon as Sal and Tony scuttled to the mangled body. They viewed with horror the gory mess. Ricky's body was contorted, and his lifeless eyes were open. Tony cradled his head and screamed. Sal lowered Ricky's eyelids. Together, they held their friend and sobbed uncontrollably.

In the distance, sirens echoed outside of the Calabrese Social Club. Patrolmen and paramedics took over the room. The gunman's mask was removed.

"It was an accident; I didn't mean to hurt nobody. My hands were sweaty and the rifle slipped," Angelo "Mats" Maffucci cockily excused his actions. The Lucchese capo appeared unfazed. He lay subdued on his stomach and defiantly raised his head as he was cuffed from behind.

Specks of Ricky's body parts matted Sal and Tony's bodies. They sat in shock, upright with backs against the plaster wall and began to maniacally bang their heads in rhythm.

26

Angry Young Man

The white Cadillac DeVille was a heavy sedan and handled the slippery pavement and turns surprisingly well. Driving in blizzard conditions, Chris took his time and plodded along at reduced speed. For extended car trips of his youth, his father had always taken the reigns in treacherous conditions. He did not think this was an appropriate use of his father's time, especially when two bodies were bound in the trunk of the stolen car.

With a plow affixed to the front of Tony's truck, his blood brothers cleared the rapidly falling snow and led the way along the sparsely trafficked thruway. The final destination was a secluded cabin, which the Tuckahoe Hunting Club members had built thirty years earlier, in upstate New York. The older residents of the village had pooled together limited resources to hunt deer and turkey in the fall and enjoy family vacations.

The southern portion of the state had received modest precipitation, but as the Columbus Avenue Boys drove through the higher elevations of the Catskills, more than twelve inches had fallen. After exiting the thruway, they continued northeast over the rolling hills. Close to midnight, both vehicles pulled into a spacious garage. Originally purchased as a tiny cabin, with an abundance of tradesman in town the structure had expanded to six bedrooms, a colossal kitchen with a stone fireplace, and an immense living room.

Once safely inside the garage, Sal unlocked the door to the interior living space. Winterized after hunting season, all of the pipes and electricity had been sealed off. Tony and Chris lugged the bodies from the trunk of the Cadillac to the living room and dumped their quarry on the frigid, linoleum floor.

John Cardullo had been identified as the gunman who pistol whipped Tony. His hands were tied behind his back, and a red bandana muzzled his mouth. He was in the clothes he had been wearing when grabbed upon leaving a bar in Ozone Park the night before. Chris Cameron had walked along the sidewalk and cold-cocked the armed-robbery suspect across the face with a devastating left hook augmented with brass knuckles. After he crumbled to the cement, Sal and Tony tossed his disoriented body in the back seat of the truck. They had been tipped to Cardullo's whereabouts by an informant of Jimmy Tree who had been working out a deal to flip on the Lucchese's and join the Gambinos. He provided additional information on the third robber, Marco Benevenco.

Shortly after the successful abduction of Cardullo, the Columbus Avenue Boys staked out Benevenco's Cadillac from the corner of his girlfriend's parent's house on Pelham Road in the Bronx. Lover boy had kissed his girl good-night from the rolled-down window of his car. Seeming like a typical college kid, Chris had strolled by once the girlfriend entered her house and asked for directions. Chris jabbed Benevenco's throat and peppered the sides of his face with punches until Tony came to assist. From the backseat, Tony pulled Benevenco over the top and subdued him as Chris drove the car away.

On the morning of the murder, Chris had been awoken by his father with the devastating news;-Ricky had been killed. Chris collapsed to the floor and cried out. He cancelled his flight to go back to school. His father had asked for him to leave the car as his was on the fritz.

Due to a lack of evidence and the fundraising guise, Sal and Tony were not arrested for hosting the poker tournament. Nobody, including the proprietors of the Calabrese Social Club, deviated from the line of the event being an innocent fundraiser. Tony was set to donate 10 percent of the proceeds to a firefighter who had died while on the job. Regardless, Sal and Tony, along with many witnesses to the tragedy had spent hours being interrogated by the New Rochelle police and the FBI.

The local news had run the story of an armed robbery gone bad with the murder of a young, decorated police officer. Major news affiliates highlighted the angle of an off-duty police officer who had turned heroic. Live reports were shot in front of the Calabrese Social Club and throughout the Village of Tuckahoe. Reporters searched vehemently to interview anyone who could shed light on the brave young man who had risked his life. Besides the prepared remarks by the chief of police, no one would comment. The entire village was in mourning and wanted space to heal.

On the morning following the tragedy, Chris visited with Jimmy Tracino, who was in the video store and immersed in a hushed discussion with Damien. "Hey Jim, how've you been?" Chris greeted his old Blue Devil teammate with a firm handshake. With his free hand he squeezed Tracino's forearm.

"Cee, been a while. You're jacked-up. Heard you're a football star?"

"Yeah, sort of; sorry I've missed you my few times back to New York. Saw you the other night at the card game, but you split before I had a chance to say hello. I'm at the University of Texas, playing ball and going to school. Hey, you heard what happened, right?" He glanced at Damien before returning to Jimmy Tree.

"Sorry, my manners; Cee, this is Damien. Sal and Tony might have mentioned him. He's on top of things."

Chris shook Damien's hand. "I've seen you around whenever I make time to come back home. It's nice to finally put a name with a face."

"Your buddy's hold you in high regard...we know who was behind this," Damien debriefed Chris on the information he had coerced from the turncoat. "After Mats was hauled off, most of his crew bugged out...hit the mattresses and shit. A live one paid us a visit last night. He spilled and gave up their names and shit. We don't have time. This was a cop killing. It's obvious the law's gonna' come hard for Maffucci's crew cause nobody kills one of their own. We need to find out who directed him."

"We need to get to them before the cops," Chris confidently stated. He was all business. "This is beyond personal for us. All you have to do is tell me where they are. Trust me, I'll get you all the information you'll need."

Back at the hunting house, Benevenco and Cardullo sat hogtied; back to back propping each other on the floor. They were visibly frightened.

"My eye is cut. Motherfucker, you have balls coming after me!" Tony punched Cardullo with a straight right to his chest. Chris had transferred the metal knuckle persuaders to Tony to help inflict the optimal amount of punishment. The blow caused them both to flounder and tip over to their sides.

"Our game was friggin' peaceful...and sanctioned. Did you think you were gonna' get away with this? Where's the money?" Sal untied Benevenco's mouth and pulled out the rag. Benevenco coughed and breathed heavy, his tough veneer shattered. Sal propped the bodies up and continued, "We're not killers, but you stole hard earned cash that belonged to good people, innocent types who had nothing to do with your war. Our livelihood's over."

"It was Mats. He wanted you bad," Benevenco blurted.

Chris grasped at Sal's forearm and stopped him from getting ready to coil. He leaned over and semi-whispered into Sal's ear, "Don't be too rough on the guy. Pal, drink this." From a one liter bottle of liquor, he poured an inch into a red solo cup. He tilted Benevenco's head and forced the thug to imbibe. Bacardi 151 burned his throat.

"How about you; is your buddy telling the truth? Come on, where's the cash hidden?" Tony untied Cardullo's mouth and Chris forced him to swallow the fiery shot in the same mode.

The dance went on for another hour. Enticed by bad cop tactics of Tony sharpening butcher knives, and Sal using the bodies of the victims for punching practice, versus the good cop persona of Chris feeding them liquid courage, the two men capitulated. They'd give half answers and in response drank the high octane alcohol, as the sharp edge of a knife pinched their cheek, or they would get slammed in the ribs with a well-placed jab. Over the next two hours, they consumed shots from two bottles and were slurring their words and swaying through the confessions.

During the fact-finding barrage, the defeated pair had divulged the location of the cash. Benevenco had the loot stored in the basement of his girlfriend's parent's house. Maffucci had not acted alone. The robbery of the Gambino protected poker game had been sanctioned by the capo, who Enzo had reported to for the Lucchese's. With the three top figures of the Lucchese's behind bars for life, Maffucci's uncle, Vito Pagnetti, had taken his place atop the criminal organization. Pagnetti had a reputation for pulling off brazen heists and had decided to execute a bold gambit to heighten his stature.

The interrogation had gone as far as possible. With dawn hours away, the Columbus Avenue Boys departed the hunting house. Chris drove the Cadillac. Sal sat in the back seat bookended by the delirious victims. Tony led the way through the blizzard. After a half-hour of driving in a southeast direction, they came to the intersection of Route 23. Both vehicles stopped at an embankment on the side of the road. Benevenco and Cardullo flopped out and stumbled against the side of the Cadillac. They were inebriated beyond comprehension.

"You're on your own, my friend." Sal lightly slapped Benevenco on his cheek and placed the car keys in the palm of his hand.

"Oh, and don't think of stopping before you get home. If I see those red brake lights go on, we'll haul your asses back and carve you like Thanksgiving turkeys," Tony stated in an icy command.

Chris slid out a windshield wiper blade and flung the projectile deep into the woods. "Be careful, seems like your gonna' have trouble with road visibility."

"Hit the road," Sal ordered the drunken duo, as he let Chris into the warmth of the truck. Tony tooted his horn and made a hand gesture for the polluted pair to get a move on.

Benevenco did not receive the desperately needed escort Chris had benefitted from on the harrowing trek to the cabin. After fifteen minutes of treacherous travel, Benevenco came upon a section of road a few miles east of the Hunter Mountain ski resort. The terrain was steep and narrow. The Cadillac hit an icy patch and slammed into a utility pole. The Columbus Avenue Boys did not stop to observe the fatal crash. Sal popped a Billy Joel cassette into his stereo; *Turnstiles* was Ricky's favorite. They sang *Angry Young Man* and headed home to bury their friend.

A FEW DAYS LATER

The United Airlines flight from LaGuardia Airport lifted off on time. Chris Cameron was awoken an hour later by the stewardess to see if he would like a snack or beverage. He nodded and asked for a can of seltzer. She scooped ice into a plastic cup, poured and placed mini-bags of peanuts on his opened tray. As he snacked, Chris reached below his seat and unzipped his gym bag and removed a black folder along with a stack of newspapers. He perused his class schedule and the associated notes he had taken to prepare for the upcoming semester. Because he was double majoring he would need a total of 132 credits to graduate. Thus far, he had completed 81 credits and needed 51 more to fulfill his requirement. This equated to seventeen classes during the next year and a half. His GPA was solid and he was happy with his curriculum. For the spring semester, he would be overloaded with six classes and follow this with no reprise; three classes in the summer session.

Chris was locked in to doing well in school and would dedicate his senior year of football to Ricky Mullino. The death of his good friend had overwhelmed him, and he was glad to leave Tuckahoe shortly after the funeral. The Columbus Avenue Boys had rallied around Joey Mullino and his mother. Reporters and cameramen had attempted to get close to the mourners but the family had been buffered by the self-appointed bodyguards. Besides grandstanding from local politicians, the Mullino family had been touched by the support of the community who had come out to pay their respects in memory of a friend and local hero.

After Chris had reviewed his notes, he perused the newspapers. The *Gannett Westchester* continued to run stories of the gruesome, cop killing on page one, but the article was buried below the fold. The *New York Post,* which had the murder on the front page in Monday's edition, had a story on page eleven. The *Daily News* had acted in similar fashion to their rival tabloid.

In the obituary section of the *New York Post* was an announcement of the death of Marco Benevenco. The twenty-nine year old from the Belmont section of the Bronx had graduated from Cardinal Spellman High School. He was survived by his loving mother and long-time girlfriend. Benevenco had died tragically in a car crash in upstate New York. A surviving passenger in the vehicle was clinging to life and in a coma.

Chris disposed of the newspapers in the receptacle in the back of the DC-10 and returned to buckle his seatbelt. The captain had announced rough air ahead, moments before the aircraft dipped, bumped and wobbled. Though his eyes watered once again as he continued to think of his friend, Chris could not help but chuckle as turbulence in the skies above Missouri were nothing compared to the turbulence set to be caused by Sal and Tony.

IN THE BRONX

Tony Albanese sat patiently in the passenger seat of Joey Mullino's Jeep Grand Cherokee. Fifteen minutes earlier, they had been mingling with friends at Ressini's. Stealthy exiting through the kitchen, they drove to their destination in the Bronx. Parked on the corner of Pelham Parkway and Morgan Avenue, they waited until the lights of a Crown Victoria pulled away from a small brick house. While the majority of people were headed to Super Bowl parties to cheer the New York Giants to a hopeful victory over the Denver Broncos, the residents of 2212 Morgan Avenue were on their way to the wake of Marco Benevenco. Juliana, the daughter of Richard and Isabella Viscano, had been dating the deceased for the past seven years.

After the mourners made a right turn into the night, Tony exited the Jeep and walked toward the Viscano home. The garage was situated directly below the living room and partially concealed on both sides. From the right, a red brick staircase fully obscured his position. On his left, a declining cement wall blocked onlookers from his large frame. The street was absent of pedestrian traffic. Tony removed a crowbar from his jacket and pried at the bottom seal of the garage door. He raised the opening half way, shimmied under and lowered from the inside. He illuminated a pocket flashlight. The door connecting the garage to the basement was unlocked. He entered, and surveyed the darkened room as a poodle was heard barking from the floor above. The money from the robbery was hidden in the boiler room. Easily finding the brown bag, Tony checked the contents and exited the property. Joey had double-parked the getaway car a few houses away. Tony bustled over and hopped in. From Pelham Parkway, they entered the northbound entrance to the Hutch and were back at Ressini's for the remainder of the Giant's Super Bowl victory.

27

He Had A Sit-Down With
The Commission

MARCH 30, 1987

While they would never see a plug nickel, Santo Tracino owed Sal and Tony a debt of gratitude. The silver lining was the deed inched them a step higher on the old coot's ladder. The elder Tracino and three of his most trusted capos were in hiding at the Tuckahoe Hunting Club's cabin in Greene County. They had hit the mattresses in the wake of the escalation in violence committed in the aftermath of the turf war that had included the poker game robbery and the unfortunate death of the off-duty police officer.

With the Commission losing control, Santo was incensed his power in the underworld had been tested. He put the word out-anyone connected to Vito Pagnetti should get clipped. "If you stole my motherfucking quarter, a hundred dollars and plenty of blood would be your penance." This had been his credo, and he became more ruthless with age.

Damien Morris was Santo's secret weapon to keep the streets flowing with blood and to restore the underworld to its rightful order. In the early morning hours, Sal Esposito snatched Angelo Pagnetti outside a rub-and-tuck on Spring Street in Manhattan. Angelo was the nephew of Vito Pagnetti and on the fast track to getting his button for the Lucchese's. Sal had waited by the vestibule of the adjoining building at the gangster's favorite late night "happy ending" locale. When he stopped to tuck in his shirt and light a cigarette, Sal slammed the recently gratified gangster's face against the brick wall, secured him in a headlock and tossed the squirming body into the back of a stolen van. The victim was dumped at the feet of Damien, who had been waiting patiently in an abandoned warehouse in the Bronx.

"Hey, you pissed, Sally? Still upset Doc Gooden's in rehab?" Damien sniggered as he lowered the evening edition of the *New York Post*.

"Kinda upset, Mets need him; but no. This asshole scratched me when I threw him into the van," Sal fumed as he cupped his big right hand and slapped the side of Pagnetti's head. Angelo tumbled onto his side and bawled.

"Come on, tough guy...I hear you're a real go-getter; can't leave this world crying like a punk," Damien declared as he removed a brand new Black & Decker hand drill from the manufacturers cardboard box. After inspecting the quality workmanship of the common hand tool, he sadistically pistol whipped Pagnetti across the side of his head. The wannabe spun backward and stumbled to the concrete.

Sal grabbed Pagnetti's head and secured his mouth with duct tape. He leaned over and accepted the power tool from Damien's hand. The tip of the bit was padded. Sal pressed the bit against Pagnetti's mane, looked him in the eyes, and squeezed the trigger. The drill whizzed to life and yanked a clump of dark brown hair, which wrapped around the entire length of the bit. Pagnetti's screams were muffled, and he flailed on the floor. Damien grabbed the tool and removed the pad from the bit. Sal firmly secured the victim by his right shoulder and arm as Damien drilled a hole into Pagnetti's right elbow. The torture continued with another bloody insertion drilled into his left knee.

"Heh-Heh, Pinocchio. Put a string through em. Let's turn this bastard into a puppet," Sal snorted in morbid amusement, as he removed the duct tape with a forceful tug.

The cruelty was paused, as a fellow wiseguy entered from the far end of the building. The clacking of shoes echoing denoted he was rapidly approaching. Smoking a cigarette, he stepped over the body, as if the prone mound were a puddle on a street corner and whispered into his lieutenant's ear.

With a satisfying grin, Damien addressed his prey. "You're lucky, Angelo old boy. You'll live...remember to tell your friends from your cripple chair what we do when you think you can run rough shot on our turf. Besides, your uncle is on a slab in the morgue. He ain't gonna be giving us any more trouble." Awkward silence followed, as Pagnetti realized his life had been spared. "Come to think, neither are you." Reneging on the reprise, Damien turned demonic, as he hauled back and beat Pagnetti's skull with the power tool. He did not stop until blood, bone and brain fragments oozed from the lifeless body.

AN HOUR EARLIER ON MULBERRY STREET

Taking in the bustling atmosphere of Little Italy on a warm spring night, Tony Albanese thought back to how a faction of the Scalamarri descendants had lived in lower Manhattan when they emigrated from Italy a century ago. His immediate relatives called Tuckahoe their home in the 1880s and had worked in the town's marble quarry. Sal's relatives had settled in Brooklyn. Chris's grandparents lived around the corner from where he stood, somewhere on Mott Street.

The Columbus Avenue Boys had been educated on bits and pieces of the family history through stories from the mouths of Vincent Scala and Joe Cavazzi. All of their ancestors had worked tirelessly to survive in an era when Italians were discriminated against. They bound together to make ends meet. Tony emulated these long-deceased relatives more than Sal and Chris. While he was no dope and extremely resourceful, Tony felt he did not have a legitimate passion to guide him toward a successful career. Chris had his book smarts and determination, which would afford him the foundation to succeed. Sal had his love for cooking. Tony, though, was growing unsure the butcher shop was his career for the next forty years. A different direction was needed.

After what had happened in the three short years since their youth had officially ended, Sal and Tony craved a return to the normalcy of life. They had matured and aged tremendously since high school and knew their association with unscrupulous characters had to scale back considerably or end. Witnessing the gruesome murder of Ricky Mullino had changed and hardened them for good. They had vowed to swallow guilt deep in their bellies and provide assistance in all shapes or forms to avenge his death.

To no surprise, unimaginable acts of violence had escalated. Before the tragedy, they were content to stay on the periphery of organized crime. The incident had triggered them to assist Jimmy Tracino punctuate his power and retain dominance in the underworld. They would not murder directly, but would participate. Their first action was to squash the dirt bags who robbed them and murdered Ricky Mullino. Then Tony shook-down the owner of a Lucchese controlled night club in Queens. He cornered the guy when he was alone by a payphone in the nightclub. Tony tossed him a roll of quarters. "Call guys to protect you...trust me, you need protection!" The owner went into his office and within five minutes came out with twenty grand in cash.

Sal had been working for Damien while Tony gravitated to assist Jimmy Tree. Tonight, he was acting as the getaway driver. Vito Pagnetti, the agitator of the current round of trouble was dining with associates at Angelo's of Mulberry Street. Santo Tracino could not do this hit off the record. As an old school, traditional mobster he held a sit-down with the Commission. Pagnetti breached mob protocol and had officially become a problem to not only his but to all of their financial enterprises. As a sweetener to get approval for the execution and to send an unmistakable message to the other families, Santo agreed to go partners with the Bonnano Family to peddle heroin and cocaine. Santo was not an empty suit. He had been a big earner for decades. The old-timer had had enough of the brazen, disregard for his stature and while he gave two shits about the killing of the kid cop, he had a strong notion Pagnetti was responsible for the disappearance of two of his top drug earners.

Jimmy acted fast. He received a call from a bartender who dealt coke for him. Pagnetti was a regular at the restaurant on Monday nights. They arrived early, in a stolen Honda Civic. Jimmy blended into pedestrian traffic on the crowded thoroughfare and spied into the window of the popular Italian eatery. Reading his weapon, he maneuvered between an alcove next to a local thrift store and the stairwell to the second floor apartments. The executions happened quickly. Pagnetti and his associates sported potbellies under their designer suits. Clustered together and lumbering, they paused to light cigarettes from a shared Zippo. Facing in the opposite direction of where Jimmy was hidden, they had no chance.

POP, POP, POP. POP, POP, POP! Jimmy shot the three hoods in the back of their heads in efficient succession. As the bodies crumbled to the ground, he tucked the untraceable, snubnosed pistol into a pocket of his black windbreaker and walked toward where Tony was waiting. The seasoned killer maneuvered close to the edge of the cars and vans along the narrow street. He removed the windbreaker, rolled the covering in a bunch and handed the bundle to a passing associate. Ten seconds later, he was in the backseat of the Civic, with Tony making his way through lower East Side traffic. A block away from the Canal Street subway entrance, Tony parked in front of fire hydrant and they scurried the steps to the uptown Six train. Jimmy exited to Bleecker Street. A red Mercedes drove him to his strip club in the Bronx. Tony stayed on to 28th Street and casually strolled the remaining fourteen blocks to Grand Central Station and bought a ticket for the 10:36 p.m. Metro North Harlem Line train to Tuckahoe.

28

No More Blood Of Any Kind

APRIL 4, 1987

The bone-jarring tackle changed the way coaches viewed a player and was reminiscent of memories from so long, or not so long ago? Rusty Greer first saw this athleticism when he was discovered on the dirt and rocks that outnumbered the blades of grass on the Tuckahoe High football field. Chris Cameron glided effortlessly across the turf of Texas Memorial Stadium and sprinted unabated toward a heralded, junior running back. He hit him squarely in one of the loudest collisions of the unseasonably warm afternoon. Chris planted his facemask between the numbers and the momentum of the impact drove his victim backward three yards.

When play resumed five minutes later, newly hired Head Coach David McWilliams had taken note, as Chris made his presence felt once more. The strong safety was instructed to cover the tight end. If the tight end stayed in to block, he checked down for potential screens to the fullback or a running play to the edge. On the snap, the tight end blocked the defensive end and the fullback swung out to receive a pass. The ball floated in the air for a second too long and with flashbacks to Bronxville's Jack Randall, Chris read the play perfectly and surged into the upper torso of number 43. The ball spit out and fell incomplete as Chris, pumped by the ferocious hit, hovered over the body.

"Yo, CeeJay, its spring drills, man."

"Whew, you like where I'm coming from Blake? Woo hoo! Little guy like me shouldn't be able to hurt you," Chris teased as he extended his hand to his friend of three years, 6'2", 220 pound, Blake Goodwyn.

Chris had a renewed focus to be the best student and football player he could be. He tackled the books, weights and offensive players with equal gusto. After the mid-term break, he had straight A's and worked out for two to three hours each day to prepare for the football season. At 6'1", 212 pounds, his bench was 375 pounds. After cranking out 85 dips and 30 pull-ups in the strength test challenge, he had unofficially been dubbed the strongest defensive player. Throughout spring drills, Chris had immersed himself in the nuisances of the complicated defensive system and seemed to be in the correct place when he had to be. Hustling his ass off in the eighty degree heat was noticed by the coaching staff, and the aloofness of his first three years of play had been replaced with maturity and a confident determination. He was committed to reclaim his form on the field and off.

After the scrimmage had ended, with the Burnt Orange squad Chris was a member of out-scoring the White squad 24-16, he was met exiting the locker room by new Defensive Coordinator Paul Jette. The entire coaching staff from last season had been replaced.

"Hey Chris, come with me. Coach McWilliams would like a word with you."

"The Head Coach wants to see me? What did I do? This can't be good," Chris tepidly replied as he followed in tow.

"I think you will like what he has to say. I don't want you going in all panicky, it's all good," his position coach reassured him and patted the soon to be senior on his upper back. The pair entered the expansive office. Cardboard boxes were full of assorted items still to be unpacked by the new head coach.

"Sit Cameron," Coach McWilliams ordered. After placing a redlined document into his Out mail box on the corner of his large mahogany desk, he stood and shook Chris' hand. "Hell of a week of practice, son."

"Thank you, sir. I feel good, no aches or pains," Chris responded with a satisfying smile on his matured, rugged face.

"I'm going to get right to why you are here. We have four other young men to speak with about this same proposition. Based on what I saw on the field this week, and the way many of the players admire you, we are proud to offer you the opportunity to be one of our defensive captains for this upcoming season. You're going to have to work hard. We feel you can be an extension to our coaching staff. This responsibility will transcend to busting ass in the dorms, weight room and around campus. Can you handle the responsibility?"

"Yes sir, coach...you can count on me. I've been through a lot this year already, and I'm confident you will see I will take this seriously...quite frankly, I have grown-up in a hurry over the past few months and I am honored you are putting your trust in me."

LATER

Chris peeked at a Jack of Hearts and Queen of Spades. He concealed the strength of the well-hidden hand by checking to the player to his left. Ron-Ron bet $2 after the third face card gave him a pair of Aces on the make shift, card table, which was primarily used as the kitchen table of their off-campus apartment. They were in the midst of a three-hour long game of Seven Card Stud. Chris was excited about winning this pot, which was growing by the second. Hopefully, he'd make a dent in repairing what he'd lost to this point-$27. Besides the hidden Jack and Queen, the three cards face up were a Nine of Clubs, Ten of Spades and King of Diamonds. This gave him a pat hand; a Straight to the King. J.R. took a swig from his can of Shiner Bock, scooped his cards and flicked them into the muck. Chris confidently made his move by raising his roommate of over three years, "Bump up to six bucks."

After a silent thirty seconds, Ron-Ron shook his head. "Boy, you can't hide your excitement about getting a straight. Dang, I fold. You're smirking; the corner of your lip rose," he sniggered and pointed to Chris' right cheek before flipping his hidden ace on the table to confirm he folded a solid hand.

Chris raked in the pile of plastic chips and stacked them by color while J.R. shuffled the deck. "Deal me in, I'm back," a voice boomed from behind the bathroom door. They all chuckled as Tony re-entered the room after an impromptu, ten minute intermission.

"Friggin' gas bubble," Tony announced, as he took his seat and peaked at two hole cards and the Eight of Diamonds dealt to him for all to see. He tossed a white chip into the center of the table. "I call. Yo, Sally, on your way back can you grab me a beer and a plate of chili. Heh-Heh; ready for round three."

"Three dude? I think your next plate will be round five," Chris teased and helicoptered his cards into the muck. "I swear, we went through a case of toilet paper."

After the hardcore, underworld fun and games, Sal and Tony were taking an extended vacation in Texas. They had arrived in Sal's truck two days earlier and had relished their time back in "fake college" and provided Chris with extra incentive to perform at the heightened level during the scrimmage. Tony's booming voice, which six hours later was horse, was heard by the other squad from the opposite sideline all afternoon.

"Give them hell Chris!"..."Go Cee!"..."Nighty Night Sweet Pee!"

Sal entered the room presenting a platter of mini-plates of chili, a few bottles of Shiner Bock and a bowl of chicken tortillas. "Hey, I'm lovin' the male bonding for the past few hours, but don't you guys think it's time we head to the bars. Let's go; last hand and eat up. The women of Austin are waiting."

An hour later, the entourage articulated encouragement from the pit of the Red River Ale House as Sal sang Billy Joel's iconic hit, *Miami 2017* from the Karaoke stage. *Before we've all lived here in Florida...Before the Mafia, took over Mexico...There are not many who remember...They say a handful still survive...To tell the world about, the way the lights went out... And keep the memories aliiii-a-iiive.*

Sal perfectly sang the tune while a tone-deaf, Chris and Tony screamed along, happily swaying to the music. The Piano Man was a foreign sound to J.R., who was into country western, and to Ron-Ron, who could moon walk better than Michael Jackson to any rhythm and blues or pop song. Regardless, they had learned to appreciate the best musical artist from Long Island. Chris had indoctrinated his roommates for the past three years.

"Whatever you say CeeJay, Billy's the master. Hey, I think some dude in the next apartment wants to hear you talk about how great he is for the millionth time."

The ballad ended, and the overflowing crowd in Austin's most frequented joints gave Sal hearty appreciation. As he was prone to do, Sal lingered on stage more than his allotment. He was an entertainer to the core and worked the room like a comedian by fake handing the microphone to the emcee and swaggering from side to side like a tiger in a cage with his sweaty burgundy colored, polo shirt collar popped. He eyed an odd, green-haired freak with four earrings, patted his own head, then pointed at the punk rocker. "This is your brain...this is your brain on drugs." As the crowd goaded him along, Sal gazed deep into the eyes of a sexy blonde he had been serenading. Suavely, he smoothed out his mullet and deadpanned, "I'm taking you to Disney World." Realizing his song and comedy routine had run its course, he good-naturedly handed the microphone to the emcee and exited the stage. To a throng of high fives, he re-joined the guys and accepted the well-earned kudos for his performance. A shot of tequila provided the fuel for Sal to make his way to his prey-the cute blonde. After he tapped her on the shoulder that was the last he was seen for the evening.

Later in the evening, Chris and Tony nursed beers from stools at the end of the bar and spoke about current events. The music was turned low and the staff of the Red River Ale House was in the midst of cleaning. "Last call, CeeJay. We close in a half hour," the bartender, who was a tight end for the Longhorns stated as he placed fresh, cold ones in front of the pair. Chris and Tony nodded appreciation, and continued with their discussion.

Tony updated Chris, "I spoke with Jimmy Tree earlier in the day. His dad was able to get a truce with the Lucchese's."

"You'll be able to restart your card game?" Chris took a sip from his last call libation.

"Yeah, real soon...and not soon enough; my cash flow's hurting bad since this shit occurred, Sal too. Ressini's is breaking even, and we need our gig. Honestly, I don't want to have to go back to work at the butcher shop." With the success of the poker room and then the subsequent actions after Ricky's death Tony had practically stopped working for his father. In his absence, he had found a few illegals to help his dad out. The little fuckers worked hard, and he did not have to pay them a full wage. "I'm too pretty to have blood all over me."

"You must mean animal blood," Chris whispered and chinked bottles with Tony.

"Well, hopefully no more blood of any kind. Making money is better than busting heads. Santo gave us a free pass for being involved. No trouble as long as we play along and give him a taste each week. We never had a problem paying our way. His cohorts gamble like crazy, plenty of profit to go around," Tony optimistically responded.

Life appeared to be back to normal. Chris knew Sal and Tony would regain their footing. The last year of college and his final steps on a football field awaited him. The trio had experienced "life" in their twenty years on earth. Chris had zero remorse for murdering Enzo and paving the way for the quasi-execution of the garbage who killed Ricky. His family and friends were his life. Even though he was halfway across the country, he would find a way to monitor his world in Tuckahoe. Sal and Tony had a reset button. Bella's was flourishing and expanding locations at the direction of his sister. 1987 began horrifically but had returned to normal in less than four months. With two-thirds of the year remaining, Chris hoped the waters would remain tranquil.

29

Scrimping And Saving

MAY 7, 1987

Chris could not hold back his excitement. On any other day, he would saunter back to his apartment after a late afternoon workout. Not today, he was bouncing with energy and needed to share his euphoria. He had busted his ass, and for the first time had earned A's for all of his classes. After a killer weight session of squats, and dead lifts, he spoke with his political science professor. He needed to pull high marks on the final exam and term paper to push his grade from B+ to an A. The professor praised his paper as one of the finest she had read during her seven years at UT.

The thesis was focused on the Great Depression. Chris had supported his contention that the big government policies of President Hoover and continued with more draconian measures by President Roosevelt had prolonged the misery. If not for the build-up of the military related to World War Two, the United States economy may have not recovered to the war production level. His analysis highlighted the New Deal as a failure. The unemployment rate rose from 14% to 19%, and the public works programs accomplished little of significance. This big government spending strategy was implemented via the recommendation of British economist John Maynard Keynes to lift the country out of its economic doldrums. His research disproved Keynesian economic policy and trumpeted supply-side economic policy as more effective in turning the country around following the 1920-1921 depression. President Harding had cut personal income taxes and reduced federal government spending.

After Harding's death, President Coolidge continued on this course, and the Roaring Twenties brought along a period of prosperity. His conclusion re-emphasized the argument with sound examples of the current success of Reaganomics supply-side doctrine.

Taking the stairs three at a time, Chris was sweating profusely. Breathing heavily, he opened the door of the apartment to the sound of a CNN anchor parroting the breaking news of presidential candidate, Gary Hart's higher office ambitions crumbling. Mr. Hart's love affair with Donna Rice aboard the yacht *Money Business* had been exposed.

"This crap's been in the news for days. Doesn't CNN have anything better to report on?" Chris derided the report as he walked to the kitchenette and the refrigerator full of beer. Sitting on opposite ends of the couch, Ron and J.R. had remained silent and did not respond to his current events banter. J.R. stood and clicked the television off.

"Hey, turn on *Cheers*. I hear Sam's going to ask Diane to marry him tonight," Chris howled.

J.R. somberly called out, "Yo CeeJay, sit."

"Dudes, get ready to party tonight; my first 4.0 for a semester!" Ignoring the sedateness, Chris took a sip from a cold Shiner Bock, clicked the TV set back on and changed the channel to NBC before plopping in the recliner adjacent to his roommates.

"CeeJay, your mom called. I took the message while you were out," Ron-Ron paused, his eyes were closed and his voice cracked. "Your grandfather had a stroke...sorry buddy...he died an hour ago."

Not another word was said. Lost in the moment, they collectively sniffled and wiped tears away. Chris had emotionally supported his roommates, for J.R. and his mom's cancer treatment and last year after Ron's sister had been injured in a car accident. They came from different worlds but had formed a bond that would never waver.

As the shock of the death of man who Chris had called Grampy as a toddler was being fully processed, happy memories darted through his brain...the image of him as a baby sucking on a bottle while resting on his Grampy's lap on their plastic-covered couch...a proud old man bundled in a winter jack braving the elements while watching his grandson play a late fall, football game...a black and white wedding photo situated on top of the living room fireplace, *oh my God, after fifty two years of marriage how was his grandmother going to survive*...a quartet of men happily toasting wine; Joe Cavazzi sharing a moment with his three *paisanos*.

The apropos lyrics to the introduction of *Cheers* sung out. Chris placed his face in the palms of his hands. He had to get back to Tuckahoe as fast as he could; Gary Portney was perceptive-Sometimes *you wannabe where everybody knows your name.*

IN MOURNING

The buzzer rang for what seemed like the tenth time over the past two hours. Sabina, wearing a white blouse covered by a black shawl with a matching skirt, excused herself. She came back moments later carrying sandwiches, a gift from the Zingaro family's deli on Fisher Avenue. Joanne assisted her cousin and placed the platter on the dining room table by the three meals that had been delivered throughout the afternoon. A plethora of fruit, meals and flowers had arrived over the past few days.

"So nice; from Frankie," Sabina meekly said, as she wiped at the corner of her eye with a tissue which had been clenched in her left fist for the past hour.

"Yeah, he had asked what we needed. I saw him this morning when I had stopped by the deli to get a coffee," Chris responded in a docile monotone.

With the end of the spring semester, Chris drove back to New York. Luckily, his father had driven down a month earlier to visit and returned the car to him. He had many road trips under his belt over the past three years and he had used this time of solitude to ponder through life challenges, aspirations, relationships, the Mets, the weather, even his purpose in the world. This thirty-hour trip was no different. He had attempted to deflect mournful thoughts with ear-piercing music. The tunes had been randomly pulled from his cassette case stored in a slender, metal suitcase on the front passenger seat. Besides Billy Joel, his taste in music consisted of U2, Van Morrison, Bon Jovi, George Thorogood and Elton John. The rhythms of the power ballads and rock anthems did not work. He could not get the vision and distinct voice of his grandfather from his thoughts.

The last his grandfather had spoken to him had been a month earlier. Chris had promised he would come to Florida for a visit before training camp in August. *Don't worry about us, boy; focus on school and get an education. Remember Christopher, no one can take what you have earned away from you. Your grandmother and I will be here when you have time.* They had always called him Christopher. Grampy had conveyed a multitude of life lessons, which at the time he did not fully comprehend or appreciate their significance to the large and fragmented family tree. They had sacrificed luxuries to make a better life for the next generation. Joe Cavazzi was born in 1912 and raised on the mean streets of Manhattan's lower east side. He stood slightly above six foot. By the time he was a teenager, he was building muscle hauling ice and coal to the tenements around Little Italy. This was where he had cast his eyes on his future bride, Julia Scalle. His Julia and her hazel eyes had taken after her mother and was an amazing cook. The newlywed's had dreams of opening a macaroni store. With relatives in the tiny village in Westchester County, they staked their claim in the country. Fulfilling their dream did not come easy as Bella's Pasta would not open until 1951. Scrimping and saving, the young couple had juggled their enterprise while raising three daughters and constructing a home. What amazed Chris was his grandparent's decision to move to the basement and convert the space into an apartment. They insisted that their daughter's family must live in the spacious, upstairs unit. The more he thought of this gesture, he realized they gave his family an amazing gift and sacrificed.

The front door opened once again but this time the bell had not been rung. Sal and Tony were family and they treated the Cavazzi-Cameron home as their own. Sal was balancing a brown bag on top of a chafing dish of pasta while Tony was dangling cases of beer from his oversized arms. They peeled off; Sal placed penne ala' vodka in the kitchen refrigerator. Tony descended the steps and put the beer into the basement refrigerator. His grandfather had called it *the Frigidaire.*

"Check these out, guys. I found pictures in a shoebox. There was a whole bunch on a shelf in my grandparent's bedroom closet. Us three in Blue Devil uniforms after the New Rochelle game," Chris said, as he handed a few dated snapshots to Sal and Tony.

After analyzing the proud moments in history, Tony asked confusingly, "Cee, why do Sal and I have messy uniforms while yours is squeaky clean? This was taken after the game, right?"

"I had three scores, my brother. I don't think I was tackled. But wait, if you look close, you'll see cleat marks on the front of your jersey. What... did someone run you over?" They burst out in laughter.

Papa Vince interjected, "You kids were fun to watch. Joe and I lived for those days and reminisced about you three playing football and baseball almost daily. Our grandkids-we call you all our grandkids-were our life. We went to dance recitals, concerts and plays for Joanne and Sabina, and we never missed any of your games...good times, great memories. I'm gonna miss him, like I miss your dad, Sal. Life isn't perfect, but blood's thicker than water. You have to try and make the best of life. What amazes me is you three became friends before you knew you were related..." Papa Vince's voice trailed off.

Tony could not keep his composure together any longer. He blubbered and hugged his grandfather. In the course of this exchange, Chris cursed under his breath. He reached into his pocket and handed Sal a twenty. "Like taking candy from a baby, Cee...candy from a baby." There was an ongoing bet for the past ten years. Whenever Tony would lose it on an odd numbered day, Chris had to pay Sal. If he had cried on even numbered days, Chris would be the victor. A quick calculation determined they had broken even as Tony displayed his feelings equally on odd and even days.

After the wake had ended and the greetings of what seemed like hundreds of family members and friends who came to pay their respects for the passing of Giuseppe Leonardo Cavazzi, the family reconvened back at the Cameron home to reminisce, imbibe and of course, eat. The night was punctuated by toasts of homemade Italian red wine and a bottle of Scotch. This was followed by a case of Black Label. Ceremoniously, they had to partake as Joe would have. He had always loved his neighbor Dom Petrillo's potent homemade red wine, which they cut with seltzer. His Irish son-in-law had turned him on to Dewars Scotch in the 1960s. On the beer front, Joe had a modest, pedestrian palate, and the rock gut brand suited him fine. The mourners had their limits. The second case drunk was Heineken.

Stories were re-enacted in a feel good manner. As the alcohol was consumed, the cadre became hysterical. Chris listened as his father's brogue became more pronounced as the family relived their own heartfelt memories. A celebration of a wonderful life was the theme, not the mourning of death.

30

Spider-Man

JUNE 19, 1987, AFTER MIDNIGHT

The Balkan Connection was dominated by ethnic Albanians centered in the New York City area. More ambiguous than their Sicilian and French counterparts, the Balkan route from Istanbul to Belgrade moved a third of the worldwide heroin supply. Processed in Turkey, the white powder was transported to Bulgaria, through Greece and into Yugoslavia. From Belgrade, couriers smuggled the highly addictive opium pod extraction to European and American metropolises.

Skender Lika emanated the persona of a law-abiding entrepreneur. Through Emina Worldwide Travel, he arranged trips to Yugoslavia, where many Albanians had originally emigrated. Mr. Lika's children were enrolled at Herbert Lehman High School, and he sponsored a recreational soccer team. The good father's line of work provided the perfect cover for drug dealers and couriers working the Balkan connection. Once the white bricks were cut and packaged, the *hard candy* was distributed throughout the Judaica shops and Chinese clothing stores dotting the Upper West Side and Harlem. Lika's merchandise tended to have a rosy gray coloration due to the sugar and strychnine added to increase volume during the cutting process. This distinct trademark was nicknamed "Horse" and had amassed over a $100 million for his powerful, illegal enterprise since the early 1980s.

Despite the early success, his crime ring had been on the verge of unraveling due to the ruthless way he protected his territory combined with the carelessness of young and inexperienced soldiers. With Old World roots, Mr. Lika was not immune to erratic behavior. A discrepancy with a business partner ended badly. Before the appetizers had arrived, Skender shot his unsuspecting associate thirteen times. The Albanians were a wild bunch and prone to cruelty of all types, even when the incident was not related to organized crime activity. In Queens, a hothead had reportedly been enraged when his wife had contracted a venereal disease. On a meth-induced rampage, the jilted lover shot three people at a clinic in Glendale before turning the gun on himself. Domestic violence incidents were commonplace, as was brazen, unprovoked gunfire in crowded restaurants and bars.

In the most recent turf war, the Gambinos had harnessed this aggression. Eager to solidify distribution channels for drugs, weapons and prostitution, Lika's men were more than willing to take out any bump in the Gambinos' road. Language barriers and a code of silence had made electronic surveillance useless by law enforcement agents and protected the Albanian-American crime factions from outside penetration.

With the good came the bad as many of these unhinged, coked-up, Third World gangsters comingled with their Italian cohorts and caused trouble wherever they went. Last summer, at a Colombo controlled strip club in Queens, two ethnic Albanians opened fire, wounding a waiter and a bouncer after a seemingly petty argument about the quality of food. Jimmy Tracino had taken notice to the hordes of these rats frequenting his strip club in the Bronx. By midnight, they would take over the establishment. Because of this, he hired additional muscle to quell arguments before incidents spiraled out of control.

Utilizing a state of the art video surveillance system monitored from a control booth stationed on the second floor of the converted warehouse, Tony Albanese was in charge of flagging all signs of trouble within Sensual Nights and for the scantily-clad women they employed. His eye in the sky had uncovered dalliances of hard-working girls doing what they do. The rehearsed dance was like shooting fish in a barrel. The wired clientele turned the switch from mingling with their pack to finding a dark corner or private room to seal the deal. Tony liked the vast majority of the young ladies in the club and sympathized with their struggles. Since he had the added benefit of viewing their appearance in pre-makeup attire, he never had the urge to partake in the generous offers granted for diligently watching their cookies.

"These girls got butter faces...all look good but their face," he would say to buddies who inquired about the sexual temptations thrown in his face on a regular basis. Besides, a few weeks back Tony had reconnected with Bernadette Petrucelli, an old flame from high school. She was a sweet girl, and he wanted to see where life took them. Coming home smelling like stale perfume and cigarette smoke would not be prudent.

While the money for this gig was good, he was motivated to get the poker room operating. Sal was remodeling Ressini's once again and planned to be done by September. On top of all the crap going on, the place had been totaled. A random drunk driver had slammed into the dining room of the restaurant. Luckily this had happened at 3 a.m. on a Tuesday when the place was empty.

The strippers, mostly of Eastern European descent, loved the almighty dollar. On a good night, the best of these Natasha's could make two thousand bucks dry humping a few johns. The faster their ready-made boyfriends came, the quicker they could be on the floor to grab hold of another quarry. If their hand was needed to get a slow one off quicker, the job would be completed. The angler's goal was to hook a live one with a pocket full of hundreds, and they were willing to pose with the fish on a big strong lap, smoke and sip from bottles of over-priced champagne until the wannabe gangster was ready to get his rocks off. At which time, they would withdraw to the VIP room, where Tony focused most of his attention. The girls could never go home with the customers. Until they paid their debt to Jimmy Tree and his Russian cohorts, they were quasi-slaves, and all dollars earned had to be accounted for. When the curtains were pulled shut, the girls would work their magic to squeeze as many *rubles* as they could. Jimmy Tree would never accept credit cards from these punks. Since he ran the scam better than they did, he was not going to get stiffed when Visa came calling. Cash was king, unless possibly from a big shot Wall Street suit on his expense account. Wiseguys could play all they wanted at Sensual Nights, but C.O.D. was club policy, even if God walked through the doors sporting his whitest bathrobe and an angel entourage in tow.

Sal Esposito parked at the far end of the *Sensual Nights* and made his way toward the neon lit entrance to the gentleman's club. He greeted the two mammoth black men with strong handshakes, as they checked ID's of a recently arrived pack of Young Turks. They let him through the velvet rope where he materialized into the blare of staccato music in the darkened den of ill repute. A bartender handed him two cold beers and Sal reciprocated with a crisp twenty. After a long pull, he ascended to the appropriately named Boom Boom Room. He ignored the intertwined couples on the high-backed couches peppering the seedy, highly profitable and exclusive area within Jimmy Tree's club. Sal marched to the far left corner and knocked on the blackened security door. Tony invited his buddy inside the high tech command center. Alone in the sound proof enclave, they perused the video screens.

"So how's construction going?" Tony asked as he took a sip from a beer Sal had brought.

"We had a problem today. Friggin' building inspector snooped around, busted my balls about the upstairs not meeting fire code and whatnot. The stupid drunk barely missed a structural beam; another three feet and the building could have been condemned. Anyway, this guy gets on his high horse and says the insulation isn't thick enough...*batta beep, batta boop*...a friggin' nightmare," Sal lamented. "Wooh, wooh, move to the side bro, the chicks going to town." Sal had forgotten about his construction woes and became fixated on a monitor of a private room session from booth number six. A dancer had dropped to her knees. Mr. John had reciprocated by standing and unbuckling his belt. After dropping his slacks to the floor, he plopped on the couch with his legs comfortably spread.

"What's she doing? Better get paid before his schlong pops out," Tony's voice grew alarmed. After she explored Mr. John's manliness, the activity abruptly halted. The sweet girl had opened the palm of her hand expecting compensation for her pre-game, hard work.

"LET's GO...MOTHERFUCKING SCUMBAG!" Tony and Sal bolted from the room and sprinted to the opposite end of the floor. The girl had been forcibly smacked upside her head with a flurry of punches by the tough guy with his pants around his ankles.

Sal yanked the red curtain of the private dance area open. Unabated, Tony leapt in and collided with the half-naked, drunken man. On impact, they surged over the back end of the couch with Tony landing on top and in a commanding position. With his left arm, Tony applied a headlock and pummeled the man's face with his massive, right fist. Sal wildly kicked at his lower body before they gained control and dragged Mr. John out of the cubicle. Tony violently escorted the uninvited guest down the three flights of fire exit stairs.

Sprawled on the curb, writhing in pain, the young Albanian voiced his displeasure in a slurred, nasally tone, "Yooouuu can't touch meee, motherfuckers. Jimmy Tree owes meee! I'll take what I want from this place." Wincing, he spit blood from swollen lips and wiped his mouth on his sleeve. "You twooo better watch out. Youuu messed with the wrong person."

Mr. John's true identity was Skender Lika's nephew, Joe Djvalac. After doing a minor job for Jimmy Tree, he had been flexing his wiry muscles like Arnold Schwarzenegger and dropping his uncle's name on all fronts. Persona non grata to all but a few of the whores who had not yet voiced their displeasure, Djvalac would be banned from the club for life. Jimmy Tree would discuss this disrespect to his place of business in the morning with his father. A sit-down was in order to handle the repercussion for the unacceptable actions of Skender Lika's nephew.

DATE NIGHT

Tony cruised along the Major Deegan Expressway. Even though his sunglasses were on, he lowered the visor. The early evening glare shone brightly off of the Bronx apartment buildings which hugged the thoroughfare. He beamed as Yankee Stadium grew larger in the distance. With all the crap going on, he took note of the fact he had been smiling a lot of late and the main reason was because of his new girl. Tony despised the Yankees and loved to tease Bernadette when she wore a Bronx Bomber T-shirt in his presence. They had sort of dated back in high school. The romance had lasted a few weeks. A year younger, he was her date to the senior prom and they had bumped into each other a few weeks back at a club in the city. Both were eager to rekindle the relationship.

The first date since high school was not a "wine and dine." He took her to see a real baseball game-the defending World Series Champion New

York Mets. The Mets crushed the Pittsburgh Pirates that night, but he did not care. Before the game, a ceremony to promote a special wedding issue of the *Amazing Spider-Man* comic took place. At home plate stood actors portraying Spidey and Mary Jane Watson. Marvel Comics publisher, Stan Lee officiated the nuptials. Bernadette could not tell if he was joking, as his eyes teared during the faux-ceremony. *He had to stop the water works.* When the marriage was consummated, Tony gave a captivating grin before placing his gigantic arm around her shoulder, peppered baby kisses on her cheek, and the deal was sealed. Officially a romantic couple for the past five weeks, he was not ashamed to state he was extremely happy and thought of her all the time.

Affectionately called Berni by her friends, the petite brunette was a 1983 graduate of Tuckahoe High. In high school, she had dated the same guy, off and on for three years, and their relationship had been intense. Always friendly with Tony, the knight in shining armor had saved her from major embarrassment when the flaky boyfriend ditched her two weeks before prom. After the frilly dress and tuxedo-clad summer evening, they had vowed to remain friends. Regardless, the two had drifted apart. Berni was taking night classes and studying for her bachelor's degree at Hunter College while working as a legal assistant within the violent crime division at the Bronx District Attorney Office over on 161st Street. Her older sister, Lori, was a paralegal and had gotten her the job.

After a quick stop at the butcher shop, Tony decided to surprise Berni at her house. He had not been able to get in touch with her all day, and missed the sound of her voice. The doorbell chimed twice in the Petrucelli raised ranch, announcing the arrival of a visitor. Radar, a German Sheppard mix galloped to the front picture window, hopped on the couch, wagged his tail and barked uncontrollably. "Radar, off the couch!" Berni commanded her excitable pooch before turning the doorknob. Radar frantically squeezed between her legs, as the door was slowly opened. Tony stood with one hand holding the screen while his other was palm-up in front of Radar's eager snout. He had brought a special treat as a gift for the pooch.

"Heh-Heh, would he still like me if I don't bring a scrap of meat?" Tony leaned in to give Berni a peck on the cheek. She flinched and her eyes watered.

"Tony, we have to talk." Berni tugged his arm and guided him to sit on the wicker love seat overlooking the front yard.

"Wow, this don't sound good. Is this why you didn't return any of my six calls today?" Tony had changed from happy to see his best gal to Gloomy Gus. He placed his hands together and wrung them uneasily.

"Anthony, I'm going to be direct. You know me and my sister work for the Bronx D.A., right?" Well, Lori heard alarming facts connected to your buddy...the guy Jimmy you hang around with. Something about Albanians, heroin and...I can't get involved. I am naive to not have seen or thought this could be true...this is bad news, and I am not a bad girl."

Deafening silence preceded Tony cautiously responding. "Berni, baby, no way am I involved. I do run my poker games, but it's no secret. I'm being honest with you! I don't get involved in drugs. Forget my father; my mother would beat the crap out of me. I work for Jimmy at his club, but no way am I connected."

The gentle giant placed Bernadette's hands into his own. He squeezed affectionately before kissing her fingers softly. Her lips turned from a frown to a slight smile before happiness shown. Tony saw his opening and scooped her into his arms and hugged tightly. She reciprocated. With eyes welling, he whispered into her ear, "Hey, I like what we have; trust me."

She grabbed his face and peered into his eyes. "I want to trust you. I like what we have, too. Promise you will keep away from Jimmy. He's trouble, mister, and I don't want you to get into any trouble."

"You have my word. In fact, I'm done at Jimmy's strip club; my surprise for you tonight...and taking you to Little Italy for dinner."

Bernadette nodded and went back inside to get her purse. Hand in hand, the young couple strolled toward Tony's truck. As he opened the door, he casually asked, "By the way, I'm curious, what exactly were the specifics about the Albanian thing you had heard about?"

As the lovebirds enjoyed their meal, Berni went over the details. Lori Petrucelli had been doing research on a case against a drug dealer who was arrested. The case had ballooned. Evidence determined he was the prime suspect in a botched robbery that had ended with one dead. With a slew of compelling evidence, the defense lawyer had worked out a deal in return for his client providing valuable insight on the elusive Albanian Mafia.

31

Grandpa Munster

OCTOBER 3, 1987-TEXAS MEMORIAL STADIUM

Spiraling in his direction, the length of the football may have been only eleven inches, but at the moment appeared to be twice the size. Chris instinctively reacted to the play. After the customary two-step drop, he noticed the Rice University halfback poorly faked a block and had peeled off to receive a screen pass. The Longhorn co-captain and strong safety sprinted toward the unsuspecting player. Chris intercepted the pass and galloped untouched, sixty-five yards to pay dirt. With the score 34-13, the Longhorns were on the way to winning their first game. After two devastating losses; a blowout at Auburn followed by a shocker at home to BYU, this win was needed to bolster their sagging spirits.

Following the easy 45-26 rout, Chris jubilantly trotted off the field with fellow defensive back John Hagy. When he noticed his father frantically waving to get his attention, Chris climbed onto the railing of the first level of the stadium seating and greeted his dad. Over hamburgers and beers at the Crown and Anchor Pub, father and son bonded. Since Grandpa Joe's funeral, Chris had been immersed with classes, studying and football training. He had limited contact with the goings on back home.

"This place opened a few weeks ago. What do you think of their Jalapeno Cheeseburger?" Chris asked before he took a huge bite out of his own Bacon Cheeseburger. Ketchup dripped on his chin. As he continued to chew, he wiped his face and took a sip from a cold, Coors Light.

203

"Very fine...hot, the jalapeno gives a good kick. Reminds me of the way your grandfather put hot pepper on his food."

"Remember watching him and Uncle Vince? Their faces would get red and sweaty but they never gave in."

"The red wine washed the fire away. You want another beer, son?"

"No dad, I have a headache. I had my bell rung, and don't think I'm going to see the guys." Chris had five tackles to go along with the interception return for the touchdown. He had held his own and was earning his captain status. He kidded his buddies that he felt like Superman getting his cape back when his request during training camp to change from number twenty to ten had been granted. Ten had been his high school number, and he felt like his strength had been sapped without the one and zero over his shoulder pads. *The third string sophomore quarterback who relinquished the jersey would be what they called "shit out of luck."*

"Don't think you have to babysit me, my boy. After dinner, I'm going to check in with your mother and go to sleep."

"How is Grandma Julia feeling?" Mike and Maria had initially traveled together. He dropped his bride off in Port St. Lucie where she cared for her mother while Michael continued on to Texas to visit with his son. Julia had been taking the death of her husband extremely hard. Her frail body had withered away even more.

"Oh son, life is moving incredibly fast. Not many of the older folk are around anymore. Your grandparents lived a full life." Michael paused and took a deep pull from his *Guinness* stout. "Wonderful memories." Michael reminisced about how he was an outsider who had married into a tight knit, Italian-American family. Chris had heard these stories a million times and never tired of listening to them. His dad was an Irish fish out of water and joked he may be the only son-in-law who wholeheartedly loved and admired his in-laws equal to the love he had for his wife-and he loved his wife more than life itself!

Chris received updates on Sabina and her hard work opening more Bella's franchise locations. The family was not rich by any stretch of the imagination. However, with five stores generating dividends, they could comfortably enjoy themselves. Ironically, this time to relax transpired when they were needed to care for Maria's mother in what was sadly progressing toward her final days. *And so is life.*

Al and Rita Albanese had wanted to take the trip, but the butcher shop was once again in a tight, cash flow period. To be prudent, they postponed the journey until the spring and would attempt to visit Chris for graduation. Tony would have paid, but his parents were awfully proud people and frugal to the core. They respectfully declined the gift.

"Anthony's a good kid. He's at the butcher shop at dawn working or having a few of his associates with him to learn the trade. He always seems to have money when Alfonse is light on cash."

"Yeah, Tony's entrepreneurial. When the NFL went on strike, he hosted a poker tournament and kept the betting on the college football games robust. Without the NFL, he's gonna' be hurting."

The players union had gone on strike, and a week of NFL games had already been cancelled. The stoppage had been called over free agency and the unwritten "Rozelle Rule" named after Commissioner Pete Rozelle. While free agency had been allowed, if an unsigned player were signed, the union argued the commissioner should compensate the original team with draft picks or players. They had contended this hampered player movement. By striking, the players believed they would have the upper hand in negotiations. To counter, the NFL owners hired replacements and the television networks showed no qualms about airing sub-par games. On the flip side, in the football crazed country, NCAA football had filled the void and Chris had his best games during a highly viewed broadcast.

Chris segued to another topic, "At least Ressini's is finally open again." The restaurant had reopened after Labor Day, perfectly timed for sports parties and late night poker games. The guys did not have to bide their time at Jimmy Tree's strip club or as bodyguard-escorts at off-sight bachelor parties. While Sal and Tony had continued their juiced-up, persona and were intimidating as hell whenever they entered a room, they were tired of the strong arm side of the world they lived in. Gambling-type operations were their forte, and they intended to be earners.

Left out of the conversation was the incident with the Albanian hothead back in June. Chris freely discussed Sal and Tony's poker and gambling business with his dad as he was a regular at the tournaments. He drew the line in mentioning the additional work they did. Santo had a sit-down with Skender Lika regarding the disrespectful conduct of his nephew. With Damien Morris standing by his side, Skender had to make good on a five thousand dollar tribute, otherwise his sister would be upset about her son's near-term health.

Besides their ability to earn, Tony had relayed to Santo the information about the rat that had provided intimate details of the Albanian's narcotic distribution network and ties to Tracino's crew. Santo severed ties with Skender Lika and moved on to a partnership with a crazy Russian. Chris amusingly recalled the telephone discussion he had with Tony the other week, "Yo Cee, the Old Man...I swear to Christ he looks more and more like Grandpa Munster...he said we get a reprise. We thank him and whatnot. The next night, he comes to the poker game; first time playing, mind you. He asks to go on the book for three thousand. We had no choice but to give him credit. The old bastard shoves all-in on the first hand against his son. Jimmy Tree calls him, of course and the old man loses. Jimmy scooped the chips and Santo waddled out before his seat was warm. Jimmy left a few minutes later with his father's money. Bastards weren't giving us nothing for free."

"Hilarious. I didn't think Santo was into the charity game," Chris chuckled from the other end of the line.

Chris stayed at the Marriott with his dad and spoke to his mother and grandmother on the phone. As Mike continued with pillow talk to his sweetheart, Chris fell asleep. He awoke in the morning to the rummaging of his father packing. The Cameron men ate a hearty breakfast and said their good-bye. Once again, in life's rollercoaster, their lives appeared to be on an upward trajectory. He hoped the fun ride would continue and not encounter another violent drop.

32

The Time Had Come

OCTOBER 31, 1987

Carefully snaking their way along Sixth Avenue, Sal and Tony shielded their dates as they wove through a frenzied, chaotic mass of humanity. A golden haired man, no older than twenty, pranced by wearing a diaper and a black top hat. He was being playfully chased by a bald, black man donned in a white sash holding an oversized bow with a quiver full of arrows on his back; obviously Cupid was chasing the Baby New Year.

"Were they Cher and Marilyn Monroe?" Sal exasperatedly asked as they dodged by a pair of giggling, drag queens. The Greenwich Village Halloween Parade appeared to be equivalent to a straight man's night at a strip club with a handful of hundred dollar bills.

"Our luck Sally, this club is right smack in the middle of the parade route," Tony kidded as they escorted the girls to their venue for the evening.

The latest trend in New York City was for real estate entrepreneurs with grand visions to convert condemned structures into the hippest nightclubs. Shout had been a historic theater. The landmark had been shuttered back in the 1970s but was the place to be on Saturday nights in Manhattan in the 1980s. Halloween was the theme and the carefree barflies were oblivious to the massive stock market correction; the ghost of Black Monday had been revisited the previous week on Wall Street. All they seemed to care about was getting drunk, snorting coke and having a good time.

Sal was donned in a form-fitting, white Satin robe, matching Champion Trunks and black boxing shoes depicting Sylvester Stallone of *Rocky* fame. The heavyweight champ weaved his way through the throng of revelers. His muscular chest was partially exposed for the ladies to admire. After receiving his order at the bar consisting of a few beers and frilly cocktails for the girls, he maneuvered his way back to a table. Tony, Bernadette and his date, Adrienne were waiting patiently as they made small talk and took in the rollicking scenery. The joke of the night was Sal had no choice but to be Rocky.

"Yo, Adrienne," Sal boisterously announced, as he approached.

Tony stood and assisted with serving the libations. Not surprisingly, he chose a Sylvester Stallone themed character as well. Big Tony wore black combat boots, olive green cargo pants with a matching, one size too small tee shirt, augmented with a bandolier pocketed belt. He was *Rambo* and every inch the part of a badass, Green Beret.

"Wish I'd a caught you before you went to get the drinks. The waitress is bringing a bottle of champagne. A friend of ours was sending his regards," Tony informed Sal of the gratuitous surprise.

"Oh yeah...did she tell you the generous friend's name?" Sal scanned the expansive room. As a converted theater, *Shout* had a dance floor pitched to a stage where costumed partygoers showcased their choreographed, rhythmic skills.

Tony and Sal yelled above the reverberation in an attempt to hold a conversation when Damien Morris made his entrance. He was wearing a sleeveless, animal skin garment with a solo shoulder strap. He was Bam-Bam from *The Flintstones,* and his date, a sexy Latina no older than nineteen, was dressed as Pebbles.

"The party can officially start!" Damien embraced his pals with gusto. "This is my new girl, say hello to Marseille." As the men bonded, Damien's date took a seat with Bernadette and Adrienne.

The waitress returned. "Did you order this?" Tony directed the question at Damien.

"Not me...I'd expect you to buy me a bottle not the other way around," Damien *kind of* joked.

Bernadette dressed as a sexy Bo Peep and Adrienne, who looked nothing like a virgin as she replicated Madonna's revealing black dress with cutouts on the sides of her waist, waited for the bubbly to be poured.

"From the gentleman sitting in the section above," the waitress commented and shifted her eyes to indicate precisely where the bearer of their good fortune was located.

Sal turned his head and raised the flute. His smile quickly switched from gratitude to confusion as Joe Djvalac performed an overzealous, one handed salute over the railing. The Albanian ruffian disappeared from view and resurfaced a few minutes later, by their side.

"No hard feelings. I wanted to show my *respects* to you. My uncle holds you both in high regard." Joe shifted his body close to speak in confidence as the girls eyed him with growing displeasure. "My crew took care of some loose ends tonight...also thanks to you."

Djvalac had received the contract to murder Zef Hulevic. The unidentifiable remains were wrapped in a plastic bag to rot on the roof of a Greenwich Village apartment building. The traitor's hands and feet were tossed into the Hudson River. As a final touch, a dead rat was shoved in his mouth to replace the tongue. Skender Lika had approved the act of retribution to his own blood and paid Santo Tracino an additional $10,000 for the information about his nephew's willingness to speak with the federal authorities. After a month of feeding the informant bogus information about his operations, the time had come for this *trajtoj* to die.

Damien had waited until Djvalac had finished his mea culpa before interjecting, "Hey, you do your thing, and we'll do ours. No hard feelings?"

"Mind your business...I do not know you," Djvulac dismissively snapped in reply.

"This is my business...and better you don't!" Damien barked back.

"Have a good night," Tony punctuated the fact that the discussion was over.

With a wry sneer, Joe slithered away in his Al Pacino of Scarface attire-a purple satin dress shirt buttoned to his naval with a pair of tight black slacks.

The men apologized profusely for ignoring their dates before segueing back to small talk. Sal and Tony had spent the afternoon watching the Texas game. Chris had a few tackles and lit a receiver's ass up against Texas

Tech. The Longhorns had won 41-27 to better their record to four wins and three losses. They could not fathom his football career was coming to an end. Four years had flown by for them all.

With a lull in the conversation, Tony excused himself. "I gotta' hit the head. Be right back." Rambo weaved his way through the pandemonium. The restrooms in the darkened nightclub were located on the lower level, and accessible by stairways descending from either ends of the converted theater. Tony waited patiently for a urinal to free. Three stalls were unavailable. Black alligator shoes were intertwined with a white pair of stilettos underneath an occupied stall. Shout was an anything goes place, and this was one of those anything goes moments. Tony zipped his fly and moved toward the long rectangular sink. Checking his costumed appearance in mirror, he noticed the door of the stall hosting the classless lovebirds had sprung open.

The giggling and sex play abruptly ended. "Sabina?" Tony shockingly peered at her disheveled appearance and threw daggers at her Don Juan-Joe Djvalac.

"It's not what you think...please," Sabina besought to no avail.

Tony effortlessly hoisted Djvalac by his satin shirt, pinning him to the white, tiled wall before hauling back and clubbing the smugness off of his face. Djvulac staggered sideways into the hallway. During the course of the altercation, Saby readjusted her appropriate-for-the-evening Slutty Nurse costume. Sniffling her nose, she grabbed a hand towel from the dispenser hanging near the counter and wiped her face clean before making her entrance into the fray.

Two bouncers had been summoned to restore order. They huddled by Tony and spoke in a non-threatening way. Another bouncer was speaking with Djvulac by an opposite stairway.

"I did nothing wrong. Çmendur burri!" Ask anyone, I was in the crapper. When I came out, he went crazy on me," Djvulac boisterously rambled. "Come my darling, your friend is a lunatic. Let's go somewhere to be alone."

Averting her eyes, Sabina complied and obediently disappeared with the Albanian. Sabina's substance abuse had reared its ugly head...again. This latest episode confirmed her addiction had escalated beyond a few too many on the weekend. Tony caught her snorting coke. Her ragged appearance and erratic conduct had been a growing concern and all of the tragic pieces to the puzzle had fallen into place.

Tony had no beef with the bouncers. They were doing their job and he was too much in shock to do or say anything, anyway. He thanked them profusely for not throwing his ass out of the club.

"About time, Anthony?" Perturbed, Bernadette channeled her irritation of his extended absence by fixing his hair. Tony had not felt the urge to check his coif after the altercation. "You're sweating, what happened?"

"Girls, can you give us a second." Bernadette and Adrienne rolled their eyes at each other before walking away from the table. Damien and his date were on the dance floor. Tony shook Sal's shoulders and spoke animatedly. "Holy motherfucking shit! Friggin' Sabina, I saw the cocksucker doing coke with her in a bathroom stall. He's been playing us all along. He don't want to pay respect, he's thinking he can get over on us by banging Saby. They split before I returned."

"We need to set her ass straight. She's out of control and can't be hanging around these types of people," Sal said before noticing Djvulac and Sabina had returned to their balcony table.

"I guess they didn't want to leave." Alarm bells went off in Tony's head. He was ready for an ambush as their immediate area had been encroached by a pack of dark haired, straggly young men not dressed in Halloween garb.

Djvulac raised his middle fingers and cursed over the thud of the music, "*Natën e mirë,* assholes!"

Tony roared back as an empty bottle struck his upper back. He stumbled forward into Sal's midsection. A fist came out of nowhere and cold-cocked Sal. He landed hard onto the table. Glasses fell, as the table tipped over. Tony reached to help him to his feet but instead grabbed for the empty 1.5-liter bottle of champagne. Reliving his days as a slugging leftfielder, he swung hard and thumped the skull of the vermin who had thrown the sucker punch. The bottle shattered, as the attackers body crumbled to the floor. Sal regained his position and gripped the metal ice bucket with his left hand. He blocked a punch and slammed the bucket on the arm of an assailant. A knife spit out and fell to the floor.

A battalion of bouncers swarmed and pulled bodies apart. Maniacal, Sal grabbed for a fistful of hair and pummeled a fresh victim's face. The strands remained clutched in his paw as the big man threw a vicious haymaker. The punk spun to the ground. Tony simultaneously applied a headlock to two assailants before hauling back and smashed their heads together. With the bouncers restoring order, a shot rang out. Tony and Sal stood frozen in place. From behind, the gunman was tackled by Damien, who had blood oozing from his arm.

If the situation had not been so scary, the vision of Rambo and Rocky systematically patting various body parts to confirm they had not been shot would have been hilarious. Luckily, the errant bullet had hit a light fixture above where they had been sitting.

33

Full Disclosure

NOVEMBER 27, 1987

The early morning sun hugging the horizon had blinded Chris for the past hour until he finally succumbed to the burning desire to rest. Driving non-stop and at high speed since before dawn, his system decompressed as he pulled off Interstate 10 on the western outskirts of New Orleans. Traversing the highway overpass, he ventured a couple of hundred yards before pulling into the entrance of the Cracker Barrel restaurant. Parking adjacent to the front porch of the traditional, general store motif, Chris blew out his breath to calm his nerves and made a bee-line for the restroom. He followed Mother Nature's calling by scoffing a plate of pancakes, eggs and home fries at the Southern comfort food establishment.

His final University of Texas regular season football game had ended in disappointing fashion. The month of November gave redemption. Solid wins against Texas Christian and Baylor soothed the devastating loss to Houston. The Longhorns had controlled their own destiny and if they had upset Texas A&M they would have been crowned Southwest Conference champs. *Coulda, shoulda, woulda, how many times had these words been said in his life.* The victory did not come to pass and they lost the nationally televised heartbreaker 20-13. Chris performed well with four tackles and two balls swatted away in the end zone, but the Aggies overmatched the Longhorns.

When he returned from College Station, Chris glimpsed at the blinking red light on his answering machine. Before he had a chance to replay the four unheard messages, the phone rang. After 1 a.m., he had a feeling this was not going to be good news; and he was correct in the assessment. Grandma Julia had taken a fall and was undergoing emergency surgery.

On subsequent calls to his father from payphones along the highways, he was informed Sabina had made an impromptu visit to spend time with Grandma Julia. She had been visiting for the past few weeks and responded quickly to the accident. Because of football and a hectic workload of classes, Chris had not heard from Sal or Tony in weeks. The brief discussion with Sabina was the first in more than two months.

Chris wished he was wealthy during times like this. The on again, off again relationship with Ally had been on for this semester and he was pleased about how their courtship was progressing. The Woods had a private jet and family members had portable phones. During the hours of solitude, he dreamed of the day when he could afford a $1,400 Motorola mobile phone or even the $150 monthly bill. On-the-fly discussions as he walked across campus or on long car rides would have appeased his thirst for hometown news.

Chris had grown concerned regarding his relationship with his sister. They had always chatted regularly, analyzing and philosophizing life's angst and euphoria, but during this semester they had rarely communicated. Whenever he had called home, Sabina seemed to always be out on a date or with friends. He longed for the days where they could have a hearty discussion on world events. Breaking news on the Iran-Contra scandal was ripe for one of their famous liberal-conservative debates. Sadly, he had a feeling the politically charged banter of their youth would feel contrived. *Was he in the right, or was Sabina?* Eerily similar to the falling out with Sal and Tony, Chris was consigned to the opinion his relationship with Sabina was changing. Maybe a better word was evolving.

THREE WEEKS PRIOR

A surly and dour mood greeted Tony on the morning after the chaotic Halloween fright night. After three hours of intense discussion outside of her house, Bernadette had officially ended their relationship. She sat in silence during the ride from New York City, crying to herself and reliving the seconds when she was yards away from where gunfire had erupted. Tony tried his best to convince her he did not associate with undesirables, but what she had witnessed with her own eyes was more than enough verification. The time had come to move on.

"Anthony, if you only ran a little poker game, why are a bunch of hoodlums jumping you and shooting in a nightclub?" Bernadette blared as she jerked away from his grasp.

"Babe, we were as confused as you were. You saw Sabina with the greaseball. The fight was related to finding out she was dating a drug dealer! The Albanians are nuts," Tony had tried to convince her that the nights mayhem was a misunderstanding. The realization of the bullet almost killing him had sunk in. All he wanted to do was wrap his arms around his sweetheart.

"Gang people shot at you. Do you think I'm stupid? Remember, I'm privy to the D.A. investigation. Anthony, I can't be involved. I am sorry, truly I am, but I have to go. I thought you were my Prince Charming. Sadly, the apple I bit into was rotten." Over and done, the love of his life had bolted out of his truck to the waiting arms of her mother on the front porch.

The dirtbag had abandoned Sabina after the shot was fired. Sal ran to the balcony and comforted his cousin as she lay huddled in the corner, confused and bawling uncontrollably. He put his jacket around her shoulders, and he and Adrienne escorted her home. With her parents vacationing, Sal sat with Sabina in her kitchen until she was in better spirits and off of her drug-induced high. He did not attempt a rational discussion, as conversation would have been useless in her fragile, psychological condition.

The next morning, Sabina walked to the butcher shop and grabbed Tony by the arm. She escorted him across the street to Ressini's, where she pulled Sal aside from his lunch menu prep.

"Okay guys, I'm going to be straight forward. I am sorry for the mess I caused last night. I've been dealing with a lot lately." Before Sal and Tony could reply she added, "I'm a social worker and have dealt with addicts. Therefore...I'm going away for a little while. I know a place in Port St. Lucie. Full disclosure, I've been treated before. I go to dry out and collect my thoughts after my world famous binges. It's an outpatient, drug and alcohol rehab place I attend when I visit Grandma Julia."

"Is this why when you go for your visits, you are gone for weeks on end?"

"Get bent Sal! Don't judge me. You guys live your life, and it's sketchy to say the least. I try to be good, but these demons are strong. Please, I beg you to not mention this incident to my brother and parents. I promise this time, I'm going cold turkey and stop this crazy life." Sabina wiped away tears in her bloodshot eyes.

Tony reluctantly responded, "Get better Saby. We'll keep quiet...this time. But you have to promise you'll end your relationship. I don't get what you see in him, but he's a sleaze and bad news."

THE RECOVERY

In the subsequent weeks, Sabina made good progress. Out of the hustle and bustle of life back home, she committed herself to getting the monkey off of her back. While staying with her grandmother, she tended to the septuagenarian's needs and carved out four hours in the afternoon to attend counseling sessions. The Arborn House was a privately-funded organization with campuses located through the country. For the past two years, she had worked out a deal to pay by the month for outpatient treatment whenever she deemed necessary. Sometimes therapy worked, and sometimes not. She had a long stretch, *for her anyway,* of being clean. After she met Joe Djvulac, he had reintroduced her back into the late night atmosphere. Since he offered a steady supply to feed her habit, she ignored the fact he was a drug dealer who partook in a reprehensible way of life. In truth, he was similar to the guys Sal and Tony associated with and she had grown to be attracted to. She had met the rugged Albanian while visiting a friend who was a graduate student at Fordham University. They had lunch in a pizzeria in the Bronx and he was standing at the counter.

"Are you friendly with two big fella's from Tuckahoe named Sal and Tony?"

"Of course, they're like my little brothers." After this revelation, Sabina's Don Juan practically begged her to go on a date.

At first he treated her well-an expensive dinner, a movie, they went to the top of the World Trade Center and took in the breathtaking view. They frequented nightclubs, which was the end for her sobriety.

After a quiet Thanksgiving dinner-*you could call a meal dinner at 1:00 pm?*-with her grandmother, Uncle Vince, Aunt Teresa and six of their closest, geriatric friends, Sabina excused herself for a solitary walk along nearby, Jenson Beach. She took the path under the pier and to the sand dunes. Stopping in her tracks, she could not believe Joe Djvulac was sitting on the hood of her deceased grandfather's late model Oldsmobile casually toking on a blunt.

"Joey, what are doing, or should I say how did you find me?" Sabina gulped before grasping at her shoulders with her opposite hands, forming a protective cocoon around her torso.

"I called your house, and your lovely mother informed me you had gone to visit your grandmother. No big deal, she gave me the address." He offered the roach to Sabina. "I do not want to bogart!" She suspiciously peered at him and refused. He shrugged, took a final toke and flicked the miniscule remnants in the direction of the ocean, blowing smoke out of his mouth and absorbing the high.

"I, I needed time to think...in private! What do you want, Joey? You were busy the night you abandoned me." Sabina fidgeted with her purse before uneasily lighting a cigarette. She averted her eyes, sternly holding a Marlboro Light and blowing a thick trail of smoke into the late afternoon ocean breeze.

Sabina stood frozen in place with shoulders slumped. Her ex-boyfriend, with all the confident charm that had seduced her in the first place, hopped off of the hood and sauntered over. She remained defiant, tapping her foot and puffing rapidly on her cigarette while maneuvering her face to admire the crashing waves in the surf. With his index finger, lover-boy gently lifted Sabina's chin, and their eyes met. Reaching in his pocket, he removed a small vial and dangled the offer about with his fingers.

"What do you say, one last time? You and me, we have fun!"

With only a few days of sobriety under her belt to fend off temptation, Sabina accepted his open arms, and they walked to the privacy of the desolate, late afternoon beach to toot their horns and escape from reality for what she promised would be the last time.

The high they received from snorting lines was amplified by swigs taken from a pint of rot-gut vodka. As the sun was setting, the intertwined couple was giddy, romantically getting reacquainted on a blanket underneath the darkness of the pier, as they mapped out a recommitted future together.

"I cannot go back to New York-my uncle needs time to cool off; better for me to stay far away," Djvulac stated as he tapped white powder onto his index finger. He placed the appendage under Sabina's nose and she blew in heartily.

"Because of what happened that night?

He snickered then moved in close to kiss her lips. "I was unaware the other fellow with Sal and Tony was Damien Morris. He was stabbed in the arm, ended up in bad shape. My uncle was summoned to meet with the powers that be. Oh, what I do when I partake in too much of this white powder. If I'd of know Damien was Santo Tracino's protégé, maybe I would not be here now. But, my life is precious to me, so I had to leave New York until Uncle Skender smooths the situation out. I hope he can."

After Djvulac's confession, they both snorted another line. She responded to the fresh high by arching her back and jerking her head from side to side in rapid fashion. "Aaahhh, oh baby!" Sabina crawled onto the love her life and kissed him passionately. Propped on top and grinding his manhood, she whispered, "We can go away, Joey. Take me, I can get money."

There was no immediate response to the offer. In a sexually aroused state, Joe and Sabina made passionate love on the blanket. She collapsed into his arms, and they lay together catching their breath, observing the underside of the pier twenty feet above them.

"So where do you think you can get this money?" Djvulac nonchalantly inquired.

The scheming pair drove to the retirement village in separate cars. Saby rejoined her man in the front seat of his Camaro. "In the top drawer of my grandmother's dresser, she keeps an envelope of cash. Could be a couple of thousand dollars," Sabina blurted out. "Her apartment should be empty. She's at my aunt and uncle's place. My brother's football game is on television. They'll be watching for hours."

"You give me the key. I'll get the cash. Stay, I saved a taste for you." Djvulac tucked a small vial of cocaine in Sabina's blouse. The addictive stimulant was nestled tightly in her bra.

In her jittery and rambling state, she nodded and sat obediently in the passenger seat of the sports car. Joe scurried off to retrieve their nest egg. Sabina's wait became impatient. Craving another blast, she sniffed her nose and rubbed her nostrils with the sleeve of her unkempt blouse. Preparing for the hit, she smacked her lips before staring at her ragged appearance in the side view mirror. Her heart surged but life had slowed to a crawl. Sabina stiffened her backbone to stop the madness. Her reflection was the image of a strung-out junkie who she counseled on a day to day basis. A far cry from the beautiful woman she was, Sabina summoned her brain to find the strength.

Sabina removed the vial from her bosom. With a desperately needed, inner fortitude, she tapped the powdery contents into the wind. Saby had come to Florida to get her act together. Instead, life had shattered and to compound matters, she had encouraged a despicable man to rob from her grandmother. *The nonsense had to stop!*

The Camaro was parked facing the two-story pink stucco complex and across a runway of grass and shrubbery. Sabina readied herself and marched toward the open doorway. Djvulac bolted out, his eyes darting about, as he scurried past her without a second glance. He leapt into the car, his arms full of more than an envelope of cash and sped away.

Sabina shook her head. *Good, I hope he's gone for good. Money well spent to get him out of my life.* She moved closer. A murmuring emanated from within. Flicking on the hallway lights, a sickening feeling grew in her stomach. Grandma Julia was lying contorted on the carpet of her bedroom.

NOVEMBER 27, 1987, LATE NIGHT

Ignoring the alarmingly low gas gauge, Chris snapped his left blinker and followed the blue H sign off of Route One toward Tiffany Avenue. He had made excellent time; the newscaster on the radio was broadcasting the 11:05 p.m. weather update. His car was the only vehicle on the road, and hopefully the security guard at the St. Lucie Medical Center would allow him to enter the intensive care unit. His father gave him an update when they spoke during his last rest stop. His mother had arrived in the morning and would stay by Grandma Julia's side for as long as her recovery took. Sabina was with her. Chris hoped to join them, even if he had to camp out in the waiting area all night.

He circled the perimeter of the hospital, following the signs for visitor parking. Chris saw Sabina standing under the brightly lit awning of the entrance, smoking a cigarette. As she stubbed the butt in an urn, a head popped out of a nearby car. Idling fifty feet to their rear, Chris sat in his vehicle and observed. He raised his eyebrows and quickly lowered the window as the conversation became more animated. While Sabina was keeping a safe distance, obviously she knew who the driver was. All Chris was able to make out was the last of her lively rant before she turned and walked hastily back through the sliding glass doors, "Go away, you've done enough harm!"

Instead of going to the ICU, Chris called an audible. He was determined to see what this was all about. He kept his distance as the Camaro sped off. Tracking the souped-up, sports car was easy in sparse, late night traffic. Before the turn for Jenson Beach Boulevard, the lead car veered into an uninhabited strip mall and continued toward the glowing red and yellow lights of the only establishment that was opened, TGI Friday's.

Chris drove past the eatery and doubled back to park. He walked past the banged up sports car and perused for clues. New York license plate, an Albanian flag sticker on the left side above the back bumper, two empty cigarette packs crumpled on the passenger seat. A suitcase was on the backseat, and a plastic bag was lying adjacent. No way was this creep from Florida. By the tone of the conversation with Sabina, he had most likely followed her from New York. *An ex-boyfriend*?

A pleasant, middle-aged hostess greeted Chris with an oversized menu held pressed to her chest. Three men mingled at the bar and a few couples were scattered at tables and booths in the dining area. She informed her guest he could order food for another hour at a table, but the bar was serving till 1 a.m. He nodded and peaked over her shoulder. The man he was following had exited the restroom. Away from the cluster of late night regulars, the stranger had ambled past the crowd and took a seat alone at the far end of the bar. Chris made his way around the horseshoe shaped bar, eyeing the television monitors strategically anchored above eye level in each corner of the lounge.

"Can I get me a Budweiser?" Chris barked out in the slight Texas drawl from his few years of living in the Lone Star State. The bartender complied and put the icy bottle in front of him. Two stools away, Joe Djvulac sat staring into space, dangling a cigarette in his hand and blowing smoke out of his mouth and nostrils. His left leg was rapidly moving on the foot rest of the barstool. Chris took a long gulp and breathed out in satisfaction. "Dang, I needed a cold beer," he voiced with a broad smile in the direction of the Albanian before he turned his attention to the television monitor. The ESPN commentator was previewing the upcoming NFL schedule. Chris made eye contact with Djvulac. "Big Dolphin game this weekend against the Bills...they beat on Dallas last week."

"Not from America, I don't follow football. I'm a soccer fan," Djvulac stated without emotion or eye contact.

"I'm a transplant, too, born outside of Fort Worth. Hey, can I buy you a beer buddy, or another one of what you're sipping on?" Chris pointed at the three quarter empty highball glass. Before he could reply, the friendly Texan called out. "Barkeep, get my friend a refill...on me...and get my ass another cold one." Chris tossed back the last of his bottle and tapped the empty on the wooden counter to emphasize how parched he was.

Halfway through a second free cocktail that Djvulac had accepted from his new friend, the Albanian spoke about his life. Playing the part of a friendly Southerner, Chris prodded the big city visitor to elaborate on his exploits. The coked-up thug willingly complied.

"My folks moved me when I was sixteen. Dad's a physical therapist. All these old people need caring. I'm trying my best over at community college, but working part-time at Winn-Dixie sure don't pay my bills. Lucky I have other ways to get cash." Chris winked.

"I came from Albania with nothing. People know I get things done," Djvulac boasted. "Twenty-four stitches to stop the bleeding." He rolled the sleeve of his tattered sweatshirt to reveal a battle scar on his forearm.

With the establishment set to close, the new chums changed the nature of the discussion. Out in the abandoned parking lot, they spoke about getting together the next day. Chris had fabricated a tale he had thought about on the fly to entice Djvulac to reconvene for a freelance job to earn a few easy dollars.

"I have some merchandise you may like to move." Djvulac unlocked his car and reached in. He re-emerged with the plastic bag. "I give you good price." The thief palmed a broach, a few assorted necklaces, and a gold wedding band.

"I can find a home for these little trinkets," Chris proposed as he studied the quality of the broach. He fought the urge to tear the thief's head off. This motherfucker had stolen his grandmother's jewelry.

"I can get my hands on more. What do you say?" Djvulac took back the items and placed them in the bag.

"Tomorrow dude. I'll give you two hundred for all this crap. This is nothing, what I need you for will pay real good!" Chris shook on the deal. Back to his car, he slammed his fists against the steering wheel and wiped the feel of Djvulac off on his pants leg. No sleep would come tonight.

34

The Monster

NOVEMBER 28, 1987

In what was odd for a Saturday morning, at slightly before 8 a.m., a businessman wearing a sharp suit and tie entered Albanese's Butcher Shop. He was in his late thirties or early forties. In decent shape, he sported a full head of salt and pepper hair and presented a cordial smile. A haggard Tony reciprocated with a warm grin and a nod of the head, eagerly awaiting the order from a new customer.

"Wow, you sure are a big one," the stranger complimented Tony with a cheery icebreaker. "Hello, my name is Ronald Brewer. Is the proprietor of the establishment available?" He placed a slim leather briefcase on the counter top.

"I'm the owner's son. Can I help you with something? We have an excellent prime rib special today."

"No, this is an unrelated matter. Can you tell me if your father owns this building?" Mr. Brewer asked as he snapped open the briefcase and reached inside for a folder.

"Yeah, the place has been in my family for generations," Tony proudly responded.

"Good to hear. To be perfectly honest with you, I represent a real estate developer, and he is inquiring about buying the shops on this corner of Columbus Avenue. If your dad wants to discuss this in greater detail, have him get in touch with me. My card is attached with this proposal."

As the business related visitor made his way to the curb, he held open the door for a bona fide customer. Still intrigued by the comments, Tony tended to the small order from a regular and returned to the counter. Bleary eyed from a late night and zoning out in his thoughts, he did not hear the first few rings of the telephone.

Tony snapped too and spun around from the counter. He excused himself and answered, "Albanese's Butcher Shop, can you hold please?... Hey, Cee. Give me a sec." He placed the receiver on the top of the wall unit and returned to complete the transaction for the mother of a high school classmate. "Thank you again, Mrs. Adams. Tell Eddie we have to get together for the holidays." As she turned to leave, he waved goodbye.

"Eddie's mom? Nice lady," Chris voiced from the other end.

"Yeah, she was our first ticket of the morning. The Saturday after Thanksgiving's friggin' slow; I gave my dad the morning off. I'm shot too. The poker game didn't end till dawn. Starving, I went straight to the diner for an omelet and came to work, you played a great game by the way...how's Nanna Julia?" Tony yawned like a bear and shook the grogginess from his system with a hearty sip of black coffee.

"I didn't get to see her last night; going over in a few minutes. Hey, what can you tell me about a creepy Albanian hanging around my sister?"

After a moment of silence, Tony responded, "You must mean Joe Djvulac. Why do you bring the scumbag up?"

"It's the answer I thought I'd get. I was sort of chumming around with him last night, in Florida. What's his deal with Saby?" Chris was direct.

"Blew us away, too...as a matter of fact. He's been dating her on the down low for the past few months. When Sal and I found out, we put the kibosh on the whole matter. The relationship supposedly ended before she went to Florida. Getting away from him was one of the reasons Saby gave for visiting the old folk. The *skeevotz* is in Florida; interesting," Tony divulged the recent turn of events. He chose to tap around Sabina's substance abuse problem. The disclosure should come from her, when she was ready.

"I caught him with Saby. They had an argument; sounded like she was ending something. I was in my car and parked across the street. I followed him, feeling like James Bond...went undercover to investigate. The bastard swiped my grandmother's jewelry and then tried to friggin' sell back to me. I bet the asshole had something to do with her falling."

"Cee, be careful. This motherfucker is real bad news. He's always packing and has killed before. Don't be a hero. This can be life-threatening, and it's not your world. The night we caught him and Saby together was nuts...we had a major brawl in the city. His gang jumped us in a club. Shots were fired, they had knives. Insane! We're lucky to be alive."

"Why the hell is Sabina with this dickweed?" Chris was annoyed by his sister's erratic behavior and string of poor decisions in life.

"You have to ask her. But in reference to Djvulac, lots of people are looking for him. He freaked out, was ordered to kill his cousin, which had apparently set him over the edge."

"Friggin' guy's desperate. He was on coke and couldn't keep still. Once I bullshitted with him, he wouldn't stop running his mouth. I dangled a bogus story I had a robbery for him to help me with. I wanted to see what his deal was."

"Does he seem like he's sniffing around for a taste of something?" Tony inquired.

"Hell yes. He practically reached into my pocket."

"But surprisingly, you don't have a clue for what to do next, hey Cee?" A long silence passed. The tables had been turned. Tony had the master plan, and Chris listened intently.

LATE MORNING

The Intensive Care Unit within the St. Lucie Medical Center was on the third floor of the west wing of the healthcare facility. Chris soberly walked into the elevator, pressed number three on the control panel, and nodded to a woman and child who he held the door for. After a few seconds, the metal doors opened and he exited directly into the waiting area of the ICU. His mother was across the room with her back turned and speaking on a payphone. Chris walked over and tapped her on the shoulder.

Maria blurted out, "Gotta' go." She slammed the receiver and collapsed into her son's chest. They had not seen each other since his grandfather's funeral. *Could six months have gone by so fast?*

Maria Cameron was a strong-willed woman who gave the appearance she did not follow sports, pop culture and the goings on of her children. Tending to the house and toiling at Bella's consumed her day. She lived on the periphery as her husband had eagerly volunteered to absorb himself in the nooks and crannies of his children's lives. Make no mistake; she knew all and was the highest ranking officer of the Cameron family. Chris and Sabina would joke as kids; *I think mom has an extra set of eyeballs in the back of her head.*

"Go to your grandmother, baby...Oh Christopher; they have her doped-up and she's in and out of consciousness. The next thirty to sixty days are critical for hip fractures." After the comment, the doors swung open. Sabina shuffled out of the ICU. Her eyes welled when she saw her brother.

"Oh Chris...if I had been a minute earlier!" Sabina had called for emergency response.

"Saby, go back to the condo and get some rest. You're haggard and have been for some time...Even before you came to visit," her mother commanded.

Chris sat with the inspiration to Bella's for the next five hours. Grandpa Joe had always bragged his wife was the most beautiful woman in the world, his *Bella Mia*. Chris had insisted his mother join Sabina and to get some rest. Alone in his thoughts, he prayed by her side and grimaced over and over again. Grandma Julia had taught him his A, B, Cs and how to color in the lines. Boasting she was physically fit, she would toss the football with him and perform toe touches to his wide eyed astonishment. The elderly saint was in tremendous pain. Opening her eyes from time to time, she was able to recognize his face and produced a slight smile or gently squeezed his fingers; but barely a word was spoken and these were in the form of faint murmurs. When in discomfort, he would kiss her forehead and caress her sunken cheeks to do anything in his power to will her back to health, *as she had done countless times in his youth.* If and when Grandma Julia's condition stabilized, the next step would be to transfer her to a rehab facility.

In the afternoon, Maria and Sabina returned to the hospital refreshed. Without informing his sister he had introduced himself to her ex-boyfriend the night earlier, Chris departed. He had coordinated to meet with the low life at *TGI Fridays* for happy hour. The eatery was bustling on the Saturday after Thanksgiving with the kickoff of Christmas shopping in full swing. Chris waited in a booth, devouring a chicken club and picking at the remnants of a Caesar Salad. He waved in the direction of the hostess stand to get the Albanian's attention. Djvulac weaved through the tables of diners and slid into the opposite side facing him.

"You're late, dude. I can't deal with unreliable folk." No handshakes were extended and immersed in his fake Texas persona; Chris took control of the situation.

"These stupid people, the traffic was horrible. My miscalculation, this will not happen again." While he had an insipid expression, the career criminal clearly did not want to pass on a potential scheme to make a few extra dollars.

Chris took a final bite from his sandwich and pushed the plate away. While chewing, he continued, "My buddy's working at the new stadium being built. Your Mets are going to be training here next year."

"Mets...no interest to me," the Eastern European dismissed the comment.

"Can I finish, or are you gonna' keep interrupting?" Chris infuriatingly snapped. "I have a big time opportunity. My friend's a plumbing assistant. He tells me boxes and boxes of copper joints and pipes are everywhere. They're getting ready to install the toilets and such at the complex. Copper is in high demand."

"I am aware. I have been taking copper rods from the railroad in New York," Djvulac responded like his Texas friend was not telling him anything new.

"Dang skippy! My kick ass connection in West Palm will take all I can give him...job's easy. The storage trailer will be unlocked. We need to keep quiet and book it...it's why I need your help. Three or four boxes each should fetch a couple of thousand bucks." Chris laid out the plan. He needed more than one car and an extra set of hands to haul enough plumbing fixtures to make economic sense.

"Sounds easy enough, when would I get my cash?" Djvulac was in.

"I'll give you two grand after we do the deed and are safely away. I'll cart those fuckers to my connection and settle without you. Meet me at midnight. In the meantime, did you bring those necklaces and such?" Chris handed his new partner a handful of twenty dollar bills and accepted the plastic bag containing the priceless, family heirlooms.

THE AFTERNOON AT THE HOSPITAL

Clenching both fists and with her head bowed at the side of her grandmother, Sabina lifted her forehead from the rumpled yellow blanket, recited the *Our Father* for the fifth time and performed the Sign of the Cross. After a two-hour nap and a shower, as well as not ingesting any cocaine or drinking alcohol for two days, she felt like a new person... physically.

Sabina was sturdily built, with a curvy feminine frame that looked incredible in a skirt or a pair of jeans. Like her brother, she had been athletic in her teen years and had run track and played soccer at Tuckahoe High. When not in her current state of confusion, Sabina found time to jog and had given Jane Fonda's workout tape a try. The smoking would have to stop...but one vice at a time.

Her mental being was another story. The passion she had for helping others, especially the less fortunate, came from within and had led her to overschedule and overpromise. The care and compassion she had devoted her life to, through counseling as a social worker, followed her home. The management of the Bella's franchises was highly stressful and did not end when the light switch was clicked off for the night. In her heart she also knew some, most or even all of her participation with the ruse of that Forgione creep was morally wrong. Yet, she never had a doubt in her mind to help Sal and Tony even with the sexual part of her commitment.

Her escalating use of alcohol and recent dabbling in cocaine was not the best life decision to make. What she had learned from the smattering of therapy sessions with *real addicts* was the underlying trouble was not the substance. The core of the problem was deeply seeded in the psyche. The craziness of life, which every other person on the planet had to deal with, was not the crux of her zest for living on the edge.

A breakthrough behind the root cause of her "issues" could have been made earlier in the day. When she and her mother had returned from the hospital, Sabina showered and took a nap. After lunching on turkey leftovers, she was in the mood to clean and tidy the spare bedroom. In the course of rearranging items under the bed, she stumbled across a dusty shoebox full of pictures. She perused the good old days stacks that were neatly bound with Grandma Julia's trademark rubber bands. The age of some of these memories were denoted by the shapes and texture of the photographs, not to mention the awful clothes they wore.

Wow, Sal had an awkward phase...I remember when Chris tried to scrub off those pimples...Mom was elegant when she wore a dress...Tony was the spitting image of Poppy...Good thing dad shaved his moustache.

Sitting with her back against the nightstand and knees bent close to her chest, she skimmed through a stack of black and whites that pre-dated her birth. Sabina keenly focused on a set of four wedding photos. They were of her mother's sister's nuptials. The bride and groom were beaming as they cut the cake. Uncle Pat was Aunt Rosa's first husband, and the marriage had lasted a tumultuous decade. When they married, Pat Fortuno was in his early twenties. Tall and gangly, he had a dark complexion and jet black hair. Aunt Rosa was stunning and a few years younger. While Rosa resembled her sister in appearance, she mostly took after the Cavazzi side and had a lighter complexion. What struck Sabina the most was the mannerisms of her former uncle. *Oh my God, he's the spitting image of Joe.* Clarity came. The genesis of her problem had been detected. Gravitating toward the lower echelon of society had been Sabina's norm. She regularly dated the hip, knockaround guys-unscrupulous, shady characters who partied to the max, smoked, and tended to thrive on boasting about their exploits of living life on the edge. Why did she gravitate to these characters? The answer became obvious. For some unexplained reason, she was attracted to men who resembled Aunt Rosa's first husband. Sabina had not seen Uncle Pat since the divorce, which was a good thing. Sabina had struggled to suppress her thoughts and memories and nightmares of her formative years with the aid and comfort of alcohol and drugs. The monster in these pictures was the crux of her pain as he had sexually molested her during her youth.

NOVEMBER 28, 1987, EARLY MORNING HOURS

Veering right onto Peacock Boulevard, both cars completed the final phase of the journey with their front headlights extinguished. The glow of the moon provided the sole source of illumination. Chris parked a hundred feet ahead of his partner in crime, on the opposite side of a dirt road, which would eventually become the entrance to the Mets' new sports complex. Djvulac exited his vehicle and crouched low, negotiating along a drainage ditch bordering a cluster of tall pines. The two accomplices met behind an enormous mound of St. Augustine grass sod to be laid around the perimeter of the new parking. Chris held two flashlights and handed one to Djvulac.

"I hope you did your push-ups today. We're gonna' have to haul ass, and these boxes ain't light," Chris empathetically whispered.

"Do not concern yourself with me. You lead where we have to go. When will I get my money?"

"Your money's in my car."

They continued through the growth of pines; carefully plodding over rocks, roots and brush of the rough. In the distance was the dimly lit array of one story trailers which appeared to be absent of any personnel.

"I made a killin' when I offloaded them items," Chris said. "The broach alone was worth three grand. Don't fret; to show you I'm honest I'll even give you an extra grand."

"Only a thousand? Seems like you are shorting me."

"Bite me, dude. You're lucky I mentioned anything. Relax; we'll be done in a half hour. Plenty of cash in my car…if we swipe a whole bunch of boxes, I'll have more for you. We'll settle when we get back." Hiding behind the massive wheel of a bulldozer, they assessed their strategy and method to employ for the heist.

"Someone's patrolling!" Djvulac heard rumpling on the far side of the yard, but could not detect the source from their hidden position.

"Don't have a cow! Ain't nobody around; some animal was rummaging for food. The garbage dumpsters not covered. It's a holiday weekend; I came by earlier to case the area out. To tell you the truth, I coulda' stole all I wanted. Thought you've done this before? Sheeitt!"

"This part of the country is unfamiliar ...wish you provided more information to the plan."

"Fuckin' A right I didn't tell you all the details. Sorry boss, you'd get the jump on me and I'd get squat. You city-slickers think I'm stupid." They crept to a position directly outside of the fence and remained hidden behind a rectangular, one-story trailer.

"I heard another bang," Djvulac whispered, as he grasped Chris' right shoulder.

"Dang, this place is supposed to be empty. I heard rumbling, too. Let's wait a sec. If any trouble, we'll come back another night. Oh heck, let's try our luck...we've come too far to not get at least a few boxes. We can hit them with the flashlights."

Chris straddled a section of the fence which was pried open. He arched his head, attempting desperately to see if they were at risk of being discovered. Djvulac surged his shoulder into Chris' back. Due to the impact, the football player was caught off guard and tumbled awkwardly to the side and into the brush.

"What the frig' did you?" Chris scolded in the direction of the unreliable Albanian but cut himself short. The beam of a flashlight shone bright in his eyes.

"Stay where you are. What the Hell are you doing, punk?" a powerful voice bellowed.

"God dang cops!" Chris exclaimed, as he raised his arms in defeat. Glancing over his right shoulder, he could see the tail end of Joe Djvulac scamper into the darkness.

"Don't move, dipstick," the angry voice commanded.

"AAAAGGGGHHHH!" Chris lowered his arms, clenched his fists and sprinted forward.

35

Reckless Abandon

NOVEMBER 30, 1987

Even though he was on Florida's Gulf Coast, an unseasonal chill was in the tropical air for this time of year. Sal was dressed appropriately in a form-fitting, crewneck sweater covered by a faded blue, denim jacket. The taxicab he had taken from the airport stopped in front of the white stucco house with the screened in porch on the side. He checked the address on a scrap of paper-2367 Coconut Drive. After paying the fare, he walked tentatively, dangling a duffel bag from his left hand. Before reaching the halfway point of the walkway, his mother had swung open the screen door and dashed over to greet him.

Deeply tanned, Dina wrapped her arms around her baby. "Sally, you look better than ever!" More than a year and a half had elapsed since he had seen his mom.

Sal was not like Tony. A lot of emotion needed to build before he shed a tear. When he pulled back, a stream was on his cheeks. He had craved the love and affection of his mother for far too long.

After Dina eloped with Angelo Palagano and moved to Fort Meyers, Sal shut her out of his life. She had attempted to call and explain the rationale behind the haphazard manner in which she handled the situation. He wanted nothing to do with her and went as far as arranging to be away on a Caribbean vacation during the week she had come to visit last Christmas. The obvious slap to Dina's face stung sharply and precipitated her miscalculated decision to not pay her respects at Joe Cavazzi's funeral.

This disrespectful slight caused her predicament to worsen. Dina was persona non grata in and around the tight-knit Tuckahoe community. With no correspondence of any kind with life back at her former home, she had been relegated to make the best of life in her transplanted, Sunshine State community.

"Hello ma." Sal had the spontaneous urge to call his mother from the airport with the surprise he would be flying in for a visit. Dina had answered the call in the midst of gossiping with one of her new girlfriends, Beth from Milwaukee, while drinking coffee on her screened in patio. After a long moment of silence, her son emotionally continued. "I miss you mom. I want to see you."

Dina screamed before bellowing, "Yes, yes, yes, I want to see you, too!" Beth must have thought something awful had happened.

After the grand tour of the Palagano one-story abode, which included a built-in pool bordering the canal, along with a flowery over-sell of the spare bedroom Dina had dreamed her son would sleep in one day, they settled into the kitchen.

"Been a lot of fits and starts with the restaurant. We were closed a few months back after a drunk driver slammed right into where you and dad always ate late night meals. Knock on wood, it's been real good lately. I kid you not, we were jammed on Thanksgiving and have four Christmas parties booked. I thought the time was right to make my amends with you before the holiday rush. My new girlfriend's managing the place while I'm gone."

"A steady girlfriend?" Dina beamed. "I have room for more grandkids. By the way, John surprised me...is wife was four months pregnant!"

"Wonderful for him...but slow down, not too fast for me. I hired her before we dated. Nice girl, her name is Adrienne. I trusted her with the place for a few days." Sal went on to blurt out random facts of his life. He missed his mother and importantly, needed to talk to her. He averted his eyes to observe the picturesque landscape over her shoulder.

"You see the little island? Alligators live there. We have to be careful when we go outside, especially in the early morning." In the awkward silence, Dina had turned to see what had peaked Salvatore's curiosity. He had been lost in thought. Dina reached over and placed her hands on top of her son's. "Sally baby, I knew you would do okay. I had all the confidence in you, even when you were a little kid; well little for you anyway. If you trust...her name is Adrienne, right? She must be a special girl. I'd like to meet her someday."

"She's been the longest relationship I've had since grade school with Teresa from down the street, remember her? We're going on three months. Heh-Heh...she's a hottie! And thankfully, no space cadet. Dre's harder on the staff than me." Tall, muscular and handsome, Sal had easy time attracting the attention of his lady friends, but because of his chaotic psyche, they never hung on for long.

"I am proud of you, and your dad was, too."

"He could have shown his love a little better."

"Honey, he was a hard man to crack, and he had those evil, gambling demons...yes, he and I grew apart...obviously...but he loved you three boys in his own way. A cousin of your fathers from Brooklyn, you never met him, Dominic Esposito. Well, Dom lives in Naples and we ran into each other. He shocked me by telling all of these vivid and detailed stories about you. Whenever he and Greg were together, all he talked about was his baby boy. You were the light of his life. Dominic knew specifics about you...the blocked kick in the Bronxville game and the supposed, secret ingredients to your Marsala sauce." Dina had thrilled her son with the statement. At first, Sal nodded curiously, in a way for her to continue on with the story. Before she had ended though, his face was gleaming.

Overall, the trip was faring well. Sal was pleased with his decision to finally see what his mother had been doing. This would not be his last visit. His emotions had been high and after he had spent Sunday afternoon consoling Chris next to Aunt Julia's bed, reuniting with his mother had been front and center on his mind. Fate had intervened as he waited for his flight to New York at the airport in Orlando.

"My nanny has Christmas presents for me." A family had sidled next to Sal at the airport and an adorable little girl decided the giant man was friendly enough to talk to. "She lives in Fort Meyers. Have you ever seen the ocean mister?" Immediately after the discussion with the adorable pigtailed angel, Sal walked back to the ticket counter to rearrange his itinerary. He even sat across the aisle from little Susie on the hour long flight.

The reason for being in Florida in the first place could have been construed as right or wrong...depending how you perceived the events. The three blood brothers had discussed in great detail the Joe Djvulac quandary. Tony had brilliantly concocted the master plan after Chris had informed him he had covertly befriended the Albanian. Through his conversations with Poppy, Tony had been following the construction of the Mets new spring training facility. He had been fervently counting the days till he could hound the players for autographs and to catch a glimpse of his favorite players in the restaurants and such around Port St. Lucie when he visited his grandparents again. A plan popped into Tony's head to coerce Djvulac to participate on an easy score and thus provide the perfect opportunity to trap him without detection.

Sal and Tony knew they would not have to get their fingernails dirty. Nursing a sixteen-inch scar on his upper arm from the knife wound, Damien had been adamant he wanted revenge. Since Sal had been more engaged with Damien on prior assignments, he accompanied the Mafia hitman to settle this dispute. The intimidating duo flew to Orlando, rented a car, and drove to Florida's east coast. Damien had a connection in Daytona Beach who supplied a throwaway gun.

From the war room of the butcher shop, Tony had mapped out the granular details to lure Djvulac to his demise without causing alarm. With his experience of canvassing locations from his work for Rodgers Oil & Gas, Chris studied the stadium site and provided detailed information of the area to plan the attack. Before nightfall, Sal and Damien arrived in Port St. Lucie. Damien hid in the tall pines, lying in wait for the volatile and desperate Albanian. He removed the battery cable and hid in the growth beneath where the Camaro was parked. Djvulac was on the lam, and he had neither time nor the resources to scurry enough money to survive after he fled from his uncle's wrath. Add a healthy drug appetite to the equation and the fact he was a thief to the core, they devised a ruse to easily whet his palate for an easy score. With Chris alternating between confidently and carelessly leading the botched robbery while broadcasting Djvulac's money was safely stored at the car, they knew the situation would be too tempting for him to not take advantage of.

Sal posed as the security guard and had alarmed Djvulac the robbery had been botched. The copper fixtures were non-existent and a security guard was not at the site. All of the major work at the Mets spring training facility had been completed months earlier. The fenced in trailers were set to be removed, and the location would soon be paved over as the northwest section of the parking lot.

Pretending to be on patrol, Sal made sure his floodlight shone bright when he nabbed Cee in the darkness. Glancing over at Djvulac scurrying off, they were confident their part of the deception had been flawlessly executed. When the soon to be deceased gangster disappeared into the darkness, Chris screamed with excitement and ran toward Sal to rejoice. Minutes later, they heard three shots ring out.

Damien worked efficiently. Chris and Sal split in his Monte Carlo as the Mafia killer scrubbed all evidence of the murder or the corpse being traced. With a blowtorch, Damien burned off the fingerprints of the Albanian immigrant. He removed the license plates and scraped the VIN number from the windshield before dousing the vehicle in kerosene. To buy himself time, he lit a small fire in the trunk and sped off. Three minutes later, the blaze was ignited. The Camaro burst into flames while Damien traveled along US-1. The charred and unrecognizable remains of Joe Djvulac were discovered early the next morning when Damien was on his flight back to New York.

DECEMBER 7, 1987

Tony always took the time to accompany his grandfather to attend church, light a candle and say a prayer on Pearl Harbor Day. In all the years the Albanese's had cohabitated with the Scala's, Vincent had never spoken about his years in the service, but Tony knew his grandfather lost an infinite number of friends in the war. In his youth, Tony would be awoken by screams from behind his grandparent's bedroom door in the middle of the night. Someday, he may strike the nerve to ask his hero about this.

He returned from ceremoniously honoring his grandfather's ritual at the Church of the Assumption. After a quick call to Pops, *Pops flows better than Poppy*, Tony turned to work related matters. With his butt comfortably snuggled on the sofa, the big man was a couch potato, lying on his back listening intently to the telephone receiver lodged in the creek of his neck while following the opening scene of the latest episode of MacGyver, *the guy is friggin' brilliant.*

"Yeah, you can count on me. I'll stop by tomorrow and get the tape... you think a movie about some suit will be a big hit?...Guess so, Charlie Sheen's a good actor, *Platoon* was way cool!" Tony had agreed to his new assignment. Jimmy Tree had a pirated copy of the new movie, *Wall Street.* They should make a killing.

With the telephone cord stretched to its limit from the kitchen wall through to the living room, Tony tried unsuccessfully to control his amusement as his father attempted to limbo. A few seconds earlier, with flair, he and Rita had made their entrance through the kitchen. After his parents danced and blocked the view of his favorite TV show, Tony had enough.

"Okay dude, later; my parents ate a bowl of Fruit Loops." Tony took a front row seat to view *God knows what.* Joanne heard the commotion and had stopped doing her homework to inquire about what all the noise was about.

Alfonse broke into one of Irish Mike's jigs and clumsily bumped into his wife, almost knocking her over. "What the heck is going on with you two?" Anthony and Joanne commented in unison before they mimicked their fathers dancing skills from the couch.

"Oh, you tell them sugar bear. I'm too excited and will flub the details," Rita beamed as she tickled the ribs of the only man she had ever kissed.

"Okay gang, here goes. We're officially out of the butcher business!" Alfonse waited for the comment to sink in. "Anthony, the guy who wanted me to call him, we had a meeting and he offered us five hundred grand to sell."

"Holy Crap Dad! I guess you accepted the offer, huh?" Tony was mesmerized by the adorable site of his parents acting like teenage love birds. *Oh no, eyes are watering...screw it, who cares!*

"A lot of money Dad, can you retire?" Joanne was smiling from ear to ear. "How about buying your favorite daughter a new car?"

"We're going to split the money amongst us. It's only fair; you two have worked hard, too...darling, what color do you like?" Rita had made her daughter's day-week-month-year with the last statement and confirmed when the sweet sixteen squealed with delight.

The Albanese family went out on the town to celebrate their good fortune. Since Alfonse had never been prone to splurge for a high-priced meal at a restaurant not named Ressini's, he deferred to his son to make the suggestion. Anthony took control. Strolling into Dominick's on Arthur Avenue like they were members of high society, Alfonse refused the menu and ordered from his heart. At any other point in time, the eye-popping check would have caused him to keel over. On this special night, he was more than happy with the delicious meal and the top-notch service. For the first time in his life, he peeled off three $100 bills and uttered the phrase "keep the change."

The car pulled into the driveway of the Albanese house on Circle Road well after midnight. Joanne had permission to go to school late and Alfonse made the executive decision to not open the butcher shop until mid-morning or whenever. *Who was he kidding? Tony knew he'd be opening the door at dawn.* Over dinner, the family dreamed about their future. Even with the mini-fortune, Alfonse remained practical. He could not stop working. They'd pay off the mortgage, buy Joanne a sensible car and put money away for her college education. Anthony deserved at least two hundred grand, but he had adamantly refused the staggering amount and settled on $50,000. Alfonse and Rita would have close to a quarter of a million dollars for their modest indulgences and retirement income. With this back of the envelope calculation, Alfonse had decided he would seek employment at a large supermarket chain while Rita continued her duties as a branch manager at the local National Bank of Westchester.

After his mother tucked him in, *a truly special night;* Tony contemplated his options in solitude. He had held off on accepting Jimmy Tree's offer to get into the construction union. The angst about leaving the butcher shop was officially a moot point. Sleepy, he closed his eyes and dreamed of being at the controls of a kick ass dump truck or heavy crane. He would be able to scale back his poker room and gambling operations while maintaining a steady income with union benefits. *ZZZZZZZZZ...*the big man would sleep well tonight.

DECEMBER 31, 1987

They Call Me Assassin was an autobiography written by Jack Tatum. The perennial all-pro Oakland Raider had penned the memoir after a devastating hit he recorded that paralyzed Darryl Stingley in 1980. During his storied career, Tatum never took a cheap shot and had played the game the way you always should-hard. He had been deeply moved by the incident but never apologized for the rough way he approached his position. Chris would read passages of this tattered paperback before practice, and on game day an entire chapter would be absorbed to get his mind in gear.

Reckless abandon had been uttered by coaches, commentators, fans and sports reporters to describe the play of defensive back and Longhorn co-captain Chris Cameron. Bug-eyed and frothing at the mouth, he had sprinted downfield on the opening kickoff of the Bluebonnet Bowl against USC. Six seconds later, he violently introduced himself to the numbers on the front of the kick returner's jersey. His credo for each tackle was to introduce himself to the numbers on the back by way of the front of the jersey.

Playing in his last football game...ever...had raised his emotions through the roof. He had a lot on his mind. This game was dedicated to his ailing grandmother. The Cameron family was consigned with the realization she would not recover and her prognosis was week-to-week. Her words spoken to him before he ventured off to Texas to "kick ass and knock'em dead" would play over and over in his head during the late afternoon.

Third and eleven for USC from their own twenty-seven yard line. "Nice play CeeJay" was excitedly hollered by Ron Grunther after Chris had deflected the ball on a pass play. His roommate was hobbling around on crutches from the sidelines. Ron-Ron's NFL dreams may have been curtailed after a crippling knee injury he had suffered in the last game.

Why couldn't Chris get his love life together? At the end of finals, Ally had informed him since she worked her cute scholastic butt off, she would be graduating a semester early. As such, she had succumbed to her parent's wishes to take over the European operations of the philanthropic division of the Woods Family Trust. The office was based in Paris, France.

Au revoir mon amour. On the bright side, any French-sounding names on the back of the USC jerseys were sure to be hit harder.

By late in the third quarter, the running back for USC, All-American Len White wore out the Longhorns front seven. Chris put a hard hit on the burly back on a second and eight running play but failed to wrap. After composing himself, Chris punched the turf in frustration, as he saw the Longhorn lead evaporate and the USC celebration ensuing in the end zone.

With the termination to his college romance, Chris had received the coincidental reply from the human resource department of Woods Energy; they would be going in another direction and not offer Chris a job within their planning and development division. He had naively been banking on this entry level position and had to reignite his career search.

Late in the game, the Longhorn's passing game came to life and regained the lead. The USC offensive juggernaut responded and with five minutes remaining, took the ensuing kickoff and methodically ran the ball on the Texas defense. USC needed a touchdown to win. With a first and goal at the Longhorn eight yard line, the UT defense held tough. Len White took a handoff for a run around the left end. Cameron darted through a cluster of offensive and defensive linemen and managed to strip the ball out of the big back's arms. With a roar of the crowd and his applauding teammates, Chris jumped to his feet and celebrated the game-changing turnover that had cemented the University of Texas's first bowl win in six years.

The picture perfect moment of his hit which had caused the fumble was captured for all to see on the cover of the next issue of *Sports Illustrated*. The satisfaction he received by preserving the victory was confirmed a week later as he narcissistically gobbled up copies of the popular sports magazine with his frozen-in-time tackle. The pats on the back, gratuitous sex from supportive co-ed boosters and an article of his four year career in the campus newspaper paled in comparison to the pleasure he had received from assisting in the extermination of the Albanian cockroach. Come to think, this paled in comparison to assisting in all of the retribution over the past four years. Reckless abandon took on another meaning entirely when you would do anything in your power to protect your family, regardless of the consequences.

36

Fish On The Line

MAY 27, 1988

Chris had been the big fish in a small pond for the first part of his life. In college, he swam amongst the trout in a lake. Could he be a Great White Shark patrolling the ocean waters, or would he be swallowed in the next chapter?

After a rewarding high school and college experience, Chris Cameron was set to enter the real world. Would the business community relegate him to guppy status or would he receive the opportunity to show what he could do? He was big man on the tiny Tuckahoe High campus and a star player among the gridiron Longhorn's. He had held his own scholastically by double majoring in U.S. History and Economics and stood ready to receive his University of Texas honors diploma with the other graduates. However, millions of college seniors from across the country would be competing feverishly for positions at large, medium and small business entities. *IBM does not care what you could bench press.*

Accepting the parchment indicating he had successfully completed his chosen courses of study, Christopher Joseph Cameron did not believe a position in a training program with a consulting firm, big corporation or broker would fulfill his desires. His entire life had been run at full throttle. Participating in sports, physical fitness, scholastic achievement, teamwork and an incredible family bond had all melded together to ignite him to be the best he could be. He needed this type of environment; Type A all the way. He would not have the patience to wait to succeed because some mid-level manger had not evaluated his work performance correctly.

Beaming with excitement, he raised his diploma to the sky and searched the pavilion to locate where his family had been viewing the festivities. Chris knew the decision he had committed to was correct. He had spent the winter and spring completing his final semester of classes and exercising in a non-football training capacity. For a brief moment, he thought about pursuing an NFL dream but knew in his heart after the final whistle blew his football career was officially over. The subsequent drop in his level of intensity had expounded the dichotomy of the way he had lived his life.

While he had confirmation the capitalist world with a salary and steady income would welcome his talent and brain power, not one of the seven interviews he went on for prospective employment excited him enough to accept their generous offers. The only position he knew was correct at this moment in his life transpired organically a few weeks back.

"Congratulations!" The throng of family members who had made the pilgrimage had all greeted Chris as one. Hugs, kisses, pats on the back and plenty of pictures were snapped.

"I cannot believe both my children are college graduates. Me and your mum are proud." Standing in the center of his son and daughter, Michael Cameron put his arm around Christopher and Sabina. "Maria, you have to take a picture."

"I'll play photographer. Aunt Maria you get in, too. A family shot would be nice." Sal accepted the Kodak Fling and maneuvered the camera around to decide whether a portrait or landscape shot was best.

"I want one alone with my baby brother," Sabina entreated. She was stunning with her hair freshly cut and wearing a sleeveless sundress showing off her toned arms and legs.

Chris stood next to his Aunt Dina. "Wait a sec, Angelo." Sal pointed at his step-father, and without saying a word, had officially inaugurated him into the family. Angelo sheepishly smiled before taking a place by the graduate. "Say money!" Sal superstitiously requested. The trio beamed as he clicked away. "Let me get one with Chris, mom, and Angelo, too." Sal handed the camera to Tony and stood by his step-father's side for the next picture.

"Okay, he saved the best for last. Uncle Mike can you take the next few." Tony handed Michael Cameron the one-time use camera as he and Sal bunched in with their blood brother.

"Oh, Maria, I can't work this contraption without my reading glasses." Michael flustered and handed the easy-to-use invention to his bride.

"So Cee, what's in store-you going to work in Texas or come back to New York?" Sal queried as they went through an assortment of cocky poses to the amusement of passersby.

"Neither. I accepted a job offer. Not great pay, but the benefits are awesome. Travel the world...work my butt off for a great cause," Chris proudly stated. "Think I'm going to be all I can be."

"Christopher, you didn't tell me about this. What kind of job, and where?" his mother said.

Chris eyed Vincent Scala before revealing his secret, "I joined the Army."

"The United States Army...Chris, how could you?" Sabina was back to her liberal form. "The government should spend money on social programs not building tanks and bombs."

The call to serve his country had grown over the past few months. After his participation in the latest mob activity, Chris knew he could blow his life potential if he came back to New York and went from skirting along the periphery of dabbling in the life to assisting his blood brothers in more formal ways. He would have a high probability of being indoctrinated into Jimmy Tracino's crew. Only so many stimuli could be received in the confines of a cubicle from an office in midtown Manhattan. Based on what he had seen and done, he knew his life would meld into Sal and Tony's. If he could be intimately involved from over a thousand miles away, what were his chances of keeping his nose clean from a few feet away? He did not think working with "Lewis from budgeting" during the day would mesh well with rolling with Damien Morris at night.

Sal and Tony would be morphing into different type of soldiers in their own right for Jimmy Tree. They were adamant to return to the life prior to the horrific murder of their buddy, Ricky Mullino. Running a poker room and gambling operations was a docile but illegal way to make a living. So far, so good. If the cops busted them, they could revert back to legitimate jobs. Tony had been happy with his career move and had been ecstatic working in and around the construction sites. Developing a bookmaking operation amongst his fellow, blue collars had been a natural progression. Sal hosted one of the poker nights at Ressini's. The eatery continued to grind away, mostly with the local residents, and was turning a modest profit.

If Sal and Tony were to get their hands dirty for Jimmy Tree again, the event would have to be of major significance. This slim possibility had been gnawing at Chris. When you chose the underworld life, you opened yourself to unscrupulous characters. Predicting the outcomes which could possibly occur would be impossible. Chris had skirted the law too many times and he knew he would assist again if he had to. The bond with Sal and Tony was too strong to think he would sit on the sideline if another flash point incident were to rear its ugly head. The law of averages for being busted was against them. While they would work their hardest to stay above the fray, zero guarantees in life's journey were promised. As a history major, Chris knew the past was a great predictor of future events.

The only way to absolve his conscious for the activities he had participated and to remove himself from temptation came together in the midst of a five-mile jog around campus one early morning. The Army Reserve Training Corps were in the midst of a training session. Chris had taken a breather to watch the ROTC cadets go through maneuvers, and he was enthralled. Sensing fate was guiding him along he continued the run into the Austin city limits and for the first time noticed an Army recruiting station situated next to a restaurant he had regularly frequented. After the workout, Chris stopped to say hello to the NCO who greeted him warmly in a sharp uniform as he sat alone in the recruiting office. The sergeant on duty had a fish on the line as he spoke proudly of his service to his country during the past six years. "Army Strong" resonated well with the disillusioned and soon-to-be college graduate. Chris believed serving his country was the best move to make. Thinking through the momentous commitment, he determined the hands on experience in the military would be far more meaningful on his resume than crunching through numbers on a spreadsheet or working to compile facts and figures to present to some B or C level corporate client. Besides, the Iron Curtain was crumbling, and there was little risk of World War III flairing up.

When he returned in four years, a mature man and not an immature, directionless college grad, hopefully the temptation to carouse with his buddies would wane and he would decide on a career choice to be passionate about. Chris did not consider this to be running away from life. The current chapter was a cleansing, a time to build maturity and face a new challenge. Each step of a journey or twist and turn of a rollercoaster had a meaning.

In Closing

The inspiration for all my creative ideas comes from my three babies; Samantha, Julianna and Amelia. My Samajumia3 may not be toddlers anymore, but I will always see my girls as chubby cheeked angels sitting on my lap or wrapping your arms around my neck and peppering me with kisses. I will cry more than Tony Albanese when I walk you three down the aisle.

I also want to thank my wife for her support and patience with my expensive hobby and the times I sequestered myself to write, edit, research, write, edit and research, write, edit and research. My family and friends as well as Teresa and her family provided the core to the life, blood, heart and soul of my characters. Et al., I love you, thanks for the memories and inspiration.

With this said, Cammie was always at my feet or by my side, keeping me company. To the greatest cockapoo and man's best friend ... Cammie!!! You have my heart.

Down to the weather of the day, the vast majority of historical facts and events in the story I tried to make as accurate as possible-*you have to love the Internet*. However, University of Texas fans may notice that I did take writers liberty with the fictitious senior year of Longhorn co-captain, Chris Cameron. To the former players and coaches at the University of Texas during that time period, sorry I also took writers liberty in the fictitious dialogue as well as on and off the field events. I would never intentionally besmirch the reputation of a member of that organization and I attempted to positively spin as much as I could. While I was not a UT fan growing up; comically, I thought I could have played defensive back for the University of Miami during their powerhouse years; I enjoyed researching the history of this storied program and the beautiful city of Austin.

If you have not done so already, I have to put a plug in for the Columbus Avenue Boys trilogy in its entirety. *Cameron Nation: Going All-in to Save His Country* and *Columbus Avenue Boys: Avenging the Scalamarri Massacre* continues the stories of Chris, Sal and Tony as well as Sabina and even Pops. Yes, they are definitely worth the read, trust me on this!

I touched on this earlier, but I want to thank all the people in my life who have inspired me to write and to continue the story; both directly and indirectly. Some of you know who you are and some of you do not. I am not being coy. Thanking everyone directly would be impossible, so let this be known, if you have touched my life you are probably in the three stories I have written in some shape or fashion.

The one person I will acknowledge directly is the memory of Joan (Mildred) Cavazzi Pinto. You had been a core inspiration to so much of my life and yes, you were my second mother. Tony has again gotten the better of me...I have tears in my eyes writing this paragraph. I love you and will always miss you Aunt Joan. I hope you and my mom are enjoying a hot cup of coffee before you head off to Heaven's Casino.

I am also thankful to have reached out to Rob Bignell; you did a great job with my final line edits to make this story readable.

I hope to continue the saga. As a first time author who could barely read, let alone write, I thought I was done after *Cameron Nation*. Thankfully, my boys, *The Columbus Avenue Boys* took over my life and I had to continue. *Cameron's Quest* had an interesting genesis which I'd like to share. For those that are believers-I am, so too bad if you are not-I went to a session with a psychic medium (not my first, mind you). In this July of 2013 reading, the spirits of my parents informed me that I have had a deceased writer who guides my craft and that I would write again. Since the *Quest* story or writing again was not even in my mind, I shrugged the premonition off. However, out of the blue in September of 2013, I began to write. I truly believe this story was my most complete work, and with over three years dedicated to bringing the characters to life, I am proud of the finished product. I hope you were as well.

God Bless and thank you so much for the support.

Printed in the United States
By Bookmasters